A CORPSE WALKS IN BROOKLYN

And Other Stories

Day Keene

The DANCING TUATARA PRESS
Books from RAMBLE HOUSE

A CORPSE WALKS IN BROOKLYN

And Other Stories

Day Keene in the Detective Pulps
Volume #5

Day Keene

Introduced by

Robert J. Randisi

RAMBLE HOUSE

A Corpse Walks in Brooklyn and Other Stories

Introduction: © 2013 by Robert J. Randisi

ISBN 13: 978-1-60543-693-7

Cover Art and Design © 2013 by Gavin L. O'Keefe

Series Edited by John Pelan
Preparation by Kathy Pelan and Fender Tucker

A Corpse Walks in Brooklyn—*Detective Tales*, October 1945
The Stars Say Die!—*Detective Tales* November 1941
Herr Yama from Yokohoma—*Ace G-Man* February 1943
Seven Keys to Murder—*Dime Mystery*, September 1944
I'll Be Seeing You—*Dime Mystery*, November 1946
Three Dead Mice—*Flynn's*, March 1944
A Corpse for Cinderella—*Dime Mystery* May 1945
Claws of the Hell Cat—*Dime Mystery,* January 1946

Dancing Tuatara Press
Special Edition

RAMBLE HOUSE
10329 Sheephead Drive
Vancleave MS 39565
228-826-1783
www.ramblehouse.com

A CORPSE WALKS IN BROOKLYN

And Other Stories

TABLE OF CONTENTS

INTRODUCTION:

A CORPSE IN BROOKLYN

AND OTHER STORIES

ROBERT J. RANDISI

By the time you reach this volume you will have learned quite a bit about Day Keene. Did you know he was friends with actors Melvyn Douglas and Barton MacLane? Did you know that he flipped a coin to decide if he should become and actor or a writer? Lucky for us it landed on the right side.

Keene is generally considered to be a cut below Harry Whittington, Gil Brewer and Peter Rabe—the Holy Trinity of Gold Medal's pulp authors—who many feel were the absolute best of the 50's and 60's paperback crew. (The Gold Medal website shows 19 books by Keene, 17 by Whittington. Maybe Keene's quality wasn't up there with Whittington's—and I say "maybe"—but he was right there when it came to high quality productivity.) And, of course, none of these authors can match the sales record of John D. Mac-Donald, Richard Prather or Donald Hamilton, but I'm talking about the quality of work done in paperbacks by the men who cut their teeth in the pulps and went on to have successful if not spectacular careers.

Keene fits snugly in the bosom of the authors who die-hard pulp-paperback fans consider the best (not best-*selling*)—Whittington, Brewer, Rabe, Charles Williams, Wade Miller, Bruno Fischer and others whose worth is not measured in sales.

But maybe I'm rambling. That's what fans of the 50's and 60's paperbacks do when they start talking books and authors.

I'm pleased that this multi-volume collection of Day Keene's stories is being produced (I think there was only one other collection before these began to appear [This is Murder, Mr. Herbert, and Other Stories, 1948, according to the Thrilling Detective website].) I'm glad to be introducing a volume called A CORPSE IN BROOKLYN. It just seemed fitting since I was born and raised in Brooklyn and wrote three novels about my own Brooklyn P.I., "Nick Delvecchio."

While "A Corpse for Cinderella" and "Seven Keys to Murder" and "I'll Be Seeing You," were also published in *Dime Mystery* from '44 to '46, and have that P.I. flavor.

Keene may not be in top form in every story—and he later graduated from *Dime Mystery* and *Detective Tales* to *Black Mask* and *Dime Detective*—but these tales are no less entertaining, as he almost always does well what he did well. I sort of wish he'd brought back Tommy Martin and Matt Mercer for more stories. (Actually, I haven't read all 11 of the other volumes in this series, so I can't say he didn't write about them, again. Did he?)

The prolific Day Keene died much too soon in 1969 at 65 years of age. This series of volumes is a must for pulp-paperback fans, and a treat for anyone who may have read Keene's novels, but not his short fiction. Once I've finished reading the other volumes, I'll have to go out and try to buy up all his novels.

Hey, that's what we pulp-paperback fans do.

A CORPSE WALKS IN BROOKLYN

CHAPTER ONE

"Let Me Stay Dead . . ."

IF A CAT CAN LOOK at a queen, a punk can shoot a king. And that was what had happened. It was not premeditated murder. It was strictly a case of a nervous trigger finger. If the old fool had not laughed at him and attempted to drive on, Morry would not have shot him. But Smith had, and he had. And now the silver-haired little gambler lay slumped in back of the wheel of his expensive car, blood trickling over his closed eyes to splotch on his stiff white shirt front, and nothing would ever be right for Morry Reynolds again. Dumb as he was, he knew that not even Lippy Courtney, or ten other mouthpieces like him, could pry him out of this jam.

This wasn't any old man whom he had shot. This was Smith. This was Silent Smith, the silver fox of Broadway who had ruled as uncrowned king of the Mazda Belt for more years than Morry had lived.

Whimpering with terror now, he shook the inert figure. "Mr. Smith. For God's sake. Mr. Smith!"

The limp body slumped lower in the seat. The trickle of blood changed its course and dripped on the four carat square-cut, good luck diamond the gambler habitually wore in his fifteen dollar ties.

Even splotched with blood the diamond gleamed like a coal of fire in the dim light from the instrument panel. For a moment avarice overcame his fear. He reached a hand toward the diamond and, whimpering, withdrew it. The diamond was too well known. Any man caught with it in his possession would never live to go to the chair. Smith had too many boys to avenge him. Homeless, unwanted boys whom he had picked out of the streets and gutters, whom he had fed and educated on the money that lesser gamblers spent to grease the law.

Sam Eagan and Bill Morrow were his boys. So was Findy, the restaurateur. And Appellate Court Judge Sam Green. And Doctor Harry Ardell. And Corbett, the special prosecutor. And Olson, and Kelly, and Kasloff, and Crandall, and Snow-Ball, the contender who, everyone said, could lick the socks off Joe Louis, if Joe ever got out of the Army.

Smith had tied no strings to his kindness. He made no distinction of race, or color, or creed. A man was a man in his book. He was right or he was wrong. If he was right, the sky was the limit. If he was wrong, God help him. All he had ever asked of his boys in return was that they keep their noses clean. Now he was dead. And the man who killed him would have to answer to his boys.

Tears coursing his doughy face, Morry shook him again, blubbering, "Please, Mr. Smith. Don't be dead. Wake up. I didn't mean it."

The silent figure lay inert. The silence lurking in the shadows of the bridge grew by leaps and bounds until it pounded on Morry's ears like mallets on a taut-skinned kettle drum.

He repeated, "I didn't mean it."

The lights of an approaching car swept up the street. The sniveling hoodlum started to run; then, fearing the wrath of the man who had hired him almost as much as he did the vengeance of Smith's boys, he forced himself to thrust a hand into the inside breast pocket of the gambler's evening clothes and extract the envelope that he had been sent to get. The back of his hand touched Smith's cheek as he withdrew it through the open window of the car. The flesh felt cold. Clutching the envelope in one hand, half blind with terror, he fled into the night, his heels making a hard clacking sound on the pavement.

Long after the footsteps had faded, Smith continued to lie inert, conscious, but unwilling to move until he could be certain that the punk with the gun was gone. The bright headlights of the approaching car pressed against his closed eyelids for what seemed like a long time.

When it was dark again he leaned both forearms on the wheel and hunched himself erect. His head burned. His eyes were hot. His face and shirt were bloody. It had been close, too close. His eyes still closed he forced the tips of his sensitive fingers to explore the wound.

Not so deep as a well, nor so wide as a church door, he decided. But it could have been enough. Maybe it is.

He opened his eyes. Across the river the silhouette of Manhattan loomed large against a summer moon. To his fogged vision the bridge lights looked like huge yellow diamonds set in a gigantic black garter that girded one of Manhattan's thighs. It was difficult for him even to think of dying, never to see Broadway again. He had lived on and with and by her for almost fifty years. They had moved uptown together. He had shined shoes on her corners as a boy. He had bet thousands on her corners as a man. He knew her as few men did. She was a gorgeous, capricious tart, who, every so often, needed her teeth slapped in to keep her faithful.

Still, whatever he was, she had made him.

He made a mental book. *I'll be damned if I die. I'll give five to four that I don't.*

He wiped the blood from his eyes but his vision was still distorted. The wound in his head had stopped flowing so freely but he was weak from loss of blood.

According to the clock on the dash it was a few minutes after one. There were two things he could do. He could lean on the horn of his car until one of the sleeping residents of the district came and investigated. Then he could ask them to phone the police or drive him to a hospital. Or he could try to drive, himself. Harry's East Side Clinic wasn't far; just a few blocks the other side of the river.

The last course appealed to him. He was weak but he knew

what he was doing. He was accustomed to doing things for himself. Besides, the police would ask embarrassing questions. And for once in his life he was stumped.

He hadn't recognized the gunman although the hood had known him. Whoever he was, he was petty. Smith searched his pockets with an effort. His wallet, his watch, his stick-pin were all where they belonged. Only the envelope was missing. As far as he knew it was valueless. All it contained was a list of names which Lieutenant Commander Kenmore had compiled—names of seamen about to be discharged, who, in the commander's estimation, deserved a little special aid in their transition to civilian life.

"It beats me," the gambler admitted.

He managed to start the car and, by driving slowly, crossed the bridge without incident. But threading Chatham Square he realized he was blacking out and tried, unsuccessfully, to curb his car. Instead he nosed it into one of the steel pillars with a shriek of crumpling chrome.

Silent Smith was well known. The first prowl car men to reach the scene set the phone wires humming. Crisp orders crackled over the air. Lights flashed at Central Bureau. Ambulance and squad car sirens tried to outwail each other. Burly detectives leaped from cars to question frightened bystanders.

When Smith came to he was lying on a table with Harry Ardell dusting sulfa powder into his wound. His eyes asked an unspoken question. Ardell winked and called for a sterilized needle. Captain Craig of homicide was scowling over his shoulder.

"You're dying, Smith," he lied. "You'd better talk. Who did it?"

"I wouldn't tell you the time of day," Smith told him.

"But you're hurt! Hurt bad, Smith!"

"Hurt?" Smith scoffed. "I'm dead, you fool. Want to bet?"

Craig grinned. "Not with you. You're mean enough to die." He hesitated, added, "Where did it happen, Silent?"

"Brooklyn," the gambler told him.

"Why?"

Smith sighed deeply. "I'll be damned if I know. Maybe someone took me for Noel Coward."

CHAPTER TWO

Snow-Ball in Hell

DESPITE THE JULY HEAT it was cool in here. The walls were stone and thick. A huge fan circulated the air. The state took good care of the men whom it had condemned to die.

Snow-Ball Johnson handed his pass, signed by both the warden and the cell captain, to the guard on the inner gate.

"You want to talk to him in the room or in his cell?"

"His cell will do," the fighter said.

There should be a lot for brothers to talk about, he thought, especially brothers who had been as close as he and Charlie. But somehow there never was. This thing that was going to happen stood between them like a screen.

The guard motioned him into the death block, calling, "Your brother to see you, Charlie."

As big a man as the fighter but darker skinned and five years older, the condemned man thrust his hand through the bars and shook hands eagerly. "Thought I tol' you not to come up heah no mo', kid."

Snow-Ball handed him the package of cigarettes and candy that had been inspected in the front office. "I'll keep coming as long as I can," he told his brother. "I keep hoping that something may break."

He tried hard to control his emotion. This was his brother. This was Charlie who had shined shoes, sold papers, busked, fought, and stolen, so they could eat after their parents had died when he had been nine years old. This was Charlie who was condemned to die for the murder of a liquor store proprietor whom he swore he had never seen.

The man in the cell thumbed open a package of cigarettes. "Ain' nothin' goin' to happen 'cept they're goin' to put me in that chair three nights from now an' fry my hide until it crackles."

"Courtney's been up to see you?"

"Yeah," Johnson admitted. "But fo' all of his big talk he ain' going to get me no commutation. My record is again' me. An' doan you go givin' him no mo' money, kid. You save it up an get you a college education like Mister Smith say you should. You learn to be a doctor or a lawyer. This fightin' business all right to pick up some quick money. But plenty our people can fight. Do I have me some education, do I talk good like you do, well, I doan' be where I am."

An awkward silence fell between them.

The block guard broke it. "Lots of company, Charlie. Here's your attorney."

A big, suave, man, overdressed and over barbered, with a perpetual smile and a protruding underlip that had given him his nickname, Courtney extended his hand to the fighter. "Glad to see you, Snow-Ball. How's tricks, Charlie."

"Fine. Jest fine," the condemned man told him. "Do I feel me any better I turn handsprings."

"Now, now," the lawyer soothed him. "Don't be like that, Charlie. I'm seeing the governor tomorrow afternoon. And I'll bet you two to one that we get a commutation."

"We," Johnson said simply.

"About that white boy that Charlie says gave him that pint of liquor and fiver to drive his car?" Snow-Ball asked. "You can't find any trace of him, Attorney Courtney?"

Courtney shook his head. "No. And we've looked for him for two years." He lighted a cigar, staring at his client. "No," he repeated. "It seems that no one saw him but Charlie."

Johnson clutched the bars of his cell so hard that his knuckles showed white. "You come in heah with me an' say that like that. Doan' you 'sinuate I lyin'." He told the story that he had told so many times before. "There I sittin' that night in the poolroom mindin' my own business. An' this dressed-up white boy come along so high on Mary he doan' know he in this world. 'You like make five dollar' an' a pint?' he ask me. I say, 'I do.' Then he tell me all I got to do is drive his car while he go make a business call. So I take the heap an' drive him where he say. Then pretty soon I heah some shootin' an' he come runnin' back an' throw a gun in the car an' say to scram on account of he have to kill a man. But before I kin get the gun out of the car the cops are all around me an' they say I stole the car an' rob an' shot the man. But I never. I jest working for a finif an' a pint."

Courtney sucked his cigar. "And if you don't think that was one hell of a yarn to make a jury believe."

Johnson pointed out, "You doan' do it, do you? An' Gawd know how much money Snow-Ball an' Mister Smith lay in your lap."

The attorney flushed slightly. "Now, now. Don't worry, Johnson. I've handled a hundred murder cases and I've never lost a client to the chair."

"That's why we came to you," the fighter said.

"Only one client," the condemned man told Courtney. "That's me. You goin' to have one black blot on your record. 'Cause I'm goin' to burn. I knows it."

The lawyer sorted some papers from his brief case. "Now, Johnson. That's no attitude to take."

Snow-Ball turned away while Courtney had his brother mark his X on the petition for clemency. He doubted that it would be granted. He believed Charlie's story. After a talk with Charlie, Silent Smith had believed it. Courtney swore that he did and had kept the case in the courts for two years, the new trials and appeals eating up every dime that Snow-Ball had made with his fists. But neither Smith's boys nor Courtney's investigators had been able to run to earth the well-dressed white youth, high on marijuana, who, Charlie swore, had been the killer. Several reluctant poolhall habitués admitted they had seen a youth talking to Charlie, a white youth, but he had never been identified.

Finished with the business that had brought him up-river, Courtney offered to drive the fighter back to town.

"I'll be back tomorrow, Charlie," Snow-Ball told his brother in parting.

"I be here," the condemned man said glumly.

Neither man said much during the long ride. Night had fallen by the time they reached the outskirts of New York. Courtney asked if the fighter wanted to be dropped off at his hotel or if he was going on into town.

Snow-Ball said he was going to Smith's casino.

"I'll go with you," Courtney decided. "I want to see Smith myself. Believe it or not, I feel like hell about this. I'd like to help."

"Charlie's got to burn then?"

"I'm afraid so," the lawyer admitted.

Smith's penthouse and Casino occupied the top and the 39th Floor of a towering set-back skyscraper that the profits of honest gambling had bought. Both the casino and the penthouse were served by a single elevator shaft, guarded at all times against holdups.

Cork Dugan nodded to Snow-Ball and glanced at Courtney's card. "There's big stuff cooking," he grinned. "The boys are trying to figure out who shot the boss last night. And when we do—"

"God help him, eh?" Courtney chuckled.

Cork admitted, "He's likely to be pushed around a little."

Snow-Ball rapped on the door of Smith's office. Bill Morrow opened it. A lean-faced man in his late thirties, with predatory eyes, he was Smith's second in command, and heir apparent, with Sam Eagan, to the throne.

"Hi, boy," he greeted Snow-Ball.

The colored boy walked on into the office.

Morrow extended his hand to Courtney. "Glad to see you, Lippy. What brings you here?"

"I wanted to see Silent. But if he's busy—"

Morrow hesitated briefly, then stepped aside to allow him to pass. "We're busy. But come in."

There were five men in Smith's office. Captain Craig of homicide, Sam Eagan, Doctor Harry Ardell, Findy, and Special Prosecutor Corbett. All of them knew Courtney and nodded. The atmosphere was slightly strained.

A bandage wrapped turban-wise around his head, Smith sat at his desk, studying the pictures that Craig had brought for his inspection. Except for the bandage and the fact that he was a trifle paler than usual, the silver-haired little gambler looked much like he always did.

"Hello, Lippy," he greeted the lawyer. "We're having a council of war."

The lawyer smiled dryly. "So I see." He nodded at the bandage. "Sorry to hear about your accident."

Smith lighted one of his long thin cigars. "It was no accident. That is, on the part of whoever sent that trigger-happy punk to high-jack me. There was something you wanted, Lippy?"

Courtney sucked at his protruding underlip. "Yes, there is." He hesitated, said, "I wonder if I could see you alone for a moment, Silent?"

Sam Eagan, just out of uniform, spoke before Smith could. "Sorry, Lippy. Nothing personal. But someone tried to knock him off last night. And no one sees him alone until we get to the bottom of this."

"I don't blame you for that," Courtney said. "Okay. It's nothing secret. But I don't want you boys to think that I'm making a grandstand play. It—well, it's about Snow-Ball's brother, Charlie."

"Go on," Smith said.

Courtney continued, "I'm going through the motions, of course. But I have an inside wire that the governor will refuse to commute, or issue any more stays."

Snow-Ball said, "Then Charlie's got to burn?"

"Why not?" Craig demanded. "He killed a man, didn't he?"

"There has been some doubt in our minds concerning that," Smith reminded him. "But go on, Lippy."

The lawyer colored, embarrassed. "Well, he'll be the first man I ever lost to the chair. You and Snow-Ball have paid me a lot of money because you figured I could spring him. My past record was your guarantee. You any idea how much you and Smith have paid me, Snow-Ball?"

The fighter told him, "Between thirty-eight and forty thousand dollars."

Smith's pale blue eyes were puzzled. "Come to the point, Lippy."

"I want to return that money," the lawyer said. "I've done my best. But it hasn't been good enough. I feel that I've let you down. So as soon as I go through my records I'll mail you a check for whatever you and Snow-Ball have paid me, minus any court costs that I've paid."

Bill Morrow felt the lawyer's pulse in mock solemnity. "To think that I should ever live to see the day—the man's not well!"

Courtney jerked his arm away. "Cut the clowning. I'm serious. The one lad in my life whom I defend and know to be innocent is going to burn. And I feel like hell about it."

Smith smiled suddenly, stood up in back of his desk, and offered his hand to the lawyer. "Thanks a lot, Lippy. I think I know how you feel. And you won't lose by this."

Captain Craig said, sarcastically, "All right. All right. You big-money guys can play beanbag with forty grand some other time. Me, I work for a salary. Let's get back to the pictures."

Smith picked a picture from his desk and handed it to Craig. "There he is. That's him."

Captain Craig read the legend. "Morry Reynolds, alias Morris Phillips. Two convictions. Armed robbery and assault."

The men crowded around him to look at the picture.

Courtney said, "I will be damned. So it was Morry Reynolds who shot you."

Smith asked, "You know him, Lippy?"

"I defended him on both charges," the lawyer admitted. "As I recall him, he's a doughy faced punk who sounds like he's crying half the time."

"That's him," Smith nodded. "Who is he tied in with?"

Courtney shook his head. "There you have me. I think he ran with the waterfront gang for a while but I don't know his present affiliations."

Findy heaved his vast bulk from his chair.

"And you wouldn't be knowing where he was living?"

The lawyer said, "It was some cheap hotel. I don't remember which one. I do know he's a Brooklyn boy."

Sam Eagan smiled without mirth. "Ah—a corpse walks in Brooklyn."

"None of that," Craig warned him. "That's what we've been afraid of. That's why I was detailed here. You boys keep your noses clean—the department will take care of this. The punk himself isn't important. It's the lad in back of him we want."

Smith agreed that was so.

"I'll tell you what," Courtney offered. "I'm on my way to my office now. I'll look up Reynolds in my files and phone you the address he gave me. It's a hundred to one that he won't be there now. But it will be a starting point."

Bill Morrow reached for his hat. "Fine. Sam and I will go with you, Lippy."

"The hell you will!" Craig roared. Then, more quietly, "You go ahead, Lippy," he instructed the lawyer. "We'll *all* wait right here for your call."

He did relent enough to allow Silent to send Snow-Ball for his car a few moments after Courtney had left.

Courtney phoned in less than ten minutes. "The address I have," he told Smith, "is the Ocean Hotel. But it's two and a half years old."

Smith thanked him and hung up.

Craig said he knew where the hotel was and they rode to the street in silence.

Craig's car was parked in front of the building on Broadway, his department chauffeur placidly reading a morning paper by the aid of the orange light from a neon sign advertising a blend of whiskey. Flanked by Morrow and Eagan, Smith pushed his way through the crowd to the cross street. His car was parked in its usual place, some distance from the corner.

Eagan remarked that Snow-Ball was taking his brother's approaching death hard.

"I feel sorry as hell for him," Smith admitted. "I know

what he's going through."

"It's tough," Eagan sympathized. "I know if I had a brother—"

Smith started to shut him up, stopped short. "Get Craig—quick!" he snapped. "Before he pulls away. And bring his chauffeur!"

Craig returned with Eagan, protesting, "Now what?"

"Something right up your alley," Smith said succinctly. "Murder!" He stabbed a finger at Craig's chauffeur. "You—did you hear a couple of backfires a moment or so ago?"

The man nodded, "Yeah—yeah. Come to think of it, I did."

Smith informed him, "Well, they weren't backfires. They were shots."

He opened the front door of his car gently and the big colored boy sagged into Bill Morrow's arms. He had been alive such a short time ago that his twin wounds were still bleeding.

But he was dead. He would never fight the Brown Bomber. He would never go on to college to be a credit to his people. He was through worrying over Charlie. Someone had put a small-calipered gun up to his left temple and had pulled the trigger twice.

CHAPTER THREE

The Corpse in Brooklyn

THE MILLS OF THE GODS grind slowly, but they grind exceedingly small. The mill of justice grinds slowly—period. It had been a few minutes of nine when Smith had left his Casino. It had been nine exactly when he had discovered Snow-Ball's body. Now it was almost eleven as they started for Brooklyn again, this time all in Craig's car.

Craig was so furious his heavy jowls were as red as a turkey's wattle. No one but his own driver had heard the shots. No one had seen them fired. The colored fighter had not been robbed. He had no known enemies. There was no known reason for anyone to have killed him.

"Damn it. It doesn't add up," Craig complained.

Slouched in one corner of the car as it raced, siren wailing, through the after-theater crowd on Broadway, the silver-haired gambler took his cigar from his mouth long enough to explain, "Murder doesn't add. It multiplies. And I'd say the common multiple in this case was time. Time is the essential factor in most murders."

The homicide captain shook his head. "What are you talking about?"

Smith said, "Snow-Ball was one of my boys. And I have a hunch that I'd better take care of this myself."

"You'll burn if you do," Craig exploded. "You're holding out on me. You know something I don't."

"I know lots of things you don't," Smith said. "Many of them have nothing to do with murder. Use your head, Craig."

Craig lapsed into a moody silence.

The Ocean Hotel turned out to be a dingy rabbit warren in the very heart of the district that had spawned the murderous ice pick killers of Murder Incorporated.

The desk clerk, a flashily dressed, shifty eyed youth who smelled of gin, shook his head at Craig's first question—then his eyes came wide as he looked at Smith, flanked by the predatory Morrow.

"Nix," he said suddenly. "I'll talk." His eyes fixed on Smith he went on, "I make you now. You're Silent Smith. Yeah. Sure. Morry Reynolds used to live here—but keep *him* off of me." He indicated Morrow.

Smith said, "Morry used to live here up until how long ago?"

"About two hours ago. Out of a clear sky he gets a call from some dame, makes like he's got the palsy, packs all of his things and scrams."

"Where?"

"That I wouldn't know."

Craig asked, incredulous, "You say some dame tipped him?"

"Yeah. Anyway she calls him."

"And who was she?"

The desk clerk shook his head. "That I wouldn't know, either. Morry was quite a lad with the wrens. And dames was always calling him. Married dames, single dames, young dames, old—"

Smith cut him short. "Never mind his love life. He was tied in with what gang? Who was he working for?" The clerk started to shake his head and Smith said, dryly, "That you wouldn't know either. All right. Let's look at his room."

The room revealed nothing beyond the fact that Morry, among other things, had been a lone drinker. Craig swore, when Silent told Eagan to get a cab.

"And where do you think you're going?"

Smith told him, "I'm going to the Navy Yard. I'm an hour and a half late now for my appointment with a Lieutenant Hanson, on a private matter."

Craig scowled. "Okay. Where'll I meet you?"

"Let's make it the morgue," Smith suggested.

Craig's face purpled with anger. "Look, Smith. We've never gotten along. But—"

Smith shook his head. "I'm not kidding. This thing has just begun. I have a hunch it's big. We're both looking for Morry Reynolds. And I'm willing to bet a grand to a dime right now that the morgue is where we find him."

Here was the scent of the sea, of ships, and of faraway places. Alert young sentries in whites and leggings padded through the summer night, armed with Garands—but the night was not silent.

Deeply bronzed men brawled orders from the decks of great, scarred ships with gaping wounds in their prows and sterns and sides. There was a constant bucketing of hammers and clang of steel on steel. Steam winches roared and rattled. Huge cranes lifted giant loads as easily as Silent Smith took a cigarette from the package that Lieutenant Hanson offered him.

"I'm sorry," he apologized, "to be so late."

Hanson said that was quite all right. "I've heard a lot about you from Kenmore," he said smiling. "All of it was good. And I have been instructed to assist you in any manner that I, can. His transfer was quite sudden and unexpected."

Smith summed up the situation from the time that he had left the Lieutenant Commander, up to and including Snow-Ball's murder.

Hanson shook his head. "The stolen list doesn't make sense."

"But murder makes sense," the silver haired gambler corrected him dryly. "Even a homicidal maniac makes a kind of sense—and the man we're dealing with is hardly that."

Hanson said, "Perhaps you'd like to talk to the yeoman who typed the original list."

Smith said he would. Hanson lifted his voice and called, "Goodwin!"

Smith liked the youth on sight. His eyes were large and intelligent. A well-built lad in his early twenties, his black hair was cropped close to his skull and his skin was deeply bronzed by a tropical sun.

He shook hands with Smith, smiling. "I've heard of you, Mr. Smith," he admitted. "And I've often thought I'd like to give your place a whirl. But the Navy doesn't pay me enough to do your kind of gambling."

"You're just as well off," Smith told him. "You can't beat the house in the long run." His blue eyes twinkling, he added, "But you don't look much like a typewriter Bertha to me."

"He's not," Lieutenant Hanson informed him. "Goodwin is sweating out an M.D. because of a knee injury he suffered in the landing at Iwo. He's just working in the office to kill time."

Goodwin grinned, "That's right, sir. But it won't be long for me now. I got it from a runner that my papers are on the skipper's desk."

Smith got back to the business at hand. "About this list of names that you typed out for Lieutenant Commander Kenmore, Goodwin."

"Yes, sir."

"Where did you put the carbon copy?" Hanson put in.

The seaman indicated a file. "Right in this file sir. But it isn't there now."

Hanson said sharply, "What's that?"

"It's been removed, sir."

"And who has access to that file?" Silent asked.

The lieutenant raised his hands in a futile gesture. "Three-fourths of the Yard. It's a sort of catch-all and nothing important or confidential is ever kept in there."

Smith sucked at his borrowed cigarette, then looked at the young seaman. "You wouldn't remember any of the names on that list, would you, Goodwin?"

Smiling widely, Goodwin told him; "I think I remember most of them, sir." He tapped a paper on the blotter of the desk at which Hanson was sitting. "And to keep the file straight, I've typed those I remembered. I put it on your desk, sir, meaning to ask for an okay."

Hanson handed the list to Smith. He skimmed it with his eyes. The names meant nothing to him. He and Kenmore had not discussed any of the men personally. He looked up at the seaman. "You're being discharged shortly. But I don't see your name on here."

"No, sir." The seaman's smile was a trifle wry. "I guess the lieutenant commander thought I had too much 'bad time'. Nothing serious, you understand. Just overstaying liberty— getting drunk and brawling with the shore patrol."

Smith chuckled. "Believe it or not, son, while General Funston and myself were civilizing the Morros with Krags in 'ninety-nine, I made the guard house in Manila myself for tangling with an M.P."

The seaman grinned. Lieutenant Hanson looked shocked. "If that's all you want with Goodwin," he suggested, "I think we can let him go. You see, I restricted his liberty, so he'd be here when you arrived."

"That's all," Smith nodded. "Good luck, son." He tapped the list. "And forget this. Drop in to see me when they hand you that paper."

"I'll do that, sir," Goodwin promised.

Alone with Hanson, the gambler asked, "About Kenmore's sudden transfer. He knew nothing about it when I talked to him last night. You don't know of any reason why he should have been transferred so hastily?"

Hanson said he did not. However, such instances were not rare—someone in Washington got a brainstorm; you got your travel orders. And you didn't ask questions—you went. There was nothing more he could tell Smith. The whole affair was a mystery to him.

"And to me," Smith admitted. His eyes had turned hard and cold again. "But all of the cards aren't dealt. And there's always a chance of catching a joker."

Bill Morrow and Sam Eagan were listening to police calls when he returned to the cab.

When he told them of his interview with Lieutenant Hanson and Goodwin, and debated his next move, Eagan brought up a point.

"Goodwin? Any relation to *the* Goodwin? You know, that lad down south somewhere who is building ships faster than Kaiser."

Smith said he doubted it very much. Any scion of *the* Goodwins would undoubtedly be commissioned. It was not an uncommon name. "We might as well," he decided, "go back to the casino." He leaned forward to tell the driver.

The move saved him a fractured skull—the half brick, wrapped in paper, crashing past him, to thud on the floor of the cab.

Morrow and Eagan were out of the cab, guns in their hands, before Silent moved again. But there was no one at whom to shoot—rather, there were too many. The sidewalks were crowded with laughing, jostling seamen returning from liberty. It could have been any of them who had thrown the missile.

Smith leaned down, unwrapped a paper from the brick. Scrawled on it in pencil was the warning—

Stop being so wise. Pull your nose out of something

that's none of your business. If you don't, its curtains, see? I missed you last night. But I won't miss again.

Morrie Reynolds

The silver-haired little gambler studied the note intently, then folded it carefully and put it in his pocket. Murder always followed a devious route. This one was even more winding than usual. But any road could only lead so far. And no killer could travel his without leaving clues behind him.

"We're getting somewhere?" he told Eagan.

"Where?" Eagan said hotly.

"Right up the killer's alley! Somebody's worried—" he stopped, pointed to the radio in the cab. The police announcer was droning.

Car Forty-six. Make an investigation in the vacant lot near Ten Eyck and Morgan. A woman has just reported that an injured drunk is sleeping in the weeds . . .

Eagan shook his head. "I don't get it."

"One gets you ten," Smith told him, "that the bum isn't injured—he's dead. And I'll give the same odds that it's Reynolds."

"But if it's Reynolds," Eagan protested, looking at the scrawled warning, "he couldn't have—" The younger man stopped abruptly and studied the curious faces of the young sailors surrounding the cab. "Yeah. I get what you mean," he said.

CHAPTER FOUR

Kitten's Britches

IT WAS ONE O'CLOCK in the morning but the usual crowd of morbidly curious, attracted by the police cars, stood three deep in front of the body, by the time that Smith's cab reached the corners of Ten Eyck and Morgan.

The Stagg Street Station squad car had been the first to reach the body. The "drunk" was lying in a patch of weeds a few feet in from the sidewalk, his face pressed into the curve of one outflung arm. In the spotlights of the parked prowlers he looked strangely shrunken and alone.

Craig was having a jurisdictional argument with one of the Stagg Street men. Smith turned to Morrow and Eagan.

"Spread out. Learn things—spend some money."

The tech men were snapping pictures of the dead man when the medical examiner drove up. He turned the body over and the crowd surged forward morbidly.

A woman in front screamed, a lost sound, "Oh, my God! He hasn't any face . . ."

Smith stood on his tiptoes to see. She wasn't far from wrong. A ball peen hammer or some similar object had been used to batter the features of the dead man into a bloody pulp. Smith glanced instinctively at the hands. The hands and fingers had not been mutilated. Here was the time element again. The killer had not attempted to prevent identification—he had been content to delay it.

Grinning, one of the Stagg Street men asked Craig if it was the lad for whom he was looking. Scowling, Craig admitted that, due to the condition of the face and the fact that all identifying papers had been removed from the body, he would not be able to tell until the fingerprint men had sent their findings through the mill.

Smith studied the corpse. He was satisfied it was Reynolds. The dead man was of the same size and build as the man who had high-jacked and shot him. More, he remembered the suit distinctly. It was a chocolate brown double-breasted, with a wide pin stripe.

Eagan came back to report that he had been unable to learn a thing. "Not that they won't talk," he reported. "But I couldn't find a soul except Mrs. Homer, the lady who spotted the body, who knew a thing about it until they heard the sirens. There were no screams and no shots."

"It didn't happen here," Smith pointed out. "The only weeds mashed down are the ones where the body is lying.

They beat in his face somewhere else and brought him here in a car."

The medical examiner got to his feet and brushed dust from the knees of his trousers. "He's been dead about thirty minutes, I'd say. And he was dead when they beat in his face—shot, I'd say, with a .22 or possibly a .32. I can tell you which one when I dig out the slugs."

Craig put in a bid for the slugs. "When you boys are through with them, of course. I'd like to match them up with the ones we dug out of Snow-Ball."

A Brooklyn homicide man asked if Manhattan had anything on that yet.

"Yeah," Craig assured him. "We have. We've got a brand new angle." He refused to amplify.

Eagan looked at Smith.

"Your guess is as good as mine," the silver-haired little gambler told him. "Craig is dumb but he's lucky. He could fall into a dead elephant and come out smelling like a Democrat."

Morrow came up between them and reported from the corner of his mouth, "I've just been talking to a Mrs. Klotsky who lives across the street. She was sitting by her front window waiting for her husband to stagger home, her intention being to give him a piece of her mind, when she saw a big black Cadillac or Packard with a bashed-in front drive up and park here in front of the lot. This was about five minutes before Mrs. Homer, who works as a subway cashier, walked by and discovered the body. The car was between her and the lot. That is, between Mrs. Klotsky and the lot. She saw no one. But she has a distinct impression that there was a woman on the front seat, beside the driver, because she saw a match struck and moved across the front of the car, as if the driver was lighting someone's cigarette." Morrow grinned. "Mrs. Klotsky remembers that because she told me that Mr. Klotsky used to light her cigarettes, while all he does now is get lit. The car parked maybe two or three minutes, then pulled on. And that was all she saw or knew until she heard Mrs.

Homer scream."

Smith digested the information. "She didn't get the license number of the car?"

Morrow shrugged. "Do they ever?"

"Oh, there you are." Craig pushed through the crowd to Smith. "So you found him, did you, Smith?"

Smith played dumb. "Found who? Don't tell me that's Morry Reynolds. If it is, you owe me a dime. I said the morgue. But this is practically the same thing."

"And you wouldn't know anything about it?"

"No. I would not."

"You didn't spot him before I did and have him, how shall we say it, taken care of?"

The smile left Smith's lips. He exploded, "What the hell are you talking about?" He studied the other man's face. "All right. Let's have it. Who put what bug in your ear?"

"I had a phone call," Craig admitted, "after I last saw you. And what do you think my caller told me?"

"Not about the birds, and the bees, and the cabbages."

Craig kept his temper with an effort. "No. They told me that you and Sol Arnson had words the other night."

"Good Lord!" Sam Eagan said. "Are you just finding that out?" He pointed to the corpse. "Bill and I threatened to make over his face, like that?"

"Stay out of this, Sam," Smith said.

He had almost forgotten Sol Arnson. A shrewd young punk around town, Arnson had tried to muscle in on a dozen rackets. Only a few nights before he had had Arnson thrown out of his casino when one of the stick-men had reported that Arnson was using switch dice.

"You're crazy, Craig," Morrow jeered. "You can't tie that lobby-gow into this."

"No?" Craig demanded. "Listen." He listed events as they had happened. "Silent quarrels with Arnson. A few nights later Silent is shot in the head by some punk. Silent swears that he'll get the punk. Snow-Ball is shot instead, while sitting in Silent's car. Now the punk is dead, and a good-sized intergang war is under way." He pounded one huge fist on a palm. "And that is exactly what I was detailed to prevent from happening."

"Who tipped you to this angle?"

Craig admitted the call had been an anonymous.

The silver-haired gambler considered. It wasn't even a frame—it was what Craig had called it, merely a red herring. But if Craig should persist in following it, it would have the same effect as Snow-Ball's death had had. His own investigation would be delayed while he and Sol Arnson answered a lot of silly questions. Time had entered the case again. Whoever it was he was bucking fighting time. He was trying desperately to make time—and Silent—stand still.

He debated telling Craig what had happened outside the Navy yard, showing him the piece of paper with the scrawled warning on it, and decided not to. He called a Brooklyn homicide lad he knew over to the group. "I want you to do me a favor, Nicky." He swung back to Morrow and Eagan. "Show Nicky, here, your guns."

Puzzled, they did as they were told. Both men had .38's swung on .45 frames.

"Break them. Smell them. Look at the butt plates, Nicky," Smith insisted.

The detective did as he was requested. "Clean," he reported.

Smith beckoned to the driver of their cab who was standing a few feet away. "Now you tell Nicky where you picked us up, where you took us, and how long we've been in your cab."

The driver answered in reverse. "I pulled my flag about—well, a little over an hour ago. I took you to the Navy Yard. And I picked you up in front of the Ocean Hotel."

"Thanks a lot for listening, Nicky." Silent smiled. "And now let's be on our way—" he looked at Craig—"that is, if Captain Craig of Manhattan has no objections."

"A wise guy," was Craig's only comment. In the cab again, Sam Eagan said, "Whew! Craig was all set for a pinch."

"So I figured," Smith nodded. "And so did the lad who called Craig. Whoever he is—we're getting too close on his tail. We're practically breathing down his neck. And he wants us out of his hair."

The girl was young, not more than twenty-two or twenty-three. She filled out the light summer dress she wore in all of the proper places. More, she was pretty, after a cheap, tawdry, fashion. But tears had streaked her makeup. The nails of the hand she pressed to her throat looked like five drops of blood.

"She won't go away," Cork told Smith. "I told her you wasn't in. But she said she had to see you and she'd wait."

Smith crossed the foyer of the building to the girl. "There is something I can do for you, sister?"

The girl stopped sobbing with an effort. "I—I want to talk to you alone. It—it's about Morry. I was his girl."

Bill Morrow opened the door of the elevator cage and silently guided the crying girl inside.

The casino was deserted except for the cleaning staff and two or three of the croupiers still working on their accounts. Smith picked a bottle and a glass from the bar en route to his office, where he poured a stiff drink into the glass. "Drink that before you try to talk," he told the girl.

She sipped at it gratefully, then sank back into one of his overstuffed red leather office chairs and crossed her legs, exposing not only her knees but a generous sample of thigh, seemingly unaware that she was doing so.

A born cynic, Morrow lifted his eyebrows.

"Now," Smith suggested. "Let's have it. What's your name and why did you come to me?"

"My name is Jane Semple," she told him. She began to cry again. "And I—I know who it was who killed Morry. I—I was with him when it happened, that is, when Sol Arnson and two of his boys dragged him out into a car."

Smith looked at his seconds in command but made no comment. "Please go on, Miss Semple."

"You see," she sobbed, "Arnson hired Morry to shoot you and steal your wallet and diamond and things, so it would look like a holdup. But Morry lost his nerve and all he took was some old envelope that he threw into the first ashcan." She looked up through her tears. "Arnson was furious with him."

"I can imagine," Smith said dryly.

She continued, "Then, tonight, in a little bar out near the Williamsburg Bridge, I heard Sam tell two of his boys to pick up Morry." Sobs racked her body. "And I knew what that meant. So I phoned Morry to scram."

Sam Eagan asked, puzzled, "Pardon me. What did you say your name was?"

She told him, "Jane Semple. Why?"

"I'm sorry," he apologized. "I still don't recognize it. Have you written any good books lately?"

She gave him a dirty look.

Smith shook his head. "Stop your kidding, Sam. This is serious. Please go on, Miss Semple:"

The girl continued, "So he did. He came straight to my flat." Sobs overcame her again. "But Sol must have followed him. Because Sol and two of his boys broke in and dragged him out—and now I hear on the radio that they've found his body in Brooklyn."

"She has good ears." Morrow nodded approvingly.

Smith sucked at his cigar. "And just what was it that you wanted me to do?"

The girl looked surprised. "Why—get Arnson. Protect yourself. It was Arnson who killed Snow-Ball. And he's going to kill you next and take over all your rackets."

"Interesting," Smith said quietly. "Thanks a lot for coming. And now you know what I think you'd better do?"

She leaned forward, asked, tersely, "Tell you where to find Arnson?"

"No. Pull down your skirt," Smith said. "You are a big girl now." He leaned forward and tapped the crisp new one hundred dollar bill folded into her stocking. "Besides, your perjury's showing."

She stood up, furious. "You can't insult me."

"I doubt if I can," Smith agreed. "Now go back to the lad who paid you that hundred and tell him your act was lousy."

She stormed out of the office.

Smith picked up his inter-building phone and called Dugan. "She's coming down, Cork. Tail her. Don't lose her. But watch yourself. We're bucking a tough combination."

"Now what the hell?" Morrow demanded when Smith had replaced the phone.

"I think I know," Smith said quietly. "And what I don't know, I think I can figure out." He stood a moment in a deep thought, added, "Get me a *Who's Who,* the telephone numbers of the deans of men at Harvard, Yale, and Princeton, a damn good fingerprint man, two quarts of black coffee, and the names and Washington telephone numbers of the senior senators from Mississippi, Louisiana, Alabama, and Florida."

Morrow stared at him. "You feel all right, chief?"

"I feel fine," the silver-haired gambler assured him. "And I'm not crazy. You just get me the things I asked for and I think I can make something of them."

"What?" Eagan asked flatly.

Smith rinsed out the glass that the girl had used and poured himself a small drink. He was old. He was tired. He had seen a lot of bright boys come and go on Broadway. He had helped quite a few on their way.

He had had his rewards, but often it had not been pleasant. For a long time now all he had wanted was peace. But it seemed that he never would have it until they threw that first clod of dirt in his face and made the well-known remark about dust.

"What?" Sam Eagan repeated. "What are you going to make of—"

Smith smiled wryly, remembering a phrase his mother had used when he had been overly curious as a child about something she had been doing. "Kitten's britches," he told Eagan soberly. "Kitten's britches for a killer."

CHAPTER FIVE

Too Damn Smart

SOMEWHERE OUT PAST the Narrows and the Hook the summer sun was coming out of the Atlantic. But here, in the deep man-made canyons of Broadway, morning was still cool and dim. Few knew her at that hour—yet it was the hour at which Smith loved her best.

Stripped naked of all her gaudy tinsel and her jewels, washed clean of her sins of the night before, she lay quiescent, plotting the day and the night to come, responding only to chosen handful of the faithful.

Weary to the point of exhaustion, Smith paused in front of an Automat, trying to decide if he wanted another cup of coffee. He decided he did not and walked on, savoring the quickening sounds of the new day's birth.

Water gurgled in the gutters. There was a clatter of milk cans and bottles, a grunting of men and a thud of boxes on the walk as supplies were delivered. Truck motors purred softly at the curb. A stocky porter was whistling Tschaikovsky's *None But The Lonely Heart,* as he scrubbed down a glittering plate glass window with a long-handled brush. There was a rising tempo to the rumble of the subway underneath his feet.

Smith walked on, content. These were his pastures. To him they were verdant and fruitful—they had been his life for over sixty years. And in more ways than one, he had had a good life, he decided. Nothing, or no one, could ever take that from him.

In front of Findy's the fat restaurateur, his back to his own closed door, broke the spell that gripped him, brought him back to the grim present. "For God's sake call this off, Silent. Stop playing pigeon. Let the cops look for him."

He walked on slowly, restless again, curiously apprehensive, as he had not often been. This time he was enmeshed in a web deadlier than he had ever known—because it was also invisible. The shot might come from the next doorway, or one after that. Rooftops and windows and passing traffic suddenly held peril, for he knew who the killer was. The killer had threatened to get him if he didn't call off his dogs. And Smith was playing bait.

As he passed the old Winter Garden a cab purred up behind him and stopped. Smith's spine stiffened as he turned, relaxed when he saw it was Sam Eagan.

"You've found him?" he demanded.

Eagan shook his head. "Not yet. Nobody but the Navy believes us—and even Lieutenant Hanson is dubious. I just came to tell you that the big shot and his wife have arrived. They've just checked in at the Waldorf. I thought maybe you might want to see him."

"He say anything to you?"

"Yeah," Eagan said sourly. "He says that it's all a lousy political gag, that you are a dirty liar, and that he is going to see to it that we all go to a federal pen for the rest of our natural lives."

Bill Morrow closed up the distance between them, one hand still thrust in his coat pocket. Smith lighted a cigar. "Well, that wouldn't be a long rap for me," he told Eagan. "But maybe we can avoid it. It might be difficult at my age to learn the lockstep."

Morrow looked at Eagan. Eagan told him, "The big shot just got in. Him and his wife. And when I left his suite he was getting the Commissioner out of bed to tell him what he'd do to him if he didn't arrest and incarcerate a madman by the name of Silent Smith who had phoned him such a fantastic story that he had been forced to charter a plane and fly here from Washington in the middle of the night."

"He came, didn't he?" Smith pointed out. "A bad conscience is a wonderful thing—for the other fellow."

"More," Eagan continued, "the girl's not talking. She merely keeps repeating that some man, some man she didn't know, phoned her that there was a hundred dollar bill in het mailbox and that there would be four more just like it in the morning if she spun you that fairy tale she told."

"She may be telling the truth," Smith said.

He was suddenly tired. This business of trapping a killer had lost some of its savor. He was bucking bigger money than he had ever bucked before. He wanted to say, "To hell with it," and go to bed.

A man he had never even seen had died two years ago—and Snow-Ball and a punk named Morry were dead. Other men had died. More men would die. All that he had to do to bow out gracefully was to say that he had been mistaken, and the whole thing would blow over.

Eagan read his mind. "So?"

Smith shook his head doggedly. "We're going on with it, of course." He looked back down Broadway. The freshness of morning was gone. The early work-bound crowd was beginning to stream out of the subway kiosks. "But we might as well go back to the place. It's getting a little too crowded for them to have a try for me now."

Cork stopped the cab a half block from the casino. The door guard was breathing hard. "There's hell to pay," he informed them. "You know our car. The one Silent smashed up the other night. The one that Snow-Ball was killed in."

"What about it?" Silent asked sharply.

"It's all over, blood in the back seat," Dugan told him. "A Mrs. Klotsky has identified it as the car she saw park in front of the lot where Morry's body was found. They found a bloodstained hammer with hair on it underneath the seat. And Craig has just sworn out a murder warrant naming you three guys."

Silent sighed. *Craig and his one-track mind . . .*

"This gun-punk is smart," Eagan admitted. "He hasn't missed a trick so far. And this looks like a grand slam."

"Not speaking of Craig," Morrow said.

"No," Eagan agreed. "Not speaking of Craig."

The silver-haired gambler sucked at his cigar. He was missing something. The man he believed guilty had been busier than the proverbial nervous cat on a tin roof. Silent debated going over Craig's head—he knew, but he had no proof—and discarded the idea.

It occurred to him, though, that now the tables had been turned—and he was the one fighting time.

"Turn this heap around," he told the driver. "Take us to the Waldorf—side door. And then forget you ever saw us."

The driver turned in his seat. "Whatever you say, Mr. Smith. I know it's a bum rap. And if there's anything else I can do—" He left the statement open.

Smith's smile was sudden and warm. "No. Just drop us off, Tony. But thanks."

There was no doorman at the side door.

"Get a room and bring me the key," Smith told Eagan. "Then you boys hang around the lobby. Let yourselves get pinched if you have to. That will keep Craig off my neck for a few hours. I'll need 'em. I've got to get about two hours shut-eye to clear my head. Then I'm going to talk to the big shot."

Eagan went inside. He had been in the Army, away from Broadway, for three years. He was the least known of the three. Morrow insisted Smith take his gun.

"I know they're against your principles," he said, dryly. "But you've found this one handy—when I used it. You're always playing hunches. Humor one of mine."

The gambler shrugged and dropped the gun in a side pocket. He was too tired to argue.

Eagan did well. The room was large and expensive. The bed was soft and wide. Smith had been dead for sleep when he had hung his coat on a chair and kicked off his shoes. But the moment his head had touched the pillow all desire for sleep had left him.

The man who had called him a dirty liar was in this same hotel. He checked what he knew in his mind. There *had* to be an accomplice to bring the time element right. No one man could be in two places at the same time. He sat up suddenly, the case complete in his mind.

I must be getting senile, he thought. He seldom swore, but he did now, softly and with emotion. All the while he had been stumbling in the dark, fitting trivia together the thing had been as plain as the nose on his face—and almost as near.

The phone on the bed table tinkled. Smith picked it up, expecting to hear either Sam's or Bill Morrow's voice. "Yes?"

"This is Sol Arnson, Silent," his caller said. He sounded frightened. "Look. What's this all about? Call off the heat, will you? I been tailing you all morning, trying to get in a word without one of your boys burning off my can."

"How did you know where I was?" Smith asked.

"I told you," Arnson said. "I been tailing you all morning. But you kept hotter than July Fourth—that Morrow is faster with a gun than I like to think about." The hoodlum pleaded, "Look, Smith. Have I asked for more trouble with you? Tell me, what is this business I hear about me hiring some punk named Morry Reynolds to burn you down? I should live so long to pull a crazy stunt like that!"

Arnson sounded on the verge of panic. After a pause, Smith said, "I believe you, Sol. Forget it. That was just a rumor passed around to blow smoke in Craig's eyes."

The hoodlum seemed much relieved. Then, "Wish you'd tell him that. Look Silent, I made a mistake about dice, but it doesn't mean that I'm running around killing people. Cool me off, will you? Hell, I even ran into a sailor last night who figured I should stick up your place—"

"Describe that sailor," Smith cut him short.

Arnson described him as young and husky with close-cropped black hair. "I never seen him before, but he talks to me like we should be buddies. I look out for that kind, and he turned out hopped up to the eyes on marijuana."

"You wouldn't know where you could find him now?"

The hoodlum admitted, "He give me his address. But I don't remember the number. It's in care of some dame named Sample or something like that. Jane, I think, was her first name."

"And where are you now?"

Arnson seemed surprised. "Here in the hotel, right on the floor above you. I seen Sam get you a room so I checked in, so we could get this straightened out."

A warning bell should have rung in Smith's mind. Fatigue prevented it from sounding. "Give me your room number, Sol. And then sit tight. I'll be right up. There's something you can do for me."

"Anything," Arnson assured him. "I'd like to get square."

Smith slipped on his shoes, threw his coat over his arm, then stopped, regarding the phone. He could get in touch with Bill and Sam by having them paged in the lobby. But that would draw attention to them and to himself. And he was stalling for time. Before he called for a showdown he had either to know several more facts, or have located the hopped up killer.

He walked up the service stairs without being seen and rapped on Arnson's door.

The hoodlum cracked it, then slipped the chain. "Come in. Anybody see you?"

"No. I don't think so," Smith said. Sudden suspicion lighted his eyes. "Why? What difference does it make?"

"My neck," young Goodwin told him from the bathroom door, over the barrel of a heavy service automatic. His face was as deeply bronzed as it had been the night before but he didn't look wholesome any more. His mouth was loose and moist. His eyes were drugged to pin points.

"Okay, wise guy," he told Smith. "You wanted me. Here I am."

Arnson locked the door. "Clever? Hell, I should have been an actor! Beat me up. Call me a cheat. Throw me out of your casino, will you? Now I'm taking over the whole thing."

Goodwin advanced into the room, his lips twisted in an evil smile. "That's what he thinks," he told Smith. He turned his gun on Arnson and the hoodlum went suddenly pale. He hadn't a chance.

Goodwin knocked him from his feet with a vicious swipe of the gun barrel that cracked the frontal bones of Arnson's skull.

Goodwin chuckled. "Sucker bait."

Smith looked, unmoved, at the bleeding man on the floor, then at Goodwin. "Not bad thinking at all. But you can't get away with it, Goodwin. Not all of your father's dough can save you. When Sol comes to, he'll talk. And you can't pay any man enough money to go to the chair for you."

There was a green cast to the young sailor's glittering eyes. "But he isn't coming to. I'm going to hit him again. Catch on? That screwy story about Arnson hiring Morry is going to hold up after all. He tricked you into this room, see? You fought with him. And just before he died, he let you have it."

Smith said, "I'll be damned. Tricked by a punk, a drugged killer, who has gone back to his old vicious habits before he is even out of the service."

He shifted the coat on his arm as if it had grown too heavy.

Goodwin lighted another pungent marijuana cigarette to nerve him. "You've been smart," he admitted. "Damn smart. That's why you've got to die. I had everyone fooled but you. Told me to come see you when I got out, did you? Hell, you didn't show it, but you were laughing at me, you goddam gambler! Well, I'm laughing now!"

"Sure," Smith told him. Under the coat, his finger squeezed the trigger of Bill Morrow's gun carefully, twice. At the distance he couldn't miss. He didn't. Goodwin died on his feet, too quickly for his expression to change—or maybe the marijuana had something to do with that.

Silent stared down at him. "Sure," he whispered sorrowfully. "You're laughing."

CHAPTER SIX

Wrong Guy

A BROAD-SHOULDERED, red-faced, self-made man weighing over two hundred pounds, it took two husky detectives to keep the multi-millionaire ship-builder from carrying out his threat to pound Silent Smith to a jellied pulp.

"Cold-blooded murder, that's what it is!" he bellowed. "And you're going to the chair for this, Smith, if it costs me every penny that I have."

"It won't," Captain Craig assured him.

Unmoved, poker-faced, Smith sat on a window sill of the hotel room studying Mrs. Goodwin's face.

She had been a pretty woman. She still was. But her face was white under her makeup. Her eyes were red-rimmed from crying. From time to time she put her knuckles to her mouth as if to keep from screaming. She was, Smith decided, on the verge of a nervous collapse.

"Well?" Goodwin demanded of Craig. "Why don't you arrest him for the murder of my son?"

Craig looked at Morrow and Eagan. Both men had their hands in their pockets. Both were fanatically loyal. Both men had spent their lives close enough to lawlessness to know its meaning, and both would shoot at a nod from Smith, regardless of consequences.

"You admit that you killed him, Silent?"

"I do," Smith answered Craig.

"You shot him, why?" Craig pounded.

Smith looked him in the eyes. "Because he intended to shoot me. I knew he would. In the first place he was drugged to the eyes." He nodded at Arnson who had never regained consciousness. "In the second place I'd just seen him kill Sol."

"That's a lie!" Goodwin said. "This whole affair is a pack of fantastic lies. Jack never killed anyone. He left college to enter the service. He served his country loyally for two years. And this is his reward. A slimy little Broadway gambler not only tries to pin a two-year-old murder on him, he shoots my son down in cold blood—and a captain of the New York homicide squad refuses to arrest him!"

"I'm not refusing," Craig protested. He glowered at Smith. "You ready to go down to Center Street?"

"Not yet," Smith answered quietly. "I think there are a few angles that should be straightened out—to that effect, Findy and Corbett are bringing up two men to look at young Goodwin's body." He added, "And I have sent for Lippy Courtney."

Craig shook his head. "You've gone too far this time,

Smith. Not even a high-priced mouthpiece like Lippy can pry you out of this one."

"Possibly not," Smith agreed. "But while we are waiting, suppose we clear up as much as we can." He looked at Lieutenant Hanson who was standing just inside the door. "Thank you for coming, Lieutenant. You looked up young Goodwin's record?"

"I did."

"And he was getting a medical discharge?"

"No. He was not. He was getting a D.D."

The ship builder stared incredulously at the Navy man. "Jack, my son, was being dishonorably discharged. Why?"

Hanson said, rather stiffly, "I'm sorry, sir. But I am not at liberty to disclose that."

"I can tell you," Smith said. "He was being kicked out as an incorrigible and a hophead. His brig time wasn't for getting drunk. It was for breaking into the pharmacist's stores for something to appease his craving."

One hand clutched to her throat, Mrs. Goodwin said faintly, "No!" She swayed slightly.

Smith continued. "It seems he became a marijuana addict in college—a fact that got him expelled, according to the dean of men, to whom I spoke last night."

"That's not so." Goodwin's tone was not as positive as it had been. "Jack left college to enter the service. Isn't that so, Grace?" The ship-builder looked at his wife. She refused to meet his eyes.

"Expelled from college," Smith continued, "afraid to come to you, knowing you would be furious, young Goodwin came to New York and tried what a lot of other fools have tried. He tried to earn a living with a gun. On one of his expeditions his drug-inflamed mind decided that he needed a driver for his stolen getaway car. So he picked up a colored boy, Charlie Johnson, with the lure of five dollars and a pint. A boy who, by the way, is in the death house now awaiting execution tomorrow night for the murder of a liquor store dealer whom your son killed."

Mrs. Goodwin said, "Oh!" and fainted.

Smith nodded to Morrow and Eagan. "Help her back to her room. There is no need for her to hear the rest of this. She has been through enough hell."

Morrow looked at Craig.

"Craig won't bother me," Smith told him. "If he does, he'll take the gold cure by eating his own badge."

"Now see here," Craig began. "You can't—"

"Shut up," Goodwin stopped him. "I want to hear the rest of this." He swung back to Smith, his eyes worried. "Admitting, for the sake of argument, that what you have said so far is true—" He nodded after the figure of his unconscious wife. "She knew?"

"I am afraid so," Smith said quietly. "And if my surmise is correct, during the last two years she has been bled for a lot of your money."

The ship-builder's body seemed to shrink. He glowered at Arnson's body. "Go on."

"It would seem," Smith began, "that—" He stopped as Courtney appeared in the doorway of the room and stood staring at the two bodies. "Come in, Lippy," Smith invited. "I know you will be pleased to learn that we have finally located the well-dressed white boy for whom you, as Charlie Johnson's lawyer, have looked for two years."

The day was hot. Courtney removed his expensive straw hat and wiped the perspiration from its sweat band. "Fine. This *is* good news. You can prove he is the man?"

"I think I can," Smith said.

Before he could continue, Findy and Corbett entered the room, forcing two sallow-faced youths ahead of them.

"That's him," one of them exclaimed, peering at young Goodwin's body. "That's the guy I seen talking to Charlie in the poolroom the night that liquor store owner was knocked off."

The other youth wasn't as positive in his identification.

Craig exploded, "So he was talking to Charlie. That doesn't prove young Goodwin killed the owner of that liquor store." He appealed to Courtney. "Does it?"

The lawyer refused to commit himself. "I'd have to know all of the facts before I'd venture an opinion." He looked at Smith. "First, just what is my position here? Why did you send for me, Silent?"

The gambler hesitated briefly, said, "You're a lawyer, Lippy. And I need you to help me clean up this affair."

Courtney beamed, "Fine. I'll do the best I can."

Craig shook his head as if to clear it. "Let's go back to the start of this. Just what is your story, Silent?"

Smith told it quietly. "After young Goodwin had killed the liquor store dealer in an attempted holdup, he was desperate. He went to a man whom he thought could protect him. And that man advised him to join the Navy and drop out of sight."

Courtney looked at Arnson's body. "I see. So that's where Sol comes into the picture."

Smith continued, "So young Goodwin did and Charlie was convicted for his crime. But matters didn't end there. This man in whom he had confided undoubtedly used his knowledge to blackmail Mrs. Goodwin on the threat of exposing her son." Smith looked at the ship-builder. "He didn't dare come to you. He knew that—for all of your money, and despite your love for your son—you were as square as a die. And he knew that you would expose your son yourself rather than to allow another man, white or black, to go to the chair for a crime he had committed."

The ship-builder's face was haggard, his eyes suddenly hollow. He said nothing.

"Mothers, however," Smith said quietly, "are unpredictable creatures. No matter what their children do they usually stand by them, commit perjury, steal for them, die for them. Mrs. Goodwin was no exception. God knows how much blackmail she has paid."

Goodwin admitted that he had been forced to remonstrate with her for the hundreds of thousands of dollars that had run through her fingers during the last two years and for which she could give no reasonable explanation.

"I will be damned." Courtney nudged the dead hoodlum's body with the toe of his white sports shoe. "Who would ever have thought that Sol was mixed up in a big time racket like that?"

"All things," Smith continued, "must come to an end, however. And the beginning of the end in this case was Lieutenant Commander Kenmore's list of boys deserving help." He looked at Goodwin. "The commander, by the way, was suddenly assigned to Iwo Jima as a favor to you, as requested in a phone call from Mrs. Goodwin to the senior senator of your state."

Goodwin's face grew even more haggard. "This is the first I'd heard of it. Go on."

"Contrary to what young Goodwin told Lieutenant Hanson and myself, his name *was* on that list. Despite his bad record, not knowing *what* Goodwin he was, Kenmore undoubtedly reasoned that he had some good qualities and that I might help to make a man of him if I could cure him of his habit. But young Goodwin knew I would investigate his background as a matter of course that murder would come out. So he went to the man in whom he had confided and asked him to have the original stolen while he destroyed the carbon. This man hired Morry Reynolds to highjack me. And Morry did. They were stalling for time, figuring that, once. Charlie Johnson had burned; the District Attorney and the police would be hesitant about reopening the case."

"Your proof of this?" Craig asked.

Smith gave him the warning note that had been wrapped around the half brick. "Young Goodwin threw that at me outside the Yard. His misspelling of the name Morry was the giveaway. He hadn't hired him himself. More, he didn't know that the man running the show, knowing I had identified Morry, had just knocked him off to keep him from talking."

Courtney scowled at Arnson's body. "He was scum. But you have to give him credit for being clever."

"Meanwhile," Smith continued, "Snow-Ball had been murdered to delay us from catching up with Morry until he had been attended to." He shrugged. "There it is. Corbett will see to it, of course, that Charlie is cleared and released at once." He looked at Craig. "And with your permission, Captain, I think I have enough influence in certain places to see that Mrs. Goodwin's name is not mentioned in this affair. She has been through enough hell."

Craig nodded, curtly.

"Thank you," the ship-builder said sincerely. "Thank you both." He took one last long look at his son, spun on his heel and left the room, his shoulders bowed with a weight that would never be lifted.

Lieutenant Hanson followed shortly. The tech squad and Craig's men finished with the bodies and they were removed.

Craig started to follow his squad, turned in the doorway and scowled at Smith. "You haven't put out all you know, Silent. There are a lot of angles to this case that are still plenty muddy. How did Arnson know we'd identified Morry? Why did he use your car to dump Morry's body? And why should Goodwin have confided in a punk like Arnson in the first place?"

"Well," the silver-haired gambler said quietly, "after all you're a detective."

Craig slammed out.

Courtney laughed. "Nice work, Silent." He crossed the room toward the door. "But seeing that you aren't going to want a lawyer after all—" He stopped, staring at Bill Morrow, puzzled, as the other man blocked the doorway. The air in the room had become suddenly heavy with silence. The lawyer licked at his lips. "What—what's the idea?"

Morrow told him, "Maybe we do want a lawyer. Bad."

Smith said quietly. "I swung all of it over on Arnson to save Mrs. Goodwin any more grief. But Sol Arnson's sole connection with the affair was being bribed by you and young Goodwin to lure me up here to be killed, after things went sour last night. I doubt if he ever even saw Goodwin until you introduced him. You are the man in whom Goodwin confided. You advised him to join the Navy. You have been blackmailing Mrs. Goodwin. It was you who hired

Morry Reynolds to high-jack me. It was you who killed Snow-Ball to delay us. You made that phone call, not from your office, but from the cigar store on the corner. You called Craig and introduced the Arnson angle. You used my car to dump Morry to back up that angle, Clever or not, you're scum. Because it meant money to you, you were willing to kill—and let an innocent man go to the chair."

"No!" The blood had drained from the lawyer's face leaving it a fish-belly white. "No. You're wrong, Silent. You know how I felt about that. I—I even mailed back the fees that you and Snow-Ball paid me."

"Sure. To cover your own rottenness."

Morrow lifted an eyebrow in question.

"I think Lippy wants to go back to his office, Bill," Smith said. "I think he's made some bad investments. And you'd better leave him a gun to protect him from his conscience."

"No!" No longer arrogant, Lippy whimpered. "I did it all. Sure. But you—you can't make me do that, Silent. I want a trial."

"You've had one," Smith said coldly.

He turned and looked out the window, ignoring the soft closing of the door. Morning was full now. Workers, shoppers, parasites, rich men, poor men, beggars, thieves, doctors, lawyers, merchants, chiefs, thronged a lusty, awakened, Broadway. She was, the gambler reflected, the only one of her kind. If a man was right, the sky was the limit. If he was wrong—well, wrong guys didn't last long.

THE STARS SAY DIE!

IT WAS, IN SOME RESPECTS, the most unusual series of murders ever committed in Chicago, that city of violence. That was due, in great part, to the prominence of at least two of the victims involved. It was furthered by the fact that an obscure astrologer who called himself Zoroaster claimed, and established his claim, that he had read of the forthcoming deaths in the stars and had at his own expense warned each of the victims.

It was complicated by the undeniable, yet seemingly impossible fact that in each of the three cases murder had passed unseen through locked windows and bolted doors, leaving each corpse blushing furiously, an embarrassed smile on its lifeless lips.

The first murder occurred at ten o'clock one unseasonably hot forenoon in the last days of Indian Summer. Secure behind locked doors and windows in his expensively appointed, air conditioned, fortieth floor office, there was no way but natural means by which the man could die. But die he did—and far from naturally . . .

The man behind the desk was advanced in years, but not yet elderly. His eyes were keenly alert. The flesh of his face was pale but firm. His mustache was two sharp spiked wisps of gray. His clothes were conservative but well cut and expensive. E.P. Marlby, a very big man, paid an income tax on seven figures.

He extended the letter in his hand to the girl before his desk.

"This, er, letter or horoscope from this man Zoroaster came in when, Miss Thomas?"

His secretary wet her lips with a pink shell of a tongue, She had been dubious as to the wisdom of allowing her employer to see the letter, but had decided it was, best. She said, "It came in the morning mail, Mr. Marlby. And I thought—"

"Please don't," he answered curtly. "That will be all, Miss Thomas. Be ready for dictation presently."

The girl said: "Yes, sir," and closed the office door as she went out. It locked with a resounding click. It could be opened again only when the financier depressed a button on his desk.

Marlby, twisting at one spike of his mustache, sat staring at the letter. It annoyed him greatly. A practical man, he despised all cranks and charlatans. Still, the writer had nothing to gain. He made no threats. He asked for no money. He was obviously sincere. Typed upon cheap bond with a colored imprint of the signs of the Zodiac serving as a letterhead, the letter read:

Mr. E. P. Marlby
27 N. LaSalle St.
Chicago, Illinois

Dear Mr. Marlby:

The writer of this letter is unknown to you but feels that it is his duty to impart the following facts.

Your life is in danger. How, or why this should be, is beyond the writer's knowledge. I do know that you were born on May 4th under the sign of Taurus, the Bull with your ruling planet Venus, and that the stars as I read them last night foretell your immediate death.

Therefore, not as an astrologer, but as a fellow man, I beg you to take whatever precautions may seem necessary to your common sense. Be guarded, be watchful, especially between the hours of nine and ten on the morning of October 2nd. It is then that the orbit surrounding your sign is filled with danger. During that time you may be maimed or harmed. The stars say—die!

Respectfully yours,

Zoroaster

It was October 2nd. The financier glanced at his watch. It was nine forty-five. A thin smile on his lips, he crumpled the letter into a ball and dropped it in the waste basket.

"I seem," he mused, as he dismissed the matter from his mind. "to have surmounted my astral difficulties."

He returned to his morning mail. But a tiny hammer had begun to beat in the back of his active brain. When a man had reached Marlby's years, death became merely a matter of time. A man's body fell heir to the sins of his flesh; a hard driven machine was bound to wear out.

Marlby raised his eyes to the windows of his office. There were four of them. Three were closed and locked. The fourth contained an electric window ventilator that sucked in the fresh outer air, always cool at that altitude, and expelled the used air.

"At the rate of one hundred and eighty-five cubic feet per minute," Marlby said dryly.

His thin smile tightened. He knew the figure to the decimal. His life had been composed of figures. He knew them intimately. The astral, on the other hand, was a vague, uncharted field. He wondered idly what the next world would be like. Above and beyond the radio cabinet type ventilator, that took up only the lower third of the window, the Lake lay a limpid body of blue water dotted with white sails. Under the other windows of his office, the Loop that had been his life lay hot and sullen in the sun. It would seem strange, he reflected, not to ever see it again.

He rapped his chest with his palm. His heart had begun to pound. It always did when he thought of death.

"No fool like an old fool," he scoffed. He poured a glass of water from the vacuum carafe on his desk to relieve a slight nausea and dizziness. "I've allowed that fool letter to upset me."

He deliberately put the thought of death out of his mind. It had no place in a business office. He addressed himself to his morning mail, sorting the chaff from the wheat, making notations for dictation, jotting down stock quotations to be checked against the opening market.

His nausea and dizziness increased. His face felt hot and flushed. He drank another glass of water from the carafe and fumbled, annoyed, at his collar. Then the piles of mail grew suddenly confused and it became an effort to think.

He reached out his hand in puzzled alarm to summon his secretary. His hand stopped just short of the buzzer, powerless to move the few inches more that would summon aid. He tried to rise from his chair—and couldn't. All strength had left his body. The thin smile on his lips became an embarrassed grimace.

Struck by a sudden thought that stabbed through his fog-misted mind, he glanced at the watch on his wrist. It was exactly ten o'clock.

Then respiration ceased entirely. He slumped forward on his desk and slept. He didn't even hear them when they battered in the door. Zoroaster had been right.

Unseen, unheard by the busy workers in the outer office, fulfilling the prophecy of the stars, Death had called for E.P. Marlby between the hours of nine and ten.

The noon rush had not begun. The girl studying the tempting food behind the glass counter of the one-armed lunchroom at Broadway and Diversey was not more than twenty-two, or three. She was hungry. She counted the change in her purse. It was a very simple matter. She had only two dimes and one nickel. She passed by the twenty cent beef stew special with a sigh. She would need seven cents for carfare.

"Just coffee and a hard roll, please," she said to the counterman.

She picked up her coffee and roll and sat in a chair near the window to study the want ads in the afternoon paper. There was little more than there had been in the morning paper. One ad alone held promise.

Wanted—Secretary with at least five years' experience. Must be able to run Burrows machine and take dictation.

Blonde beauties please save your time and mine . . .

The girl looked at herself in the mirror walls. A plain but intelligent face framed in unbecoming brown braids stared back.

"It might just be I'm the type," Fran Harlan sighed. "God knows I've more brains than beauty. Still—" She blushed at the thought of the scene that had terminated her last employment after four years of faithful service. "Why, the nasty old thing," she sniffed.

She finished her coffee and roll and walked west on the Boulevard to her hotel. The morning mail had not come in when she had left at seven on her fruitless search for work. It might just be that there would be an answer to one of the numerous applications she had filed.

The hotel was old. Even its garishly painted lobby couldn't quite hide the smell of mold. Without rising from the switchboard the single clerk reached behind him and handed the girl her mail.

"About your bill, Miss Harlan," he began. "The manager told me to tell you that he'd have to have some money on it by the end of the week."

Fran Harlan smiled, frightened.

"I—I'm certain I'll have a job by the end of the week," she assured him.

"I hope so."

Once in her room, Fran Harlan leaned against the door and locked it. It wasn't much of a room. There was a bed, a dresser, a cheap writing desk and a chair. A solitary window opened on a narrow, noisy alley in the rear of the hotel. To make the room habitable, the management had installed an electric window ventilator. It kept out most of the alley noises and the smells. The filtered air was fresh and pure and cool after the blazing heat of the streets.

The girl sank down wearily on the bed, kicked off her shoes and ripped open her mail with a hair pin. There were a half a dozen letters. The replies were stereotyped. They might have come from the same firm. "If you will contact our employment bureau in several weeks it is very possible that . . ."

"I'll be dead of starvation in two weeks," the girl muttered. She let the letters fall on the floor beside the bed and opened the letter she had saved until the last. It was typed upon cheap bond with a colored imprint of the signs of the Zodiac serving as a letter head. Her blue eyes were bitter as she read it. The letter was cryptically ironic.

Dear Fran:

Despite the recent unpleasantness which caused you to leave my employ after four years of mutually pleasant relations, I feel it my duty to warn you of the following solemn fact.

Death is very near to you, Fran. I cast your horoscope last evening I was alarmed to find that a very sinister shadow is entering the orbit of Virgo, the Virgin.

Please, Fran, take care of yourself. Watch your every step, your every move. The stars foretell that on mid-day of October 2nd, or 3rd, death will be very close to you. The stars say you will die. Be forewarned. Consult me if you care to.

Sincerely alarmed.
Zoroaster

The girl wadded the letter into a ball and threw it from her. The man was mad. He was also a fake. She knew. She had been his secretary for four years. She had mailed out hundreds of mimeographed horoscopes to the gullible curious who had been able and willing to part with a dollar.

"Virgo, the Virgin," she snorted.

She buried her face in the pillow and cried. She was admittedly frightened. Not of death, but of living. What was she going to do?

She was too hungry, too worried to cry for long. She *had* to find a job. She had to keep shelter over her head, she had to eat. Still, it was pleasant just lying on the bed and looking at the ceiling. What was the use in answering ads? There were no jobs.

A wave of nausea and dizziness swept over her. She wondered how long the human engine could sustain itself once it ceased to be fueled by even rolls and coffee. She pounded her clenched fists on the bed.

"I've got to get a job. I've got to eat." Her eyes turned, slightly puzzled, towards the dresser mirror. Her voice had sounded faint and far away. She got to her feet and stared at herself in the glass.

Her braids had fallen in loose, soft waves against her cheeks. Her cheeks were flushed. The combination made her look somehow strangely beautiful and wanton.

"I'm going mad," she thought. "I even look like that kind of a girl."

She lay back on the bed, an embarrassed smile on her lips. She closed her eyes and found it difficult to open them again. She tried to speak, and couldn't. It felt to her dulled senses as if a softly caressing hand had clamped down upon her lips. She gasped, in fear:

"I'm not alone!"

She forced her eyes to open, saw no one.

But her last conscious words had been correct. So had the stars and Zoroaster.

Unseen, unheard by the yawning clerk at the switchboard in the lobby, Death had needed no key to steal into Fran Harlan's room.

CHAPTER TWO

Herman the Great

THE AFTERNOON SUN was still a brazen ball of fire. Night was long in coming. The humidity was intense. There was no breeze at all. The sweating blond giant in uniform pants and shirt sleeves sat in what shade was afforded by the back of the station garage as he studied the "EXTRA" filled with the sudden and somewhat mysterious death of E.P. Marlby, the great philanthropist.

"That guy," he tapped the paper with a massive finger, "no more died natural than you will, Phinny. He was murdered." He added without much hope. "Two gets you ten he was."

His working partner considered the odds and was tempted. He was a cautious little man mostly neck, ears, and nose. He had driven the Diversey Precinct Wagon since its horse power had been actually horses.

"Mebbe, but I ain't a gambling man." He shuffled the deck of cards in his hand accidentally to get at a buried black nine to play on his ten of diamonds.

"Why it's a cinch," the blond giant expanded. "And if I was down on Homicide where I belong, instead of—"

A bell clanged inside of the garage. It was followed by a bellow from the dim depths of the station.

"Herman! You, Stone! Herman the Great!"

A burst of smothered laughter rippled through the drowsing precinct station. Phineas Ott lay down his cards.

"Hell! For twenty years I try to beat this game. And every time I get four aces out, that damn thing rings." He disappeared into the double doors of the garage.

Herman (the Great) Stone, Shield 2413, former plainclothes ace of the Headquarters Homicide Squad, lowered the front legs of his chair to the pavement and struggled into his uniform coat. It buttoned with an effort. Up until two weeks before, he hadn't worn it in ten years.

But it was fortunate that he had kept it packed in moth balls. There are no detectives in Chicago. All are regular police assigned to detective duty. And Herman the Great was being disciplined for his own good. He had made the grave mistake of thinking that a certain old line politician was subject to the law. He had, in fact, arrested him and almost convicted him of murder.

"For God's sake, Herman, are you nuts?" his immediate superior had bellowed. "What you need is a touch of the sticks in uniform, my boy, maybe herding the goats out at Cragin."

It hadn't gone as far as that. It had been worse. H.Q. had

assigned him to the wagon at Diversey. Instead of roaming with the gravy squad and picking murderers out of thin air, the feat that had won him his newspaper title, "Herman the Great," he now picked drunks out of the gutters, and helped Phinny trundle the remains of careless pedestrians and suicides to various hospitals, undertakers, and the Morgue.

"Yes, sir. You have a run for me?" he asked as he reported to the sergeant at the desk.

Desk Sergeant Mack, a dour-faced man whose home life was unhappy, glowered at the fallen star.

"A run for Phineas," he corrected. "You just go along for the ride. And don't try to make a murder of it, Stone. McCarthy's in charge over there. All you have to do is pick up a stiff in 412 at the Diversey Terrace Hotel, have her certified, then dump her off at the nearest undertaker for a post by the Coroner's Office."

"Yes, sir."

Sergeant Mack didn't like the big ex-homicide man. He never had. He scowled:

"That's all, Herman the Great. Let's see you get a headline out of this one."

The blond giant grinned unpleasantly. "You never can tell. I might."

The usual crowd of morbidly curious still clustered around the outer door of the hotel, while the perspiring patrolman on the beat ordered them to move on. Stone talked to him as his partner got the stretcher from the wagon.

"You find the body?" he asked.

"Not me." The patrolman wiped the sweatband of his cap. "The clerk seen her go up about noon. About two a maid uses her pass key to leave fresh towels and finds her stretched out on the bed." He put his cap back on his head. "Poor kid. McCarthy thinks she must have had high blood pressure and died of a stroke. But she looks to me like she died of starvation."

"No sign of foul play?"

"If you don't mind, Stone," McCarthy's voice was cool as

he walked out of the lobby followed by the district squad, "we've made the investigation. It's merely a sudden death and not a homicide." He called to the wagon driver as he climbed into the squad car. "It's okay, Phinny. You can move her."

Stone stood staring after the squad car; his gray eyes the consistency of slate. Phinny came up with the stretcher.

"Well," he demanded, "what are we waiting for?"

"A break," Stone told him. "Just one corpse that some wiseacre slips up on."

Death had been kind to Fran Harlan. He had left her with a smile on her lips. Her plain face framed in soft brown curls would have been beautiful but for the general duskiness of her skin and the too high color in her cheeks.

Stone didn't like it and said so. It wasn't a heat prostration. Heat victims are pale. And he doubted she had died of a stroke. She was too young and too thin.

"What the hell," he growled, "does that young punk of a McCarthy mean saying she died of a stroke? I can tell that duskiness of the skin and that flush a block away. That kid's a carbon monoxide victim."

Phinny scratched one of his ears. "On the fourth floor of an air conditioned hotel room?"

Stone scowled from the corpse to his partner.

"Look, son," the little wagon driver told him. "I know how you feel. You want to climb back on the top of the heap. But we're just the wagon men. If McCarthy's made a mistake, the post-mortem will bring it out. Come on. You take her head. I'll take her feet."

He spread the stretcher on the floor and glanced up impatiently at his partner. Herman the Great was staring at the electric window ventilator. He held his hand before the draft, then stooped and smelled of it.

"It's pure, fresh air," he announced.

Phinny grunted, "What did you expect it to be? Attar of carbon monoxide?"

"Yes," Stone nodded, "I did." He looked around the small, bare room. "I suppose," he said to the beat patrolman who had followed them upstairs, "that McCarthy and his boys took all her clothes, and letters, and personal possessions?"

"Don't they always?" the patrolman countered. "Unless it's a case for Homicide. And this dame just died. She only had one thin dime in her purse." He paused. "There was one funny thing about it, though."

"Yeah?"

"Yeah. She got a letter this morning from some guy named Zoroaster. He warned her that she'd die."

Stone's nostrils tightened. He had been right. The old sixth sense wasn't gone. He still could smell premeditated murder. And one good case would put him back where he belonged.

"Hmm. That's interesting:" His tone was disarmingly casual. "McCarthy make much of it?"

The patrolman shook his head. "Naw. He paid it no attention. That guy Zoroaster is a crank. He sent the same kind of warning to that big shot banker who dropped dead of heart failure this morning. He claims he can read death in the stars."

Stone said nothing. Phinny wrinkle his nose, disgusted, and picked up the dead girl's shapely ankles.

"If it isn't too much of an effort, a little co-operation, Officer Stone."

Dusk was creeping in from the Lake but bringing no relief from the sticky, penetrating heat. On the front seat of the wagon Phinny whistled cheerfully off key as he hurled the big patrol down Clark Street against the steady stream of rush-hour, north-bound traffic. In the back, Stone stared at the corpse on the stretcher.

The flushed cheeks had not faded, nor would they soon fade. The dead girl had been murdered—he knew she had. But how a girl behind a locked door on the fourth floor of an air conditioned hotel could die of carbon monoxide poisoning was something that stumped even Herman the Great. Still, he knew that, despite McCarthy's error in calling it sudden death, the Coroner's Inquest would prove him right and the H.Q. Homicide Squad would raise hell because they had not been called.

He compared her death to the newspaper account of the death of E.P. Marlby. But for a difference of two hours and thirty-six floors they were identical in all details even to the letter from Zoroaster: He wished he could read those letters.

"Damn it, this is murder, Phinny," he shouted through the grating at the driver. "Two gets you twenty it was."

The little driver considered the odds as he leaned on his siren and shaved a curl of yellow paint from the fender of a cruising cab. Twenty bucks would buy a lot of beer.

"Well," he decided, "not that I'm a gambling man, but just to learn you a lesson, it's a bet. You got homicide on the brain. You're so anxious to—"

The blast of a squad car siren cut him short as it swung to his left and curbed him. A few yards further on the squad car skidded to a screaming halt and four plainclothesmen swarmed out of the car and across the sidewalk, doubled barreled shot-guns in their hands.

"Hold the wagon, Phinny," McCarthy called over his shoulder. "We may have another stiff. A call just came in that Ed Faber's been knocked off."

The four officers bolted through the doorway of the Pink Star Inn.

Herman the Great opened the back of the patrol and joined Phinny on the sidewalk. A big grin split his rugged face. He beamed: "Boy. And is that good news. But I only wish whoever got him had gotten the dirty son before he had me busted. Did I ever tell you, Phinny, how Ed Faber—"

"Twelve times," the little wagon chauffeur stopped him.

One of the plainclothes men returned to the squad car for an axe.

"You guys better give us a hand," he said. "Faber's locked in his private office."

Phinny asked: "You mean it's locked from the inside?"

The plainclothesman wrenched the axe out of its holder. "Yeah. And he's been in there for three hours according to the barkeep."

The two wagon men followed the squad man into the Inn.

It was one of the oldest places in Chicago and one of the most profitable. To the right of the bar; through an alcove, rows of tables lined a dance floor. On the floor above, an open gambling house had run for years. The third floor was opened intermittently according to the extent of pressure from reformers and the whims of the Morals Squad. Ed Faber's private office was in the rear of the first floor and on the alley. When Phinny and Stone arrived, McCarthy was giving the barkeep hell.

"But why phone the station that Faber's been knocked off? How do you know he's dead? How do you know he's in his office?"

The bartender wiped the palms of his hands on his apron. His eyes bulged slightly either from excessive thyroid or from fear. He nodded at the door.

"Don't bull-doze me, McCarthy. It's locked from the inside, ain't it? And if Ed ain't dead, why ain't he answered when I called him? He had a date for seven o'clock and I banged on the door for fifteen minutes before I called the station."

The plainclothesman with the axe swung it against the door. The wood was thick and hard. The axe glanced off and sank into the jamb.

"How about the windows in back?" McCarthy wanted to know.

"Not a chance." The barkeep shook his head. "They got half inch steel bars on 'em. This is the only way you can get in."

Stone reached out his hand for the axe and the sweating plainclothesman let him have it. The blond giant swung it and the head bit cleanly through the wood. Stone wrenched it out and applied his eye to the crack.

"Faber's in there all right," he informed them. "He's half sitting in a chair and half laying across his desk."

He renewed his attack on the door. The wood splintered around the lock and he kicked it open. It swung open the length of a short chain.

Phinny, peering under the big man's arm, gasped: "Gawd!"

The politician, gambler and tavern owner had been a big, red-faced man in life. In death his face was scarlet. He lay, one fat cheek on the back of one arm, a half smile on his lips.

Stone forced the chain with his shoulder. McCarthy strode into the office and felt the fat man's pulse.

"Get a doctor and an oxygen squad," he ordered. "And one of you call the station and tell Mack to notify Homicide."

Stone grinned unpleasantly. "Why Homicide? Ed looks just like the dame that we've got outside in the wagon."

"So I was wrong," McCarthy admitted. "So she didn't die of a stroke. Suppose you tell me how she did die?"

"Of carbon monoxide," Stone told him. He pointed at the politician. "Just like Faber there. And maybe E.P. Marlby, too."

McCarthy scoffed: "Ahgh! You only die of that in garages." He tugged at a letter half hidden by the politician's beefy arm. It tore and he had to piece the two halves together. It was typed upon cheap bond with a colored imprint of the signs of the Zodiac serving as a letter head. A puzzled frown on his face, McCarthy held it up:

Mr. Edward Faber:
Pink Star Inn
1582 N. Clark St.

Dear Mr. Faber:

The writer of this letter is unknown to you. And while he highly disapproves of politicians of your stamp he never-the-less feels it his duty to warn you of the following facts:

You, having been born on August 12th under the Sign of Leo, with your ruling planet the sun, are entering into a very dangerous period of your life. In fact, according to your horoscope, death will be very close to you at twilight on the evening of October 2nd. The stars say you will die!

As one fellow man to another I beg you to heed this warning. Perhaps you can circumvent Fate by going to the police, showing them this letter and asking them to assign you a body guard.

In what manner death will strike is beyond my astral knowledge, but believe me, I am sincerely alarmed for your safety.

In haste—
Zoroaster

McCarthy searched for the envelope of the letter and found it. It bore a special delivery stamp cancelled at three-thirty the same afternoon. No other evidence.

"It come just before Ed locked himself in the office," the bartender offered. "But I didn't know what it said."

McCarthy laid the letter back on the desk. His eyes were worried. "Look, Stone," he said extending the pipe of peace to the former Homicide star whom he and most of the boys at the station had ridden for two weeks. "You had a lot of experience in this sort of thing. You really think—"

"I don't think at all," the blond giant told him coolly. "I'm only the wagon man. You're the officer in charge."

The plainclothesman scowled at him, then scowled at the expensively furnished, mahogany paneled office. There was no means of entrance save by the door they had chopped down. There were three windows opening on the alley. But they were barred and locked from the inside. One of them contained an electric window ventilator. McCarthy crossed the room, stooped down and smelled the rush of air. It was fresh and sweet. Moreover, the alley was a busy thoroughfare for scores of delivery trucks.

"Well," he said uncertainly. "We—we'll see what the Coroner's office has to say. Then I think we'd better have a little talk with this here guy Zoroaster."

CHAPTER THREE

Zoroaster the Prophet

HERMAN THE GREAT smiled wryly. He knew. Once H.Q.

Homicide had reached the scene, the district plainclothes squad wouldn't talk to anyone. Homicide didn't like the district plugs to butt in on their cases.

"If—if it should be Herman's right and it is carbon monoxide," Phinny asked uneasily, "would oxygen bring the little wren out in the wagon back to life?" He was thinking of his two dollars.

McCarthy said: "Hell, no. Whatever she died of, she's dead." He felt the politician's pulse again and added glumly, "And from the looks of him, so is Faber."

An awkward silence followed.

"Well." Phinny scratched one bat-like ear. "I hope you saved your uniform like Herman did . . ."

It was night. The clock over the back bar said midnight. Stone looked like a well-dressed actor. He was merely wearing his usual clothes. He sat on a stool in the Sherman Bar with Phinny, drinking beer and culling the late extras. The little man was tired.

"But I don't like it," he kept saying. "I don't like it at all."

The bartender looked up perturbed.

"Something wrong with your beer, sir?"

"No," the little bat-eared wagon driver told him. "Not with the beer. With my partner. He's nuts."

"I'm glad, sir," the bartender said, relieved. "We pride ourself on our beer." He eyed Phinny suspiciously and retreated down the bar.

The little man relapsed into sullen silence. He felt awkward out of uniform. He also felt they were wasting time. He lowered the ring of foam in his glass an inch and tried again.

"Look, Herman. You say that the two guys and the dame were murdered, and the Coroner's office admits that they didn't die natural. But you ain't never going to prove how it was done by sitting here."

Herman the Great looked up, pre-occupied, a slight frown creasing his forehead. "How it was done? I know how it was done. What I'm trying to figure out is—why?"

"You know how it was done?"

The blond giant nodded. "Sure. At least I think so." He

scribbled a name and address on the back of an envelope and handed it to Phinny. "Look. You call up this dame and ask her these two questions." He scribbled the questions under the name and looked up at the clock on the back-bar. "By that time the Homicide boys should be through pushing Zoroaster around and we'll drop in and have our fortunes told."

Phinny climbed wearily off of the stool.

"This the way all you Homicide guys solve cases?" he demanded. "You park your keysters on a bar stool and have your stooges rout dames out of bed at midnight to ask 'em," he read the last question again, "to ask 'em when their office building was last cleaned by a sand blasting crew?"

"Most of us," Stone grinned. "But I'm not a Homicide guy. I'm just your wagon helper. Go on and give the dame a ring. I'll buy another beer when you get back."

The little wagon driver trudged off wearily to the battery of phones in the northeast corner of the Sherman Lobby, belching slightly. There was no justice in the world. When you paid for your own beer, you couldn't enjoy it for thinking of the expense. When it was free, you drank too much and the hang-over cost you Bromo Seltzer.

Stone continued to read the paper. The headline screamed in great block type:

FABER FLIGHTS FOR LIFE!

The story was a reprint. He skimmed through it again in snatches. "Police this evening admit they are baffled by a Coroner's verdict that the three deaths believed at first to have been by natural means, are possible murders. Carbon monoxide ... behind locked doors in air conditioned rooms. Still being questioned was a meek little charlatan who at his own expense had informed all three of the victims that the stars foretold that they would die ... Protesting any guilty knowledge in the matter, Zoroaster, who styles himself a prophet of the stars, is expected to be released from custody as up to a late hour this evening no formal charge had been preferred against him ... Missing from the usual scene, however, was Herman the Great, colorful Homicide Ace, who was dismissed from the H.Q. Squad two weeks ago for an alleged infraction of . . ."

"Hey! How do you do it, Herman?" Phinny's eyes were as big as his ears. "Marlby's secretary says that a cleaning squad was working on the building this morning. Also, she says that Ed Faber owed her boss two hundred thousand dollars."

The blond giant merely grunted. "Hmm. I thought that must be it." He held up his finger for two beers. "Come on. Drink up. Then let's go over and talk to Zoroaster."

"But look," the little man protested. "Tell me. How in heaven's name do you do it?"

"With mirrors," the big man told him solemnly.

Zoroaster combined office and home in a studio apartment east of Michigan on Rush. The building was a warren of cheap apartments and assorted smells. Two cars, one from the *Morning Times* and one from the *Post* were parked at the curb. But there was no police stake out, at least none that Stone could see.

"We're apt to get in trouble," Phinny warned.

Stone grinned. "Hell. I'm in trouble now. Just let one report get back to Sergeant Mack that I've been posing as a Homicide man and you'll have a new helper on the wagon in the morning."

"If I have a wagon," the little man said glumly.

The lights in the lobby were dim. Stone ran into the girl studying the names above the bells before he saw her. He apologized:

"I'm sorry, Miss—" He gasped as the light fell full upon her face: "My God! You're dead."

She stared up at him, puzzled. Her face was plain but intelligent. She might have been attractive but for her glasses and the way she wore her hair. It was bound in tight brown braids around her head.

"No. Not quite," she told him dryly. "But you try going without eating for two days and see how you look." She stared at the row of bells again. "I wonder if you could tell me which one of these wakes up Zoroaster?"

Phinny stretched out a timid hand and touched the girl's arm cautiously. "Gawd!" He whistled through his teeth. "She's real! Hey! Who let you out of the morgue?"

The girl looked puzzled.

"Out of the morgue?" She smelled the beer fumes then. "Oh. I see. I'm being welcomed to Chicago by two drunks." She tried to brush past them to the stair.

"Just a minute, sister," Stone stopped her. "Your name is—what?"

"Harlan. Joan Harlan, if it's any of your business," she told him. "But it isn't. So I must ask you to please take your hand off my arm."

Stone removed his hand from her arm. "You had a sister?" he demanded. "A twin sister by the name of Fran?"

Her eyes widened slightly. "No. We aren't twins. But I have an older sister by the name of Fran. She works somewhere in this building for a fake astrologist by the name of Zoroaster. I'm trying to locate him to learn her new address. She's moved from the last address she sent me."

"You, er, have been out of town, or something?" Phinny asked.

The girl's voice was apprehensive. "I have. I just came in from New York an hour ago. On the bus. But say—what is this?"

Stone showed her his shield. "Look," he said gently. "You said something about not eating for two days. Suppose we step down to the Greek's on the corner and introduce ourselves over a steak."

The girl gasped: "Fran's in' trouble!"

"She's dead," Phinny told her bluntly.

The girl said: "Oh." And fainted in Stone's arms.

"Now how the hell," the little wagon driver said, "was I to know that she'd do that?"

The girl stared into her mug of steaming coffee. "And that's my story. I knew Fran had a good job here. And even if we hadn't been friendly for these last six months I knew that she'd give me a lift until I found a job of some kind."

Stone drew a Nazi swastika on his notes. Then added an American flag to each terminal of the sign. The girl had been a god-send. The pieces of the puzzle were falling into place. There were only a few gaps left. He asked:

"And you say that your sister had worked for Zoroaster going on four years?"

Joan Harlan nodded. "That's right. She met him when she was a probationary nurse and he was being treated for carcinoma of the mouth."

"For *what?*" Phinny asked.

"Cancer of the mouth. They were treating him with radium. One of the capsules disappeared. Fran always thought he'd swallowed it. Anyway, they kicked Fran out of training, and because he felt responsible, Zoroaster gave her a job in his office."

"But if he had swallowed the radium," Stone asked, "wouldn't it kill him in time?"

The girl said: "I don't know. I'm not a nurse. But Fran was always certain that he had swallowed it. She'd mention it every once in a while in her letters."

"She mention anything else?"

Joan Harlan thought a moment. "N-no. Only in the last letter that she wrote before we quarreled, she said that he was growing amorous in his old age." She paused. "And knowing Fran—"

"Yes?"

"Well, that's probably why he fired her."

"Probably," Stone agreed. He glanced at his watch. It was after one. "Look," he told the girl. "There's no need of your seeing Zoroaster. You've someplace you can stay tonight?"

"No," the girl admitted candidly. "I haven't." She added bitterly: "It seems Fran's luck and mine ran out together. She had a dime more than I have when she died."

Stone reached for his wallet.

"Put it away," Phinny told him. "She can go home with me." He explained: "I'm married. I've got two girls about your age."

Joan Harlan smiled. She said: "I'm not worried." But it was obvious that she was.

"You're okay, kid," Stone told her. "And so is Phinny. Now you two run along and I'll go have a little talk with the guy who reads the stars." He paused. "And, Phinny—"

"Yeah?"

"If my hunch on this thing is right, we're playing with dynamite. Mum is the word."

"I'll keep it under my arm," the little man assured him. His big ears stood out, indignant. "Hell. I've looked at enough of 'em in my life, but I'm not the rear end of a horse."

On impulse Stone stooped and kissed the girl. "Good night, kiddo."

Shaping his expensive light-weight beaver on his head, the blond giant strode out of the restaurant door.

The girl sat staring after him. Her eyes were shining. Her face was no longer plain. She said:

"That's the first time that a cop ever kissed me. And I like it." She smiled.

"There are cops, and cops, and cops." Phinny shrugged philosophically.

Two men were sitting on the top step of the landing. One dim bulb burned on the wall. Jackson of the *Morning Times* was the first to recognize Stone. He greeted him enthusiastically.

"Hi, Herman. You back on Homicide?"

"Just on my own," Stone told him. "And keep me out of your re-hash or it's likely to cost me my job." He stared at the door of the front apartment. "Zoroaster come in yet?"

"Just now." Web of the *News* got up from the steps and screwed a flash bulb into his camera, not very hopefully. "And after me waiting here four hours the crumb won't even let me shoot one picture of his layout."

Herman the Great asked: "Why?"

Jackson rattled the apartment doorknob. "He said he'd already talked to three million, four hundred and twenty-four cops and reporters, and that was enough."

"I'd sure like to see him," Stone said simply. He waved the reporter aside.

Jackson grinned. He knew the big man's methods.

Stone took hold of the doorknob, leaned his bulk against the door and shoved. The lock tore out and the door swung open. Stone looked surprised. He said:

"Hell. It wasn't locked after all."

"You get out of here," Zoroaster shrilled from an inner door of the apartment. "You get out of here or I'll call the Law!"

"I am the Law," Stone told him.

A flash bulb popped.

"Thanks, Herman." Web grinned cheerfully. "The Loop ain't been the same without you."

"I'll be back," the big man said grimly. He showed Zoroaster his shield.

Zoroaster scowled. He was a skinny little man in his late fifties. He wore white shoes, a light gray shepherd check suit, and a bright purple tie that bulged over a white linen vest. He looked more like a successful race track tout than a student of the stars.

"What more is there for me to say?" he demanded. "I do a simple Christian act of charity, and this is my reward. The Homicide Squad grilled me for five hours and now you break into my apartment."

"I missed the session at headquarters," Herman the Great told him coldly. "You fired Fran Harlan—why?"

"That," the astrologist stood his ground, "is a personal matter concerning only Miss Harlan and myself."

Stone let it pass. "And you sent the warnings to Marlby, Harlan, and Faber—why?"

Zoroaster sniffed. "My good man and you call yourself a detective? That's been in all the papers. I sent all three of the warnings because when I cast their horoscopes I read in the heavens that the stars had ordained that they die.

"But you had nothing to do with their deaths?"

"Don't be absurd." The little man was indignant. "I've established an alibi beyond question. Besides, they didn't die mortal deaths. It was a death sent by the stars."

"They died, those who did, from carbon monoxide poisoning," Stone corrected.

Zoroaster smirked. "On the fortieth floor of an air conditioned office?"

The reporter lighted a cigarette, and through the match flare said: "That's the sticker, Herman. You got the answer?"

"Yeah. I think so. But it's not for publication yet." One of his big arms shot out like a drag-line and lifted the little astrologer off of the floor to dangle at arm's length. "Come clean now, Zoro. How much did Ed Faber pay you to send those warnings?"

"Put me down!" the skinny man protested. "You're mad! Mr. Faber was one of the victims."

Stone said: "Let's see." He nodded at the reporter. "Call Mercy Hospital, will you, Benny, and inquire as to Faber's condition?"

Jackson picked up the phone on the desk and dialed a number. A flash bulb exploded again.

"Don't print that, Web," Stone warned him. "I'm officially not here." He dropped Zoroaster into a chair.

"You'll be fired for this," the astrologer spluttered, fighting for the breath that his collar had choked off. "You'll be fired!"

"Maybe," Stone admitted, "and maybe not. When a guy is in back of the eight ball he's got to take some chances. Well?" he demanded of Jackson, "what's the dope?"

The reporter cradled the receiver. "Give, Herman. Ed Faber recovered completely. He walked out of the place under his own power an hour ago."

Stone said: "I thought he would. You ready to talk yet, rat? Or do I have to smack the truth out of you piecemeal?" He lifted the astrologer out of his chair and sat him down again—hard. "As Benny says, give. I haven't much time to fool with you. I'm not supposed to be here, and—" He stopped, too late.

Zoroaster's eyes were pin points of cunning. He opened his mouth and screamed:

"Help! Murder! Police! There's a mad man in my apartment."

CHAPTER FOUR

The Pink Star

IT WASN'T A RAIN, it was a deluge. The heat had broken in a cloudburst. Sheets of water raced across the streets and stormed along the gutters to flood the street car viaducts and basements of the business houses fronting Clark Street. It was four o'clock in the morning.

Parked in a cab a block from the Pink Star, Stone tried to figure his best move. If he had still been a privileged member of the roving squad it would have been a simple matter. He could have crushed in and talked to Faber with all the might and majesty of H.Q. behind him. But a wagon helper didn't have any such powers as that.

The big man grimaced wryly. If Zoroaster, or Jackson, or Web should talk, as they undoubtedly would, it was very likely that after a second session with the trial board he wouldn't even be a wagon helper.

He wiped the steam-fogged rear window of the cab. A block behind his cab, another cab was parked. Somewhere he'd picked up a tail.

"Still there?" the driver asked laconically.

Stone nodded. "Yeah. Still there." He looked ahead through the rain at the neon sign of the Pink Star. "But there's no use me stalling any longer. Drop me off in front of the Pink Star."

"And wait for you?"

"And wait for me."

The Chicago closing hour is two. The Pink Star never closed. Ed Faber claimed that he had lost the key. There were no customers at the bar, and very few at the tables lining the dance floor in the dimly lighted alcove.

Faber, showing little effect of his close brush with death, sat half way down the bar, a glistening expanse of chrome-and-leather stools on either side of him. The slightly pop-eyed bartender with the over active thyroid was still on duty. Several waiters studied a *Racing Form* at the far end of the bar.

Stone sat down on a stool next to Faber. He had a feeling that he had been expected. "A double rye," he ordered. "And no chaser."

Faber turned his bulk slightly on the bar stool, asked:

"Not looking for trouble, are you, Herman? Because if you are, you've come to the right place. After what happened to me this afternoon I'm in no mood to argue with a dumb cop."

"I figured that," Stone nodded. "That's why I didn't bring one with me. They have much trouble in bringing you around?"

The red faced politician glowered at the pop-eyed barkeep. "They damn near didn't make it. It's lucky I'm alive."

"It's a shame," Stone assured him.

The fat man transferred his glower to Stone, then nodded to one of the waiters. "You always were a wise guy, weren't you, Herman?"

"No." The former Homicide ace shook his head. "I was lucky." He felt his way. "But when I get you next time, Ed, I'll make it stick."

He looked toward the alcove. The waiter to whom Faber had nodded was talking to one of the couples. As Stone watched, they glanced in his direction. Then the man got up, helped the girl with her wrap, and laid some bills upon the waiter's tray.

"They're clearing the joint," Stone thought. *I'm right. Faber's nose is as dirty as hell. He's making a play for a showdown.* He reached in his side coat pocket ostensibly for a cigarette and thumbed the safety off his gun.

"You say something?" Faber thrust his red face into his.

Stone shook his head. "No. Just talking to myself."

The red-faced man talked loudly, obviously for the benefit of the wary couples filing out into the rain. Stone wondered what the waiter had told them.

"Okay, okay. Go on and have your drink," Faber blustered. "But I don't care if you are a cop. Don't start any trouble in here. I'll talk to you any time you are sober, but I've no time to waste on drunks!"

Faber inched his bulk off the stool and waddled along the bar back toward his private office. Stone watched him closely, puzzled by the move. The last of the couples filed out. A waiter began to pile chairs on the tables. A colored porter came out of the kitchen with a mop and pail and began to slop the tile before the door. Faber's office door slammed behind him.

Stone ordered another rye. It was up to Faber to make the move that he knew would not be long in coming.

The metal snout of the bottle rapped his glass sharply as the bartender poured his drink. Stone grinned wryly:

"Not nervous, are you, Billy?"

The bartender gulped. "I'm nervous as hell." His eyes were almost popping from his head. He stooped and began to arrange some bottles under the bar, still talking. "Look. Get me out of here, will you, Herman!"

"Get you out of here?" Stone talked into the hand that held his cigarette, trying to figure out the play.

Sweat beaded the bartender's forehead. "Yeah. I'm in bad with the boss some way. I tried to leave when my shift was up and they wouldn't let me." He spoke with a rising inflection. "I'm afraid that I'm on the spot—and I don't know why!"

Stone thought a moment. "What time did Ed tell you to call him this afternoon?"

"At five o'clock," the bartender admitted. "And I forgot all about it till five-thirty." He mopped his forehead with the bar-towel. "But, gees! I didn't know what was going to happen. That ain't no reason to finger a guy. I was busy and I forgot."

Stone nodded slowly. "It was reason enough in this case—if I'm right. How many pots of black coffee did Ed drink this afternoon before he locked himself in his office?"

The bartender gaped at him. "Hey, you weren't here until we bust in the door. How did you know that Ed was on a coffee binge?"

"I'm Herman the Great," Stone told him. "I know all, hear all, see all. He was on a coffee binge?"

"Hell, yes. He drank enough to float a battle-cruiser."

Stone said: "Sweetheart, that's all that I wanted to know. No wonder you're in wrong. You damn near murdered Ed."

"*I* murdered him?" the barkeep gasped. "I—" He stopped short, his eyes staring wildly at the kitchen door.

The big man didn't turn around. He didn't need to. He could see Joe Mattuchie, flanked by two minor gunmen, in the back bar mirror. He puffed at his cigarette, one hand in his coat pocket.

"Don't try to pull it, Stone," the gunman warned him. "You don't need to let us see it. We know it's there. It's just like the one in my hand." He stepped to one side of the kitchen door to allow the other two hoods to pass him. "Get his rod," he ordered.

Stone swung his stool around so his back was against the bar. His hand was still in his pocket when one of the hoods reached out a tentative hand.

"Burny-burny," Stone warned. "Right through your little guts."

The hood backed up a step. Faber came out of his office. A fat smile on his doughy face, he jeered at Stone:

"You ought to get wise to yourself, fellow. You can't come into a respectable bar like this and try to bust it up just because you're sore at me."

Stone smiled unpleasantly. "So that's the way it's going to be." He flashed a quick glance at the door where the porter still mopped the tile. It was a mistake. There was a flash of movement behind him and a half filled whiskey bottle crashed down upon his head. The big man staggered to his feet half blinded by the whiskey and the sudden veil of blood.

"See? See, boss? I'm with you all way!" The pop-eyed barkeep danced behind the bar still clutching the neck of the shattered bottle.

Faber nodded at Mattuchie. "Okay, Joe. Let fly!"

Unable to see, Stone hurled himself forward at the knees of the two hoods, who had been closing in, to use their bodies as a shield until he could clear his eyes. It was his second mistake. The shot hadn't been meant for him. It tore through the bartender's cheeks and shattered the back-bar mirror. A second shot caught him in the temple. His arms embracing air he waltzed around and pitched face down on the drain boards.

Mattuchie circled the struggling men upon the floor.

Faber warned: "Don't shoot him. Joe!"

Mattuchie shook his head, stepped into the tangle of thrashing arms and legs and swung his gun barrel viciously against the big man's temple. Stone's legs kicked out spasmodically. Then he lay still.

The two hoods with whom he had struggled got unsteadily to their feet.

Faber jerked his head at the kitchen door, said: "Out!"

They went, unsteadily. Mattuchie stooped and tugged Stone's gun from his pocket, wiped his own fingerprints off the one that had killed the pop-eyed bar-keep and forced it in Stone's hand. It was a regulation service .38.

Faber brought a bottle of whiskey from the bar, holding it by the neck.

"Look all right?" he demanded. He stepped back to survey the scene. "Perfect," he decided. "Okay. You can go now, Joe." He waited until the gunman had swaggered out through the kitchen door, then told the porter: "Remember now, Habeas. You're my witness. You and Stone and Billy and I were alone when Stone started to get tough. After he shot Billy, I had to hit him in self-defense."

The colored man said: "Yes, suh."

Faber stood over Stone's unconscious body and lifted the

bottle over his head. "This," he smirked, "is going to be a pleasure." He tensed his muscles for the blow.

"Hold it, Faber," a thin voice warned. "I ain't no astrologist and I ain't no bettin' man. But if you swing that bottle one gets you ten that you kiss a handful of lead stars."

Faber lowered the bottle slowly and glowered at the front door of the bar.

His thin nose twitching, his long neck thrusting his bat ears forward until he looked like a pint-sized turkey buzzard, Officer Phineas Ott, wagon chauffeur of the Diversey Avenue Station, stood dripping on the welcome mat of the Pink Star. He was holding a .38 on a pearl-handled .45 frame.

CHAPTER FIVE

Turn in Your Shield

THE DAWN was as veined with red as the whites of a drunkard's eyes. The rain of the night before was steam upon the pavement. Even in the dimness of the Pink Star bar the heat that had awakened with the sun was making itself felt. It was going to be another scorcher.

Stone sat at a table up against the wall, his head swathed in a blood-stained bandage. Faber sat on a stool at the bar. Phinny was lost in the swarm of district men and downtown technical experts who had been rushed to the scene. Only the H.Q. Homicide Squad was missing.

"Now look, Mack," Stone told his station sergeant who had been routed out of bed. "You've got to believe me. I wasn't drunk. I didn't start any fight! And I didn't kill the barkeep."

"You're lying," Faber contradicted coldly. "Your whole absurd story is a lie. And once H.Q. gets here they'll laugh at you."

Stone said: "Maybe," curtly.

He was worried. He had reason to be. Faber had influence. Stone had none. Faber had broken him once. He might be able to send him to the chair. All that Stone had was a theory. And theory isn't proof. In the cold analysis of day, he didn't even have a sound motive for his theory. Zoroaster had made a play for Fran Harlan. True it had been no dice. But that was no reason he should kill her or want to see her dead. Likewise, the two hundred thousand dollars that Faber had owed E.P. Marlby was undoubtedly a legitimate business loan on sound security. The blond giant sighed. Besides, he had no proof of the tie-up he was certain existed between Faber and Zoroaster. It was his word against Ed Faber's—and he had played that game before—and lost!

Phinny wriggled his way through the crowd and stopped beside the table. "How you doing, Herman? Okay?"

"Okay." Stone tried to smile, and couldn't. Needles of pain had sewn the muscles of his face into knots. "And thanks for sending the little wren home in a cab and tailing me, Phinny. I guess I wouldn't be here if you hadn't." He looked at Faber.

Faber laughed. "Don't be ridiculous, Stone. I only hit you hard enough to subdue you until the police arrived." His small, deep set eyes singled out the porter leaning against the wall. "Isn't that right, Habeas?"

The colored man nodded. "Yes, suh. Tha's right, Mist' Faber."

"Then it's a good thing," the little wagon driver said, "that the police arrived as soon as they did. You sure weren't trying to pour a drink down Herman's throat when I walked in."

There was a mild commotion in the front of the bar as the Homicide drove up. Harry Purvis, the officer in charge, was as big a man as Stone, and as immaculately well dressed as Stone had been. But his face was gray from lack of sleep and his eyes were tired. He said:

"All right. Let's have it, Herman. You knocked off the bartender, or you didn't?"

"He did according to the gun that we found in his hand," a technical man said.

"I've told you that wasn't my gun," Stone insisted. "It was Joe Mattuchie's gun. He put it in my hand while I was out."

Purvis looked at Faber.

The politician shook his head. "He's cracked, Harry. I haven't seen Joe in a week. Look. This is the way it happened."

Faber told his story convincingly. It was well known that Stone didn't like him. He had walked into the bar hunting trouble. Faber had sent his few customers home just in case that the big man got nasty. Homicide could question the customers. Alone in the bar with Faber and the barkeep, Stone had accused him, Faber, of being involved in the mysterious series of murders in which Faber himself, had almost been a victim. Billy the bartender had resented the implication. Herman the Great had drawn his gun and Billy had smashed at him with a bottle just as the big man had shot him. Faber's part had been simple. He had merely picked up another bottle and stood by ready to smash him again if he tried to get up before the police arrived. Officer Ott could testify to that effect.

"You see anyone else?" the homicide man asked Phinny.

"N-no," the little man admitted reluctantly. "But—"

"Save it," Purvis cut him short. "All right. What's your story, Herman?"

Stone breathed a mental prayer. "Ed's lying, Harry. Look. This is the way it was."

"Yes?"

"Somehow Ed Faber is tied up in the murder of E.P. Marlby and that Harlan girl."

A choked silence filled the bar at the flat accusation. Stone continued:

"There was some reason he wanted them out of the wav. So Ed had that phony Zoroaster send them a note warning them that they were going to die. He got one, too. Just to keep his nose clean as far as you homicide boys were concerned. But Ed damn near did die. And it was Billy the barkeep's fault. He was supposed to call Ed and become alarmed a half hour before he did. That's why Ed was sore at him and had him bumped by Joe Mattuchie. Billy knew too much. He knew that Ed had been swilling black coffee all afternoon before he locked himself in his office."

Sergeant Mack scowled, puzzled: "Black coffee?"

"Yeah," Stone nodded. "If a guy is loaded on black coffee, and maybe has a shot of methylene blue in his arm, he can take a hell of a belt of carbon monoxide and still be brought around. It's an old gag but it always works as long as a guy's ticker is sound." He looked up at Purvis. "Remember that phony suicide pact that we had up at Sheffield, Harry?"

The squad leader admitted he did, but wanted to know: "So you've got that figured, Herman. Then where did the carbon monoxide come from?"

"Through the electric window ventilator. Those things work automatically. They keep circulating air so many hundred cubic feet per minute. And once you stop pouring the carbon monoxide through the vent, it's all sucked out again without leaving anything but a corpse."

Purvis looked thoughtful. Sergeant Mack scoffed:

"Baloney. And just how do you 'pour' carbon monoxide in an office window forty floors above the street? Or even four floors, for that matter? Answer that one, will you, chum? Go ahead and answer it!"

"You let down a scaffold," Stone told him. "And you pretend you're a sand blasting crew cleaning the face of the building. Only you haven't got sand in your tank or your hose. You've got carbon monoxide. Go on and check. I have. A crew was working on every building—including this one—where one of the murders was committed!"

Purvis' face was an inscrutable mask. "And you figure then, Herman that Ed Faber here and this Zoroaster had a big steal on of some kind, a steal big enough for Faber to risk his life?"

"I do. They're planning a racket of some kind. A big one. But I'll be damned if I can figure out what it could be—not this short a time."

"And that's your story?"

"That's my story."

The squad leader's voice was regretful. "Then I'm afraid that you're stuck with it, Herman. You see we just came from Zoroaster's."

"Yes?"

"And he's dead. Dead of carbon monoxide in his own apartment with all the windows open and not a sand-blasting crew in sight. There's no way that he could have died of carbon monoxide, but he did." The squad leader's voice was weary. He took a letter from his pocket and tossed it on the table. It was identical in format with the ones that E.P. Marlby, Fran Harlan, and Ed Faber had received. "He's got some crazy stuff in there about returning from the grave in his present form; re-incarnated, he calls it, to serve as a liaison officer between the living and the dead. The man was nuts." He added bitterly:

"And I'm not far behind him. Boiled down to a police report, he died of something that he couldn't possibly die of just because the stars said—die!"

Faber laughed thinly, nervously. Stone fired a cigarette. He had difficulty making contact with the match.

"And—me?" he asked unsteadily, his face full of anxiety.

"I'm sorry, Herman," Purvis told him. "But you'd better turn in your shield. I'll have to believe Ed Faber's story and take you in for murder."

CHAPTER SIX

Return of the Dead

WHETHER IT WAS still hot outside, Stone didn't know. It was difficult to tell if it was day or night. A high war bulb burned constantly above the door of the tiny, inside cell at the detective bureau in which he himself had kept so many other men. The place reeked of antiseptic. He talked to the girl through the bars.

"That's swell of you, Joan," he told her. "But there's nothing you can do. I don't know what anyone could do to help me except possibly Ed Faber. If it had happened in a story I'd have made a break from the Pink Star, I suppose, and cleared myself somehow." He added glumly, "But I guess it's up to my lawyer now."

Joan Harlan looked different somehow. Perhaps it was the way that Phinny's wife had helped her fix her hair, and the fact she wasn't wearing glasses. Or it might have been the fact that for the first time in her twenty-two years she was in love and fully conscious of being a woman.

"Herman," she said softly, she began to cry. "I—I'm so worried about you."

Stone smiled grimly. "Yeah? I don't feel so chipper myself. You bring me the papers, Joan?"

She thrust them through the bars.

"Okay, sister." The turnkey took her arm. "Purvis said five minutes."

Stone kissed her goodbye through the bars. "I should have ought to have met you years ago," he told her ungrammatically but sincerely.

Alone with the papers the big man spread them on the steel cot swung from chains in one corner of the cell. His alleged murder of a bartender was given small attention. The spread still went to Zoroaster. The *Morning Times* had printed his last letter in full. It was dated Two A.M. October 3rd. It read:

To Whom It May Concern:

I write this in haste. Having but this past half hour compiled my own horoscope; I have learned that the stars ordain my death before the coming dawn.

However, if my faith be strong, I need have no fear. I die but to live again. The stars revolving in their orbit ordain that I return to earth, reincarnated in my present form to cast confusion upon the skeptical and to serve as a liaison officer between the living and the dead.

I have no fear. I know this prophecy to be true having had proof in the deaths of E.P. Marlby and Miss Fran Harlan, and the near death of Mr. Faber. That which I read in the stars is infallible.

Those of you who know me, and love me—who have consulted me in the past, and who will wish to consult me in the future, I say to you—have no fear. Though I die I shall rise again, and ye shall know me.

Arrangements pertaining to the cremation of my mortal form will be found in a separate enclosure. All who may care to attend are invited.

Affectionately,
Zoroaster

Stone fired another cigarette and turned the pages of the extras slowly, skimming through each story. Despite the spot that he was in, it amused him that he wasn't on Homicide. The three p's—the Papers, the Public, and the Powers—were giving the boys hell. They were stupid, unfit for their jobs, blundering fools. His own theory of the introduction of the carbon monoxide was disputed by the latest death. Found dead on his own bed, in his own apartment, with all of the windows open, there was no way that Zoroaster could have died of carbon monoxide poisoning. But he had.

Stone turned to the classified ads. The one that he thought he remembered reading was under the heading PROFES-SIONAL SERVICES. It read:

Have you a loved one, one perhaps about to enter the Armed Forces of the United States? Would you like to know his future, know if your son, your sweetheart or husband will return safely to your arms?. . . If so, consult Zoroaster. Each mortal lives and dies according to his astral chart. I read the stars. ZOROASTER THE PROPHET, Apartment 3A, 42 East Rush St.

It was, Stone thought, a neat racket, but a small one. Zoroaster hadn't lived long enough to—Struck by a sudden thought the big man climbed to his feet, grasped the bars of his cell and yelled at the turnkey.

"Hey, Mike! Tell Harry Purvis I got to see him right away. And, Mike—?"

"Yeah?" the other man asked placidly.

"Do you think it's possible for a guy who's been cremated

to come back from the dead?"

"Well," the turnkey summed up the matter succinctly. "It ain't never been done before."

The building was low, impressive, white—and jammed with perspiring women and a sprinkling of men incited by the reams of publicity that had been given the case in the newspapers. They spilled down the crematory steps, perched like eager vultures on the nearby tombstones to catch the first glimpse of the smoke that would waft the soul of Zoroaster to the stars he claimed to read.

In the crematory chamber of the building, Stone, handcuffed to his former chief's left wrist, stared at the body on the slab. The astrologist was still dressed in his white shoes, light gray shepherd check suit, bright purple tie, and linen vest. But all of his self-assured dignity was gone. He looked older, shriveled somehow. It was as if death had been a pin that had deflated his mortal ego.

"That's him, all right," Stone identified the astrologist stolidly. "Sorry I dragged you out on a wild goose chase, Harry. But I thought for a minute I might have something. I thought maybe a switch had been made."

"Forget it." The squad leader's voice was heavy with fatigue. "I don't want to see you go to the chair. I don't like Ed Faber any better than you do. I hoped we could tie him into this someway. But hell, you can't buck a buzz saw with wishful thinking." He nodded to the crematory attendants. "Okay. You can push him in the furnace whenever you're ready."

Purvis, Stone handcuffed to his wrist, waited through the ceremony and until the ashes had been gathered and put into a small metal container.

"And what happens to them?" he asked.

The undertaker led the way to another wing of the building kept locked for the day against the crowds. There he slipped the metal container into a small receptacle built into the wall. It was not unlike a safety deposit box. It was one of a hundred similar vaults that lined the wall. In time a small metal plate would be engraved with the name Zoroaster.

"And that," Purvis said, "is that. Let's see our fortune telling friend get out of there."

Stone said nothing.

It was mad. It was incredible. It was fact. The skinny, smiling, nude little man was real. He had been picked up by two Grant Park policemen, wandering along the Lake Front as naked as the day he had been born. Because one of them had thought he recognized his face, the park police had draped him in a blanket and brought him to detective headquarters.

The man said he didn't know why he was naked. He said he didn't know his name. But Purvis knew it. Or rather he knew the name that the little man would claim.

"Keep those damn reporters and cameramen out of here. And one of you bring Stone from his cell. Herman's hunch that there would be a switch was right. He just had it turned around."

Two detectives left the room. Purvis scowled at the prisoner.

"Give," he demanded. "Don't think you can get away with this. Who are you?"

The skinny little man clutched his blanket with one hand, the other pressed to his brow in thought. He whispered frightenedly: "I don't know. It's all so strange. All I remember is an intense heat, and then a blaze of stars, and—"

"Okay," Purvis stopped him wearily. "But when we get through with you, you'll see more than stars."

A detective brought Stone in.

"Your story," Purvis told him, "is beginning to stack up, Herman. We're up against a racket, and a big one. Take a look over there in the corner."

The blond giant turned and stared.

He gasped: "By God! Zoroaster!"

"Zoroaster!" the skinny little man cried eagerly. "Of course. That's who I am. I'm Zoroaster the prophet who died that he might be born again!"

His voice was high and shrill. It carried out through the

transom to the hall where the reporters and cameramen were gathered. They began to clamor.

Purvis said wearily: "Okay. Let them in. If this story goes out half baked, it'll raise all kinds of hell. Let the boys in for the pay-off."

"Pay-off?" the little man puzzled.

The homicide man ignored both the question and the sudden pop of flash bulbs. "You, Murphy," he ordered. "Bring me everything we have in the file on that Zoroaster guy. And ask the Bureau of Identification to send up a man."

Stone stood staring at the little man.

"He is a fake, isn't he, Herman?" It was Jackson of the *Times*.

"He has to be," Stone told him. "But so help me, he looks enough like the guy I slapped around last night and saw cremated this afternoon to be his brother."

Murphy returned with the file and an Identification man.

"Okay. Pipe down, you guys!" Purvis drummed on his desk for silence. He glowered at the little man, clad only in a blanket and a worried frown, as he talked to the reporters. "You lads all know the story. What's back of it is my job to find out." He nodded at his former homicide ace. "But Herman here was right in some details. He claimed that E.P. Marlby and the Harlan girl were murdered for some purpose. And it begins to look like it was the build-up for a shake-down of Mr. and Mrs. John Q. Public. If this little rat in the blanket was really Zoroaster, dead and come to life again, he could make ten million dollars. I'd pay a pretty penny myself to be tipped off when I was going to die by a lad who was really in the know."

A nervous titter rippled through the office.

"But he, or they, forgot one thing. They forgot there was such a thing as fingerprints."

The little man who claimed he was Zoroaster, returned from the dead, protested strongly. Two husky detectives grabbed him and forced his fingers down upon the pad.

Purvis sorted through the file that Murphy had brought him. "But we've the real Zoroaster's fingerprints right here.

Fingerprints that we took out of his apartment and from the fingers of the corpse." He laid them in front of the Bureau of Identification man.

The Bureau of Identification man straightened slowly. His lips were a thin, straight line.

"Well?" Purvis demanded.

"They're the same," the B. of I. man told him. "He *is* Zoroaster. *His fingerprints match with those of the dead man!"*

CHAPTER SEVEN

The Weakest Link

IN THE DISTANCE a prowl car siren wailed like a predatory tomcat. Stone winced and crowded his bulk still further back into the corner of a booth in the small bar where he had asked Phinny and Joan to meet him. In the confusion that had followed the positive identification of Zoroaster, he had walked unchallenged out of the Detective Bureau.

"They want me bad, Phinny?"

"Bad," the little wagon driver told him solemnly. "Every cop on the force, but me, is looking for you. Purvis has hit the sky. First this guy Zoroaster has made him a party to his racket and then you walk out on him. There's orders to shoot you on sight."

Joan gasped: "Oh!"

Stone grinned and put his hand on hers. "It's okay, honey. Most cops are rotten shots. I had a reason for walking out." He asked Phinny: "You saw Jackson?"

"I did. And he swears the letters and telegrams are pouring in to that slimy little charlatan's apartment by the hundreds. The newspaper boys estimate that unless he is proved a fake, he'll make ten million dollars on the racket."

"But if he is Zoroaster returned from the dead—" the girl protested wide eyed.

Stone shook his head. "Like Mike, the turnkey says, it ain't never been done before. It's a racket, honey. But it's the first racket I ever heard of that used the Homicide Squad as an angel. On the surface it looks fool proof. But I don't think it is." He tightened his big hand on the small, clenched fist of the girl. "Look. You told me, didn't you, honey, that Zoroaster suffered from carcinoma of the mouth, and that he had been taking radium treatments? That it was even thought at the time that he had swallowed a radium capsule?"

"I did. That was how Fran met him."

Stone grinned. "Then it's okay. If Ed Faber has a guilty conscience, this thing's a cinch."

"Yeah?" Phinny brightened in admiration. "You mean that you've picked a solution right out of the air?"

"No," the big man told him soberly. "But I am going to bluff a solution right out of a crematory." He bent forward and lowered his voice. "Now look, Phinny. This may be dangerous. But it's our only chance. Here's what I want you and Joan to do. It's a simple case of blackmail."

Oakwood Cemetery lies on the outskirts of the city, but just inside the boundaries of the city proper. It is, at best, a lonely stretch inhabited at midnight only by the dead, and a rednecked crematory watchman.

The watchman knocked the dottle from his pipe and stared with avarice at the fifty dollar bill folded lengthwise between the fingers of the other man.

"Well, it ain't regular," he grumbled. "But seeing as it's your vault and the undertaker give you the key, I guess I might make an exception."

The bill changed hands. The watchman unlocked the big steel door to the vault wing of the crematory and switched on a blue ceiling light.

"It's probably over there in the second tier," he pointed. "That's where the ashes are of the guys they burned today."

The little man who had paid fifty dollars for the privilege tip-toed breathlessly across the tile as though he feared to wake the dead. The bronze plate had not as yet replaced the single word—ZOROASTER. He inserted a key, removed the metal urn, and replaced it with an identical urn that he took from the brief case that he carried. Then he closed and locked the small vault door with an audible sigh of relief.

"Thanks," he whispered huskily. He handed the red-necked watchman a second fifty dollar bill. "Forget all about this, will you?"

The watchman switched off the light. "What the hell. I ain't no fool!"

The little man didn't hear him. He was hurrying between the monuments and tombstones to a black sedan parked behind a clump of bushes on the drive.

Ed Faber sat perched on the rear seat. Bound hand and foot, their eyes dull and worried above the wide strips of adhesive tape strapped across their mouths, Phinny and Joan Harlan lay on the floor-boards at his feet partially covered by a blanket. Joe Mattuchie crouched behind the wheel.

"You got it?" he demanded tersely.

"I got it," the skinny man panted.

Faber reached out a fat hand for the brief case. "Then give it to me and let's get out of here." He laid the case on the seat beside him as the little man scrambled into the car beside Mattuchie. "Get going, Joe." Faber tapped the gunman on the shoulder. "We're hot as long as we have the dame and the copper and the ashes in the car. They know too damn much to live."

"They're as good as dead right now," Mattuchie assured him.

"I doubt it." Herman the Great had materialized out of the night to stand beside the car. He held a gun in his hand. He reached through the open window and smashed the gun butt into Mattuchie's teeth while his other hand switched off the ignition.

"This is the pay-off, Ed," he told the politician. "I told you that the next time that I got you, I'd get you right." His voice was grim. "And I have. This time you're going to burn. Zoroaster's ashes in that briefcase are going to send you to the chair."

The big man calmly lifted Phinny and Joan out of the car and unbound Phinny's hands, his gun muzzle never wavering a second from the bottom button of the fat politician's vest.

"You get out of here," the politician blustered. "The police have orders to shoot you down on sight. And you won't get away with this. It's nothing but a dirty, high jacking frame-up." He filled his lungs with air and bellowed: "Police!"

"Right here, Ed," Harry Purvis told him quietly. He stepped out of the night back of Stone, his homicide squad behind him. "But it looks as if we aren't needed. It looks as if Herman's lived up to his name and picked a couple of murderers out of thin air."

The thin little man who had cowered in terrified silence began to whimper: "I'm not a murderer. I'm not. I—"

Stone slapped him.

"The hell you're not. If you didn't kill the real Zoroaster, then why were you so anxious to get his ashes out of the vault and replace the urn with an empty one?"

Faber said sharply: "Don't answer him." He turned to Purvis. "And you've no right to hold and question us. We aren't guilty of a thing."

The squad leader looked at Phinny and the girl.

"You're wrong there, Ed," he told the politician quietly. "You're guilty of kidnapping for one thing. If your hands are clean, what are you doing here this time of night with Phinny and the girl?"

The girl sobbed: "He was going to kill us. He said so."

Faber said: "I want to see my lawyer."

Herman the Great shook his head. "No. We're settling this right now." One crane-like arm shot out and picked the little man from the car. "You going to turn State's Evidence?" the big man demanded as he shook him.

The little man began to sob.

"I'll talk. I'll talk," he promised. "I don't want to go to the chair. I didn't kill anyone. And I'm afraid to die."

Stone grinned mirthlessly. "That's quite a statement from a man who's just been re-incarnated." He shook him ruthlessly. "Who are you? Talk!"

"I'm Zoroaster's brother," the little man babbled between

sobs. "His twin brother. Faber brought me on here from the Coast. He said we could make ten million dollars. He said that every woman in the country would want to know what the stars had to say about the chances of their sons, their husbands, and their sweethearts in the army being killed."

"But you needed a sure fire publicity buildup," Stone continued the story. "So you send out the phony letters and the first guy to be killed was Marlby. Ed killed two birds with one stone as far as E.P. Marlby was concerned. He knew what a splash his death would make, and he owed him two hundred grand."

"And the Harlan girl, Herman?" Purvis asked.

"Was murdered," Stone shook the little man again, "because this slimy little heel couldn't keep his paws to himself. And Ed was afraid that the girl might talk. He was afraid she might suddenly realize that the twirp who had tried to make her wasn't the guy she had worked for, for years." He threw the little man back in the car and bellowed: "How did you kill your brother?"

Faber said: "Shut up!"

The skinny little man refused to heed him. He sobbed: "I didn't kill my brother. Faber and Mattuchie did. They kidnapped him weeks ago and kept him in a hideout until it was time for him to die. Then they gave him carbon monoxide and left him on his own bed dressed in the clothes I had been wearing."

"It sounds, Herman. It sounds," the squad leader nodded. "But how about the fingerprints on the corpse matching up with this guy's?"

"They didn't," Stone shrugged. "That was simple. There was a switch in the B. of I. As I recall, Ed has several stooges working there."

The graveyard was filled with silence.

"Well," Faber admitted dully, "it rather looks like you have me, boys." He tried slyly to tug the metal urn out of the briefcase and scatter its contents.

"Don't try it!" Purvis warned him. He yanked the politician from the car and slipped a handcuff on his wrist. "Just leave the real Zoroaster's ashes where they are. They're going to burn you."

"I'm afraid so," Faber admitted. His voice was bitter. "But after the dame and Phinny told me how the real Zoroaster had been taking radium treatments, and how there were detectors that could prove its presence even in a dead guy's ashes, I had to get them."

Stone grinned: "The hell you did. All you had to do was just sit tight. He was the first guy that's ever been reincarnated and until you got stampeded and made a bull and grabbed his ashes they didn't mean a thing. Now, like Harry Purvis says, they're going to burn you. But if you hadn't had a guilty conscience and had left them alone, it wouldn't have meant a thing if they were filled with radium. It would merely have proved what a drag Zoroaster had with the other world. He'd died a sick man and was re-incarnated cured."

Faber exploded, "And that dirty little tramp had the nerve to come into my bar and try to blackmail me, told me that unless I split half of the take with her and Phinny she'd see that those ashes burned me." His fury knew no limit. "Why the lying, scummy, brazen—"

Stone slapped him hard across the mouth. It was a pleasure.

"Easy, louse," he cautioned, one big arm around the girl's slim waist. "You're talking about the future Mrs. Stone."

HERR YAMA FROM YOKOHAMA

CHAPTER ONE

Nobody Killed the Corpse!

STANDING ON THE CORNER of Pell and Matt Streets listening to the moon fiddles in Ed Liwang's Lotus Bud Cafe sob *towsey mongclay,* the Chinese words that meant eternal farewell, Lee Sin's face was grim. He could sense death in the air.

"One gets you ten it's Yama, General Yama." he said.

Brad Hatfield, standing beside his Chinese partner grinned crookedly. To him it was just another case. To Lee Sin it was in a sense a triumphant homecoming. He had been born in New York's Chinatown. He had played all its streets as a boy. Fourth generation American, educated at Harvard and Oxford, he was Chinese in racial background only. But that background had made him invaluable to the F.B.I. Doors through which occidental agents might not pass were often willingly opened to Lee.

Lee and Hatfield were of a size. Both men were six feet four. Both carried two hundred and twenty pounds of well-coordinated dynamite on their huge frames. They were known in the department by two names. Some called them the trouble twins. The big boss called them his corpse makers. They were assigned only to the toughest most dangerous cases—and they had sought General Yama in forty-eight states.

The man was a wraith, a shadow. No man ever saw him and lived. Some said he was a renegade Chinese. Some said that he was a white man. All that was really known about

him was that he was the smartest agent the Japanese espionage service had. Hate, sabotage and sudden death followed
him like a plague—and here men had died.

And here, Lee sensed, others were about to die.

Hatfield demanded. "But what's it all about, Lee? Why
have three prominent Chinese-Americans been murdered?"

"I don't know," Lee admitted frankly. "All the Chinese I
have questioned are afraid to talk." He turned to light a cigarette, cupping his hands against the wind.

The move was all that saved his life. Lead spat against the
wall behind him. The shot came from an upper window of
the ancient rookery that housed the Lotus Bud Cafe—and the
music was suddenly silent. The two agents blasted the glass
from the window, then raced across the street now filled with
screaming bedlam.

The heavy, brass-studded door of the cafe was locked.
Brad shot the lock off the door as Lee reloaded his gun. Side
by side they raced up the stairs.

The moon fiddle players were gone. The Cafe floor was
dark. Lee pulled down a dangling bamboo curtain that led to
the third floor, and hell burst loose in a blast of gunfire. Lead
peppered the plaster walls in a stinging spray of death.

A machine gunner stood on the top step, firing over the
railing. Lee's second shot caught him in the forehead. A
rosebud blossomed on his skin, then burst into full, bloody
bloom.

There was no one in the upper hall. Lee kicked in the door
of the room from which the shot had been fired. He had expected to find it empty. He was wrong.

A black haired, golden-skinned girl in a form-fitting crimson Mandarin robe turned dull-eyed from the window. Her
slightly slanted almond eyes were filled with tears. She
clasped a heavy rifle to her breast. Lee tore it out of her
hands, shot the bolt and sniffed the spent gasses in the firing
chamber.

The girl sobbed: "I'm sorry I missed you, I prayed to Kwan
Tai I would kill you."

"Applesauce," Lee grinned tautly. He knew the Chinese

beauty well. They had gone through school together. The daughter of Ed Liwang who owned the Lotus Bud Cafe, Broadway knew her as the Oriental Gypsy Rose Lee. "Who fired that shot, Mary? Whom are you trying to shield? Who has been killing the ancients? Why did that slant-eyed *Bo do* out in the hall try to chop me down? What the hell is this all about?"

"As if you cared. You—who are no longer one of us!" Her hand made a quick gesture toward the shot-shattered window.

Lee Sin intercepted her. He took a small metal object from her hand. It was a miniature model of a four-motored long-range bombing plane. The big federal agent changed his tactics abruptly.

"It is written," he told the sobbing girl in fluent Mandarin, "that only a fool conceals the truth from a friend. Trust me. Believe in me, Mary. What is this all about?"

"Teeth," the girl said bitterly. "Teeth for the Chinese dragon."

The secret room built into the walls on the second floor of the Lotus Bud Cafe was large and lined with crimson folds of silk. It had one door, no windows. In one corner of the room huge copper bowls of incense glowed red before the ugly features of Kwan Tai, the god of war. The lazy, thick bodied, gray snakes of war spiraled upwards to the ceiling and misted the seven dim, small-watt, electric bulbs that burned in a solid gold candelabra.

The seven bulbs were the only lights but for the red glow of incense.

At the downstairs door of the Cafe two uniformed police stood guard. Two more guarded the rear door. All four would have sworn that the building was empty.

Lee Sin had known better. He had known that the ancients would meet as soon as he had sent Brad down to the detective bureau with Mary Liwang with instructions to charge her with attempted murder. Now, as he stood in the secret passageway that led up between the walls, he could see that there were five ancients and four tong gunmen in the room.

Death, Lee knew, was very close to him. Chinatown guarded her secrets well. Unless he could make himself believed, his bloated corpse would be found in the river in the morning. He wondered if the ancients would believe him; accept him as his father's son and not as a spying federal agent. There were doors in Chinatown through which not even he might pass.

He knew four of the ancients. Ed Liwang, Mary's father, sat in one corner of the room. Chang Fu, the multimillionaire importer, Yuan Liang, the poor poet and philosopher, and Ch'en Yang, the fat-bellied merchant, sat at the judgment table. In front of them, a dozen feet away from Ed Liwang, a seemingly enfeebled old man with parchment-like skin drawn taut upon his cheeks sat stroking a straggly Chinese beard and sipping a glass of *ng ka pay* which one of the hatchet men replenished from time to time. Lee gathered from the staccato conversation that he was the famous General P'u who, Washington had been informed, had been sent by Chiang Kai-Shek to solicit financial and moral aid from the American-born Chinese.

The big agent walked in boldly and laid his guns down on the judgment table before the aged Chang Fu. "I come in peace," he said.

The four hatchet men sprang forward, their gun-snouts rammed into his body, their fingers itching on their triggers.

"Kill him! Kill him!" the aged General P'u screamed shrilly. "He is an enemy to our cause. He is a spy!"

"A spy. A spy. A spy!" The deadly word circled the room.

Lee Sin bowed to the judgment table, then turned and bowed to the old man in the chair. "If I were a spy, honorable ancient," he answered General P'u in Cantonese, "I would not have come unasked to the judgment chamber. True, my heart is of this country, but my skin and the roots of my being are still in the soil of China."

Chen Yang the merchant nodded. "He speaks with a well-considered tongue. I knew his father well. He died an old man full of years and many honors with a dutiful son to mourn him."

General P'u spat on the floor but made no answer.

Yuan Liang the poet broke the awkward silence. "Why have you come to us?" he asked the big federal agent gently.

"To help you," Lee said frankly.

"Promises, promises, promises," General P'u shrilled as he pulled at his thin beard. "Where are our planes and guns? Where is our ammunition? Men and boys die like flies as they fight with their bare hands against the devil-men from Nippon and your statesmen continue to—promise."

The F.B.I. man flushed. There was truth in the old man's statement. England, Russia, Australia, Central and South America, even India, had been manned with American planes and guns and ammunition under the Lend-Lease program while China had fought on unaided except for the gallant group of American volunteer fliers under General Chennault. Things were better now but supplies were still inadequate.

Ed Liwang spoke for the first time. "You say you have come to help us. We have need of help. We are hemmed in on every side by death. No man can truthfully say who will be the next to die. Yet my daughter was torn from my bosom. She has been unjustly accused of attempted murder."

Lee said: "A shot was fired. Your lotus bud admitted that she fired it, that she had prayed to Kwan Tai she might kill me."

"She lied," the old man said heavily. "It was the disembodied voice of General Yama who told her what to say. He said I would be slain did she not lie."

Lee considered briefly. "I believe you." The scowling hatchet men's guns still in his ribs, he picked up the phone from the judgment table, dialed Central Bureau and asked for his waiting partner. "This is Lee, Brad," he said crisply. "Withdraw the charge against Mary Liwang and see that she is released. She was lying to save her father."

He placed the phone back on the table. Yuan Ling nodded to the hatchet men. They returned their guns to their pockets and stepped back against the wall.

"I think," Ling told the others, "it is time that the truth was told. This man is of the F.B.I. I vote that we trust him and ask him for his help."

"The F.B.I. is strong," Lee tempted. "Its arms are long," he added, still speaking in Cantonese. "Unburden your hearts to me. Tell me how we can help China."

"No," General P'u spluttered. "No! How do I know that we can trust this man? All is lost if we weaken now. I vote not to trust him with our secret."

The other ancients voted soberly. General P'u lost four to one. He sat back scowling in his chair and clapped his hands for another glass of *ng ka pay,* the Chinese rice brandy that tastes like orange shellac with a fusil content of crude oil.

Ed Liwang shook Lee's hand. He was no longer a solemn Chinese ancient. He was a successful American businessman who had run a shoestring into a fortune. He spoke in crisp, incisive English. "You're okay, Lee," he said. "We should have come to you in the first place. But we can't be too careful. We're fighting the devil himself. A devil who can change his form at will. This Yama can be a man, a woman, a voice—just as he pleases."

Lee smiled wryly. He had never seen a disembodied devil that his .45 couldn't blast.

"But it is true," Ch'en Yang assured him. "This Yama is not mortal. He is a voice from Hell."

"I'll take a chance," Lee grinned. He turned back to Ed Liwang. "Your daughter tried to destroy a little model of a four motored Seversky long range bombing plane. Where does that model fit into the picture? And what did Mary mean by the words, 'teeth for the Chinese dragon?'"

"It's this way, Lee," the Cafe owner told him. "We've collected forty million dollars in cash from the Chinese-Americans of this country. And dealing in the black market we intend to—"

Ed Liwang never finished his sentence. The seven bulbs in the gold candelabra dimmed low—then blinked out entirely.

Ghostly moon fiddles began to sob. The only light was the red glow of the incense in the censers before Kwan Tai the God of War.

Lee snatched back his guns from the table. But there was nothing, no one at whom to fire. There was no sound but the hoarse breathing of the ancients and the sputter of the smoldering punk.

Then a woman's voice sobbed, *"Eh yeh!"* It seemed everywhere and nowhere, a ghostly voice that danced around the room.

"Death," Yuan Ling muttered hoarsely from the darkness, "is among us. I can smell the stench of blood!"

The lights came on as abruptly as they had been turned out. No man had moved from where he had been sitting. But Yuan Ling the poet was right. Death had struck again. Ed Liwang slumped in his chair, a dozen feet from any of the others. His white shirtfront had turned crimson. His throat was cut from ear to ear.

General P'u staggered to his feet. "A judgment! A judgment!" he shrilled in Cantonese. "It was not General Yama this time but the voice of Mother China who sealed the honorable Liwang's lips."

Lee Sing dropped his guns back into his holsters with an oath. Instead of advancing the case, his thrusting himself upon the ancients and Ed Liwang's willingness to talk had merely brought about another murder.

"Get me Brad Hatfield," he demanded when he had dialed Central Bureau again. "He'll probably be up in Homicide talking to Inspector Flynn. This is Lee again," he told his partner. "And if Mary Liwang hasn't left, hold her until I get there."

His partner hit the ceiling. "Why the hell don't you make up your mind!" he bellowed. "The dame has been gone for five minutes. You want me to ask the local boys to put out a pick-up on her?"

"No," Lee told him crisply. "Never mind. Meet me at the Astor Bar in twenty minutes." He paused and studied the impassive faces of the ancients as they stared at the dead man in the chair. "And if Flynn isn't subject to heart failures," he continued, "you might tell him to start the meat wagon and a homicide squad for Ed Liwang's Lotus Bud Cafe. That's right." he answered Brad's question. "We've another stiff with his throat cut—and nobody who could've done it."

"Who," Ch'en Yang quavered as the big man set the phone back on the table, "do you think did it, Lee?"

"Well," Lee told him. "It wasn't the pixies, and it wasn't Mother China."

CHAPTER TWO

Score One for the Corpse-Makers

BEHIND THE BLACKOUT CURTAINS of the Astor Bar, business was booming. The after-theatre crowd filled every table. Brad Hatfield stood at the bar alone, scowling into his beer. Lee was a half-hour over-due. It was then that he heard the pageboy.

"Paging Mr. Sin. A telegram for Mr. Sin."

The few patrons who heard him laughed. They thought it was a gag. Hatfield stopped the boy, laid a dollar bill on the tray and picked up the telegram.

"I'm Mr. Sin," he lied.

The telegram was brief and to the point. It read:

DEAR LEE:

I HAVE JUST BEEN TOLD OF MY FATHER'S DEATH AND OF THE FACT THAT HE WAS ABOUT TO CONFIDE IN YOU. PLEASE COME TO ME AT ONCE. I KNOW WHO IT WAS WHO KILLED HIM. I KNOW WHO THE TRAITOR IS WHO IS THREATENING OUR CAUSE.

An apartment number and street address followed. The telegram was signed—Mary Liwang.

Brad Hatfield was no fool. He realized that it might be a

trap. He hoped it was. He was growing tired of inaction.

"Look," he told the barkeep who had served him. "If a big fat Chinese-looking lug as tall as I am pops in here in the next few minutes tell him that the man he's looking for has gone to see a girl about a dog."

He slid a folded bill across the bar to keep the man's memory green.

"Yes, sir," the barkeep grinned. "I'll keep an eye out for him."

"You couldn't miss him if you tried," Brad said.

He hailed an eastbound cab on 44th Street and gave the swank Sutton Place address to the driver.

"No. Don't bother to announce me," he told the uniformed doorman of the apartment house before which the cab had stopped. "Miss Liwang is expecting me."

The door to Apartment E 4 was open slightly. Brad made certain that his gun slid easily in their holsters, then rapped on the door jamb sharply.

"Yes—? Who is it?" a girl's voice called.

Brad opened the door with his foot and walked in. "I'm Lee's partner—"

The F.B.I. man stopped abruptly and flipped both of his guns from their holsters as he realized he was talking to air. He had heard the girl's voice distinctly. It had sounded like Miss Liwang's voice. But Mary Liwang was not in the room. The one room apartment was empty.

"What the hell?" Brad swore.

Then the girl's voice called again. This time it was mocking and seemed to come out of the bathroom. "So sorry, Mr. Hatfield. So sorry you're such a fool. It is almost a shame to kill you."

Brad started slowly across room towards the door from which the voice had seemed to come. As he did, a closed door behind him opened silently. A pair of beady black eyes peered our. Then a glittering razor-sharp knife, seemingly floating in air, began to inch across the room toward the back of Brad Hatfield's neck.

The agent opened the bathroom door. The room was empty.

"So sorry," the girl's voice mocked behind him.

Brad whirled, too late. The knife was at his throat. It swept sideways for the death stroke. Then the glass of a window crashed. The heavy roar of Lee Sin's .45 filled the room. There was a loud *pling* of lead on metal. The knife hurtled across the room—*then seemingly rebounded and floated hurriedly back into the closet!*

Lee flipped two more shots at the closet door, then bounded from the fire escape into the room through the shattered window-pane. He and Brad reached the closet door together. It had slammed with a solid thud and locked from the inside. The trouble twins broke it down. Another door had been cut in the closet wall into the adjoining apartment. That apartment, too, was empty. The killer had escaped again.

Brad thought of the knife and said, "Thanks. But how did you know I'd come here?"

"I planted where I could be reached," Lee told him grimly. "Then I waited across the street until I saw your cab drive up. I had a hunch that Yama would bait a trap for me with Mary Liwang. I knew if he did that you'd try to get in on the fun. I thought we could catch him red-handed."

"In other words," Brad grinned, "you were sticking my neck out for me."

"Go to the head of the class."

He strode into the bathroom. There were grim signs of a struggle. A half used roll of adhesive tape and a torn towel lay on the bowl. Two crimson splotches stained the floor. Lee touched them with his fingers. One was blood. One was a scrap of silk from the crimson robe that Mary Liwang had been wearing.

A jeering voice broke the silence. It seemed to come from everywhere and nowhere.

"That's right," General Yama read Lee's mind. "I have the girl."

Raging, Brad raced around the room tearing pictures from the walls and upsetting furniture as he looked for a dictograph with a two way hook-up.

Lee stood where he was, trying to figure from just what spot the voice was coming. It could only come, he decided, from the fire escape.

The chatter of a sub-machinegun proved him right.

"So sorry you must die." the thin voice jeered above the snarling of the gun.

Brad had thrown himself flat on the floor. His guns were barking in answer. The thin voice stopped abruptly and so did the machinegun. There was the smack of lead in flesh and a man screamed shrilly in pain. Lee raced to the window.

Four men lay dead on the grating. Two were Japanese. One was Eurasian. One was white. As Lee watched, a fifth man dropped from the end of the iron ladder four floors below and raced towards a waiting car.

Lee took careful aim and fired. The racing figure stumbled, regained his feet and leaped on the running board of the car. The car leaped forward like a plunging jeep and rounded the corner on two wheels before Lee could fire again.

Brad got to his knees slipping fresh shells into his guns. Blood streamed down his lace from a nasty flesh wound on his forehead. Something had torn Lee Sin's right ear lobe. Yama had been shooting with murderous accuracy.

"I got how many?" Brad demanded.

Lee sponged at his ear with a towel. "Four with four shots," he said. "That's pretty good."

"Pretty good, hell," his partner scoffed. "That's perfect."

Two hours had passed. It had begun to look as if for the first time in their careers the trouble-twins had smacked into a wall they couldn't smash. Not a soul in Chinatown would talk. They were afraid of the knife that floated and the disembodied voice.

"Of what good is gold to a dead man?" Ming Po the manager of Ed Liwang's cafe had shrugged. "One can't placate the devil with cash."

"Confucius say," Lee told his partner grimly. "No can get in through one door, then kick in door on other side of house."

The morgue was cold and smelled of formaldehyde and death. Swollen-eyed with sleep, shivering in the damp night air, Lieutenant Phillips of the Bureau of Identification turned up the collar of his topcoat.

"This is a hell of a time to get a man out of bed," he protested.

Lee came directly to the point. "You're known as Camera-eye Phillips? You know most of the known hoodlums and Bundbums in New York by sight?"

"I do," Phillips admitted.

Lee led the way into the ice room and pointed to the four naked bodies of the men whom Brad had shot on the fire escape outside of Mary Liwang's apartment.

"Finger just one of them for us," he said. "Tell us who he is and what his connections were. We'll pick it up from there."

Phillips came fully awake abruptly.

"This is more of that General Yama stuff? These are some of the gang who kidnapped Mary Liwang the dancer?"

Brad nodded curtly. "That's right."

Phillips passed by the two Japanese and the Eurasian but stopped beside the dead white man. "I know this lad," he said. "He's a registered enemy alien by the name of Otto Swartz." He thought a moment then added a street address in Yorktown to the information.

"Thanks. It's a starting point," Lee said.

"At the other end of the Axis," Brad grinned. "Chop-suey town to Heinieville. We ought to be running a sight-seeing bus."

"But what's it all about?" Lieutenant Phillips demanded. "Who is this guy General Yama and what is it that he wants?"

Lee eased his guns in their holsters. "We'll know by morning," he promised.

On the corner of 42nd Street and 2nd Avenue a newsboy was shouting, "Wuxtra!" Lee parked their borrowed squad car at the curb and bought a paper. The headline read:

F.B.I. BAFFLED AS MYSTERY
KILLER SLAYS AGAIN!

There was a three-column picture of Mary Liwang dressed in little but a G-string and some beads. The caption was:

Oriental Gypsy Rose Lee kidnapped from her apartment as G-men seek to question her concerning brutal slaying of Ed Liwang, her father, a wealthy Chinese-American cafe owner.

The sub head of the main story was a slap in the face to the department. It stated:

Famous Chinese-American G-Man Present But Failed to Prevent Murder!

The tone of the rest of the story followed suit. Lee's cheeks burned as he read it aloud.

"To hell with them," Brad said. "It's easy to second guess."

Lee meshed the car back into gear and roared north down the silent street. He knew Mary Liwang would talk if they could find her. Now that her father was dead, filial loyalty would not seal her lips. But he was racing with death and he knew it. Yama, whoever he was, could not afford to let the girl live.

"The case doesn't make sense," he told Brad. "Chinatown is as afraid of the F.B.I. as they are of General Yama. Remember, Ed Liwang's throat wasn't cut until he started to confide in me."

Brad asked, "Could the killer be one of the ancients?"

"He could," Lee admitted curtly. "But I don't know which one it could be, or what he could hope to gain." He pushed the accelerator to the floorboards and thought aloud. "Mary Liwang had a model of a four-motored long range bombing plane in her hand that she tried to destroy just after that shot was fired at me. Why couldn't it be planes that they intend to buy with that forty million dollars her father said they'd collected here—'teeth for the Chinese dragon.' "

"That listens," Brad admitted crisply. "But even if they could buy the planes how could they get them out of the country?"

"They could fly them out. And if that's what they intend to do they wouldn't dare appeal to the F.B.I. even after General Yama moved in on them. They know we'd try to stop them."

"We'd have to," Brad protested. "It would be a suicide flight. Besides, the W.P.B. would never approve of the deal."

"It is written," Lee said grimly, "that a drowning man doesn't stop to inquire if a pair of water wings are union made."

He parked the car two doors from the address that Lieutenant Phillips had given them and walked up the stairs of the house. It was an old fashioned brownstone in a solid residential neighborhood. A surly blond brute in a dirty undershirt and trousers opened the door in response to their heavy pounding. His breath was heavy with cheap whiskey.

"Der Teufel," he swore. He doubled his big fists into balls. *"Ich weide—"*

"The hell you say," Brad stopped him. He knocked the German down, then picked him up. "That's for nothing, *mein freund,"* he told him. "Now start talking. You're Otto's brother, aren't you?"

"I am," the man admitted sullenly.

"We're Federal men," Lee told him. "We want to know who Otto was working for and where the gang hangs out."

"I will tell you nothing, Schweinhund," the big German sneered.

What followed wasn't pretty. Lee had no time to waste. He had a knowledge of vital nerves. Five minutes later he and Brad were on their way again with the information that they sought.

The place was a neighborhood biers tube not far from the

East River. Venetian blinds had been lowered over the front window and the door but through the chinks in the blinds they could see men standing in front of a dimly lighted bar.

Lee tried the door. It was locked. He rapped on the glass panel sharply.

"Ja!" a guttural voice demanded.

"Open up. Otto Swartz sent us," Lee lied.

"Otto ist dead," the man on the inside jeered. "Und if you are officers, show me first your warrant."

Brad kicked in the plate glass of the door and covered the startled men at the bar while Lee reached in through the shattered glass and unlocked and opened the door.

"We've four warrants between us with six subpoenas in each one," he said. "Who wants to see the first one?"

There were ten men at the bar. All stood in frozen silence.

Lee addressed the short, pot-bellied German nearest to him. "Where is General Yama?" he demanded. "Where is he holding Mary Liwang?"

The German stormed, "You have no right to question me. I stand on my constitutional rights. I—"

The G-man cuffed the Bunder with his open palm. "You stopped being one of 'We the people' and became just another punk when you joined the Bund. You rats want your cheese and you want to eat it, too." He slapped the man again. "Start talking. Fast!"

"But I do not know this Yama." the German protested, "I did not even know Otto very well. He but drank here on occasions."

The bartender, a red-faced man with no neck at all and a bullet-shaped close-shaven head, came out from behind the bar.

"You guys are Federal agents?" he demanded.

"We are," Brad informed him in a flat, level voice.

"Then maybe I can give you the dope you're looking for." The bartender nodded towards the rear of the saloon. "Suppose we go back in the boss' office and talk this over."

Lee winked at his partner. "Thanks a lot." he said.

The two G-men followed the red-faced German to the rear

of the saloon. He opened a door to a darkened room and stood aside to let them enter.

"After you," Lee said.

With a sweep of his powerful arm he propelled the now screaming, cursing German into the room. It had been a booby trap. A thin, almost invisible wire had been stretched across the doorway. As the bartender's body struck it the wire released an automatic burst of machinegun fire that almost tore the man in two.

"A clever little gadget," Lee said dryly. "We must have been expected."

Brad was too busy flipping shots to answer. The rats at the bar had dropped hands with guns the moment that the G-men had passed by them. Now they were raking the rear of the saloon with a murderous blast of gunfire.

Only an L in the wall had saved the two men briefly. Lee broke the wires across the doorway with his gun barrel. He swung his partner inside the room and slammed and bolted the door just as the Bundpunks who had been lined against the bar gathered the courage to rush Brad's now empty guns.

Brad grinned, "I'll do as much for you sometimes."

Lee put one finger to his lips and pointed to the ceiling. "Listen!" he said tersely.

The gunfire outside the door had died down briefly. In the sudden silence Brad could distinctly hear the girl's voice calling:

"Help! Help! Help!"

The cry seemed to come from the room directly above the one in which they stood.

Brad swore, "We've found her! That's Mary Liwang's voice!"

There was a door in the rear of the office. Behind it a dimly lighted stairway led up to the second floor. Lee started cautiously up the stairs, stopped and flattened himself against the wall as two blond gunmen appeared around the angle of the staircase and let loose a burst of shots that tore Lee's hat off his head. At the same time a withering blast of gunfire made a sieve of the office door. They were caught between two fires.

"Down! For God's sake, down!" Lee bellowed, simulating fear.

The two now over-confident gunman came back around the angle of the stairwell, but Lee had leaped up—not down. The giant G-man caught a gunman in each hand and smashed their heads together.

Brad swept by his partner to cover the upper hall. It was an old-fashioned railroad flat; the hall ran the length of the building. Only one of the rooms was lighted. A woman sobbed broken-heartedly behind the door, then whimpered in pain and terror as a hard palm smacked on flesh.

Lee kicked in the door, his guns ready in his hands.

Mary Liwang, her crimson robe half-torn from her lovely golden body, crouched terror stricken in one corner of the room. A thin-faced German, a monocle gleaming coldly in one eye, stood over her, holding the barrel of a Lueger to her temple. His face was vaguely familiar. Lee had a feeling that they had met before.

The thin-laced German bowed lightly. "Herr Oberst-Leutnant Eric Roeheim of the *Deutsches Auslands Gestapo* at your service." He added coldly, "But unless you would care to see the young lady die, I would suggest that you drop your guns as you enter."

The Oberst-Leutnant meant what he said. Lee could see the knuckles of the Nazi's trigger finger whiten as he spoke.

"No Lee! No!" The Chinese dancer pleaded. "My life doesn't matter. Shoot him! Kill him, Lee!"

The G-man hesitated. If Mary Liwang died, the information that he wanted would die with her. He and Brad could kill the Nazi by allowing her to die. But Roeheim's death would gain them little while General Yama still remained at large.

"So—?" the Gestapo man demanded sharply.

Lee tossed his guns at the Oberst-Leutnant's feet. His partner grimly followed suit.

"The corpse-makers," Roeheim sneered. "Bah! You will

both be corpses by morning. You are fools of a nation of fools, you Americans—like little children. You still believe in Gott and Santa Claus, and in such fairy tales as decency and honor."

The bund-killers from the bar swarmed up the stairs and down the hall and over the G-men like rats. Both men went down swinging, bare fist, against steel gun butts.

"Tie them securely," the Gestapo agent ordered. "But do not kill them yet." He paused, smiled thinly. "It is possible that General Yama might wish us to question them before they die."

The pot-bellied little Nazi whom Lee had slapped in the bar laughed shrilly. It was the last thing that Lee heard. A viscously swung gun-barrel chopped through his guard and crashed against his temple. The big man sprawled his full length on the floor.

CHAPTER THREE

Flame Dance

THERE WAS NO SOUND in the dimly lighted room but the soft sobbing of the girl and the vicious squeals of the four-legged rats that infested the old wooden building. They were as real and could be as deadly as their human counterparts who were questioning Brad Hatfield in a room across the hall. Lee and the girl were alone.

Lee sat up slowly. The rats who had been attracted by his blood, scampered back through their holes in the baseboard as he moved. Now that he was fully conscious he could hear the flat smack of a leather strap on flesh, hear Roeheim's thin voice swearing.

Brad's voice came faint with pain but defiant, "Go to hell, you lousy crumb."

The slap of the strap and the questioning continued.

"You are conscious, Lee?" Mary Liwang asked softly.

"I'm conscious," the big man said.

His head ached like a throbbing boil.

"What is this all about, Mary?" he demanded. "And who is this lad, Roeheim? Is he working with General Yama?"

"I think so," she said. "It was his men who kidnapped me." She began to cry. "But he isn't as bad as Yama!"

"Stop crying and talk fast," Lee said sharply. Brad's defiant voice across the hall was growing fainter. Lee knew it would be his turn next. "Have you ever seen this Yama?"

"I don't know," the girl admitted. "We first heard of him in Chinatown six months ago."

"Shortly after General P'u came here?"

"That's right."

"And it was General P'u's idea to collect the forty million dollars and buy hot planes for China?"

"I don't know." Mary said. "I think Yuan Ling the poet first suggested it. I do know that General Yama tried to kill General P'u the night the ancients first met to form a ways and means committee to help China." A sob crept into her voice. "His neck was badly gashed by the knife that floats."

Lee's battered lips twisted in a scowl. The attempt on General P'u's life would seemingly remove the aged Chinese General from his list of suspected men. It left only Chang Fu the importer, Yuan Ling the poet and Ch'en Yang the fat bellied merchant. Lee had known the three men all his life. It was hard to believe that any of the three could be bribed or coerced into plotting with either the Nazis or the Japs.

"How did you intend to get the planes," Lee asked.

"I don't know," the little Chinese-American dancer admitted. "My father and General P'u were handling that angle of the deal. I believe that a large share of the money is to go for *cumshaw.*" There was triumph in her voice despite her fear. "And no one can stop us now—not even General Yama. General P'u and the remaining ancients are to meet with executives of the plane plants and a man from the War Production Board in Chicago this afternoon."

"You don't know where in Chicago?"

"I do not," she admitted. "But I do know that the money is

to change hands this afternoon."

"And you have never seen this General Yama?" Lee persisted.

"No one has seen him and lived," she sobbed. "He is a voice, a man, a woman, just as he pleases. Walls cannot keep him out. He is evil, invisible spirit."

Lee said, "Baloney," and leaned back against the wall to think. It was the damnedest case in which he had ever been involved. It had begun in Chinatown, to wind up in Yorkville with those who should have been his friends arrayed against him, and an Oberst-Leutnant of the *Deutsches Auslands Gestapo* taking over for his Japanese ally.

Lee considered Roeheim briefly. Both the man's face and his name were familiar. He felt again that he had seen the man before, not once but many times. But try as he would, he could not place him.

Her slim wrists and ankles cruelly bound with rope, Mary inched her way across the floor until she sat beside Lee, "Have we any chance at all?"

"I don't know," he admitted frankly. Then he grinned. "But it is written that no ball game is over until the last man has struck out." He paused a moment, demanded, "No one heard all those shots? The prowl car on this beat never even took a look-see?"

The girl said tonelessly, "There is a trucking garage next door. And I heard Herr Roeheim boast to Mr. Hatfield that the squad car men who investigated a reported shooting were told that it was a cold truck motor backfiring and went away satisfied."

"Then that's that," Lee said curtly. It was up to himself and Brad.

The door from the hallway opened, flooding the windowless room with light. Two Bund-rats, followed by Roeheim, dragged Brad Hatfield into the room, rebound his wrists and ankles and threw him into a corner. Barely conscious the G-man muttered:

"Didn't tell 'em a damn thing, Lee."

"Stay with it, boy," Lee said.

The two Nazis pulled him to his feet and dragged him across the hall to the room that his partner had just quitted. A blazing white light hung from the ceiling. The room was bare of furniture save for a sturdy table with stout straps looped through steel rings on each of the four corners.

"Tear his shirt off and spread-eagle him," Roeheim ordered.

Four more Bund-punks stepped from the wall to help. Had Lee's arms and legs been free the six would not have been enough. Bound as he was they wrestled him onto the table and strapped his wrists and ankles securely.

"If you are sensible, Agent Sin," the Oberst-Leutnant said as he soaked the lash of a heavy dog whip in a bucket of bloody water. "You will spare yourself much pain. Your partner Hatfield is a fool. All that he would say was, "Go to hell.""

"I can't think of a better place for you to go to," Lee answered soberly, "Unless you crawled back under a stone."

The Nazi's monocle glittered fiercely. He handed the bloodstained whip to a husky German almost as large as Lee. "Soften him up!"

The whip slashed Lee's back to ribbons—the pain ate into his brain like liquid fire . . .

"Enough," the Oberst-Leutnant said finally. "He should be in a mood to talk."

Lee swam back through a sea of pain. "What do you want to know?" he asked.

"Just how much does your Federal Bureau know concerning General Yama?"

"Not much," Lee admitted. "We've been looking for him for some time. We believe him to be responsible for most of the sabotage on the west coast, the dynamiting of several dams, and the attempted rising among the Japanese in the San José concentration camp."

"Good," Roeheim beamed. "I am glad you have decided to be sensible." He glanced at the watch on his wrist. " I have not very much time to waste on you."

Lee grinned wryly as he spat the blood out of his mouth. He hadn't said a thing that anyone with three cents to buy a daily paper hadn't read.

"And what," the Oberst-Leutnant continued, "do you know of General Yama's connection with the recent executions in Chinatown?"

"Why not say murders?" Lee asked dryly.

The Bund-rat with the whip slashed at the raw flesh of Lee's back. "The Oberst-Leutnant asks the questions."

Lee admitted that he knew little but the names of the ancients who had died. "But from the looks of things," he added, "you and your boys must have had a hand in some of them. How does it feel," he taunted, "for an Oberst-Leutnant of the Gestapo to take orders from a Jap?"

Roeheim nodded curtly to the man with the whip. He flogged Lee again until his arm was tired.

"That is to teach you respect," he said.

As sometimes happens, the intense pain made Lee's mind razor sharp. He knew now where he had seen Roeheim before. It was small wonder that the man's name and face had seemed familiar. For years he had toured the Keith and Orpheum time with his own vaudeville act. He had been known as the Marvelous Roeheim. Lee tried to remember what the act had been and his mind went dull again as Roeheim's voice intruded.

"Now let us get to more important matters. In your Federal Bureau of Investigation there is a small group of ace agents who for various reasons have been publicly dishonored and discredited but who still take orders from the Bureau. This small group of men have done more damage to our cause than all the other agents put together. I know that you know who they are. Tell me their names and describe them."

Lee knew now why Brad had kept repeating, "Go to hell!" The words came to his lips instinctively.

His face crimson with rage, Roeheim snatched the whip from the man who held it and lashed brutally at Lee's back. As he did so a grimace of pain contorted his lips and Lee caught a glimpse of a bloodstained bandage under the other man's coat.

"Well I'll be damned!" he gasped.

He had all of the picture that he needed. The Department had been mistaken in thinking that General Yama was a Jap. It was but another of his disguises. No wonder the pot-bellied little Bund-punk had laughed so shrilly at the mention of Yama's name. No wonder that Yama had been described as a man, a woman, a voice. The Marvelous Roeheim could be all three. In his halcyon vaudeville days he had been a quick-change artist, a ventriloquist and a magician.

"Talk, damn you, talk!" Roeheim roared. "Who are they?"

"I'd see you in hell before I'd tell you," Lee told him soberly.

The former vaudeville actor, now risen high in the Gestapo threw the whip from him in disgust. "Bah! These American G-men swine are all alike, even those with yellow skins. Throw him back in with the others." He glanced hastily at his watch. "I have but time to catch the morning Chicago plane."

The pot-bellied little Nazi saluted. *"Und* the girl—?"

"It is a shame," the Gestapo agent said, "but she must die when the two men die. Let it take place tonight."

The hall door slammed, cutting off most of the light. A key turned in the lock. Men's feet thudded down the hall. For a moment there was no sound but Lee's heavy breathing and the shamed sobbing of the girl.

Then Lee rolled to a sitting position and began to tear with his teeth at the rope around his wrists.

"Roeheim is really General Yama," he informed the others.

Brad swore deeply and with feeling. Even the girl stopped sobbing.

"He's a former ventriloquist, quick-change artist, and a magician," Lee continued. "That's why he can be a man, a voice or a woman as he chooses. And ten gets you one that when General P'u and the three remaining ancients meet with their contact men in Chicago this afternoon Roeheim will be posing as either an airplane manufacturer or as the

War Production Board man whom they hope to bribe."

His own hands and ankles freed, he untied Brad and Mary.

The little dancer was too terrified to move. "There are too many of them. We can't escape."

"We can't tell till we try," Lee said curtly.

The trouble twins made a circuit of the room. There was only the one door leading to the hallway. Brad looked at the ceiling. The only window was a tiny skylight too high for them to reach.

"I guess this is it," he admitted.

"The hell it is," Lee said. "There is some way out of here."

He sat down on the floor and tried to think. Emboldened by the silence in the room and attracted by the sweet sickening stench of blood, a mangy, hungry rat scampered across his legs. A slow smile lighted Lee's battered face.

"It must be my Chinese blood," he grinned. "Darn clever, we Chinese." He looked at his own shirt and then at Brad's. "Our shirts won't do," he said. "They're both too wet with blood. Tear off the rest of that robe and let me have it, Mary."

Lee tore two long strips from the robe, each about three feet long and six inches wide, Then, crushing the silk into a ball he could hold in the palm of one hand, he saturated it with the fluid from his lighter.

"I get you, Pal." Brad grinned. He added the contents of his own cigarette lighter to the silk.

His preparations made, Lee cautioned the others to be silent and sat as motionless as a great yellow Buddha until the rats, emboldened by the silence and the scent of blood came back into the room. First there was one, then two, then three, then four—Lee's big hands shot out and grasped two screaming rodents by their bodies. Mad with fear they twisted, biting at his hands and arms.

Brad tied a strip of silk to each rat's right hind leg and set the material aflame with his lighter. The impregnated strips of silk burned with a steady flame that would last for a long time. Lee released the rodents. Squealing with fear they circled the room then disappeared into the walls dragging the flaming silk behind them.

Lee sat sucking at the bites upon his hands. The old frame building should burn like tinder. They hadn't long to wait. An acrid smoke began to coil out of the rat holes in the baseboard.

"We'll be burned alive!" the dancer screamed.

"Perhaps," the G-man admitted. "Then, on the other hand, the fire department may get here first. That is the gamble we're taking."

As he spoke there was a sound of voices in the hall. Brad and Lee got to their feet and faced the door. A key was inserted in the lock. The doorknob began to turn.

Lee lunged against the door as it began to open and slammed it shut again.

"Quick! Quick!" a hoarse voice bellowed. "Gedt oudt before the fire department gets here. Fire in every wall has out burst!"

Then the key turned in the lock again and the voice of the pot-bellied Little Nazi screamed maliciously, "All right. So stay in there and fry."

Running feet pounded down the hall to safety. Inside the room the acrid smoke was pouring through the rat holes in thick grey sluggish coils. Then a red tongue of flame licked after the smoke, caught at a loose piece of wallpaper and danced up the wall.

Somewhere in the grey of dawn, fire sirens began to wail. But both men knew that they could not arrive in time. The fire was spreading too rapidly. No one knew that they were in the building but the Bundrats who had fled. The top floor of the biers tube was not known to be occupied. By the time that the firemen found them their bones would be pieces of charred lime. Even the floor was growing hot beneath their feet.

Lee told his partner curtly, "We'll try to smash through the door." He tore his blood soaked shirt from his back and tossed it to the girl. "Keep that over your nose and mouth." He hesitated, added, "And if we shouldn't make it, Mary, well—I'm sorry."

The little dancer stood on her tiptoes suddenly and kissed him. "I'm not afraid," she whispered.

The two big men smashed their shoulders against the door. Something had to give—and the steel lock split from the panel.

The hall was a murky haze of acrid smoke, the staircase a mass of living flame. Brad felt the floor begin to sway beneath his feet. "Look out!" he bellowed. "The floor is caving in!"

Lee picked up the girl and raced through the searing heat towards the front of the hall where a smoke-smeared pane of glass showed grey in the early dawn. Just as the G-man reached it, a red-faced Irish fireman standing on the top of an extension ladder shattered the pane of glass.

Brad said, "Back down that ladder, Paddy. And back down fast! We've a date with a lad in Chicago!"

CHAPTER FOUR

Blood on the Rising Sun

ED FERRIS, divisional head of the mid-west sector of the F.B.I. stopped his nervous pacing and strode out through the plane gate and down the runway as the big B-17 circled the Cicero Airport and swooped down in a perfect landing.

Lee Sin and Brad Hatfield got out of the great bomber stiffly. A few handfuls of salve and a few yards of gauze had been all the medical treatment that either man would stop for. The yards of gauze beneath their clothes made both men look even larger than they were. Their grim and battered faces were unbandaged.

"You're sure of your facts, Lee?" Ferris demanded. "I've just been talking to Washington on the phone and there'll be hell to pay if you're making a bull."

"Where," Brad asked him dryly, "do you think we spent the night? Sleeping with a buzz saw?"

Ferris looked at the raw cuts on their faces. "Okay," he said. "That's good enough for me. But this General P'u came damn well recommended by Chiang Kai-Shek himself."

Lee exploded "So? Does that keep him from making a fool of himself and buying a bill of goods when he bumps into a Gestapo agent as smart as Roeheim?"

"And you think this Roeheim is General Yama?"

"We know he is," Brad said, and Lee asked, "Did you check the morning plane?"

"I did. And that's what has me worried," Ferris said. "I checked the plane myself. And no one even faintly resembling this Roeheim, as you described him to me over the phone, was on it. There were only General P'u, Yuan Ling, Che'en Yang, Chang Fu, four other Chinese who might have been tong gunmen or bodyguards, and two young Army nurses."

"He could have been one of the nurses," Lee said.

There were three other agents in the car that was waiting for them. Phil Mercer told Ferris, "They're meeting at Wang Po's place. We just had a flash on the two-way from the boys you put on their tail."

The big car moved off slowly. Ed Ferris shook his head. "I don't like it. Lee," he admitted. "Chinese or no Chinese, Wang Po is one of the smartest business men in Chicago. And I doubt if even this Roeheim could pull the wool over his eyes."

The strain the Trouble Twins had been through had been too great for them to be doubted now. Brad opened the car door. "Okay," he said hotly. "To hell with the Bureau. Stop the car and let Lee and me get out. We've handled this so far on our own. We can take it the rest of the way."

Ferris closed the car door. "Hold it, Brad," he clipped. "We'll take a look."

A grim silence filled the car. Mercer, driving, cut east down 72nd Street, then south again to stop before a huge stone mansion near the South Shore Country Club. A high stone fence studded with broken bottles surrounded the mansion completely. As the car stopped in front of the gate two bland Eurasian guards with their hands in their coat pockets walked out to the curb.

"Shove on," one of them said. "Mr. Po isn't seeing anyone today."

Lee showed them his shield.

"No dice," the other guard snarled. "There's a big deal going on inside. And the only way you could bust in, pal, would be with a Federal warrant."

"I've got just what you want," Brad said curtly. He stepped from the car and rammed both of his guns into the guard's slim belly.

As Lee did the same for the other guard, the guards' sallow faces turned sullen, but they made no attempt to draw their guns. Ferris disarmed them and turned them over to Phil Mercer. He detailed several of his men who had been waiting across the street to guard the four sides of the house.

"It begins to look as if you boys were right." Ferris said grimly.

Lee and Brad led the way down the drive to the front door of the mansion. It was locked and no one answered the bell. But Lee had expected that. He plunged one big fist through a panel of the glass then reached in and unlocked the door.

The front door opened into an entrance hall as large as the average living room. A heavily carpeted winding staircase led up to the second floor. Rare tapestries and drapes hung on the walls. The pottery was priceless. A pair of heavy doors inlaid with mother-of-pearl led off the entrance hall into what Lee assumed must be the library. He drew his guns and started for the door just as an elderly Chinese in a well-cut business suit came down the winding stairs.

"Who are you, gentlemen?" he demanded curtly in flawless English. "What are you doing in my house?"

Ed Ferris recognized Wang Po. "We're Federal men," he told him quietly. "You are entertaining guests, Mr. Po?"

The elderly Chinese-American businessman shook his head. "No. I am not entertaining," he said. "But a business transaction very important to my native country is being consummated in my house."

"It's a phoney." Brad said tersely. "General P'u and China are being taken by a Nazi slicker." He banged on the library doors. "Open up in there."

On the other side of the door General P'u screamed shrilly in Chinese. "Shoot! Shoot! Shoot for Mother China. It is General Yama come to rob us!"

A withering blast of gunfire echoed his words. Lead poured through the door in a murderous hail. Jim Peters, one of the G-men, clutched at his heart then sank slowly to his knees. He tried to grin and blood gushed from his mouth. Wang Po, too, had been hit—and badly. A look of intense surprise on his lemon-tinted features, he stepped down another stair towards Lee and fell flat on his face.

"Stop it! Stop it, you damn fools!" Lee tried to make himself heard above the bellow of the guns. He didn't dare to return the fire for fear of hitting General P'u and the three ancients. "You can't get away. Guards are posted all around the house."

Brad crawled across the hallway on his hands and knees toward a heavy straight-backed chair that he intended to use as a battering ram. "You should know better, Roeheim," he jeered. "Once you tangle with the F.B.I., you're through."

There was staccato order in Chinese and the gunfire from inside the library stopped abruptly.

"The F.B.I.!" a man on the other side of the door cried out. "Then why didn't you say who you were? We have forty million dollars in cash in here. We thought we were being robbed."

A cold chill swept down Lee's spine. Ed Ferris looked at him sharply. Then the heavy inlaid doors were opened by one of the three-tong hatchet men whom Lee had seen in the council chamber in Ed Liwang's Lotus Burl Cafe. The other three hatchet men, puzzled but alert, stood covering the men in the doorway.

Across a table covered with papers and plane specifications, Yuan Ling, Ch'en Yang, Chang Fu and General P'u faced two pallid American businessmen whose names and faces were well known to every citizen. One was Harvard Pile, the aeronautic head of the War Production Board. The other was Bill Stacey, the famous West Coast airplane manufacturer.

Bill Stacey looked from Lee to the two dead men in the hall then back to Ed Ferris whom he knew. "And just what the hell is the meaning of this?"

Grim-faced, Ed Ferris said: "We had a tip that one of you was a phoney, Bill." He glanced at Lee, continued, "We were informed that one of you would be General Yama, otherwise known, according to Agent Sun, as Herr Oberst-Leutnant Roeheim of the Deutsches Auslands Gestapo."

"But that is ridiculous," the plane manufacturer said quietly. "You can see for yourself that there is no such person here. This is a legitimate business deal. You see," he explained, "realizing the desperate need of General P'u's country for planes and more planes, the W.P.B. has just given us the go-ahead and waved all priority rights. We've agreed to supply Chinese Army pilots waiting on the West Coast with five hundred fighter planes and long range Seversky type bombers."

General P'u rose to his feet stroking at his scraggly beard. "I think," he said in his shrill voice, "I can explain." He spoke in Cantonese looking straight at Lee. "You will please to interpret my words."

"First," General P'u said, "it is much to be regretted that this lamentable mistake has happened. It is in a way my fault. When there came a great pounding on the door I thought that it was this General Yama and so ordered our bodyguard to shoot.

"Yama has killed five of our council. He wanted the forty million dollars we had collected for China." Here the General slapped a bulging brief case on the table that was both locked and sealed with wax. "But we were willing to die," he said simply, "before we would give it up. The money did not belong to us. It belonged to Mother China."

Again Lee Sin translated.

General P'u slapped the brief case a second time. "At first we expected to buy planes in the black market, but your War Production Board has realized our necessity." He looked out into the hall at the crumpled figure of Wang Po. "Again I can only say it is regrettable that this has happened. We have been through so much. So many of us have died. We thought that we were being robbed."

"And that's the way it stands," the War Production Board man said grimly. He looked out at the dead Chinese and the federal agent in the hall. "I'm afraid there'll be hell about this." He fingered the crimson sealing wax on the lock of the brief case. "General P'u and Mr. Ling and Mr. Yang and Mr. Fu are representatives of an important ally of this country. And someone is going to pay for this unwarranted intrusion and for the death of Mr. Po."

Ed Ferris took a deep breath. "This is the worst break," he admitted, "that the Bureau has ever made." He looked at Lee. "You'll be lucky if you're only broken and not indicted for murder."

General P'u and the three ancients rose.

"This is not our affair," Yuan Ling said courteously, "however lamentable the accident has been." He bowed in turn to Harvard Pile and Bill Stacey.

"True, true." General P'u echoed the poet in shrill Cantonese. "The deal has been consummated. Our responsibility is now over."

Followed by their bodyguard the four old men started for the door.

"But—wait!" Brad shouted. "There's a Nazi in the woodpile somewhere!"

It was then that Lee got the picture. He slipped both of his guns from their holsters. "Hold it! Everyone!" he ordered. He crossed to the table and glanced briefly at the bulging briefcase. "There are forty million dollars in that?" he demanded.

"There are," Harvard Pile said coldly.

"And what are you going to do with it now?" Lee asked.

"Put it in a vault in the Treasury intact," the W.P.B. man said curtly, "until the first plane has landed in China. Then it will be opened and applied on China's credit under the Lend Lease Program."

"Open it!" Lee ordered and covered Pile with his guns. "Open that brief case!" he ordered.

Pile did so, unwillingly. The brief case was filled with neatly stacked pieces of newspaper cut to the size or bills. Pile and Stacey stared at it unbelievingly.

Yuan Ling. Chang Fu and Ch'en Yang began to jabber.

"We paid the money. We did!" Yuan Ling insisted. "I saw it put into the case. It was not our trick but yours."

General P'u tottered toward the door shrilling in broken English. "Chiang Kai-Shek shall hear of this. He—"

"Hold it," Lee ordered him curtly. He flipped a shot past the general's ear to emphasize the order. Brad held Ed Ferris back as he tried to grab Lee's guns. "And the next one goes right between your eyes Herr Roeheim," Lee exulted. "You are a mighty damn good actor, the best one that I've ever seen. *But you weren't quite good enough to pull the old switch game for forty million bucks.*"

The tong hatchet men stood uncertain, their eyes on the guns in Lee's hand.

"You're crazy, Lee," Ed Ferris shouted, still struggling in Brad's arms.

"Like a fox," Brad jeered. "No wonder General Yama could be anywhere in Chinatown at will. He—look out!"

Roeheim had dropped his pose. He was no longer the enfeebled oriental general that he had pretended to be. He was Oberst-Leutnant Roeheim, a deadly Gestapo killer. His hands came out of the sleeves or the flowing Chinese robe that he was wearing. One held a spitting gun. From the other hand a glittering knife blade shot across the room propelled by an almost invisible extension rod.

One of the tong hatchet men screamed, "The knife that floats!"

The knife blade missed Lee's throat by a hair's breadth;

then Brad shot the spitting gun out of the Nazi's left hand as Lee shot Roeheim between the eyes.

The Nazi staggered and collapsed across a chair. Brad released his no longer struggling superior and ripped the dead man's robes aside. Hung from a stout thong fastened to his belt and slung between his legs there was a second briefcase identical to the other one.

The G-man broke the seal and lock. Packets of five and ten thousand-dollar bills spilled out.

Yuan Ling stared at the dead man.

"But the real General P'u—?"

"He was probably killed on the high seas before he ever reached this country," Lee told the ancient soberly. He explained to Pile and Stacey. "Roeheim stood to win three ways. Once the switch had been discovered no planes after the first one would have been sent to China under this agreement. The United States would feel that they had been tricked. Yuan Ling, Ch'en Yang and Chang Fu, all honorable men, would swear that they had seen the money paid. An ill feeling would have been engendered that nothing could have explained away. In the meantime Roeheim and the Nazis would have had forty million dollars to spend."

Chang Fu demanded. "But why all the killing of the ancients?"

"The less eyes to spy out a thief," Lee answered in Mandarin. "He killed Ed Liwang in the Council Chamber because he was about to confide in me. The pretended attempt on his own life, the floating knife, the disembodied voices, the ghostly moon fiddles playing *towsey mongelay*—all were tricks of the magician to divert us."

Lee piled the bills back into the briefcase. "The deal still stands?" he asked Pile.

"More so now than ever," the W.P.B. executive said earnestly. "I am only sorry that previous commitments first led the Chinese to believe that they might have to deal in the black market. China has need of planes and she shall have them."

Lee remembered something he had forgotten, "I've got to

get right back to New York," he said. "I've got some unfinished business there."

Ed Ferris grinned, "Forget it. Six of the boys are flying down from Washington to round up what's left of the Roeheim gang."

"I wasn't thinking of that." Lee admitted. His battered face split in a happy grin. "I just happened to remember that Mary Liwang kissed me and I didn't kiss her back!"

SEVEN KEYS TO MURDER

CHAPTER ONE

Hound of Doom

THE JOB MEANT A LOT to McGinty. He needed the money desperately, because he hadn't made anything to speak of in three years. Now he wondered if he had been wise to risk it. The storm flags had been flying when he left Miami. He didn't like the feel of the air. He didn't like the country.

The highway wound through miasmatic thickets of mangrove swamp, sparse stands of moss-draped cypress, and across long barren wastes of sand and white coquina. The only signs of human habitation were the occasional closed up juke joints, a few shabby fishing camps. In places, if his arms had been a little longer, he could have reached out the window of the car and touched the Gulf of Mexico with one hand and the Atlantic with the other.

As another white culvert flashed by, he glanced at his speedometer. If the mileage that Green had given him was correct, he should be on Seventh Key. Another three miles down the road, his headlights picked up the high stone wall for which Green had warned him to watch. Glass and pieces of broken bottles embedded in cement glittered along the top. The iron gates were closed but not locked. On one gatepost there was a sign:

Seventh Key Lodge—
Peddlers, Solicitors, Uninvited Guests, Stay Out!
THIS MEANS YOU! Silas T. Martin

He lighted a cigarette with fingers that shook slightly and reviewed what he knew of the man. What little he knew was bad.

Martin had been a Capone gunman whom the gang had run out of Chicago. He had come to the Keys in the first lush days of prohibition and had made a fortune running whiskey. He had died in his own bed, an old man full of years, with the first dollar that he had ever stolen clutched in one clawlike hand.

It takes all kinds, McGinty thought.

He opened the gates and drove in. In its day, Seventh Key Lodge had been a mansion. The house itself was built of co-quina block. It loomed huge and black against the shore line of the Gulf, impervious to rot, hurricanes, and time. Tall white, Ionic pillars rose out of the ground to disappear into the night. Through slightly sagging shutters he could see a four-foot pine log blazing in the fireplace. Mixed with the tang of salt spray, the fragrance of gardenia was strong.

He got out of his rented car and locked it. In the exact center of the circular drive was a more than life sized statue of a man. He had a flock of gulls on one shoulder and a ragged pickanniny or a conch kid on the other. McGinty struck a match and studied the inscription on the base. It read:

Silas T. Martin July 3rd, 1884—January 1st, 1943

Under that, in larger Gothic letters, were carved the words:

Blessed Are the Pure In Heart

Tied in with old Silas Martin that was a laugh. McGinty threw back his head and howled.

The voice came out of the dark behind him. It was masculine and very English. "You find the monument amusing?"

McGinty's hand dropped to the gun in his pocket, sweat starting on his cheeks. The fragrance of good whiskey was strong.

"Yeah. I do. So what?" he demanded.

"So, so do I," the speaker told him. "Ha." His pipe bowl glowed red, illuminating a long and bony face above a silk cravat and loud tweed jacket. "Towers—Lord Jerry Towers is the name. And I hate the whole bloody place. Migawd! Building a statue to a gunman!"

Before McGinty could speak, he was gone, the glow of his pipe wavering down the path that led to the shore. Whoever Lord Towers might be, McGinty decided, he was sailing three sheets in the wind but tacking with an experienced hand.

There was a solid brass knocker on the door. He squared his shoulders and banged it. He had to begin again some time. This job was as good as any.

The girl who opened the door was young, not more than twenty. Her hair was a rich dull copper. Her eyes were green and smiling in the ivory of her face.

"Yes—?" she smiled. "There was somethin' that you all wanted?"

McGinty nodded. He wanted to ask where she'd been all his life. This was it. He knew it. There had been that certain something when their eyes met.

"Why, yes," he hesitated. "I'd like to see Miss Fay."

The smile faded. "Come in," she said coldly. "You must be Mr. McGinty. You are expected."

She spoke with a southern drawl that had been tampered with at Vassar. Her eyes took in the prison pallor and the three year old cut of his sport clothes in a single glance.

"And you're about what I expected," she added.

Before he could explain, she was gone.

McGinty started after her down the hall only to be intercepted by a black haired girl who threw herself into his arms.

"Sweetheart! Darling!" she shrilled. She slipped her arms around his neck and pulled his lips down to hers.

McGinty kissed her mechanically. It was one of the things that he was being paid to do.

The girl in his arms pressed closer. "You *are* Jim McGinty, aren't you?" she whispered. "Attorney Green *did* send you?"

"That's right," he said.

Her voice grew even more intense. "Then respond to me, you fool. After all, we're *supposed* to be engaged."

He kissed her again, more soundly. She wasn't the little red head but she wasn't difficult to hold. Her body was firm and slim and young. It was good to have a woman in his arms again.

"That's better," she admitted. "Now let's talk before the others come down to supper." She led the way into the living room. "How much do you know?"

"Not a hell of a lot," he admitted. He sketched what Green had told him. "You're the heir to Martin's money. You have reason to believe that your life is in danger."

"I know damn well it is," she told him. Her pretty face was contorted with hate. "They're jealous of me. But if I can get through the next two nights, they all can go to hell."

McGinty had most of the picture then. She was the type of greedy little baggage for which old Martin would have fallen. Her beauty was just a veneer.

"Anyone made a try?" he demanded.

She shook her tight black curls. "They haven't dared. They're afraid of Clause Five in his will. But with only two days to go, they're getting desperate. That's why I had Green get you." She studied his face. "You're not a bad looking devil," she admitted, "but it seems to me that Green would have done a lot better to hire a private detective than an ex-con just out of stir."

"I—" he began.

"Sure, I know," she said coldly. "You were framed. I've used that gag myself."

McGinty hesitated, shrugged. What difference did it make? This was a strictly business proposition.

"Let's get the household straight," he suggested, "so I'll know what I'm up against. How many other heirs are there?"

She shook her head. "None. Unless I die. Then six of them split the estate."

"An estate of how much?" he demanded.

"Seven million dollars," she told him.

McGinty whistled. Seven million dollars would buy a lot of murder.

"They're all here at the Lodge?" he asked her.

She nodded. "All but Green. I thought that you'd drive down together. He called me this afternoon all hot and bothered about something and said that he wanted to talk to us all."

"This was at what time?"

"About four thirty," she answered.

McGinty mentally checked the time. He had been on his way an hour by then. "Now, tell me this," he said quietly. "If you're so afraid of these other heirs, why do you allow them to stay here at the Lodge? Why haven't you asked them to leave?"

Surprisingly, the girl began to cry. "Because that's also in the will. They were to have free run of the place for a year. Old Silly wanted them to kill me."

"Silly?"

"Silas," she explained. "He hated me because I wouldn't," she hesitated, "well, because I wouldn't. That's why he drew up his will the way he did. But none of them inherit a penny unless they can kill me without getting caught. You see?"

McGinty shook his head. "No. I don't," he admitted.

"That's paragraph five," she told him. She quoted it verbatim:

"In the event, however, that any of my said heirs, real or prospective, shall within the twelve months immediately following my demise, be charged and convicted of theft, assault, or murder, such charge and such conviction shall automatically be construed as disqualifying them as heirs."

"Perhaps you'd better let me see a copy of the will," McGinty suggested.

Angela got one from a desk drawer and gave it to him. Stripped of its wherefores and whereases, it boiled down to a simple contest whereby any of six named provisionary heirs could inherit one or more million dollars by killing Angela Fay in a manner that would escape detection.

He handed the copy of the will back to the girl. "That isn't a will," he told her. "That's a murder lottery." He checked the named heirs on his fingers. "Who's Caleb White?"

"His first cousin, a religious fanatic," she told him.

"And Phillip Martin?"

"A grandson."

"And Lady Jeffry Towers?"

"She'd be the best of the lot," Miss Fay admitted, "if she weren't so desperate for money. She's Teeny Martin, the big time vaudeville actress who used to sing *I Don't Care* and *Shine On Harvest Moon,* and songs like that."

McGinty nodded. "I remember her very well. And this Swami Sajahanhpur?"

"A fake out of some mitt camp," the girl said scornfully. "In his last few years the old man was afraid of Hell and the Swami set himself solid by getting messages for him from Heaven."

"And Mary Lee Gaspiralla?"

Angela's face turned sullen. "That's that red haired gal who let you in. Her father used to own this place—before he went partners with Martin."

McGinty lit a cigarette and hoped that his gun-shattered nerves wouldn't shy. He had a hunch that he would earn the thousand dollars that Green had promised him.

"And old Martin left you his money, why?"

Miss Fay's face colored slightly. "I was his secretary."

"Is that so?" McGinty asked politely.

A door opened at the head of the stairs and a woman's voice begged: "Just this once, Jeffry. Please."

"Dem it. I told you no," the clipped English voice of Lord Towers answered. "I'm too tired from my stroll. If you want me to eat you can jolly well bring up a tray. And bring a fresh bottle while you're at it."

Angela sat closer to McGinty. "He treats her like a dog," she confided. "He makes her wait on him hand and foot. He's only been down to supper once in the ten days that they've been here."

McGinty studied the woman on the stairs. Teeny Martin had changed. She looked old and tired. Her hair was too blond. Her long bony face was over-rouged. Her shabby evening gown did little for her flat body.

She offered her hand to McGinty, smiling. "Well, so this is the much talked of fiancé." Her smile turned cynical. "Bit of a surprise, eh, learning that your fiancée had inherited seven million dollars, taking the bread right out of the mouths of Silas' rightful heirs, so to speak."

Angela stood up, furious. "That will be all of that, Lady Towers. I had nothing to do with the making of that will."

"So you say, Miss Fay."

The oily voice from the hallway swung McGinty towards its source. A dark-skinned little man stood in the doorway. Against the olive skin, his teeth were as white as the turban he affected.

Angela glared at him coldly. "Swami Sajahanhpur, Mr. McGinty."

McGinty merely nodded.

The Swami seemed amused. "You've been avoiding the sunlight, it seems."

The red haired girl came in with cocktails on a tray. "If anyone wants them, here." She placed the tray on table, asked, "You say Mr. Green is coming?"

Angela nodded. "He said it was very important, that he had just found out something and he wanted to talk to us all."

The small talk that followed was strained.

Lady Towers merely nibbled at her cocktail and went to prepare a tray for her husband. "There's only the cook," she explained. "The other servants are gone. They don't like Jeffry. When he's drunk, he throws things at them."

Mary Lee offered to take up the tray.

"With that shape? No thank you," the older woman told her.

One by one the others drifted out. McGinty made a mental check of the heirs. There still were two he hadn't met when a car roared up the drive.

Angela said, "There's Green." She walked to the door and into the night before McGinty could stop her.

He and the red haired girl were alone. She studied his face intently. "Perhaps I had you wrong," she admitted. "You couldn't be *the* McGinty?"

This is it, McGinty thought. This is the girl.

The red haired girl came close to him and looked into his eyes. "I think that you are," she told him. "And I don't think you're engaged to Angela. I think that you came here because—"

What she thought was drowned in a burst of gun fire from the drive.

McGinty strode to the door and tore it open. The echo of the shots had died away. There was nothing but the night, and somewhere a girl who was sobbing.

CHAPTER TWO

The Line Is Dead

McGINTY FELT HIS WAY through the darkness, shouting, "Angela! Miss Fay!"

A man's voice shouted something from a distance. A beam of light began to bob along the path up from the shore. To McGinty's left there was a crackling in the underbrush.

"Angela! Miss Fay!"

The girl sobbed out an incoherent answer not five feet from where he stood. He strode to her and shook her. "You all right?" he demanded.

She laughed, hysterically. "A lot you care. All you're worried about is the thousand dollars you were promised."

A wizened-faced little man materialized out of the night behind them shining an electric torch on his face. Then he directed it toward the ground and knelt by a silent figure. "Yeah. Sure. She's all right," he cackled dryly. "But Lawyer Green is dead. She's kilt him!"

The girl turned, screaming, in McGinty's arms and tried to claw at the little man. "I didn't. It was somebody else who shot him!"

"Yeah. I'll just bet," the old man cackled.

Swami Sajahanhpur came panting up the drive. "What is it? What were those shots coming from?"

Caleb White looked up from the body, his eyes shining with fanatic zeal. "Angela's shot Green. Now she'll go to the chair and we'll all inherit what's due us. Hallelujah. Praise the Lord."

Angela Fay twisted free from McGinty. "I didn't shoot Green," she screamed. She stooped toward a metal object glittering dully on the drive.

McGinty tried to stop her and couldn't. She already had the gun in her hands.

"Someone else shot him," she panted. "They shot him with this revolver, then threw it at my feet so I'd be blamed."

"A likely story." A second light had bobbed up the path to spotlight the lawyer's prostrate body.

That, McGinty decided, would be Phillip Martin, the last of the old man's heirs. He tried to take the gun from the now hysterically sobbing girl and the Swami brushed him to one side.

"If you please," he objected suavely. He wrapped a handkerchief around his hand and took the gun from her fingers. "There will indubitably be fingerprints," the Swami explained blandly.

I'm slipping, McGinty thought. I've been away from all this too long. I ought to bust him in the jaw and tell him who I am. He realized suddenly that there had been gunfire and he hadn't flinched. He hadn't even thought about it.

"All right. Let's get down to business," he said coldly. "Which one of you shot him?"

McGinty made a brief examination of the body. There was no doubt the lawyer was dead. There were three small brown puckered holes in the left breast of his coat. All together they could easily have been covered by a silver dollar.

"The police. Someone call the police." Caleb White stumbled to his feet. " 'The wicked flee when no man pursueth; but the righteous are bold as a lion.' "

"Who shot him?" McGinty repeated.

Swami Sajahanhpur smirked, "I think that is obvious. Who walked out in the night to meet Green? Who, perhaps, had a guilty conscience and wished to seal Green's lips against the something he wished to tell us?"

Angela Fay's oval face was a granite mask standing out in bas-relief against the night. She said, her lips scarcely moving, "It's a frame."

Lady Towers appeared out of no where, lifting her trailing skirts to save them from the crushed gravel of the drive. The dead man was worth a million dollars to her. She stared at him with satisfaction. "That's the prettiest sight I've ever seen," she admitted candidly. She turned back to the house.

McGinty stretched a restraining arm across her path. "You didn't shoot Green, did you?"

The former vaudeville actress snorted indignantly. "I did not. I was fixing a tray for Jeffry when I heard the shots."

Caleb White took Angela's arm and shook her. "You did it, you wicked girl." He marched stiff-legged toward the house. "Don't anyone move the body. I'm going to phone for the police."

McGinty asked the Swami, "Where were you when the shots were fired?"

"Suppose," the Swami suggested smugly, "we leave that to the police."

McGinty helped Angela to the house. "And you?"

"Not ten feet away," she admitted. "He'd just stepped out of his car." She looked at the swift scudding clouds that were racing across the moon. "For a moment I could see him plainly. Then all I could see were the flashes. They seemed to come from the house. Then something heavy thudded at my feet—"

"And you picked it up. It proved to be the murder gun. And that's all that you know about it," Phil Martin finished for her.

She nodded. "That's right."

Young Martin grinned. "Listen, sister. A D.A. just out of kindergarten could play hell with that yarn. He'll say that you dropped the gun then picked it up again in front of witnesses to alibi the prints that you left on it when you shot Green."

"But I didn't kill him," she protested, sobbing.

"The hell you didn't," he snorted. "You're going to the chair. And with you out of the way and Green dead," he licked his lips at the prospect, "there will just be five of us now to split up the old man's millions."

A high wind had begun to blow. McGinty sat slumped in a chair watching the others in the room. They sat staring at the sobbing girl in obvious satisfaction. Any of them could have killed Green with the exception of Mary Lee. She had been with him when it had happened. The problem was to prove it. Time was when it would have been easy. Now all that his head did was ache. A year in a fox hole on Bataan and another year in a Japanese prison had sapped the virility of his mind, slowed his usual quick decisions.

Angela twisted in her chair and stared at him. She seemed to be coming to some decision. "How do we know?" she demanded, "that McGinty didn't kill Green? He's no fiancé of mine. Green sent him here to guard me." She searched frantically for someone on whom to put the blame. "Look at his hair cut, his clothes. Look at that prison pallor. That's it. One of you double-crossed me and hired him to shoot Green and then put the blame on me."

A dead silence followed her hysterical disclosure.

Phil Martin broke it with a chuckle. "Well, I'll be damned. So we have a stir-bum in our midst."

The Swami Sajahanhpur smiled. "How interesting. Perhaps there will be a reward for his return."

The red-haired girl looked at McGinty. He shook his head. As long as they mistook his pallor and his clothes they would talk freely. Once they knew that he was a detective they would clam up.

Caleb White tottered into the room. "The phone line is dead," he announced. "There's someone here who don't want the law to come. The wires have been cut."

Angela Fay laughed shrilly. "Now try to blame that on me. I haven't been out of this room."

The Swami stared hard at McGinty. "Perhaps it was your convict friend."

Mary Lee spoke for the first time. "That's a lie. I was here in the room with him when the shots were fired."

"Perhaps you killed him," Angela suggested. "You could have shot him from the porch, then cut the wires. You've been in the house all the time."

McGinty got up shaking his head. "That's out. I didn't shoot Green. Neither did Mary Lee. And I don't believe that Miss Fay did." Some of his old-time strength came back in his voice. "I think that one of you three men killed him. All right. Which one? Start talking."

Young Martin sneered, "Nuts."

McGinty slapped him out of his chair. "I said, start talking. Where were you when the shots were fired?"

Martin eyed him sullenly. "I was down on the beach."

"You can prove it?" McGinty fired.

"No." Martin stood up and faced him, swaggering. "Can you prove that I wasn't?"

McGinty started another blow and Martin blocked it easily with his forearm.

"But if you want to play rough," he continued, "there are two who can play at that game. I've handled stir-bums like you before."

His eyes telegraphed the blow that was coming. McGinty read the message but his reflexes wouldn't work. Before he could raise his guard the younger man's fist caught the point of his jaw and sent him spinning into the wall.

McGinty's nerves screamed in protest. Keep your mouth shut, they told him. We can't take this anymore. Too many little yellow men beat us in Manila and Kobe. Keep still and wait for the law.

McGinty got stolidly to his feet ignoring the pain in his knee where a piece of shrapnel had shattered his knee cap.

This is my game he told his nerves. McGinty doesn't wait

for anyone. He is the law.

He hobbled across the room, out-feinted Martin, and belted him off his feet. "You want to learn to hit harder," he told him. "Most times you only get one chance."

Angela glowered at him sullenly.

Mary Lee's eyes glowed with pride. She knew what the effort had cost him.

"I didn't kill Green," Martin whimpered. "And I can prove I was on the beach. Caleb and I were there together. We were watching the sharks in the harbor. There have been two big ones in there for days."

McGinty looked at the old man.

White nodded. "That's right. We suspicioned that someone's been feeding 'em meat."

McGinty turned to the Swami. "And how about you?" he demanded. "Where were you when the shots were fired?"

The East Indian shook his head. "I have no alibi. I was walking in the garden holding a psychic communication with the stars. In your earnest effort to help the girl you are making a big mistake. It was Angela who shot Green."

Caleb White echoed him soundly. "Hallelujah. Praise the Lord."

Angela faced the others ranged against her with aloof composure. "You mean that you'd *like* to prove that I shot him. But there's no judge or jury who'll believe it. You haven't a leg to stand on. They'll know that no one would throw away that much money."

It was a good point and it scored.

Young Martin crumpled a cigarette in his fingers. "You watch," he warned the others. "She'll wriggle out of this yet."

"I doubt that very much."

Lady Towers' head appeared over the high Chinese cabinet at the head of the stairs. Her long, too-yellow hair streamed down over her shoulders and she held a brush in her hands.

"I'm not dressed," she admitted. "But I've just heard something that I want you all to hear." She repressed a shudder with an effort. "It seems that Jeffry was standing in the window when Lawyer Green drove up. He saw the whole affair."

"You don't mean," Phil Martin demanded, "that he saw Angela shoot Green."

"I mean just that," she said crisply. She disappeared into their room, her voice trailing behind her. "I'll send him down immediately."

There was a rumble of voices in their room.

"Oh bother. What difference does it make who shot the blighter," Lord Towers said distinctly. "But very well, if you insist."

Caleb White knelt in prayer, rubbing his thin dry hands together. "A Daniel come to judgment! Yeah, a Daniel!"

CHAPTER THREE

She's The Woman!

ALL EYES TURNED on a common pivot toward the stairhead.

"Now be careful and don't fall, Jeffry," Lady Towers warned from their room.

Lord Jeffry backed through the door and slammed it. "You mind your own dem business and get on with the packing. As soon as the Police Johnnies finish, we're leaving heah— t'night."

"A nice lad," McGinty said in an undertone to Mary Lee. "Is he always drunk?"

"I've never seen him sober," the red-haired girl admitted.

Lord Jeffry stood for a moment at the top of the stairs surveying the group in the living room owlishly, then began to weave a perilous descent. McGinty watched his progress with a speculative eye. His Lordship was even drunker than when he first had met him, but was holding his liquor well. Not quite so tall by an inch or so as his equally angular wife, he might have been called intelligent looking, but for his puffy drink-reddened face.

On the second step from the bottom, he staggered sharply,

recovered himself and stood holding onto the newel post, staring coldly at the faces watching him through the monocle screwed in his right eye. The monocle settled on the Swami's face and stayed there.

"I say, old chap," he asked. "Where are the Police Johnnies that Teeny said were on their way?"

Sajananhpur's smile was half apologetic. "I'm sorry, Lord Jeffry," he dry-washed his hands, "but when Mr. White tried to phone for the police, he found that the phone wires had been cut."

The Englishman focused his eyes on White. "But why should you cut the phones wires?" he puzzled. "It wasn't you who killed Green."

"I didn't cut 'em, you drunken fool," Caleb shrilled. "All I did was try to *use* the phone."

McGinty made a mental note to check the phone as soon as Lord Jeffry had finished. The case, when it broke in the papers, would be big and if he could crack it before the police arrived, the resulting publicity wouldn't harm his newly refounded agency. It might even put him back in the money. And he could use it. He glanced at his three year old suit and grimaced. A man couldn't save much money on a buck sergeant's seventy-odd a month.

"Oh," Lord Jeffry Towers said. "I see."

It was obvious that he didn't.

Angela clawed at the arm of the chair in which she was sitting like a nervous cat. "Stop stalling," she demanded. "Who was it that shot Green?"

Drunk as he was, the Englishman looked embarrassed. "Why, it was you, my dear," he said quietly. "She's the woman," he told the others. "I distinctly saw her cross the drive and shoot him!"

The girl sprang to her feet, screaming. "That's a lie!"

Phil Martin grinned, "That tears it. I guess one of us had better hop in a car and get the cops."

He looked at McGinty. The detective shook his head. The whole set-up smelled phony to him. Angela spoke his mind.

"You're drunk," she accused the Englishman.

"Indisputably," he agreed.

The blood had drained from Angela's face leaving only two red splotches of rouge high on her cheek bones. She was fighting for more than money. She was fighting for her life. "By saying that I killed Green you automatically eliminate me from the will. That means that your wife will inherit one-fifth of seven million dollars. With Green dead, there's only Mary Lee, Phil, your wife, the Swami, and Caleb White left."

"Hallelujah!" Caleb shouted. "Praise the Lord. Blessed are the pure in heart. Blessed—"

Angela cut him short with a vicious, well-aimed kick. "Shut up, you lecherous old fool. You haven't gotten your million yet." She whirled back to Lord Jeffry and pounded on the newel post like a slightly envenomed Portia. "And you're nothing but a drunken liar. There isn't a court in Florida that would believe you."

Lord Towers, looked embarrassed, then said triumphantly, "Then I shan't tell them. T'ell with the money. Have plenty of my own. Didn't want to come heah in the first place. Told Teeny so. Beastly place. Dead men all over the yard."

He started back up the stairs. Phil Martin stopped him. "Now just a minute, Sport. You want to see justice done, don't you?"

"S'ppose so," the Englishman admitted.

"You take this down," young Martin told the Swami. "Then we won't have to *bother* his Lordship again. But he's going to tell us just what he saw."

Mary Lee leaned close to McGinty and whispered, "Hadn't you better tell them who you really are?"

He successfully resisted an impulse to kiss her. "They're doing swell," he grinned.

His fountain pen poised over a pad of paper, the Swami cleared his throat. "Now, if you would tell us in your own words, Lord Jeffry—"

"I was standing in my window," the Englishman began, "thinking what a ghastly place this was to live in, when I saw a motor come up the drive.

"Barrister Green got out of the car," he continued. "Knew him as soon as I saw him. Detested the beastly beggar." He fought with a hiccup and lost. "Excuse me. Then a woman crossed the drive to meet him."

"What woman?" young Martin pounded.

The Englishman looked puzzled for a moment. "Must be losing my memory. Thought I had told you that." He screwed his monocle in his eye, then fixed it on Angela. "It was this young lady heah."

McGinty got up from the love seat and crossed to the stairs. "You are sober enough to realize what you are saying?" he demanded. "You're positive that it was Miss Fay to whom Mr. Green was talking?"

"Pos'tive," the other man assured him.

"Then—?" the Swami suggested.

Lord Jeffry weaved, caught at the post to steady himself, then cocked a thumb and finger to imitate a gun. "Then she shot him, right through the chest. Saw the whole thing distinctly."

"How could you see her?" McGinty demanded pounding softly on the rail. "How could you see her from the house when it was so dark outside that standing five feet away I couldn't see her?

Angela flashed him a swift look of gratitude. "I had you wrong."

"You still have," McGinty said coldly. "All I want is the truth of this matter." He turned back to the Englishman. "Well?"

The Britisher seemed puzzled. "Never thought 'bout it being dark," he admitted. "But I know what I saw." His bleary eyes lighted briefly. "Of course—the moon. Sometimes the clouds obscured it. First it was dark, then light. Remember that distinctly."

Phil Martin sighed with relief. "That's good enough for me." He took the statement from the Swami and handed it with the pen to Lord Towers. "Now if you'll just sign this, your Lordship, I'll jump in a car and drive down the road for the cops."

Towers signed his name with an exaggerated flourish. "Sorry and all of that," he told Angela when he finished. "But one must do one's duty."

Martin put the statement in his pocket and went upstairs for a coat.

McGinty returned to the love seat. There's something wrong with this picture, he thought. That girl is being framed right before my eyes and there's nothing that I can do to prove it. I'm a hell of a detective. I must have left all my brains in Kobe. At the thought of the prison camp, he shuddered.

The red-haired girl took his hand. "Steady, soldier," she whispered.

"How did you know?" he asked her.

Mary Lee smiled wryly. "You were my pin-up boy at college," she said quietly. "I cut your picture out of a Sunday supplement right after Bataan and kept it on the wall of my room until old Martin died, the allowance that he made me stopped, and I had to come back here to live."

"Disappointed?" McGinty grinned.

"You don't look much like your picture," she admitted. "You look like you've been through hell."

"I'm two weeks out of a hospital," he told her. "Give me a chance to fatten up."

Lord Towers was still staring at Angela. "You don't believe me? You don't believe that I saw you?"

"I know that you didn't," she said coldly.

He staggered the last two steps and tucked her hand under his arm. "Come," he insisted. "C'n prove every word that I've said. I'll show you just where you stood. Show you where Green was standing. Show you the window where I stood."

The girl ran the tip of a coral tongue across her lips. A cat could be skinned in many ways. "I—er—wish you would," she told him.

They walked hand in arm to the door.

Sajahanhpur who had gone to the fireplace to spread his

hands, looked up and demanded sharply. "And just *where* are you two going?"

The black-haired girl smiled at him thinly. "Out to the scene of the murder."

Caleb White got up from his chair. "I'll come along," he offered.

Angela steered Lord Jeffry through the door. "You stay where you are," she told White. "You weren't invited."

The door banged solidly behind them.

Caleb White licked at his withered lips. "An evil woman," he said dryly, "is an abomination before the Lord."

The Swami looked at the door and shrugged. "What difference does it make? Let her try to change his testimony. Lady Towers will take care of that. Besides, young Martin has his signed statement."

Somewhere in the house a grandfather clock struck nine. The wind that had died down briefly had begun to howl again. A blow, a big one was in the making.

McGinty considered the couple that had just gone outside, then turned back to the girl beside him.

"Look. Give me the picture," he told her. "Give me these people's backgrounds so I'll have something to work on."

It was fifteen minutes after nine when Phil Martin came down stairs. Caleb White was not in the room. Angela and Lord Towers had not returned. The Swami was reading, or pretending to read, by the fireplace. McGinty and Mary Lee still sat on the love seat with the redhaired girl doing most of the talking.

McGinty summed up what she had told him. It hadn't changed the picture. He tabulated it in his mind.

Angela Fay had been engaged by Martin to type his memoirs when he had begun to write his unpublished book.

Lord and Lady Towers had been in Africa when the old man had died. He was reputed to have loads of money. They had arrived only ten days before, Lady Towers coming on ahead, and Lord Towers following her from Miami by a day. He had been drunk on his arrival and had stayed drunk ever since, spending most of his time in their room at the head of the stairs.

Her own father, Lee Gaspiralla, had been victimized by Martin in a large real estate development and had taken his own life. Martin had made her a small allowance ever since. "Conscience money," she told him.

Phil Martin was a petty hoodlum from Chicago who had admired the old man greatly but who had as greatly amused Martin by mincing along in his own seven-league criminal footsteps.

The Swami was from Miami. Mary Lee knew very little about him except that old Silas Martin had been interested in the occult for some years before he had died.

Caleb White was his first cousin from some little town in Vermont. He was a self-admitted religious fanatic and had spent the whole year at the lodge ogling herself and Angela.

"And there it is," she concluded. "Old Martin hated us all, including Green. I think that he deliberately drew up his will the way he did hoping that we'd all kill each other off to build up the money we'd get."

Young Martin chuckled. "I'm satisfied with my share. Where did the others go?"

"White said he was going to bed," McGinty told him. "Miss Fay and Lord Towers went out to the scene of the murder."

Martin strode to the outside door and wrenched it open. "What the hell did you let them go for? She'll do anything to change his testimony."

Swami Sajahanhpur shrugged, "We have his signed statement. Besides, Lady Towers—"

A door in the upper hallway opened.

"Jeffry!" Lady Towers called. "I'm finished packing. And if you've finished with the police, please have one of the younger men come up and help me with these bags."

Mary Lee got to her feet. "Excuse me," she smiled wryly. "A hair pulling on top of this other, would be just too much for one night." She walked back down the hall to the kitchen.

Lady Towers' blonde head, a chic traveling turban perched

slightly awry atop it, peered over the Chinese cabinet. "Isn't Lord Towers down there?" she demanded.

McGinty shook his head. "No," he admitted, "he isn't. He went out to the scene of the murder with Miss Fay."

"He went out to the scene of the murder with Miss Fay?" Lady Towers demanded. Her high French heels beating a worried tattoo, she hurried down the stairway and into the room. "But why should he go anywhere with that murderess? Jeffry told me that he saw her shoot Green. He said—"

A scream from the kitchen cut her short. Before McGinty could get to his feet, Mary Lee stood white-faced in the doorway.

"There—there's another dead man in the kitchen!" she gasped.

Lady Towers screamed, "Lord Jeffry!"

The redhaired girl shook her head. "No. It isn't Lord Jeffry." She weaved on the verge of a faint and McGinty caught her.

"Who is it?" he demanded.

"I couldn't see him plainly," she said wanly. "But I think that it's Caleb White!"

CHAPTER FOUR

"You Killed Him!"

THE WIND HAD RISEN to a scream. It tore at the sagging shutters on the windows and banged them up against the house. A dried frond wrenched from a palm thudded against the kitchen door.

McGinty knelt beside the body. It was White. The old man lay half under the kitchen table in a pool of his own blood. His throat had been cut with a knife. The knife lay where the killer had thrown it, at the foot of the service stairs that led to the second floor.

Phil Martin lighted a cigarette with trembling fingers. His voice was strained with fear. "So someone has upped the kitty with old Caleb's share. It looks like old Silly knew what he was doing when he drew up that damn fool will."

Sajahanhpur turned from the body, gagging. "Don't look at me. I was in the other room all the time. I can prove that by Mr. McGinty."

Lady Towers stared at the body dry-eyed. "It was Angela who killed him. Caleb was outside. He too must have seen her shoot Green. He attempted to blackmail her—and she killed him."

McGinty, still kneeling, asked dryly, "And Lord Towers?"

The former actress caught at her heart. "How long have they been gone?"

McGinty told her that it had been at least twenty minutes and she began to sob hysterically. "She's killed him. She's killed Jeffry, too. I know it!"

McGinty got to his feet and shook her. "Stop it! Hysteria won't get us anywhere." The time for evasion was over. He laid his shield on the table. "And just so there won't be any further doubt as to my right to ask questions, I'm not Angela's fiancé. I'm not an ex-convict. I *was* sent here by Green to guard her. I'm a private detective from Miami with an agency of my own."

"If you'd read the papers," Mary Lee said scornfully, "you'd have recognized him. He's *the* McGinty, the one who held out for days all alone on Bataan until the Japanese captured him. He—"

"That's past," McGinty cut her short. His voice held its old time ring. "Don't anyone touch a thing." He pointed at Martin. "You jump in a car and head for the nearest phone. Get the State Police if you can." He dropped his shield back in his pocket and strode down the hall. "You come with me, Swami. It's going to blow hard, and soon. And if Miss Fay and Lord Towers—"

The front door banged open in a gust of wind and as suddenly banged shut. Breathless, her black curls blown across her eyes, and her skirt spotted with flying fume and powdered shell, Angela leaned against it panting breathlessly.

"Of all the damn dirty tricks," she began. "I almost didn't

make the house."

Lady Towers strode past McGinty, picking nervously at one lapel of her smartly cut traveling suit as if to keep the hand from reaching out and clawing at the girl. "Where is my husband?" she demanded.

Angela stared at her, puzzled. "Where is he? He came back here to the house."

Phil Martin shook his head. "Stop stalling, Angela. What have you done with Lord Towers?"

The girl shook her curls from her eyes. "I haven't done anything with him. I haven't even seen him since he left me in the summer house."

"In the summer house?" Sajahanhpur asked softly. "But we were given to understand that you were just going out in front to the scene of Mr. Green's murder."

"What have you done with my husband, Angela?" Lady Towers repeated.

Angela answered her hotly. "I haven't done a thing. But that wasn't his fault. It was *his* suggestion that we go to the summer house to talk over what he had seen. Then he parked me there and left me, telling me he'd be back as soon as he got a drink."

McGinty asked quietly, "You expect us to believe that?"

"It's the truth."

Lady Towers lifted her hand and slapped her. "It's a lie. *You killed my husband, Angela, just as you killed Caleb White, because both of them saw you shoot Green!"*

The wind that had risen to a scream dropped suddenly away. Only the breathless, sticky heat and the swift scudding clouds that raced across a dusty looking moon foretold what was to be. The tall, shallow-rooted palms that lined the drive from the gate to the house again lifted their ragged fronds into a velvet sky. There were no stars.

McGinty had been through blows before. He knew what they could do. "She'll hit in a minute," he told Martin. "You won't dare to go for the cops now. If it caught you on the road it would blow you into the Gulf."

He led the way down the path toward the beach and the summer house on the pier.

Swami Sajahanhpur panted beside him. "You *do* think that Angela killed them?"

McGinty shook his head. "I don't know," he admitted frankly. "Let's find Lord Towers or his body first."

"Towers! Lord Jeffry!" Martin shouted.

The only answer was the scrunch of their feet in the sand and the drum of the surf on the beach.

"We'll have to move Green when we go back," McGinty said. "We'll put him in the kitchen with White."

Sajahanhpur pointed out, "Angela could have killed Jeffry, come back to the house, cut Caleb's throat, then come in panting through the front way as she did in an attempt to establish an alibi."

McGinty wished that his head would stop aching. The picture still wasn't right. He had a feeling that he had missed something. Angela might have killed Towers. The girl was desperate. Still, it hardly seemed likely that she would have doubled back to the house and have killed Caleb White in the kitchen. She wouldn't have known where he would be for one thing. He had said he was going to bed. Either of the men beside him might have killed White.

Or he might have been killed, he thought grimly, by either Lady Towers or Mary Lee. The body was still warm when we found it. His death increased both of their shares in the will by a quarter of a million dollars.

Lady Towers had been upstairs. She could have slipped down the back way. Mary Lee had excused herself for a moment. It was possible, but not probable, he decided. Lady Towers had been busy packing. She had thought the police had arrived. Outside of the money angle, Mary Lee had no reason to kill him. He *knew* that she hadn't shot Green.

There was no one on the T-shaped concrete pier with the thatched roofed summer house at one end. McGinty started to pass it by, spotted a small dark object in the moonlight, picked it up and stopped.

"He's been here," he told the Swami and Martin. "He

dropped his hat."

He ran his fingers along the sweat band. They came away sticky with blood.

Martin spotlighted the hat with his flashlight. "And it looks like he didn't leave."

The Swami shook his head. "Poor Lady Towers. He treated her like a dog. But from the way that she acts, she loved him."

The pier was sticky with salt spray. Blown spume festooned the concrete benches. The water was dark and angry.

McGinty walked out to the end and studied the small protected harbor. "Someone said something about sharks," he said quietly.

"I did," Martin admitted. "There have been some big babies in here for days. I was watching them tonight when Green was shot."

The small veins in McGinty's temples began to throb. He said at the time, he thought, right after I knocked him down, that he and Caleb White were together. Now White is dead. It could have been Martin who killed him to protect his alibi.

Martin tore a rotted cork crash fender from the piling on which it hung and threw it into the water. There was an angry swirl beneath the pier. A long black shape broke water. Rows of white teeth flashed briefly in the moonlight.

"That's the smallest of the two," Martin grinned. "The other one's twice that size."

The Swami sat down on a bench. "There goes the *corpus delicti.* Angela lured him down here and pushed him into the water." His face, in the moonlight, was a sickly lemon. "She knows that the sharks are here. Because she told me last night that if Caleb White didn't stop praying for her to die that she was going to feed him to them."

McGinty considered briefly. The sharks could have been lured into the harbor by feeding them bloody meat. Even after one feeding, they would have remained in the neighborhood for days.

"Let's search the pier," he suggested.

Young Martin jeered, "For what? What do you expect to find?"

"I don't know," McGinty admitted. As he spoke, his sharp eyes caught the glitter of glass in the angle of the concrete rise in which the low hand-rail was imbedded. He picked it up and held it on his palm. It was the broken half of a monocle.

"That tears it," Martin swore. "It fell out of his eye when she pushed him."

They searched the rest of the pier minutely. It was the only thing they found.

It's enough, McGinty thought grimly, to send her to the chair and my thousand bucks along with her. Still, the proof was too pat, too perfect. And there was White's death to account for.

A drop of rain splashed into his face. A blast of wind screamed in from the Gulf whipping the black water to froth.

"This is it!" he shouted. "Head for the house—and fast!"

The beach was ankle deep in water when they reached it. The wind was a screaming fiend that tore at them with greedy fingers. The air was filled with powdered shell and grains of sand that stung like bird shot. There was a steady roaring in the air that drowned out the pelt of the rain.

Martin and Sajahanhpur raced by Green to the front door of the house. McGinty called them back and made them help carry Green into the kitchen.

Rain streamed from their clothes and faces. The world outside the door had become a roaring void of sound. They had to shout to make each other hear. All three men had been battered by the flying debris that filled the air and thudded against the walls of the house and the shutters.

McGinty fought the door shut and dropped the bar. The house was suddenly cold and black. A whimpering wind, frantically fleeing the very havoc that it wrought shrieked through the air vents, screaming murder in a hundred unknown tongues. McGinty shuddered. It was like an animated tomb, the quick buried with the dead.

Martin tried the light switch and cursed.

McGinty shouted in his ear. "The power lines are probably down. They are usually the first to go."

Mary Lee's disembodied face bobbed down the hallway toward the kitchen, illuminated by the yellow glow of a candle encased in an etched hurricane lamp. "All of the lights went out at the first blow," she shouted. She clung to McGinty's arm. "Tell me. Did you find him?"

Her long, bony face a tragic mask framed by her too-yellow hair, Lady Towers floated close behind her, and behind her came Angela Fay. All three women were faces, nothing more.

"Did you find him?" Lady Towers shouted. "Did you find my husband, Jeffry?"

McGinty looked from her to the girl behind her, then felt for the blood stained hat and the broken half of an eye glass in his pocket that might well send a woman to the chair and decide the ultimate disposition of seven million dollars. He thought that he had the answer. Now all that he had to do was prove it.

He cupped his hands and shouted, "Yes. I guess you could say we found him."

CHAPTER FIVE

Return Of The Dead

THE HELL OF THIS CASE, McGinty thought, is that it is like the wind. It veers. No sooner do I make up my mind who is guilty than there's a blow from another quarter.

He stood watching the girl by the fireplace, shouting to make herself heard against the drone of the hurricane.

"Listen, all of you," Angela was shouting.

The others eyed her expectantly.

"I'll make a deal," she shouted. "I didn't kill Green. I didn't kill White. But I'm afraid." The black haired girl's eyes rolled wildly. "There's a killer in the house. I want to make a deal."

The Swami's lips formed the words distinctly. "What sort

of a deal?"

Angela strained her voice against the storm. "Let's split the money five ways. There is enough for us all."

Lady Towers told her, "I'll make no deal with you." She took one of the hurricane lamps from the table, fighting against tears and failing. "We shouldn't ever have come here. If only I had listened to Jeffry."

McGinty watched her ascend the stairs in a small circle of candle glow that shrunk to a pin point of light then disappeared entirely with the closing of her door.

Mary Lee put her lips to his ear. "I feel so sorry for her."

He nodded, his eyes flicking back to Angela. The girl's terror was not assumed. She was afraid.

There was a loud burst of static from the radio. Martin switched off the power of the old battery set. "The hell with it. All I can get is static and Cuba." He looked at his watch. It was five minutes of four. "I think that we'd all better go to bed." He nodded his head at the fury of wind that was battering at the shutters. "How long does one of these things last?"

"Sometimes for days," Mary Lee told him. "But they often times come in two sections. And there's usually a lull between blows."

McGinty borrowed his flashlight. The younger man sneered, "What's the big idea? Aren't you going to bed?"

"I doubt it," McGinty shouted.

If Angela's fear was genuine, if the girl hadn't killed Green and Towers, the killer would strike again.

It's too good an opportunity to miss, he thought. You can only burn once for murder, and each additional heir that he kills will up his share by over a quarter of a million dollars.

Martin and Sajahanhpur climbed the stairs sharing one hurricane lamp between them. McGinty lighted Mary Lee's way to her door.

"Keep it locked," he warned her in parting.

She clung to him a moment, breathless, and was gone.

He flashed his light over the closed doors, then walked the long upper hallway to the stairs that led down to the kitchen.

Green and White lay where he had left them. He searched

the pockets of both men minutely. Their contents told him nothing that he had not learned before.

He sat squatted on his heels studying the faces of the dead men. Both of them were placid and relaxed. They had been that way when he had found them. Neither man had strained in terror or tried to flee from death. Both of them had known and trusted the person who had killed them.

He sensed footsteps in the hall, saw a faint glow of candle-light and looked up to see Angela Fay staring at him from the kitchen doorway.

"Do you think that I killed them?" she asked him.

McGinty told her frankly, "I don't know. The evidence is all against you, but—"

"But there's too much of it," she shouted. "There's a killer in this house."

Above the wind, the words came as a faint whisper.

McGinty considered the girl. Innocent or guilty, it was needless to lock her up. There was no way she could leave the house. No one could live five minutes in the storm that was hurling itself at the Keys.

"You'd better go to bed," he told her.

She whimpered like a frightened child. "I'm afraid."

He watched the candle bob back down the hall and saw it ascend the stairs. Either the girl was innocent, or she was a clever actress.

He threw a log on the fire and sat where he could watch the stairs. There were only five of them left. One of them was a killer. He checked them on his fingers. There was the Swami, Phil Martin, Angela, Mary Lee, and Lady Towers.

The Swami and Phil Martin were definitely suspect. Both had been outside when Green was shot. Both stood to gain a million dollars by pinning the blame on Angela.

On the other hand, there was Lord Tower's testimony. He had been insistent about what he had seen. A half hour later he had disappeared.

McGinty thought of the swift swirl in the water and the rows of white teeth that had flashed in the moonlight and shuddered.

Coupled with the known facts, any jury would undoubtedly accept the bloodstained hat and the broken half of a monocle as circumstantial proof that Angela Fay had killed him.

On the other hand, the solution was still too pat. There was too much evidence against her.

He thought of the thousand dollars that Green had promised him. Why had Green, who had been one of the heirs who would not inherit a penny unless Angela Fay died or was charged with theft, assault, or murder, been so eager to protect her life? McGinty suspected a secret agreement.

He struck a match to light a cigarette, then blew it out and moved swiftly to one side, the hackles on the back of his neck rising. The jungle had sharpened his senses. He could both feel and sense eyes staring at him through the dark. He dropped one hand to his gun and stabbed at the dark with the flashlight.

There was no one on the stairs. There was nothing, no one in the room or in the hall. There *was* something that reflected light on the floor of the hallway in front of the front door. McGinty crossed the room and played his light on it. It was a pool of water. Someone had come in out of the storm and had stood there, dripping.

His nerves beginning to pound, he examined the door. It was bolted from the inside. The great storm bar was in place. There was no wet spot on the ceiling. The sill of the door was dry. There was no place that the water could have come from.

He flashed his light down the hall. Perfectly outlined on the floor there was a file of wet men's footprints that led back to the kitchen.

He forced himself to follow them. There was a second pool of water by Green's body as if someone had paused beside him. There was a third, smaller pool by White. From there, growing fainter as they climbed, the footprints ascended the stairs. A speck of color caught McGinty's eyes. He stooped and picked it up. It was a piece of slimy sea weed.

Cold sweat beading his forehead, McGinty climbed the stairs one at a time, stabbing the darkness before him with the light to make certain that no one was waiting. By the time he had reached the upper hallway, the footprints had disappeared.

He paused, uncertainly, playing his light on the closed doors. Here, close to the roof, the sound of the storm was intensified. He took a step forward and stopped.

Someone had climbed the stairs behind him. He could feel his cold breath on his neck.

He spun on one heel, shooting. In the spurts of orange flame, he could see lead smack into sodden tweed. Then a gun barrel slashed savagely at his wrist. His flashlight fell to the floor, winked out. Then a second blow of the gun barrel caught him flush on the temple and sent him reeling against the wall.

The figure, a hulking blob of deeper black, followed, still beating at him.

McGinty fought back grimly. He could feel but he could not see or hear. It was like fighting in a nightmare. His hands gripped a dripping coat sleeve and came away wet with slime. A blow knocked him to his knees. He wrapped his arms around wet trouser legs and a knee rose in the darkness, thudding into his jaw.

We told you, his nerves screamed. You've been away too long. They never come back, you fool. You're not a hot shot private agency man anymore. You're nothing but a shell and torture-shocked ex-soldier who belongs in a veteran's home making brooms or weaving baskets.

Half out on his knees, McGinty fought for consciousness. He thought he saw a match flame leap into light. He knew that he smelled the pungent fragrance of tobacco as the faceless apparition applied it to a pipe bowl.

The thing's movements were unnatural. The arms rose jerkily. It seemed to have no face. A strand of still dripping sea weed had caught behind one ear and trailed down over its shoulder like some monstrous green curl.

Then the match flickered out. McGinty tried to get to his feet. The gun barrel slashed through the dark. Already numb with pain, all that he felt was shock. He reached out, caught at nothing, and fell forward on his face.

The roar of the wind had subsided. The darkness was less intense. McGinty rolled from his face onto his back and lay staring into the gray. The thing with which he had fought was gone.

He fumbled his hand across the floor and found his flashlight. He rapped it sharply against the baseboard and a weak yellow beam formed a vague spot on the ceiling. He got to his feet and fought nausea.

His gun lay where it had been beaten from his hand. He picked it up and swung out the cylinder. All six shots had been fired. He examined the floor for blood spots. There were none. He had held the gun to the *thing's* body when he triggered but there was no blood on the floor.

If I faced a judge and jury with a yarn like that he thought, they'd send me to a padded cell in Chattahoochee. I wouldn't believe it myself.

He flashed the light on his wrist watch. It had been about four-thirty when he had followed the footprints up the stairs. It was now ten minutes after six. He had been out almost two hours.

He retraced his steps to the kitchen. The wet footprints on the stairs had dried. There was no sign of water by either body. He walked down the hall to the door. The pool there, too, had dried.

There was a mirror over the fireplace. McGinty studied his face in the yellow glow of the flashlight. A great purple welt ran from his forehead to his cheek. The beating at least had been real.

He left the mirror and went to the door. The last of the wind was dying. It could mean that the blow was over. It could be a lull. He unbarred the door and swung it open.

The dawn was gray with a heavy overcast of yellow. The Gulf lashed at the beach and broke over the concrete pier in a fury of dirty spume. The lawn and the drive were littered with debris. Half of the palm trees had blown down.

You're stalling, his nerves accused him. Another heir is

dead. That scene last night was staged to get you out of the way and to destroy the value of your testimony.

McGinty closed and barred the door.

His mind was beginning to function. The pools of water, the wet footprints on the stairs had been made deliberately to confuse him and to decoy him up into the hallway where he had been slugged. By starting at the top and walking backwards they, whoever it had been, had left a trail that seemingly began at the front door. Then they had slipped down the front stairs and up the back stairs behind him.

He climbed the front stairs and rapped on Lady Tower's door.

Her voice sounded faint and far away. "Yes—?"

"It's McGinty," he said. "Open up."

A bolt shot on the far side of the door. Lady Towers peered out at him cautiously. Her bleached yellow hair was done up in rag curlers. She clutched a shabby dressing gown together with one hand. "Someone else has been murdered!" she said. It was a statement, not a question.

"That's right," McGinty nodded.

"Who?"

"I don't know yet," he told her. "Get some clothes on. I want everyone in the living room."

"I hope that it's Angela," she admitted, and slammed the door.

McGinty walked on to the next door and rapped.

"Who is it? What do you want?" Mary Lee demanded.

He told her that it was McGinty and asked her to dress and come to the living room.

The door across the hall opened as he was speaking and Angela looked out. "What is it? What's happened?" she asked him.

McGinty studied the girl's face in the faint light that was seeping in through the shuttered window at the far end of the hall. Her eyes were red and swollen. She looked like she had been crying. He accused, "You haven't slept at all."

"Could you sleep?" she asked frankly, "if you stood to lose

seven million dollars and faced a double murder rap that had been pinned on you by a lot of greedy liars?"

He shrugged and rapped on Phil Martin's door.

Angela called after him, "Green sent me one hell of a detective. Who are *you* splitting with, that baby-faced red haired wench across the hall?"

She slammed the door.

"Open up," McGinty ordered.

Bed springs creaked in the room as Martin sat up. "The door isn't locked," he called. "Come in."

McGinty walked into the room. Martin sat on the edge of his bed staring at him owlishly. A half-emptied fifth of rye stood at his elbow. "What's happened?" he demanded.

"Murder," McGinty said succinctly.

Martin came awake with a start. "Murder! Who's been killed now?" he demanded.

McGinty told him, "Sajahanhpur."

Lady Towers appeared in the doorway. Her face was still shiny with cold cream but she had exchanged the wrapper for an equally inexpensive dressing gown. "How do you know?" she demanded. "You told me—"

McGinty crossed the hall and rapped on Sajahanhpur's door. There was no answer. He rapped again, louder, this time.

"He has to be dead," he said grimly. He looked from Martin to Lady Towers to Angela who had opened her door again. "Whoever it was who batted me around last night wasn't doing it for fun."

He tried the door. It was unlocked. The Swami lay half in and half out of his bed in a pool of clotted blood. The wooden handle of a kitchen knife protruded from his chest.

McGinty caught a gleam of color in his hand and stooped to examine it.

"Oh, no," young Martin stopped him as he attempted to open the stiffening fingers. "You leave that right where it is until the cops get here."

Lady Towers hurried into the room. "Leave what, where?" she demanded.

Martin pointed to the dead man's hand. Entwined in Saja-hanhpur's fingers was a strand of long red hair.

CHAPTER SIX

Exit Laughing

NOW THAT THE WIND had ceased, the heat in the hall was sti-fling. The drum of the surf was plain. McGinty could hear his own heart thumping. He hated doing what he knew that he had to do.

Mary Lee stared at the Swami, her green eyes round with horror. "I didn't kill him. I didn't." Tears starting in her eyes, she appealed to McGinty, "You believe me, don't you?"

"Why should he?" Angela demanded coldly. "Why should any of us believe you? I get it now. It was you whom Lord Towers saw on the drive. *It was you whom he saw shoot Green.*" She raised her hand and slapped the other girl. "Admit it."

McGinty caught at her hand, too late. "Stop it," he warned her sharply. "Mary Lee didn't shoot Green. I was with her when the shots were fired."

"So you say," Angela sneered.

"Yeah," McGinty said coldly. "So I say."

The dryness had gone from his throat. His heart had stopped thumping. His moment of weakness had passed.

Martin warned Angela, "You'd just love to pin the blame on someone else, but if I were you, I wouldn't try. You shot Green and fed Lord Towers to the sharks because he saw you. All Mary Lee did was knife the Swami."

"I don't believe it," Lady Towers said crisply. "Why should she kill Sajahanhpur?"

"You know that as well as I do," Martin told her. "Both Caleb and the Swami were always making passes at her." His lips twisted in a wry smile. "And well, it looks as if Saja-hanhpur made one pass too many."

The red haired girl shook her head. "I didn't kill him."

"No?" Martin scoffed. He pointed to the strand of hair in the dead East Indian's hand. "I suppose whoever knifed him put that there just to—" he paused, uncertain.

"That's right," McGinty told him. "Go on. To cut her out of Martin's will according to Clause Five."

Angela said, "I don't believe it."

"I can prove it," McGinty said coldly.

"I hope so," Lady Towers said. She took Mary Lee in her arms and tried to soothe her. "Don't cry so, honey. I don't care what's in his hand. I don't believe that you killed him."

Angela stared at him coldly. "What do you mean, you can prove it?"

"Just that," McGinty said quietly. He thought of the thousand dollars that Green had agreed to pay him. That was over a year's Army pay. "How about it?" he bargained. "If I can prove that you didn't shoot Green and didn't kill Lord Towers, is it worth a thousand to you?"

"Cash on the barrel-head," she assured him.

McGinty lighted a cigarette. "Of course," he admitted, "I can be wrong. But I don't think I am. Most murders follow a pattern. This case has been no exception. They—"

Martin broke in coldly, "Stop stalling and start talking!"

"Why not?" McGinty agreed. He began with a description of the *thing* that he had trailed by its footprints and fought with in the hall.

"And you expect," Martin scoffed, "any sane jury of twelve men to believe a wild yarn like that?"

"No," McGinty admitted frankly, "I do not. That was a part of its purpose, to destroy the credibility and the sanity of anything to which I might testify. After all, I'm a shell-shocked veteran. I'm two weeks out of a hospital after a year in a Jap hell hole. And if I turned up with a yarn like that, it would prove that I am nuts."

Lady Towers shook her head. "I'm afraid that I don't understand."

McGinty sucked hard at his cigarette. Let's put it this way," he suggested. "According to the terms of old Martin's will, who still stands to inherit? You," he pointed to Angela, "have been accused of two murders, possibly three. That lets you out." He hurried on over her protests. "Green and Caleb White and Swami Sajahanhpur are dead." He touched the strand of hair in the dead man's fingers. "This undoubtedly belongs to Mary Lee." He studied the girl admiringly. "You say that he's been making passes at her. Any jury would believe that. And it wouldn't be *too* difficult for a jury to believe that the Swami forced his way into her room last night, she fought with him, stabbed him, and he crawled back in here to die. What's more," he concluded coldly, "I'll bet you ten to one that her fingerprints are on the handle of that knife."

"But he didn't, I didn't," Mary Lee protested. "That is—"

McGinty ignored the interruption. "A conviction of murder or manslaughter automatically cuts her out of the will." He paused, added quietly, "leaving only two of the original heirs, Lady Towers and Phil Martin."

The former actress sniffed. "I'm not proud of the company I'm in."

"Now wait just a minute," Martin began. He licked his dry lips nervously. "You don't think—"

"I don't *think*. I *know*," McGinty cut him short. He leveled an accusing finger. "You have a criminal record?"

"So what?" the younger man snarled. "What the hell are you driving at?"

"Murder," McGinty told him. "How's chances on searching your room?"

"Okay. Why not?" Martin shrugged. He dropped his hand in the pocket of his robe. "Just what do you expect to find, another corpse?"

"You never can tell," McGinty told him dryly.

Mary Lee warned, "He has a gun."

"That's just fine," McGinty told her. "So have I."

He led the way across the hall. The room was high-ceilinged and huge. The furniture was old and massive. Beside the bed and highboy there was a massive carved sea chest. McGinty studied it briefly, then touched it with his palm. The edge of the wood was damp. "I imagine," he told Martin, "that what I'm looking for is in there."

He raised the lid of the chest. It was filled with yellowed linens and gave off a smell of camphor and moth balls.

Lady Towers stared at it, puzzled. "Just what is it that you are trying to find?"

"A suit of your husband's clothes," McGinty said shortly. "There is a tweed suit missing?"

Lady Towers dabbed at her eyes with a wisp of lace. "I don't know," she admitted. "I can look."

"If you will, please," McGinty asked her.

She left the room still dabbing at her eyes.

Martin took McGinty by one shoulder and swung him around to face him. The younger man's face was ugly. "Now just one minute, soldier. What the hell are you trying to pin on me? Why should I have a suit of Lord Tower's clothes?"

McGinty grinned. "You're a hell of a hood if you can't figure that out."

"I get it," Angela gasped. *"It's been Phil right along.* It was Phil who shot Green because Green knew that he had a criminal record. And then, it was Phil who killed Caleb in the kitchen to make good the alibi that he had given!"

Young Martin jeered, "You're crazy! Next you'll be saying that it was me who fed Lord Jeffry to the sharks."

Lady Towers hurried into the room. "There *is* a suit missing. One of Jeffry's favorite gray tweeds."

McGinty removed the linens. The top few layers were dry. Under the bottom layer he found the water-sodden tweed suit for which he had been searching.

Lady Towers cried, "That's Jeffry's!" She pointed a dramatic finger at Martin. "It was you who slugged Mr. McGinty to get him out of the way so you could kill the Swami. Then you tried to lay the blame on Mary Lee to build up your share of the will."

His thin face rat-like in the half light, Martin whipped a gun from his dressing robe pocket and backed to the wall. "It's a frame, a dirty frame," he whimpered. "I never even saw the suit before. I don't know how it got into the chest."

McGinty demanded, "And with your record as a hood, you expect a jury to believe that?"

"No," Martin admitted, "I don't."

Quit stalling, McGinty's nerves urged him.

"But I do," McGinty said shortly. "Sure you were framed. Our killer was too damn clever. And now she's outsmarted herself." In the sudden silence that followed, he added. "Slip off your robe and jacket and let me see your chest."

Martin stripped to the waist. The flesh on his chest was unblemished. "So what does this prove?" he demanded.

McGinty looked at Lady Towers. "Do you want to tell him," he asked her, "or shall I?"

She said, distinctly, "I don't know what you are talking about."

"I think you do," he told her. "If young Martin had been convicted of assault who would that have left in the clear? Who would have inherited *all* the money?"

Lady Towers fluffed her curl papers and wiped some cold cream from her nose. "But that's ridiculous!" she sniffed.

"Is it?" McGinty asked her.

"I get it," Angela gasped. "It was Lady Towers who shot Green. Then she and Lord Towers pinned it on me deliberately. They planned it that way from the start."

Mary Lee puzzled. "But Lord Towers—"

McGinty told her. "There never was a Lord Towers, at least not at Seventh Key Lodge."

"That's ridiculous," Lady Towers repeated. Her long bony face had turned pale. Twin spots of rouge stood out on her high cheek bones underneath the film of cold cream like the make-up of a clown.

"What was her former profession?" McGinty asked the others. "She was an actress, an impersonator. And one of the best impersonations that she did was that of an English Lord. I saw her act a half a dozen times."

"Damn you!" Lady Towers fumbled in the sleeve of her robe and her hand reappeared with a deadly looking little automatic.

"You mean," Martin demanded, incredulous, "that she planned all of this from the start. You mean that she shot Green, and killed Caleb and the Swami?"

McGinty nodded. "And the payoff came last night when she put on a suit of Lord Towers' clothes, played ghost, and slugged me."

Mary Lee still didn't get it. "But Lord Towers—"

"Did you ever see them together?" McGinty demanded. "In the ten days that they were here, did any of you ever see Lady and Lord Towers at the same time?"

"By God," Martin swore. "I get it now. There never was a Lord Towers. We saw either one of them or the other. It was Lady Towers who walked down to the beach with Angela, planted that hat and monocle—then snuck in through the back door of the house and disappeared!"

"Leaving Angela neatly framed for the murder of a man who never existed," McGinty added coldly. "But Caleb White was in the kitchen. He saw her so she had to kill him. And as long as she had gone that far, a few more murders didn't matter."

"You'll never prove it," Lady Towers panted.

McGinty reached out a hand before she could back away and caught at the too yellow hair. The wig came away in his hand. Her own hair was close cropped and gray.

"What's more," McGinty continued, "the *thing* that slugged me last night was wearing a bullet-proof vest. And a vest stops lead but not the impact. Suppose you go in the other room with Mary Lee and Angela and disrobe. And if your chest isn't covered with purple bruises, then I'll apologise."

Lady Towers had recovered her composure. "And if it is—"

"You're going to the chair," he told her.

"No," she said quietly. She smiled wryly. "Oh, you have me all right. I'm guilty. But I thought I'd been fairly clever. At first I only meant for Green to die and for 'Lord Towers' to disappear. But the storm gave me other ideas. I'd been poor for *so* long. The real Lord Towers *was* a drunken beast." Her knuckle whitened on the trigger of the little gun. "But that doesn't matter to you. I gambled—and I lost. And so—"

McGinty sprang toward the door and tried to knock up her arm—too late. By the time that he had reached her, the little gun had barked three times.

Lady Towers swayed in the doorway, her lips still in the same set smile. "And so—exit laughing. I—" She clutched at the jamb of the door and slid down it slowly to the floor.

Angela Fay said smugly, "You get your thousand, McGinty!"

He said, "To hell with the money," and strode down the hall and the stairs and wrenched open the big front door. The dawn was still overcast with yellow. The air was hot and sticky. He fought a desire to be sick.

Murder was so senseless, and so futile.

He wondered if the storm was over, or if this was just a lull. He strode back into the living room and switched on the battery set. There was a burst and crackle of static, then Miami came in clearly. . .

Flash. And I mean Flash!. . .

The rest of the newscast was a jumble interspersed with static:

"Federal men in Miami last night. . . strange culmination of. . . strangest will ever filed for probate in history of. . . working secretly. . . income tax evasion. . . after such penalties as will be imposed there will be little more than several thousand dollars left. . . Horace Green, Martin's attorney left immediately for Seventh Key Lodge to inform the hopeful heirs that. . . "

Static drowned out the announcer completely and McGinty tuned off the set. *Green had been on his way to Seventh Key to tell them there were no millions, that the Government had stepped in.*

Martin planned it this way, you jerk, his nerves jeered, and deep in hell, he's howling.

McGinty crossed back to the door and stared out. It was beginning to rain again. He closed the door and returned to the living room to find that Mary Lee had come down stairs.

"I thought I heard a newscast," she began.

"It was nothing important," he lied. He was right back where he had started. Angela wouldn't pay him now. He wouldn't have a dime. "No, nothing important," he repeated.

The red-haired girl came closer to him. "You've been grand, McGinty," she told him. "And I only wish that I—"

"Forget it," he said gruffly.

They stood a moment in embarrassed silence, her lips only inches from his.

Go on and kiss her, you big palooka! his nerves urged him. She doesn't care how much money you have. She isn't that kind of a girl. She's broke, too. What the hell, you can start together.

"Look, Mary Lee," he began. "I—"

Then somehow she was in his arms and he was kissing her. She seemed to want him to. He didn't need to be a detective to know that.

I'LL BE SEEING YOU

O'HARA'S OFFICIAL POSITION in the City Hall was undefined, and, of late, untenable. Although he had ruled Rossville for years, he held no elective office. He had no desire for one. An elective office would cramp his style. He preferred to take the cash and allow his elected stooges to take the credit, and the blame.

It had been a pleasant and remunerative arrangement. But that had been in the good old days before J.M. Before John Martin.

Although handsome, well educated, and of good family, O'Hara was a former racketeer and labor slugger before he had turned his talents to politics, and had muscled his way into power. He was known as a man without fear. He was also known as a killer, although he had never been brought to trial. There was small danger of such a thing ever coming to pass. He nominated the local ticket. He said who would be Mayor. He appointed the Chief of Police. A nod from him could make or break a detective. The only fly in his sticky ointment was the District Attorney's office. We The People had crossed him there and in a frenzied last minute 'write in' campaign had elected recently returned John Martin instead of O'Hara's hand picked candidate. There had been so many 'John Martins' written in that not even O'Hara's well oiled election machine had been able to throw out enough ballots to keep him from being elected. It had been John Martin ten to one.

Now, sitting well back on the platform of the Good Government Rally that District Attorney Martin had called in the public interest, O'Hara studied the young man thoughtfully.

A former platoon sergeant of Marines, Martin was a fighter. It showed in his jutting jaw, in every gesture that he made. He meant every word that he said.

"A certain amount of vice, corruption, gambling, theft, malfeasance of office, and general official stupidity, is normal in every city," Martin said. He spoke without raising his voice. He gave his words no particular intonation. But they carried with an electric spark to the last seat in the rear of the big hall. "I said, a certain amount," Martin continued. "But it would seem to me that Rossville has more than its share."

Nervous laughter swept the hall.

"The kid is clever," O'Hara thought. "I'm going to have to take care of him." But how? He had tried both bribery and threats, and Martin had laughed at him. There seemed to be no weak spots in his armor.

The youthful District Attorney continued. "The war in Europe was over on V.E. day. The war in Japan was over on V.J. day. But the fight for good government has just begun. And we, I speak as a veteran, didn't lick Germany and Japan to allow a gang of greedy, stupid, politicians here at home to steal our birthright out from under our noses."

The audience applauded loudly. So did the officials on stage. So did O'Hara.

Martin went on to substantiate his charges. On taking office he had found, still buried in the files, murder, attack, and grand larceny charges, that had been gathering dust since long before he had joined the Armed Forces. If a man was willing to pay the price he could commit murder with impunity. On the other hand a common citizen who dared to inquire concerning the disposition of a confidence racket charge involving his life's savings had been beaten within an inch of his life and told to go home and mind his own damn business. Because someone in the City Hall (Martin spelled it out. "H-a-u-l") wanted a new Cadillac, veteran and non-veteran alike had to pay twenty-seven dollars and fifty cents for a building permit that formerly had cost ten dollars. Businessman, labor, and management, were preyed upon alike. Known criminals walked the streets while a man with a family to feed was arrested and given thirty days in jail for daring to peddle from door to door without the fifty dollar vendor's license he couldn't afford to buy.

One by one the youthful District Attorney touched on the sore spots O'Hara had created.

"Tonight," he drew near to the end of his address, "I am not going to mention names. But this much I will say. Our elected officials are not entirely to blame. They are under the thumb of a man," Martin looked deliberately at O'Hara so no one would mistake whom he meant, "who with the exception of myself has all of official Rossville in his vest pocket. But I have called this meeting to serve notice that I am not afraid of anything or anyone with the exception of my conscience and with the help and consent of the electorate I intend to clean up Rossville. To that end I will welcome any and all complaints, criminal or civil," he raised his right hand, "and here pledge myself before God that I will prosecute them to the full extent of my strength and my ability."

O'Hara applauded mechanically with the rest, his cheeks a bright brick red.

A reporter paused by his chair. "Anything to say, O'Hara?"

"Mr. O'Hara to you," O'Hara said coldly. That was the way it was. Let one ram jump over a fence and all of the curly lambs followed. Martin decidedly had to be stopped before the whole flock got out of hand. He added, "Why should I have anything to say?"

The reporter shrugged and walked on.

O'Hara caught Mayor Arnst's eye. A rabbity little man the mayor looked like he was about to up-chuck his cookies. "Get Klein, the City Sealer," O'Hara told him. "We're going to play some poker in my office."

Arnst began a feeble protest

O'Hara cut him short. "And you'd better get Judge Thompson and Chief Bailiff Green. Meet me there in five minutes."

"But, O'Hara," Arnst protested. "After what young Martin had just alleged, do you think it wise to—"

"Do as you're told," O'Hara said curtly. "A neglected fire

spreads. We can't afford to neglect this one." His smile was wry. "For example, would you want the Simpson girl's parents to lay the whole of that sordid little mess before our fearless new district attorney?"

Feeling his throat, his gills green with fear, Arnst went in search of the men he had been ordered to contact.

O'Hara hesitated briefly, crossed the stage to where Martin was shaking hands with enthusiastic attendees of the rally. "A great speech, Mr. District Attorney," he complimented. "And I want you to know that I'm behind you all the way. It's time Rossville was cleaned up."

Martin ignored his extended hand. O'Hara shrugged and turned away. It didn't matter. A half dozen reporters had written down his statement. At least two city editors would blue pencil it as a 'must'. He knew where their bodies were buried and they, in turn, knew on which side their grey bread was spread with oleo.

Once outside the theatre he drove directly to his office in the City Hall. Arnst, Green, Thomson, and Klein, were already there. All four men were frightened. They knew what his poker games meant. They had played 'poker' with O'Hara before.

"I don't think—" Judge Thompson began.

"I didn't put you on the bench to think," O'Hara cut him short. He took a five hundred dollar bill from his wallet and dropped it on the green baize table at which Klein, the City Sealer, was nervously stacking chips. "Chips for that." O'Hara added a one dollar bill from a crumpled wad in his pants pocket. "Also one white chip extra."

"For luck?" Klein laughed nervously.

"For luck," O'Hara said grimly. "Not that I think I'll need it. Now—deal me out the first hand. I—I've got to go to the John."

The long rows of houses were heavy with sleep. Swift scudding clouds obscured the moon. There was no one on the street but O'Hara and the man whom he had come to kill.

He had known Martin would walk from the street car. Eager to avoid even the appearance of wallowing in the easy money the other city officials enjoyed, Martin never rode in a cab.

"The fool!" O'Hara thought. It was almost a shame to kill him. He was that almost extinct public official who meant what he swore when he took his oath of office. Martin really intended to give the public an even break. The fool. He had been offered a chance to feed with the other pigs at the trough. But he was too noble minded. And a lot of good it had done him. As feet sounded on the frosted walk, O'Hara thumbed the safety off his gun. Young Martin had lived through Bougainville, Guadalcanal, and Saipan, to die on a lonely suburban street in Rossville.

And O'Hara intended to make certain he did die. That was why he was attending to the task himself. He attributed his success, and rightfully so, to the fact that he had never sent a boy to do a man's job. The saw was old. It was corny. But if a man wanted a job well done, no one could do it like himself.

Parked half a block from Martin's home, he waited. He doubted that Martin would be armed. After tonight's open declaration of war he would carry a gun. But tonight he would be carrying nothing more deadly than a transcript of the script of the speech he had made. He would not expect O'Hara to strike tonight. Well, neither had the Army or the Navy at Pearl Harbor.

The thud of feet on the walk came closer. The fool was whistling the Marine Battle Hymn. He thought he was good. He thought he was a big shot. He'd told O'Hara off.

"I intend to clean up Rossville," he'd boasted.

There was no need for O'Hara to nerve himself to kill. He had done it too often before. He stepped from the car as Martin passed and called, "Oh, Martin," softly.

Martin recognized his voice and turned, as O'Hara had known he would. His eyes were wide with disbelief. "You wouldn't dare."

"No?" O'Hara grinned, and pulled the trigger.

The heavy slug slapped Martin's chest with the impact of a

baseball bat, but he continued to advance.

Cold sweat beading his forehead, O'Hara backed away from him. "Die, damn you, die!" He fired twice again. The third of the shots stopped Martin.

"I will be damned," he said thickly.

He stood a moment longer, swaying on his feet, then crumpled to the ground. Bold now, O'Hara stood over him and fired the four remaining shots into his back to make certain he was dead. Then he took the dead man's wallet and his watch and got back into his car.

Lights were beginning to blink on as aroused householders stumbled out of bed. A porch light flicked on half way up the block. A woman stepped out on the porch and screamed—"Police!"

O'Hara grinned. "You'll have to yell louder than that, sister." Meshing his big car into gear he drove away rapidly without turning on his lights. No Polly Pry would get his license number.

Four miles from the scene of the killing he stopped his car on the bridge linking the business section of the town with the residential district and threw the gun he had used into the river. Martin's watch and wallet followed the gun. He peeled off the gloves he had worn and threw them in too. There were no pedestrians on the bridge. No car passed as he was parked. No matter what happened now, no one could prove a thing. Meshing his car into gear he drove directly to the parking lot in back of the City Hall. He had been gone, he noted by his watch, a little less than twenty minutes.

He entered the City Hall through the boiler room door after first making certain that the colored fireman on duty was snoring soddenly, a drugged fifth of whiskey beside him. Green, at least, was worth the money he allowed him to steal. He had seen to the doctored whiskey, as he had seen to it twice before. O'Hara considered running Green for Mayor in the next election as he climbed the cement stairs of the silent fire well.

His office was back of the Mayor's office, connected by an ante room. The four men were playing a round of roodles.

Arnst, Thompson, and Klein, studiously studied their cards as he entered. Green raised his eyebrows slightly.

O'Hara nodded as he hung up his overcoat and suit coat. "Any phone calls?"

Green said, "One. About five minutes ago. That wise punk on the city desk of the *Evening Eagle* wants to know if you want to comment on District Attorney Martin's refusal to shake hands with you." The city sealer dealt a round of hands as he spoke.

"And what did you tell him?"

Green grinned. "I told him to call back, that you were in the John."—O'Hara picked up his hand, laid it down again as the phone rang. "O'Hara speaking," he answered it.

He listened briefly to the caustic questions of the *Evening Eagle's* city editor. "No," he replied. "I haven't the least idea why young Martin refused to shake hands with me. Sure, he beat out my man in the election but there are no hard feelings on my part. I think he's a clean cut young fellow and a credit to the District Attorney's office. More, I meant what I said. It was a great speech he made and I'm behind him all the way. It's time Rossville was cleaned up."

He listened a moment longer, chuckled, and hung up.

"What did he say?" Mayor Arnst wanted to know.

"It sounded like 'nuts'," O'Hara grinned. He tossed a blue chip in the center of the table. "And a five buck ante just in case somebody catches a trey on the first up card."

The phone rang again but O'Hara ignored it. There would be a stink over this killing. He might even be asked to drop down to Headquarters for a friendly talk. Not that he had anything to fear from the police. Young Martin had called the turn. Both the Chief of Police and the head of the Detective Bureau were in his vest pocket. But a man could never be too careful. There was still the State Patrol. And he didn't want his alibi too tailor made. A lot of wise lads had gone to the chair by being over clever. He really had no alibi. He had merely put the burden of the proof upon the law. But to convict him a jury would have to discredit the testimony of the mayor, the city sealer, the head bailiff, and the presiding judge of the criminal court.

Mayor Arnst caught a trey on the first round of up-cards, put in five blue chips to stay and bet ten dollars more. His face grey he asked O'Hara, "Did he—? That is, I mean did anyone—?"

"I don't know what you're talking about," O'Hara said blandly. "See your ten and raise you ten more on my deuces in the hole."

Judge Thompson turned down his cards and for the next twenty minutes they played in a silence broken only by the grunted mechanics of the game, the click of chips, and a constant ringing of the phone. It was still ringing shrilly when Lieutenant of Detectives Bartlett walked into the office.

He was another returned soldier. Federal law had blocked O'Hara's attempt to refuse him the job he had held when he had obtained a leave of absence to enlist. But Bartlett knew that O'Hara had tried, knew that he was gunning for him. And that was all right with Bartlett. He was gunning for O'Hara. The rank and file of the Force were still honest. If they cut corners at their superior's request, it was because they had families to feed.

O'Hara looked up, smiling, pretending a pleasure he didn't feel. "Hi there, Lieutenant. Long time no see. Draw up a chair and buy chips."

White-lipped, Bartlett said, "So that's the way what's going to be, eh?"

O'Hara looked surprised. "So that's the way what's going to be? Why so grim? What's happened?"

"You wouldn't know?"

"I wouldn't." O'Hara looked in simulated surprise at the two plainclothes men. "My, God. What is this, a raid? Don't tell me that since young Martin was elected District Attorney that it's against the law to play poker?"

"Martin is dead," one of the plainclothes men told him.

"Dead!" Mayor Arnst knocked over his stack of chips. "My goodness! How did it happen?"

"You wouldn't know?" Lieutenant Bartlett asked O'Hara.

O'Hara chuckled, "You asked me that once before when I asked you what had happened. How did young Martin die, choke on a malted milk?"

Lieutenant Bartlett clenched his fists to keep from striking him. "No. He was killed a half block from his home in a phony stick-up, a stick-up during which seven shots were fired into his body, to make certain he was dead. And believe it, or not, O'Hara, you were the first guy I thought of."

"How nice of you." O'Hara's voice turned cold. "Quit kidding, Bartlett. I wouldn't dirty my hands on that sniveling Y. M.C.A. punk. I thought Marines were men until I—"

Unable to contain himself any longer, Bartlett knocked O'Hara out of his chair, picked him up and knocked him down again.

"Here!" Judge Thompson cried. "Yon can't do that."

"I'm doing it," Bartlett said, "if it costs me my shield. Johnny is dead. but there are a lot of us who feel the way he felt."

O'Hara got to his feet spitting blood and nursing a badly split lip. Furious, he forced himself to speak calmly. "I think you are rather exceeding your authority, Lieutenant Bartlett, but I'll forgive that blow because Martin was your friend. However, I assure you, if he has been murdered I know nothing what-so-ever about it I—"

"I know," Lieutenant Bartlett said bitterly. "Ever since the rally broke up you have been playing poker with the mayor, the city sealer, Judge Thompson, and Bailiff Green. You haven't been out of their sight for a moment."

Klein giggled nervously. "He went to the men's room."

"That's right. I did." O'Hara forced a smile. "But you can't arrest a man for that, can you?"

Bartlett searched O'Hara for a gun. He didn't expect to find one. He didn't.

His split lip making him lisp slightly, O'Hara asked, "Satisfied?"

"Not by a damn sight," Bartlett said sourly. "Get your hat and coat on, O'Hara. I'm taking you down to the Bureau to record your statement. The rest of you better come, too." He massaged the knuckles of his right hand thoughtfully. "Or would that be too great a strain, I hope, on your constitutional rights?"

"Not at all," O'Hara assured him. He counted and cashed in his chips. "I'm glad you broke up the game."

The phone was still ringing shrilly as the eight men left the office.

The trip to the Bureau had been, as O'Hara had known it would be, merely a matter of form. Mason, the head of the Detective Bureau, had merely recorded his statement and the freely proffered alibi tendered by Mayor Arnst, Chief Bailiff Green, Judge Thompson, and City Sealer Klein. O'Hara had insisted that a paraffin test be made of his hands to prove that he hadn't fired a gun within the last twenty four hours. The test had come out negative. It hadn't even been necessary for O'Hara to disturb his lawyer. On the contrary Mason had rebuked Bartlett for allowing his feeling for his dead friend to get the best of his judgment.

Green drove O'Hara to his hotel. "And that's that," he chuckled in parting.

"That's that," O'Hara assured him. "The nerve of the young punk. Going to clean up Rossville, was he?" As he stepped from the car, he added, "We'll have to get Bartlett next. These returning vets are a pain in the neck. They really believe in the things that they were fighting for."

"We'll figure out something," Green said.

As the desk clerk gave him his key, he told him, "There is a young lady waiting for you in the cocktail lounge, Mr. O'Hara. She has been waiting since shortly after the rally. And she asked me to tell you that you seeing her is important, vitally important to her."

O'Hara tapped his key on his palm. "She didn't give her name?"

"No, sir. She did not."

"Young?"

The clerk outlined a woman's figure with his hands. "Young, and very pretty, sir."

"Then I'll see her," O'Hara grinned.

The cocktail lounge off the hotel lobby was dimly lighted. The headwaiter met O'Hara at the door. "Good evening, sir," he greeted him pleasantly. "The young lady had just about given you up. If you will please follow me, sir."

O'Hara followed him across the lounge to one of the leather-upholstered booths on the far side. "Mr. O'Hara, Miss," the headwaiter said, and left them.

In the shaded glow of the table light, the girl's face looked vaguely familiar but O'Hara couldn't place her. But she was pretty, very pretty, and young. "I'm afraid I haven't the honor," he began—then he saw the silver object in her hand.

"Sit down, O'Hara," she said calmly. "You don't know me. But I'm Gwen Martin, Johnny's sister." She took a deep breath, continued. "And I want to have a little talk with you about my brother."

O'Hara stared at the glint of silver in her hand. He could think of nothing to say.

She continued, "I've been waiting for you for hours. Six gin bucks to be exact."

O'Hara shifted his weight to his toes, fear sweat misting his eyes. Why didn't she shoot?

The girl smiled wryly. "I want you to order me another drink. And I want you to promise not to harm Johnny. He's young, hot-headed. He doesn't realize that Rome wasn't built in a day. And he hasn't the least idea of all of the ramifications of the office to which he has been elected."

O'Hara exhaled audibly. The girl didn't know that her brother was dead. He stared hard at the silver object. It wasn't a gun. It was a silver compact. "Thank you. I will sit down." He pressed the service button and ordered two gin bucks. "I take it then, that you were at the rally?"

She said, "I heard it over the radio. And I can't say that Johnny was exactly diplomatic,"

O'Hara chuckled. "You know, I think I could like you."

Her voice was low but melodious rather than throaty. "Don't strain yourself, O'Hara. But you're not so bad looking yourself."

The waiter arrived with the drinks.

Amused, O'Hara lifted his glass. "Now I know I could like you. To us."

"To us," she sipped the toast. "But about my brother, O'Hara."

"God bless him," O'Hara lied, "I wouldn't harm a hair of his head. But he really does me an injustice."

"I doubt it," the girl said frankly. "You run Rossville. Anyone with any sense knows that. But on the other hand, all big cities have bosses. It's a part of our political set-up. And I can't see anything particularly wrong about it. It is, in a sense, I suppose, an application of the old law of the survival of the fittest. No one has any use for a sucker. And that's what Johnny made of himself tonight. He should have kept his mouth shut until he had the goods on you instead of tipping his hand."

O'Hara laughed heartily. He liked this girl. Now that his eyes had become accustomed to the dim light he could see that she was even prettier than he had thought she was. She was tall, and dark, and sultry. And from what he could see of her figure under a smart traveling suit the desk clerk had done her an injustice. "I didn't know Johnny Martin had such a pretty sister. Where have you been keeping yourself?"

"The Philippines," she told him. "I'm an Army nurse." She corrected herself. "That is, I was. I just got into town this evening in time to hear Johnny make a fool of himself."

O'Hara ordered two more gin bucks and moved around to her side of the table. He liked the scent of her perfume. It was feminine without being cloying. Nor was there anything coy about her. This girl knew her way around. He wondered how she'd act if she knew he'd killed her brother. "And just why did you come to see me?"

"I know how these things are done," she said. "I know what will happen to Johnny if he continues to get in your hair. And I know that you'll probably go Scot free because his charges are probably true that you have most of the city officials in your vest pocket."

She allowed him to kiss her, laughed, "Not so fast, wolf. Let's settle Johnny first. Promise me that you won't take any notice of his childish outburst tonight."

He raised his right hand. "I promise."

"Word of honor?"

"Word of honor."

She pressed the button for the waiter. "Two more gin bucks. And make them double this time," she told him. "What's the matter with your bartender? Is he Scotch?"

O'Hara kissed her twice while they were waiting for their drinks. As they drank them he suggested, "I could have a bottle sent up to my suite."

"It's an idea," she admitted. She kissed him, hard, her teeth against his split lip. "But I'm afraid I'd better get home to Johnny. You see, I haven't seen him in five years. But well, some other time maybe."

He continued ordering drinks, trying to persuade her. She allowed him to kiss her at will but refused to be persuaded. She drank drink for drink with him but they seemed to have no more effect on her than if she had been drinking water.

He remembered dancing with her several times. Then things began to blur and the next he knew the tall sultry girl who was Johnny Martin's sister and the obsequious head-waiter were helping him across the floor out of the cocktail lounge into the hotel lobby and up to the elevator bank.

O'Hara insisted on kissing her again. Gwen mashed her lips against his in parting, her teeth meeting playfully on the lip Bartlett's fist had split.

"Thash a promise?" O'Hara asked drunkenly.

"That's a promise," she told him. "I'll be seeing you."

It was late afternoon when O'Hara awakened. He had a sour brown taste in his mouth. His head ached dully. He couldn't ever recall having been so drunk before. He lay thinking of Gwen Martin. She was a nurse by her own admission. He wondered if she had drugged him and if so for what purpose.

He decided that she had not. The little fool hadn't even known that Johnny was dead. And she had gone for him in a big way.

"I'll be seeing you," she had kissed him in parting.

The hell she would. O'Hara shrugged into a dressing gown. He wanted no part of Johnny Martin's sister. The breed was dangerous. Besides, Gwen knew by now that her brother was dead. Still, the evening had served its purpose. Gwen Martin would not believe no woman could believe that he had been able to make ardent love to her within an hour of the time he had killed her brother.

He phoned room service for his breakfast and studied his face in the bathroom mirror while he waited for it to arrive. The little devil had bitten him. He could still see the marks of her teeth. His lip was puffed and slightly discolored. And that reminded him. He had a score to settle with Lieutenant Bartlett. These returning G.I.s thought they were hell on wheels. But Bartlett would learn different, shortly.

His grapefruit was iced and laced with sherry. A morning paper was folded on the tray. Life, O'Hara thought, was a pretty fine affair if a man had sense enough to take from it what he wanted. He must remember to send a spray of flowers to District Attorney Martin's funeral. It was a pity his tenure of office had been so brief.

Martin's death, as he had expected, occupied almost all of the front page. Robbery was the accepted motive. O'Hara dug his spoon in his grapefruit and began to read:

> . . . District Attorney Martin's body was discovered by his sister, who returned to this city from the Philippines last evening. "I was waiting for Johnny to return from the Rally," Miss Martin said, "when I heard seven shots and saw the proverbial long black sedan race from the scene of the crime. My brother was dead when I reached him."
>
> Asked why she had disappeared from the scene before the arrival of the police and had waited until a late hour to report what she had seen. . .

O'Hara swept the dishes from the table to make more room

for the paper.

Gwen Martin had been the woman on the lighted porch. Gwen Martin had been the woman who had screamed 'Police'. She had known that her brother was dead all the time she had allowed him to make love to her.

. . . Miss Martin, formerly an Army nurse who was on Bataan when it fell, added a new note of tragedy to her brother's death when she told Lieutenant of Detectives Bartlett that during her flight from the Japanese she had been forced to take refuge in a small leper colony in the Islands and had, herself, contacted the disease . . .

O'Hara shuddered. No. Not that. It couldn't be. That couldn't happen to him. His eyes in their sockets, he read on . . .

. . . "I am technically under custody of another nurse," Miss Martin explained, "and on my way to the leper colony in Louisiana for treatment. But my brother and I have always been very close and I wanted to see him just once more before I reported to the hospital in Louisiana. It is believed I can be cured but at the present time the disease is in a highly contagious state and it was for that reason that I did not immediately contact the police for fear—"

Allowing the paper to fall to the floor unnoticed, O'Hara walked into the bathroom and studied the tooth marks on his lower lip. It seemed to him that his lip was even more discolored and inflamed.

". . . but at the present time the disease is in a highly contagious state. . . "

No! No! This couldn't happen to him. *I'll be seeing you,* the girl had told him.

O'Hara shuddered. He was damned if she would. There was

one way out of this. He studied his lip. Her tooth marks were very plain. He even thought he could see a faint, shiny, silver sheen. She might be cured. He couldn't. His luck had run out at long last.

His feet leaden, he walked back to the living room, took a pistol from the drawer of his desk.

His face frozen with horror, he did what he had to do.

~ ~ ~ ~ ~

To Lieutenant Bartlett, waiting in the hall outside of O'Hara's elaborate suite, the report sounded faint, like an uncorked bottle as O'Hara's life spilled out.

"And that's that," he told the white-faced girl beside him. "Knowing O'Hara, I thought he would."

Gwen Martin nodded, white-faced. "He had it coming."

The reporter who had paused by O'Hara's chair to ask if he had anything to say, following Johnny Martin's speech, wrote 'O'Hara takes own life in mystery suicide,' on his note pad.

It was, in a way, he thought, a shame, not to let all of Rossville in on the story. But it would be difficult to explain that the copy of the paper O'Hara had read had been the only one containing the leper story.

It was enough to know that Rossville would benefit. It was one of the things all three of them had learned in the Army. If a thing couldn't be done one way, it could be done another.

THREE DEAD MICE

CHAPTER ONE

Return of the Dead

TO PORT LAY STATEN ISLAND. Right ahead to starboard the towers of Manhattan rose out of the cold, gray waters of the Bay. A drizzling December sleet was falling. The woman lifted one corner of the lifeboat cover and peered out.

The throb of the motors had ceased. The big ship rode at Quarantine. The repatriates it carried expressed themselves in various ways. Some laughed. Some cried. Some knelt on the deck in prayer.

The woman in the lifeboat pulled the cover further back and slid down to the boat deck. No one saw her. All were too busy with their own affairs. She half walked, half crawled to a deck chair and studied her fellow refugees with worried eyes.

The shawl that she clutched to her throat was a rag. A thin dress covered her emaciated body. Her hair hung in limp gray locks. Her cheeks were the color of wax. She sat, a hunted animal, no longer entirely sane, her· lips mumbling the nursery rhyme:

"Three blind mice . . . See how they run . . . They all ran after the Farmer's wife . . . She cut off their tails with a carving knife . . . Three dead mice . . ."

The reporters swarmed aboard as soon as the anchor was dropped. A refugee ship was news. A few reporters came up to the boat deck. Morg Baker of the *Clarion* was one. He passed the woman twice before he recognized her. Even then he wasn't certain. He squatted beside the deck chair and studied her face, incredulous.

"Cynthia! Cynthia Dalton!"

She reached out a white, wasted, hand and clutched hard at his coat sleeve. "Get Larry Miller," she whimpered.

Baker was a good reporter. He knew a story when he saw one. This was big.

"But, Cynthia," he protested. "How—Where—"

Her haunted eyes filmed slightly. "I'm afraid," she whimpered. "They want to kill me. They don't want me to tell. Get Larry Miller. Please."

The waterfront bar was small and dimly lighted. Baker, acutely conscious that he had been followed since he had left the ship, glanced nervously over his shoulder as he spun a dime across the bar.

"Two nickels, please."

He dialed the *Clarion* rapidly and asked for Miller's extension.

"This is Morg, Larry," he said crisply. "Meet me at the Half Moon Bar on Front Street as fast as you can get here. Cynthia Dalton just came in on the *Stockholm* from Lisbon."

Miller said, "You're crazy."

Baker shook his head doggedly. "She looks like a witch. She's been through hell. Somebody wants to kill her. But it's Cynthia. And she won't talk to anyone but you. She says—"

Fingers reached over his shoulder, tore the receiver from his hand and replaced it in the cradle. The two big men had entered almost on his heels. One of them spun Baker around to face them.

"What stateroom is she in? What does Mrs. Dalton look like? What's the name on her passport?" he demanded.

The bartender attempted to intervene. "Here. None of that rough stuff," he protested. "This ain't the Astor, but—"

One of the big men smashed his fist into the bartender's mouth. The other demanded of Baker:

"How much did she tell you?"

Baker attempted to brush away the hand that clutched his coat lapel. The man banged his head into the wall.

"Talk, damn you. Talk!"

Baker told the truth. "She didn't tell me a thing. She said that she wouldn't talk to anyone but Larry Miller."

"You're lying," the big man said coldly.

He drew a gun and shot Baker three times, through the chest. One of the shots pierced his heart. The reporter died instantly.

The second man kicked the body, made a sneering remark, and both men left the bar.

Miller arrived at the Half Moon minutes behind Homicide. Lieutenant Pierce was questioning the bartender.

"And you didn't recognize the guys?"

The bartender spat a mouthful of blood on the floor. "Naw. Both of 'em looked like they might be sailors. But I never seen them before."

"And they walked right up to Baker, pulled him away from the phone and shot him." It was a statement, not a question.

"That's right," the bartender told him.

Pierce swung around to Miller. "Does that make sense to you?"

"Not yet," Miller admitted.

The bartender hesitated, added, "And then when the guy that was shot was lying on the floor, one of the guys who shot him kicked him and said, 'Give our regards to the Fuehrer.' "

"He said what?" Lieutenant Pierce demanded.

" 'Give our regards to the Fuehrer,' " the bartender repeated stolidly.

Pierce turned back to Miller. "There's one for the book," he said.

A lean-faced, gray-eyed man in his late thirties, Miller had covered Manhattan crime for twenty years. When he was sober, he was reputed to be tops in his line.

"Baker was phoning me," he admitted. "In fact he was talking to me when they tore him away from the phone."

"They, meaning whom?" Pierce asked him.

The reporter shook his head. "I haven't the least idea. Was

Baker drunk or sober? Or don't you know?"

"He didn't have nothing to drink in here," the bartender offered.

Lieutenant Pierce knelt on the floor, smelled the dead man's lips, and fingered back his eyelids. "The M.E. can tell us that to the degree. But my guess is that he was sober. Why?"

Miller hesitated. The information that Baker had given him was fantastic. Cynthia Dalton was dead. "No particular reason," he evaded the question. "I just wondered."

Pierce got to his feet and brushed at his knees. "The hell you did. What did Baker phone you about?"

Miller told the truth. He didn't expect to be believed. He wasn't disappointed. "Morg phoned to tell me," he told Lieutenant Pierce, "that Cynthia Dalton was aboard the *Stockholm* that just dropped her hook at Quarantine."

"Nuts," Pierce snorted. "You're slipping, Larry. Cynthia and the Farmer drowned in that Clipper that was shot down off the coast of Ireland five months ago."

"So we printed in the *Clarion,*" Miller agreed.

The Homicide man crossed the room and waggled a finger under Miller's nose. "Someday you're going to cover up for someone once too often, Larry," he exploded. "And I'm going to slap you in the Tombs with an accessory after murder charge against you. Who killed Morg Baker? And why?"

The reporter shook his head. "I don't know."

Pierce turned from him, disgusted. "I'll come back to you later, Larry."

Cole, the medical examiner, stomped in, blowing on his hands to warm them. The tech squad and a police stenographer arrived.

Miller walked out on the sidewalk and stared through the late afternoon drizzle at the outline of the big ship lying at Quarantine. Baker's tip-off had been fantastic. Cynthia and the Farmer were dead. Their bodies had been recovered by fishermen and buried near Downpatrick Head. Still—

He walked briskly along Front Street to the nearest small boat landing.

"No," the purser of the *Stockholm* told him, "we have no one by that name aboard. However, you are welcome to look at the passenger list."

Miller scanned it carefully. The name Dalton was not on it.

He went back out on deck and walked slowly through the groups of excited repatriates, his sharp eyes searching their faces.

Joe Carr of the *Star* stopped him. "What's cooking?" he demanded. "I thought Baker covered the water-front for the *Clarion.*"

Miller considered briefly. "I'm looking for Morg," he lied. "You seen him here, Joe?"

Carr shook his head. "Not since just after we came aboard. He was talking to some old witch up on the boat deck." The reporter shuddered, not from the cold. "So help me. Someone ought to knock off that louse Hitler. You should hear the stories that some of these folks who have been in concentration camps can tell."

"I have," Miller told him curtly.

He walked to the nearest deck ladder and on up to the boat deck. It was deserted except for two seamen busy shining brass. Both of them were big men. Miller studied them thoughtfully in the half gray of early twilight.

This thing was mad. It couldn't be. The Farmer and Cynthia were dead. Their bodies had fallen in the ocean, had been fished out, identified, and buried.

Still, if what the bartender had said was true, one of the big men had kicked Morg's dead body and muttered, "Give our regards to the Fuehrer." That could mean only one thing.

Miller's pulse began to beat a little faster. The day of the scoop was gone. Wireless, cable, radio, the airplane, had all conspired to destroy it. But this, if true, was a scoop.

Here the wind was bitter and biting. He turned up the collar of his coat and regarded the lifeboats. If Cynthia was alive, if the impossible had taken place, she would not have dared to travel under her own name. They had agents everywhere. They would want to kill her to keep the news from getting out. She would have been a hunted outcast, her life in constant danger, even on such a ship as the *Stockholm*. She would not have dared to tell her story. The purser, the captain, the United States Consul in Lisbon would have believed her to be mad.

Miller walked down the row of port lifeboats, examining their lashings carefully. All of the heavy canvas covers but one were laced down tightly. He rapped on the boat, called, "Cynthia," softly.

There was no answer.

Miller glanced over his shoulder at the seamen.

As he looked at them, they started toward him. "You like life-boats, huh?" one said.

Miller backed against the boat, his right hand in his coat pocket. "Let's hold it there," he said. "Who are you two guys and what do you want of me?"

"You're Miller, Larry Miller of the *Evening Clarion?*" one of them demanded.

Miller admitted his name.

The first of the two big men smiled thinly. "Fine. You're the lad we've been waiting for."

Miller jabbed his hand deeper in his pocket. "Hold it," he repeated.

"Nuts," the big man said succinctly. "Reporters don't carry guns."

He drove a vicious right at Miller's temple.

Miller parried the blow with his left forearm and lashed out with own right hand. The blow caught the man flush on the jaw. It was like hitting a solid brick wall. The seaman merely shook his head and continued to bore in.

The deck below was crowded with laughing, talking people, seamen, officers, reporters, and federal and customs men. A short rifle shot away, Lieutenant Pierce was investigating Morg Baker's murder. The lights on Front Street and in Manhattan had blinked on, ringed with triple halos by the fog.

Here there was only the half dark and death.

Miller opened his mouth to shout for help and a hard fist

smashed into his lips.

"Don't kill him," the second seaman said. "He may have guessed the truth and phoned a lead to his paper before he came aboard. Finding his body would confirm it. We'll smuggle him ashore tonight and question them together."

A sap swung through the murk to cut a deep gash in Miller's temple. He fell, limp but still conscious, to the deck. Strong arms lifted him into the lifeboat on which the cover had been loosened and dropped him on one of the thwarts.

Almost blinded by blood, Miller stared at the bound and gagged gray-haired woman who lay in the bottom of the boat.

As her eyes met his they blazed fiercely.

They did it, Miller exulted. *She and the Farmer did it.*

One of the seamen tied his wrists and ankle. The other man thrust a gag in his mouth and bound it securely in place with his soiled neck cloth.

As they worked, the motors of the ship began to throb. A winch chattered noisily. A cheer rose from the deck below. The *Stockholm* had passed Quarantine.

The seaman finished gagging Miller and laced down the cover of the lifeboat. "We'll see you tonight after we dock," he said in parting. "But I don't imagine that either you or Mrs. Dalton will enjoy the *kaffee klatsch*."

CHAPTER TWO

From the Files:

POLICE DEPARTMENT

December 23, 1943
Tel. Typewriter
Telephone X
Radio

Bureau of Telegraph Shall
Transmit by:

To: P. Comm.
Ch. Insp.
Asst. Chief Insp.
Borough Carom.
Manhattan Det. Commr.
Homicide Sq.
Photo Gallery and Fingerprint
D. A. Office
Medical Examiner
Night Inspector
MURDER. HANS VOGEL, KARL SCHLACTER, IDENTIFIED. TWO SEAMEN UNIDENTIFIED. LOCA-TION VOGEL APARTMENT CENTRAL PARK WEST. REPORTED BY PATROLMAN WEINBERG (52nd St. Station) AND WAITING HOMICIDE AND MED. EX. ALL CONCERNED NOTIFIED.

Signed *Wm, Kuens*
Title *Lieut. H.Q.*

FORTHWITH X
Rec. at Bur. of Tel. by Lamb T. C. 23/12/43
11:46 P.M.
Trans. frm Bur. of Tel. by G. Harris Sergt.
23/12/43 11:51 P.M.
POLICE DEPARTMENT
Report Of Lieutenant Pierce to-Deputy Chief Insp. Kelly
Subject=Vogel murder Case 4-325. Open

On receipt of a telephone communication from Lieutenant Arnold that a homicide had occurred at Central Park West and 81st Streets, I proceeded to the address given, accompanied by Detectives Phillips and Meyers, arriving at 12:24 a.m.

The Vogel apartment is on the fifth floor. We were admitted by Patrolman Weinberg who had been guarding all parties concerned, four of said parties being dead.

The walls and the floor of the room in which the bodies

were lying had been liberally splattered with blood and there were obvious signs of a struggle, broken chairs, a smashed china lamp, *et al.*

I was able to identify Vogel and Schlacter at once, both men having criminal records and being the object of a recent search by the F.B.I. all charges of espionage. The other two dead men I do not know. From their clothing I presume them to be seamen. All four men had been shot and were dead on my arrival.

Present also was Larry Miller, criminal reporter for the *Morning Clarion,* sought for questioning in the Baker Homicide this afternoon in the Half Moon Bar on Front Street.

Miller was in a wildly incoherent mental state and kept babbling that someone whom he called Cynthia had to be protected. On the advice of Dr. Cole, the medical examiner, that it would be unwise to question Miller at this time, I had him transferred, under guard, to the psychopathic ward at a city hospital and confined my questions to Patrolman Weinberg and the neighboring residents of the building.

There was little Weinberg could tell me. He had been passing the building on his usual tour of duty when he was attracted by loud shouts and gunfire coming from the Vogel apartment. He states that the four men, Vogel, Schlacter, and the two as yet unidentified seamen, were dead or dying on his arrival and that Miller was standing over them with a revolver in his hand, laughing in an insane manner, and shouting, "Give *my* regards to the Fuehrer."

Weinberg states that Miller made no resistance when he took the revolver from him and placed him under arrest other than to insist that "Cynthia" must be found and given medical attention and a police guard at once.

Weinberg further states that there was no woman in the apartment when he arrived. However, Miller's incoherent insistence is substantiated to some extent by our finding a ragged shawl in the apartment and the statement of a man living across the hall who swears that he positively heard a woman screaming.

Detectives Hooper and Slade from the fingerprint department should be able to clarify this matter.

While there seems little doubt in my mind that Miller is guilty of all four murders, I am, as I have said, waiting on Dr. Cole's advice until his mental state has improved before I attempt to question him.

Meanwhile a search for the missing woman (if she exists) is being very vigorously prosecuted.

A more detailed report will follow.

POLICE DEPARTMENT

Memo, from Dept. Chief Insp. Kelly
to—Lieutenant Pierce Case 4—325, Open

Pierce. Get somewhere on this Vogel case and get there fast. The D.A. has called six times demanding to be allowed to take it out of the department's hands.

This make five murders in less than twelve hours with only one reputable criminal reporter committed to the Tenth Street Psychopathic Ward to evidence any police work. Who killed Morg Baker? Have you had the bartender of the Half Moon attempt to identify the bodies of the two alleged seamen found in the Vogel apartment? If not, why not?

Are you positive that Cynthia Dalton is dead? Suggest that you check with the State Department.

I want action.
Signed: T. Kelly
Deputy Chief Inspector

TENTH STREET HOSPITAL

Psychopathic Ward
24/12/43 7:32 A.M.

Memorandum from Dr. R. Vaughn
to—Lieutenant Pierce, Horn. Sq.

Re Larry Miller committee under guard for observation 23/12/43 1:22 A.M.

This man has been severely beaten and is in a weakened if not serious physical condition. In my opinion, however, while in a highly emotional state of mind, he is entirely sane and may be questioned at your convenience.

Within two hours after having been committed, he so far recovered his faculties that he asked to phone his paper and, being denied that request, asked for paper and pencil with which to write a statement.

Not being able to reach you by phone I took the liberty of sending to H.Q. for a police stenographer whose notes you will find attached. I believe they are self-explanatory. I am also crossing my fingers and hoping that Miller is right and that his statement is not the fantasy of a disordered mind.

POLICE DEPARTMENT

Report of Police Steno. Monroe

for—Lieutenant Pierce

Subject—Vogel murder Case 4—325. Open

Taken Tenth Street Hospital, 24/12/43 5:22

A.M. Miller's statement follows verbatim, the italics being the words he emphasized.

Statement of Larry Miller

Psychopathic Ward

Tenth Street Hospital

In the first place, I'm not mad. And I *am* not saying that this is true. I am saying that I believe it. For twenty years my job has been to ascertain and publish facts. This case began, for me, one day last fall. That was September of 1943.

It began at five minutes after three on a Friday morning. The paper had been put to bed. Morg Baker had staggered off to drink himself into a stupor. I was alone in the office when Cynthia and the Farmer stepped off the elevator and came into the city room.

I said, "Hello," but neither of them spoke. Both were too stricken with grief to be articulate. It had been five years since I had seen them, but I knew why they had come to me.

You may remember Cynthia. You do, if you ever saw her. Men don't forget her kind. The Farmer married her out of the Follies of 1923 when she was seventeen. At thirty-seven she still was beautiful. There wasn't a line in her face. She still curved in the proper places, not too much, not too little. She was as slim and as vibrantly alive as any girl of twenty-five. She wouldn't have looked that old except that she had been crying.

You remember the Farmer. His record is on the books. He should have been killed or electrocuted a dozen times during prohibition. Each time that he beat a rap, he boasted that the devil was saving him for bigger things. I know so now. His right name was Robert Dalton but no one ever called him anything but the Farmer because he was so big, and because of his plowboy stride. He came, originally, from one of the Dakotas and he wasn't as bad as he was wild. He killed, but he wasn't vicious. He had merely been born too late. Whiskey running spelled adventure. He retired from the rackets the day that repeal was made final.

We had little occasion to meet after that. I never saw his name on a blotter again. The last time that I had seen him he owned several dozen apartment buildings, a big garage, and a farm out on Long Island. He and Cynthia also had a boy. It was the boy that they wanted to see me about.

It was Cynthia who spoke first. She forced a smile that had once brought ten dollars a ducat. "Hello, Larry. Long time, no see."

I nodded and looked down at my desk to give her a chance to blink away her tears. She was taking it pretty hard.

The Farmer was taking it even harder. He wasn't a hard-boiled lone wolf any more. He was a graying, slightly pot-bellied father who had lost his only son. "We—we were listening to the radio," he began, "and well—"

He tried to go on and couldn't. Like all hoods he was superstitious. He was afraid that saying would make it so.

"We thought," he continued with an effort, "that—" Sweat stood out on his forehead in drops as big as pearls. "Give it to us straight, Larry. We know that you'll tell us the truth."

I wished I could tell him it was a mistake. I couldn't. It was why Morg Baker was getting stinking. He had washed out of the same pre-flight class in which young Dalton had been commissioned. The wire editor had tossed the story on my desk.

I handed the Farmer a proof sheet. The head and the sub-head read:

U.S. FLYERS MURDERED
Entire Crew Of U. S. Flying
Fortress Executed In Berlin

The story began:

Acting under direct orders from Chancellor Hitler, pre-sumably in a desperate attempt to bolster failing German morale, a Nazi firing squad acting contrary to all international law, this afternoon publicly executed Lieutenant Robert Dalton, Jr., pilot of an ill-fated Flying Fortress shot down in a recent raid on Berlin, and all the members of his . . .

The Farmer put the paper back on my desk. "That's dirty pool. We were notified by the War Department a week ago that Bobby's plane was missing, but—" He gulped.

Cynthia cried openly. She was beautiful even when she cried. "I—I suppose it was foolish of us," she admitted, "but we knew if there *had* been a mistake that you would tell us. Such—such things do happen, you know."

I agreed that they did, but said I was afraid this was no mistake. The report had come via Stockholm.

The Farmer looked east out the window. He didn't seem so gray. The bulge at his waistline had disappeared. He put the blame where it belonged. "Someone ought to kill that louse."

I said I imagined that Hitler was pretty well guarded.

"So was Dutch Shultz," he said coldly. "A good smart hood could get him. All he'd need would be a clever gimmick and a gun!"

I didn't argue with the Farmer. I had gone to the funeral of lads who had.

Cynthia began to cry in earnest. "He—we were so proud of

him," she told me. "He—he was everything we aren't. We—we're going to miss him."

The Farmer picked her up in his arms as if she had been a doll and carried her back to the elevators. "Don't cry so, honey," he tried to soothe her. "They can't do this to us. I'll get that guy."

Take it, or leave it, that's it. That was all there was to it—at the time. I didn't even play up the story.

Four days later word came in that they were dead. How the Farmer had wangled passports and places on a Clipper is something I'll never know. I imagine that a few of his wires were still hot. He still knew where some bodies were buried.

I thought at the time, *he tried it.* He was headed for Berlin or Berchtesgaden. *The crazy hood really meant it. He thought he could knock off Hitler.*

CHAPTER THREE

From the Files:

POLICE DEPARTMENT
Report of Police Steno. Monroe
for—Lieutenant Pierce
Subject—Vogel murder Case 4—325. Open
At this point, 5:47 a.m., a nurse interrupted Miller to take his temperature and pulse. Both were slightly above normal. Dr. Vaughn, who had not left the bedside, ordered that a mild sedative be given to the prisoner. It seemed to have little, if any, effect. Miller said that he felt like talking and Dr. Vaughn allowed him to continue. At this point Miller also demanded to know if the police were searching for Cynthia Dalton, and on being assured that they were, seemed to be greatly relieved. "She's been through hell," he told me.

Statement of Larry Miller
Psychopathic Ward
Tenth Street Hospital

(Continuation)

What happened this afternoon is on the blotter. Pierce thought I was lying. I wasn't. Morg Baker called me from the Half Moon Bar to tell me that Cynthia Dalton had arrived in Quarantine on the refugee ship *Stockholm* out of Lisbon.

I got to the ship about four. It was beginning to grow dark. Cynthia was not on the passenger list. I had not expected she would be. It stood to reason that if she and the Farmer had been successful, she would have had to stowaway.

Joe Carr said that he had seen Morg talking to a gray-haired woman on the boat deck. Morg had said that Cynthia had aged. I went up and looked around. I saw no one but two seamen shining brass.

I did see an unlaced lifeboat, but before I could lift the tarp, the two big seamen had braced me. Both of them had saps. I had the story then—too late. These were the boys who had killed Morg—Ausland Gestapo men . . .

(Here I interrupted Miller to ask if he knew the names of the two men. He replied that he did, that they were the same two men who had been killed in Vogel's apartment. He said that Vogel and Schlacter had seemed much afraid of them, calling one of them Herr Oberleutnant Prager and the other Herr Doktor Harsch. I asked one of the two detectives guarding Miller to phone this information to H.Q. at once and he said that he would.)

This was death. I could smell it. I pretended I had a gun, but they knew better.

One of them sapped me and threw me into the boat, the other man warning him:

"Don't kill him. He may have guessed the truth and phoned a lead to his paper before he came aboard. Finding his body would confirm it. We'll smuggle him ashore to-night."

I wasn't alone in the boat. Cynthia was lying on the floor-boards, bound and gagged. It was difficult to recognize her. She wasn't pretty any more. Only her eyes were the same. They blazed as they met mine. Then she began to hum. At first I thought that she was mad. She wasn't. She was telling me what had happened:

"Three blind mice ... see how they run ... they all ran after the Farmer's wife ... he cut off their tails with a carving knife ... did you ever see such a sight in your life as three blind mice ..."

I substituted the word dead for blind and I had it. I had the biggest story that ever hit this town—and there wasn't a thing that I could do about it.

That night, after the boat had docked, they smuggled us ashore in two big hampers and took us to Vogel's apartment. I knew Vogel well. He was a heel, a louse, and a Ratsi. Schlacter was his yes man.

Herr Oberleutnant Prager hauled me out of the hamper, set me on my feet, and Vogel knocked me down.

"It will be a pleasure to kill you," he assured me.

The other three men laughed. All of them were nervous. All of them were mad. They acted like men working against time, trying to stopper a break in the levee with the Mississippi pouring through.

Schlacter tore the gag from my mouth. "Go ahead und yell," he told me. "The walls and floors are sound-proofed."

(Suggest that this point be checked as I noted in the lieutenant's report to Deputy Chief Inspector Kelly that you made mention of a party in a neighboring apartment claiming to have heard a woman scream. Initialed M.)

The Gestapo agent whom Vogel called Herr Doktor Harsch lifted Cynthia from her hamper, unconscious. He applied a restorative from a medical kit that he took from his pocket, saying coldly:

"Come, come. We do not want you to die so easily." He unbound her hands and feet and removed the gag from her mouth. "We have many pleasantries in store for you—before we return you to the man with the axe in Berlin."

She screamed and fainted again.

"Damn her!" Vogel bellowed.

He kicked her heavily. I snatched up a table lamp and hurled it at his head. Behind me, Oberleutnant Prager cursed:

"You *verdammt Amerikaner!* You all fight up to the

grave."

I asked him what he expected me to do, sing *Deutschland über Alles* or the *Horst Wessel* song? He slapped me unconscious with his sap.

When I came to, I was lying on the floor of a small room. There was a dim bulb burning in the ceiling. Cynthia was crouched, crying, in a corner. I could hear Vogel, Schlacter, Prager, and Harsch arguing on the other side of a closed door. They were discussing how best to dispose of my body.

I looked for a window. There was none. The room was merely a large closet.

"Hello, Cynthia," I said quietly. "Too long time no see."

She stopped crying and looked up. There wasn't a trace of her beauty left. She looked like a hag. "They're dead," she told me. "They're dead, Larry. Both the Farmer and Bobby are dead."

Her mouth went slack. The light went out of her eyes. She began to sing *Three Blind Mice*.

I crawled across the floor and tilted back her chin. "Look in my eyes," I ordered. "Tell me, Cynthia. The Farmer sent you back to tell me."

Sure, she was mad. Her mind was hanging by a thread. She had been through too much for it to be otherwise. But she knew what she was saying. I believe it was the truth. The Gestapo wouldn't have hounded her all over Europe and back to the States if it wasn't.

"Keep looking at me, Larry," she begged me. "And keep tight hold of my hand. My mind—it wanders—there are gaps."

I tried to help her. "The Farmer said that a good smart hood could get him. All that he needed was a clever gimmick and a gun."

She nodded, her eyes never leaving mine. She clutched hard at my hand and began to talk.

(Here I asked Miller if he was about to tell the story that the alleged Cynthia Dalton had told him. He said that he was. Therefore in order to avoid confusion re the party speaking and quotation marks, the remainder of this report,

until otherwise specified, is written in the first person as told by the alleged Cynthia Dalton to the prisoner Larry Miller. Initialed M.)

She began:

Most mothers would have felt as I did. Shooting Bobby wasn't fair. They had a right to hold him as a prisoner of war. But they had no right to shoot him. As the Farmer said:

"It's like putting the snatch on a gee and then shooting him down in cold blood before you even send out the ransom note."

No. Don't look away, Larry. Keep hold of my hand. We talked all that night after leaving you at the paper. Neither one of us had been much. We knew it. The Farmer had been a hood. I was a show gal. Our lives had revolved on Bobby. He was to be a gentleman, well educated, everything that we hadn't been. Now, he was gone.

Toward morning the Farmer got out his gun. He said that he had a plan but he doubted if we'd live through it. I told him that was all right with me. I knew what he was talking about. He didn't need to tell me. I'd seen that look in his eyes before. He had made up his mind to kill Hitler.

He told me to pack and be ready, that he'd have to brush up some wires. I didn't ask any questions. The Farmer knew his business.

In four days we left for London. We were two of eight passengers on the Clipper. There were lend-lease men from the State Department. Senator Corson and his secretary, a woman about my age, made five. The sixth was a high-ranking Naval officer.

All of them knew about Bobby. They all were nice to me. The Farmer said we were going to London in the hope there was some mistake. They'd have thought we were mad if we'd told the truth.

We were two hours out of London when it happened. The Farmer cursed then like a madman. He had hoped to slip into Germany via Holland. He hadn't figured on the Luftwaffe.

Slugs ripped through the sides of the Clipper like hail. One of them struck the pilot. The relief pilot took over, but the controls had been shot away. We started to fall, planes screaming around us like hornets.

Two of the lend-lease men were hit. Senator Corson's secretary screamed, then stopped. Her face had been shot away. We learned later from the Gestapo that there had been a leak in Washington and that it was the high-ranking Naval man whom they were after.

He was the next to die.

All of the time we were falling. It seemed as if we fell for miles. They shot at us as we fell. There was a constant blast of shots through the metal. Most of the shells were tracers. Streams of flame criss-crossed the cabin. The Farmer unfastened his safety belt and bent across me, both hands gripping the sides of the seats until the big veins stood out in his forehead.

"We'll make it, honey," he shouted.

He had to shout to make me hear him.

The water rushed up to meet us. The big plane seemed to level for a moment—then everything blacked out.

I was cold. I was wet. The seat was rocking. I could taste blood on my lips. The Farmer was calling to me. His voice sounded faint and far away.

I opened my eyes. We still were in the plane. We were down but floating on the water. It gurgled in through bullet holes. It gushed in through a hole in the hull.

The Farmer was inflating a life raft and yelling at me to come alive. I looked around the cabin. It was a shambles. There were dead people everywhere.

I closed my eyes again and the Farmer slapped me.

"You've got to make it, Cyn," he shouted. "Come on; Make a try—for Bobby."

He unfastened my safety belt and helped me out of the seat. The hull was tilted almost on its side, and was filling fast. Then I was in the water and the Farmer was pushing me upon a raft.

The planes were still diving overhead, but none of them

strafed the raft. I was to learn why they didn't, later.

Only the two of us made it. The Clipper turned on its side, but floated. Those who hadn't died outright were drowned. All I had on was a dress. I'd lost my coat and my purse in the plane. That's why people thought we were dead. I was to wish we had died.

To the Farmer it was an omen. He was already making new plans. He still had his gun and his gimmick.

The planes swept even lower. There was a phosphorus streak in the water. The Farmer saw it first.

"There's a submarine broaching," he said. "They must have been after some big shot and they wanted to make sure that they got him."

It looked like a black whale with metal scales. A round door in the top of it opened and a man in uniform came out. He was followed by another man, and then a third.

All of them lighted cigarettes. All of them looked at me. Then one of them looked at the Farmer and asked him: *"Amerikaner?"*

The Farmer said he was an American.

One of the other men asked, *"Sprechen sie Deutsch?"*

I started to say that I did, that my *Grossvater* had come from Schleswig Holstein, but the Farmer shook his head.

"No. Neither of us speak German." He pointed at the three-fourths submerged Clipper. "But what the hell is the big idea?"

The three officers nudged each other and rocked with laughter.

"He asks what is the idea?" one of them told the others in German.

The Farmer dropped his voice and told me not to admit to any of these men that I spoke German.

Then one of the officers barked a command down the hole, or hatch, or conning tower, or whatever it is they come out through on a submarine, and a sailor came out on deck and pointed a sub-machine gun at us.

One of the officers made a stiff little bow and said in perfect English, "Believe me, *Fraulein,* we regret this."

"You'd be a fool to shoot us," the Farmer told him. He shrugged. "But then most Heinies are dumb."

Color spread into the officer's cheeks. "What do you mean by that?"

"Just what I said," the Farmer answered. "If you're smart, you'll take us aboard. I was on my way to Berlin when the Luftwaffe shot us down."

"You were on your way to Berlin?" the officer asked, incredulous.

"Berlin or Berchtesgaden," the Farmer said.

"Why?"

I saw the veins in the Farmer's temples beating. He knew that his answer had to be good. "I don't talk to office boys," he said finally. "My business is with Herr Hitler, Herr Himmler, and Herr Goering."

The officer said, "You're crazy."

The Farmer smiled. "You think so? Okay. Go ahead and shoot us."

He fished a soggy cigarette packet from his pocket, stuck a cigarette between his lips, turned his back deliberately and sat down on the roll of the rubber raft.

It was his turning his back and sitting down that got them. They held a hurried consultation.

When it was finished, the one who spoke English demanded:

"Who are you?"

The Farmer gave up trying to light his wet cigarette. "I'm Farmer Dalton," he admitted. "You ever hear of Al Capone and Johnny Torrio?"

"Jawohl." One of the German-speaking officers nodded.

"Well," the Farmer said coldly, "I'm the hood who ran them out of New York. I'm a tough, hard-boiled, two-gun killer. And I've an appointment with Herr Himmler."

The three officers looked at me.

"She is very beautiful," one of them said in German. "I would like to know her."

Another said, "He is lying. He is just trying to save their lives."

The English-speaking officer hesitated. "It could be that he is connected with the Ausland Gestapo. It is a foolish lie, if he is lying. It would but put off their time of dying." He called in English, "You have proof of this appointment with Herr Himmler?"

"Sure," the Farmer sneered. "I've got a great big swastika tattooed on my chest. I had to show it to the F.B.I. before they'd let me on the Clipper."

The officer barked a command. The submarine came up alongside, and they helped us up onto the deck.

"*Gott* help you," he said, "if you're lying." He hesitated, added, "just what is this business of yours with Herr Himmler?"

"Quoting a price for murder," the Farmer told him.

CHAPTER FOUR

From the Files:

TELEPHONE MESSAGE
Case 4—325 Open

Received by Kuenz from Monroe, 24/12/43 at 6:10 A.M.

Get this through to Lieutenant Pierce wherever he is. Tell him to come to Tenth Street Hospital. Miller's story is fantastic but it has the ring of truth. Suggest that you also notify the F.B.I. and ask Deputy Chief Inspector Kelly to put out a radio pick-up on Cynthia Dalton. Five-feet-two, gray-haired, two front teeth missing.

When last seen she was wearing a gray light wool dress and old-fashioned foreign high-button shoes. If Miller's story is true, the Wilhelmstrasse has issued orders to all foreign agents to shoot her on sight. For God's sake send Inspector Kelly or Pierce or someone to the hospital.

POLICE DEPARTMENT
Tel. Typewrite

Telephone
Radio X
Bureau Of Telegraph
Shall Transmit by:
TO; Lieutenant Pierce
Homicide Squad
Real, or alleged, I have put out a pickup on Cynthia Dalton. Drop whatever angle of Vogel case you may be working on and proceed to Miller's bedside, Tenth Street Hospital at once. Will meet you there. Police Stenographer Monroe taking Miller's statement is having heebies.
Signed T. Kelly
Title Dep. Chief Inspector
FORTHWITH X
Rec. at Bur. of Tel. by Lamb T. C. 24/12/4.
6:15 A.M.
Trans. frm Bur. of Tel. by G. Harris
24/12/436:19 A.M.

POLICE DEPARTMENT

Report of Police Steno. Monroe
for—Lieutenant Pierce
Subject—Vogel murder Case 4—325.
(Continuation)
Directly following Miller's dramatic disclosure of Cynthia and Farmer Dalton's rescue by the Nazi submarine, Doctor Vaught insisted that it was necessary to re-dress the severe cuts and contusions that Miller allege that he sustained in the Vogel apartment.

After asking Miller how he had received them and on being told that he had suffered them during the fight he had staged to allow the alleged Cynthia Dalton to escape from the apartment, I phoned Lieutenant Kuenz at H.Q. and asked that he contact either you or Inspector Kelly personally and ask that you come to the hospital. I sincerely believe this is big.

Statement of Larry Miller

Psychopathic Ward
Tenth Street Hospital
(Continuation)
(On being assured by Miller that he was still telling Cynthia Dalton's story, to avoid confusion re party speaking and quotation marks, the remainder of this report, until otherwise noted, is written in the first person as told by the alleged Cynthia Dalton to the prisoner Larry Miller. Initialed M.)

We were landed in Hamburg, not Kiel where the Farmer had told me that he thought the submarine would dock. It wasn't a pleasant trip. The officers eyed me constantly and made remarks about me in German. The Farmer did not know the language.

They had taken the Farmer's gun from him when we had boarded the submarine.

It was a cold gray day when we went ashore in Hamburg. Two Gestapo agents were waiting. One was an Oberleutnant Prager. The other was Herr Doktor Harsch. Both of them were big men, but not as big as the Farmer.

Oberleutnant Prager asked the Farmer, "What's the gimmick? Are things getting so slow in New York that you had to come all this way to get a bellyful of lead?"

"I'll be damned if it isn't Squarehead!" the Farmer answered. "Well, that settles one thing in my mind. I've always wondered what lobby-gows grew into."

Prager raised his fist as if to strike him. He didn't, then.

We were bundled into a car with big swastikas painted on both doors.

Prager seemed to amuse the Farmer. He told me that when he had last seen him he had been a petty hood running errands for Mad Dog Coll.

Hamburg had not yet been bombed. All of the buildings were standing, but what people I could see on the streets looked pinched-faced and very shabby.

We hoped to be taken directly to Berlin. We weren't. The car stopped in front of a dingy brick building and we were hustled inside and into the office of a horse-faced man in uniform whom Prager called Herr Kommandant Dietrich. He seemed to know all about us, and he referred occasionally to a thin dossier of papers on his desk.

"You are Herr Robert Dalton, an American citizen?" he asked the Farmer.

The Farmer said that he was, and the Kommandant looked at me.

"And you are Frau Dalton?"

"I'm Mrs. Dalton," I told him.

He winked at Herr Doktor Harsch. "A tasty tid-bit, eh, Herr Doktor?" he said in German. He glanced at the papers on his desk. "It is difficult to believe that she is thirty-seven. These *Amerikaners* pamper their women."

"Let's get to business," the Farmer said sharply. "I didn't come here for my health."

"No, *mein freund,*" the Kommandant chuckled. "I can believe that."

He nodded at Prager and Harsch.

"I wouldn't!" the Farmer warned them.

They did. Both of them had saps. He had only his fists. They beat him to the floor and kicked him, then pulled him to his feet.

"That was just to limber up your mental muscles," Dietrich told him. "Now talk. Why were you aboard that Clipper? Why did you tell the submarine commander that you had an appointment with Herr Himmler?"

Both of the Farmer's eyes were closed. Blood was trickling from his lips. He spat a mouthful on the floor. "I'll tell Herr Himmler," he said.

Harsch and Prager beat him again.

"As if Herr Himmler would bother with the likes of you," Oberleutnant Prager sneered.

"He got the cablegram which I sent via Rio," the Farmer said doggedly. "I see a copy of it there in the dossier."

Kommandant Dietrich picked up the copy and read the message:

Arriving Germany via Holland. Have important business

matter to discuss. For twenty million dollars well spent the Third Reich still has a chance to win this war.

The Farmer continued, "More, Himmler thought enough of my cablegram to send a punk"—he nodded at Prager—"who knew my reputation, to sit in on the preliminary questioning. Now, do I get to see him or not?"

"You do not," Prager screamed. He took a gun from his pocket and beat at the Farmer with the barrel. "Talk, damn you. Talk! Vas ist your game?"

The Farmer blocked the blows as best he could. "I'll tell that to Himmler," he repeated.

Dietrich stopped the pistol whipping. "You are the father of Lieutenant Robert Dalton, Jr., the young *Amerikaner* aviator, who was executed in Berlin a week ago?"

Weaving on his feet, the Farmer nodded.

"Und still you have a proposition to offer Herr Himmler? A proposition favorable to the Third Reich?"

The Farmer spat out three front teeth. "I have."

The three men looked undecided. Oberleutnant Prager scowled at me. "How about it, Blondie?" he demanded. "What brought the Farmer to Germany?"

When I could stop sobbing I told them what the Farmer had told me to say. "I don't know. The Farmer never tells me his business."

It worked, as the Farmer had said that it would.

"We can kill him, but he won't talk," Prager told the Kommandant in German.

Kommandant Dietrich shrugged.

"Then I guess that all we can do," he replied, "is to patch him up a bit and send them on to Berlin."

(Here, Miller says, the alleged Cynthia Dalton became hysterical and began to scream the words of the nursery rhyme, Three Blind Mice *at the top of her lungs, substituting the word "dead" for blind. He heard the door of the closet in which they were confined being unlocked and feigned unconsciousness! Vogel, Schlacter, Prager, and Harsch came in. Prager shook the alleged Cynthia Dalton roughly, warned*

her that he had a score to settle and that he would cut her throat on the spot unless she quieted down. The threat seemed to calm her. When she stopped screaming they left. She then had a prolonged fit of weeping after which she continued with her story.)

I had imagined Himmler as a big man. He wasn't. He was a slimy little man with thick glasses. I had met his kind before. He looked me over with interest.

"You are either a very brave man or a fool," he told the Farmer when Oberleutnant Prager and Doktor Harsch escorted us into his office. "I admit that you have piqued my curiosity."

The Farmer said as coldly, "I am not a religious man, but I do believe in one of the laws of Moses—an eye for an eye. You fellows shot my son. I want vengeance."

Prager and Harsch drew their guns. Squealing in fear, Herr Himmler pressed a button and four big Storm Troopers entered. I almost laughed. Himmler was as pale as a ghost.

The troopers rushed the Farmer. He picked up the first one to reach him, hurled him at the others, and before Prager or Harsch could trigger, he had torn Prager's gun from his hand and backed up against the wall. "No, by God," he bellowed. *"You're going to listen to me!"*

Himmler's face was paper white. I imagine that he could hear dead men laughing.

"I am listening," he faltered. "But in this matter of your son. I assure you that I had nothing to do with his execution. It was the Leader himself."

"It wasn't Hitler who killed my boy," the Farmer shouted. "It was the authorities back in the States who dragged us into this war."

Himmler's pent-up breath squeaked out like hot air from a penny toy balloon. "Ah," he said. "Ah. I see." His eyes were still on the gun in the Farmer's hand. "I seem to have been under a misapprehension. Just what is it you propose to do?"

"Get even with them!" The Farmer crossed to Himmler's desk and laid his gun down on the blotter. He began to sell his bill of goods. "I have the organization," he told Himmler eagerly. "I have the guts. I have the brains. I've thumbed my nose at Federal men for years and made a fortune." He jerked his head at Prager. "Ask Squarehead here. He knows."

Himmler picked up the gun and looked at Prager. Prager was anxious to reingratiate himself.

"Much of what he says is true," he admitted.

Himmler asked the Farmer, "And what is your plan?"

The Farmer said, "I have a network of underworld machinery at my disposal in America. I can plant destruction in a hundred places at once, and at a single broadcast signal. It will be more effective than an air raid, because it will hit a dozen cities simultaneously."

Himmler's lips formed a thin white line. "And this is what you came here to sell me?"

"Yes, and I want cash on the barrelhead," the Farmer told him. "I can't get things moving without money and there must be some payment to me for the job."

"Why should we trust you?" Himmler asked.

The Farmer shook his head. "I don't expect you to. I'll leave my wife here in Berlin when I go back to do the job. The day that your agents send you word that the job has been completed, you pay the money to her and I'll meet her in some neutral country, say Sweden or Brazil."

Himmler took a perfumed handkerchief from his coat sleeve and patted at his lips. "The man is mad. He is also a fool," he told Doktor Harsch in German. He hesitated, nibbled at the bait. "In your candid opinion, Herr Doktor, is there a possibility that he could accomplish such a thing?"

Harsch answered stiffly in German, "There is a *bare* possibility, Herr Excellency. The *Amerikaners* are a very trusting people and this man is a killer by profession."

"Let's talk English," the Farmer suggested. Himmler pursed his lips and resumed looking me over. "This is a very serious matter," he admitted. "I would have to discuss it with the leader and with Reichsmarshal Goering. Your proposition is fantastic. I doubt your sanity. Still—"

The Farmer looked at me, then looked away quickly. I

knew what he was thinking. We still had a long way to go, but we had climbed one more rung of the ladder. As he had told me before we started:

"Hitler's basic Philosophy is sound. If you tell a big enough lie, tell it loud, and tell it often enough, people will believe you."

CHAPTER FIVE

From the Files:

POLICE DEPARTMENT

Report of Police Steno. Monroe

for—Lieutenant Pierce

Subject—Vogel murder Case 4—325. Open

On Deputy Chief Inspector Kelly's arrival at 6:32 A.M. he read the first pages of this report and interrogated Miller briefly.

Question: You swear this is the truth, Larry? *Answer:* So help me, Inspector.

Q. It's not just a build-up for a Sunday feature story? *A.* It is not.

Q. And this same Oberleutnant Prager and Herr Doktor Harsch that we found in Vogel's apartment are the men whom she told you met her and the Farmer in Hamburg? *A.* That's right. After what had happened in Berchtesgaden they knew that their only chance to save their own necks from the axe was to find her and return her alive to Germany, if possible, and failing that to kill her before she could tell her story to someone who would believe her.

Q. And you believe her? *A.* Implicitly. Her mind was unbalanced by all that she had been through, but she was sane.

Miller then asked Deputy Chief Inspector Kelly if Cynthia Dalton had been located, and on being informed that she had not, expressed a belief that she certainly would not be found alive.

He then, on Deputy Chief Inspector Kelly's insistence,

continued with his statement.

Statement of Larry Miller
Psychopathic Ward
Tenth Street Hospital
(Continuation)

All the time that Cynthia was telling me her story, I could hear Harsch, Prager, Vogel, and Schlacter arguing in the other room. Vogel and Schlacter were for killing her outright and disposing of her body at the same time that they disposed of mine. Prager and Harsch, however, maintained that if they could return her to Berlin alive and have her publicly beheaded, some of the prestige of the Gestapo would be restored when the truth could no longer be kept from the general public. By this I gathered that the Junker generals had taken over but were still using the three dead men as figureheads until their own organization had been perfected.

It would be funny, I thought, if the news broke on this side of the ocean first and all the commentator lads who once had broadcast from the Bundfunk in Berlin, could broadcast from New York to Berlin that *Hitler, Himmler,* and *Goering* were dead.

And they are dead. Cynthia told me—

(At this point I again asked the prisoner if he intended to continue the story the alleged Cynthia Dalton told him. He said that he did. The following therefore, unless otherwise noted, is written in the first person as told by Cynthia Dalton. Initialed M.)

Outside of Himmler's office we were separated. They took me to one prison. They took the Farmer to another. It was a month before I saw him again. That was at the airfield the night that they flew us to Berchtesgaden. His face was a mass of half-healed cuts and bruises. He had a white patch over one eye. He looked as if he had been through hell, but he was grinning.

"It's in the bag, kid," he told me.

I noticed that the Storm Troopers and Gestapo men treated him with respect. Herr Doktor Harsch and Oberleutnant

Prager, who were to follow in a second plane, almost fawned upon him.

"I've been showing the boys how to do it," the Farmer told me from the corner of his mouth. "This superman gag is the nuts. If these guys had been Feds during prohibition, I'd have come out of that owning the White House."

In the plane he told me what had happened. He had been beaten, and third degreed. He had been questioned by Nazi psychologists for days. In the end they were forced to believe that he and I had come to Germany for the sole purpose that he stated. Then they had wanted proof that he could do what he said he could do and he had given it to them.

He asked how they had treated me. I told him fine. It didn't matter. Nothing mattered any more but getting even for Bobby. The Farmer and I had lived our lives.

When we got out of the plane he kissed me. Neither of us spoke. Words weren't necessary.

Maybe Berchtesgaden is pretty. I don't know. It was night when we arrived. The halls leading to the "Presence" were lined with uniformed guards, all of them heavily armed. None of them knew the Farmer. All of them looked at me. I had *willed* myself to be pretty. I *had* to make Hitler like me.

Prager and Harsch showed us to a room to refresh ourselves from the journey. It looked like a movie Queen's boudoir. The furnishings had been used.

Harsch told Prager as they waited for us to change into the evening clothes that had been laid out, *"Der Teppichfresser* has an eye. He and old Fat-belly will go to the mat over this one."

Prager chuckled.

The Farmer asked me what they were saying. I told him that they had called Hitler a carpet-chewer and Goering an old fat-belly.

We had hoped for an intimate conference. It wasn't. The room was almost as large as the main concourse of Grand Central. Herr Hitler sat in a straight-backed chair with Herr Himmler on his left and Reichsmarshal Goering on his right.

Four Nazi secret service men stood behind him. Two more guarded each door. I saw the Farmer's lips turn down. We had been fools to think that they would talk to us alone.

It wasn't to be as simple as we hoped.

Hitler stopped biting his nails when we entered. He nodded curtly to the Farmer as we were presented, but offered me his hand. It was like shaking a cold, wet flounder.

"I am honored, Frau Dalton," he said in German.

I gave him a big, toothy smile.

Goering looked at me, then patted at my bare shoulder. His hand was hot and sticky. He looked like a fat old woman.

Herr Himmler looked down at his hands. All three of them were madmen. They knew how the wind was blowing. They were clutching at straws. The Farmer's proposition was fantastic. They knew it as well as we did. But they were desperate. It *might* work. It might give them a breathing spell. They didn't intend to pay him. Whether it worked or failed it wouldn't cost them a dime.

I saw the Farmer shoot his cuff. I knew that he had a knife. I hoped he'd have time to use it. *We didn't want one. We didn't want two. We wanted three. We owed that much to Bobby.*

Hitler opened the conference himself with a torrent of very bad German. Herr Himmler translated as he spoke.

"The Leader says that you have claimed that you can do and will do a certain thing for a certain stipulated sum of money," he addressed the Farmer.

Sweat beaded on the Farmer's cheeks. "That's right," he admitted.

The Fuehrer fingered some papers on his desk. "In proof of your earnestness in this matter," he continued in his low German, "and to show us the size and the ability of your organization, you have caused certain acts of sabotage to occur in the United States by sending word of your desire to certain assistants."

Herr Himmler translated and the Farmer nodded.

Hitler read from a piece of paper, "On the night of October

twenty-first you caused an incendiary bomb to ignite and demolish the gigantic Queen City Garage, destroying considerable valuable property."

The Farmer had planned that with Tony before we left. He had a right to burn it. It was his own garage. He had planned to give it to Bobby.

Hitler continued, "On the night of October twenty-ninth, by cabling your assistants, you caused fire to completely gut a sixty-four-apartment building near one of the big plane plants, making homeless innumerable defense workers."

I knew then why the Farmer had canceled the insurance on the buildings. This was his party.

Hitler continued to read from the list. It sounded impressive. The Farmer had meant it to. He had wiped us out completely.

"All in all," Herr Hitler concluded, "you have given convincing proof that you may succeed in carrying out more widespread destruction." He extended his hand to the Farmer. "And I pledge you my sacred word that we will abide by our agreement." He forced a nervous smile. "Your wife will remain here at Berchtesgaden under our protection as a hostage to your success. You may be assured that we will treat her well. You will return immediately to Berlin with Oberleutnant Prager and Herr Doktor Harsch, where arrangements will be made to transport you to the States. *Auf Wiedersehen.*"

The Farmer knew that much German. This was dismissal. Things hadn't gone at all as we had planned. We had hoped for a day, a night, an hour.

Herr Himmler smiled thinly. He wasn't a fool. I think he knew. I think he had known all the time. He nodded to two of the secret service men. They stepped on either side of the Farmer. One of them touched his arm.

"I will show you to your plane, Herr Dalton."

The veins on the Farmer's neck stood out like cords. Hitler was less than three feet away. He might as well have been three thousand miles.

There was a guard on both sides of the Farmer. There were

four more in the room. Before he could even touch Hitler, one of them would kill him.

We had failed.

Then the Farmer suddenly relaxed. "Okay. Thanks. That's swell," he told the man. "I'll be seeing all you boys later." He pulled me to him and kissed me. "And I'll be seeing you, baby," he said with a chuckle, "when the Highwayman comes riding."

He left with the two secret service men. An awkward silence followed. I forced myself not to scream. I was alone with three madmen.

The Farmer and I had failed.

The rest of the evening was a blur. I believe that we ate. I know that we drank.

Herr Goering was drunk and getting drunker. He paid considerable attention to me.

Himmler boasted of men he had killed, men who had tried to fool him. I wondered if the Farmer was dead.

Hitler's eyes never left me for a moment as he ranted of his destiny as written in the stars and what he still would do if the Farmer's mad scheme was successful. From time to time he pressed my hand.

The night grew late, and wetter. All three were frankly high. They acted like visiting firemen from the sticks, back home, who were in New York for the first time. I was a Follies girl.

I wondered if a scissors was a weapon. There were scissors in my traveling bag.

Hitler ended the party at three. Goering was almost too drunk to stand but he winked as he told me *Gute Nacht.*

Herr Hitler clutched my hand. "I'll see you again," he whispered in German.

Herr Himmler merely smiled.

I went up to my room. Someone had taken the scissors. I searched the room for a weapon. There wasn't a bottle or piece of glass. There was nothing that I could use.

I went to the window and looked out. The room was on the top floor. A coarse growth of ivy matted the wall. In the distance a pale moon was slowly climbing up over the mountains. I got myself ready for bed and sat down in a chair and cried.

The Farmer and I had failed. Nothing else, *nothing else* mattered.

I heard, or thought I heard, cautious footsteps in the halls, then whirled to face a voice from the window.

"I'm in time?"

The Farmer crawled over the sill. There was a deep cut on his forehead. He had no coat. Blood had clotted on his left shoulder. His face was a fish-belly white, but his eyes were flame.

"Prager and Harsch?" I gasped.

It was an effort for him to speak. He was bleeding internally. "We made a forced landing," he said grimly. "In the mountains."

Over his shoulder I saw that the moon had risen. I had been foolish to be afraid. I had been foolish to think that we had failed. He had told me that he would come when the Highwayman came riding. Remember?

> Look for me by moonlight;
> Watch for me by moonlight;
> I'll come to thee by moonlight; though hell
> should bar the way.

The footsteps in the hallway grew louder. There was a light tap on the door.

The Farmer drew a long thin knife from his shirtsleeve.

"The first of the mice," he said coldly.

(Here, Miller states that Cynthia Dalton again became hysterical and began singing Three Blind Mice, *substituting the word "dead" for "blind." Again the closet door was unlocked and Vogel and Schlacter entered.)*

CHAPTER SIX

Auf Wiedersehen

Beyond the window, the East River was silver in the dawn. A fog horn moaned in the harbor. From near Hell Gate came the sharp jangling of a ship's bell. There was no sound in Miller's room but the hoarse breathing of the men.

Ignoring Dr. Vaughn's protests, Miller sat up in bed and lighted a cigarette. His face was an interlocking mat of cuts and bruises. "Don't worry about me. I feel just fine," he said.

Lieutenant Pierce came in with the morning clatter of breakfast trays that was beginning in the hall. His eyes were tired. "What the hell gives?" he demanded.

Deputy Chief Inspector Kelly handed him the completed pages of Police Stenographer Monroe's report. "Read and keep quiet," he told him. The inspector swung back to Miller. "Keep talking, lad. What did they do to the lass? How much more did she tell you?"

Miller sucked at his cigarette until the tip was a glowing fire. "Not much," he admitted. "She'd come to the end of her rope. Nothing she said after that made sense." He asked Lieutenant Pierce, "You've found her?"

Pierce looked up from Monroe's report and shook his head. "No. But we know she exists. We trailed her, or a woman answering to her description, from Vogel's apartment to the morning boat to Atlantic Highlands."

Kelly tapped Miller's knee, insistent. "Go on." He prompted, "Vogel and Schlacter came into the closet—"

The reporter snuffed out his cigarette. "One of them, Vogel I think, hauled Cynthia to her feet and tried to shake her silent. It was Vogel. Because Schlacter saw that I was conscious and kicked me. Then he told me to get up, that they were getting rid of me."

"I staggered into the other room. Prager and Harsch were sitting at a table, just drunk enough to be nasty. Prager looked at Cynthia and asked Vogel, 'Is she crazy, or just pretending?'"

"Vogel said that he didn't know, and didn't care, but that he wanted her out of his apartment. He said that the Feds were close on his heels and he didn't want a murder rap added to the other charges against him."

Pierce said, without looking up, "That checks. The F.B.I. are up there now."

Inspector Kelly asked Pierce, "And how about that bartender of the Half Moon?"

"He's identified the bodies of Prager and Harsch as the two seamen who shot Morg Baker," the homicide lieutenant said shortly. "I'd like to get a murder just one time in my life that didn't have complications."

Inspector Kelly nudged Miller. "Go on. What happened then?"

Miller lighted a fresh cigarette.

Monroe looked at Pierce and coughed.

"Take it down," Pierce told him. "And then have Miller sign it. It all goes into the files."

Monroe wrote:

POLICE DEPARTMENT

Statement of Larry Miller
Psychopathic Ward
Tenth Street Hospital
(Continuation)

This was it. They had made up their minds to kill us both. Oberleutnant Prager said so.

"Under existing circumstances it is not worth our effort to try to return to Berlin." He poured a drink he didn't need and scowled at me. "How much has she told you?"

"Nothing," I lied.

Harsch got to his feet and knocked me off mine. "You lie. All the time we have been debating I have heard her voice. *You know.*"

I tried to get up. He kicked me. "Okay. So I know," I admitted.

"A shame you can't print it," Schlacter sneered. "But you are leaving here in a barrel. Instead of smearing it in your paper you can tell it to the fishes."

He looked around for approval. No one laughed.

Cynthia lay on the sofa where Vogel had thrown her. She had stopped singing *Three Blind Mice* and was babbling of an appointment that she had with the Farmer and Bobby. Her mind was gone. She was mad.

"How did she get out of Berchtesgaden?" I asked Prager.

He smiled thinly. "She didn't. Harsch and I weren't far behind the Farmer."

Harsch scowled into his empty glass. "We were too far." He hurled the glass at the wall to hear it shatter. *"Gott in Himmel* what a people. Had I lived as long as Prager in this country, I would have known which side to choose."

Cynthia stopped babbling and pointed a finger at him. "I know you," she cried. "You're the man who shot the Farmer in the back." She threw back her head and laughed. It made my hair stand on end to hear her. "But you didn't come soon enough. By then the three mice were dead."

Vogel shook her roughly. "For Gott sake shut up!"

Cynthia whimpered like a frightened child. "I don't like it here. I want to go to the Farmer and Bobby."

She started to get up and Vogel struck her with his fist.

"Shut up and sit down!"

I couldn't take any more. What could I lose? I crossed the room and belted Vogel in the jaw.

His head smacked into the wall like a wet towel.

(Here Lieutenant Pierce interrupted Miller to ask him if he was certain that he had struck Vogel with his fist and not with a chair leg or a hammer. He said that Miller at the most weighed one hundred and thirty pounds while Vogel had weighed over two hundred and Dr. Cole, the medical examiner, had reported that Vogel's jaw had been fractured in six places. Miller insisted that he had struck Vogel with his fist and Lieutenant Pierce told him to continue.)

Miller admitted:

I tried to kill him. I hit him with everything I had. I'd always been fond of Cynthia. It made me half crazy to see what they had done to her.

"She's lost her mind," I told them. "And even if she hadn't, no one would believe her. She can't hurt you any more. Let her go."

Prager cursed me in German, and said something about wading in blood. Vogel picked himself off the floor and began fumbling for his gun.

"This is it," I thought.

I hurled the bottle on the table at the window, trying to break the glass.

Harsch swung at me with a sap. I ducked and took it on the shoulder. Before he could swing again, I belted him into the floor lamp. They crashed to the floor together. It was one of those big, three-way bulbs. It popped like a mortar shell.

Someone, Schlacter I believe, yelled for Vogel to switch on the ceiling lights.

He was too busy shooting at me. Each time he triggered I could see a little feather of orange flame.

The room was dark but for a belt of moonlight that laid a runner across the carpet.

Harsch was still on the floor, tangled in the lamp cord. Then his hand flashed into the moonlight holding a gun. Before he could trigger I stepped on his wrist, tore the gun from his fingers, and stepped back.

On the far side of the room I could hear Prager cursing. "You dumkopfs! We'll have to run for it now! In the name of Gott why did you shoot?"

I fired at his voice. He grunted as the slug smacked into his flesh.

Harsch screamed, "Kill the woman before we go!" He caught at my ankles and I kicked him in the face.

Cynthia was still sitting on the couch. The moonlight streaming through her hair had turned it from gray to gold.

"Get down. Hit the floor!" I shouted.

She got up and moved out of the moonlight and I lost her.

I had my hands filled with Schlacter and Vogel. One was sniping at me. The other swung a sap at my head. The man with the sap was Schlacter. I pushed Harsch's gun in his face and pulled the trigger.

He screamed and fell over Harsch's legs. Harsch cursed him and groped for me. I flipped another quick shot at Vogel—and missed him. I heard the lead shatter a mirror.

Prager was stalking me now. I could see his big bulk as a deeper blob of black against the shadows. The light made him seem even larger than he was. I fired at him and missed. The shot seemed to go right through him. He must have thought I was Vogel. He continued on to where Harsch was still struggling to get up and I saw his arm lift and fall.

Harsch screamed in terror. "This is Harsch, you damn fool. You have killed me. Miller is over there by the wall. He—"

I shot at his voice and got him. "By the wall" were the last words he said.

The darkness must have confused me. Prager's voice came from the far side of the room. It held a note of terror. "Vas ist? To whom are you talking, Hans?"

Vogel moaned from somewhere near the door of the apartment, "I give up. The lights. Turn on the lights. Mein Gott! I am bleeding to death!"

I threw the last shot in Harsch's gun at him. He sobbed and folded up. I heard his body hit a chair and then the floor.

That left me alone with Prager. He had a gun. I didn't. I froze, trying to hold my breath.

Prager was doing the same. Then he decided my shells were gone and stalked me.

I backed from the wall to the sofa, from the sofa to the table, avoiding the runner of moonlight. He got me near the closet door. His bulk rushed out of the darkness. I could feel his hot breath on my face. His fists battered at my body.

I clinched with him and yelled at Cynthia, hoping she was sane enough to understand me. "Run, Cynthia. Run. Get out of here!"

Prager ripped loose a German oath and kneed me, trying to break free. I wrapped my arms around him and held on. Then he suddenly went limp. His breath rattled in his throat.

He said, *"Ach Gott!"* and became a dead weight in my

arms.

When I let go of him, he fell.

Then the hall door opened briefly. There was a light in the hall. Cynthia stood in the doorway. Her lips were moving as if she were talking to someone.

I tried to call to her and couldn't. The words seemed to stick in my throat. Then everything blacked out. The next I knew, Patrolman Weinberg was shaking my shoulder and asking me what the hell had happened.

(Miller said that finished his statement. Deputy Chief Inspector Kelly asked him if he realized that all or any part of it could be used against him. Miller said that he did, but that he had acted throughout in self defense and in defense of Cynthia Dalton, and believed that such homicide as had occurred was justified. His attested signature follows.)

Witnessed:

John R. Vaughn, M.D.

Grace Hopple, R.N.

12/24/43 7:26 A.M.
Tenth Street Hospital
Signed: Larry Miller

Inspector Kelly took back his fountain pen from Miller, slid it into his vest pocket, and asked quietly: "Off the record now, Larry. What you've told us is the truth, the whole truth, and nothing but the truth?"

"So help me, God," Miller told him.

Dr. Vaughn nodded. "It sounds like a straight story to me." He picked the memoranda he had written Pierce from the pile of pages on the table and shredded it thoughtfully. "There's only one point that bothers me. How did she leave Berchtesgaden? How did she get to Lisbon, even with Prager and Harsch on her trail?"

He looked at Miller.

The reporter shook his head. "I don't know," he said frankly.

Lieutenant Pierce lighted a cigar and tapped the statement.

"You going to run the story, Larry?"

Miller broke a cigarette in half, and then in quarters. "How can I?" he demanded. "There are too many holes in it. We haven't positive proof that it's true. There aren't five hundred people in New York who would believe it."

He hesitated, asked, "Where do I stand with you?"

Pierce looked at Kelly and shook his head. "We don't want you. Not if your story is true. And I believe that can be established. You see—"

He broke off as Detective Hollis and Gilman of the Harbor Patrol entered. Hollis reported:

"It was her, all right, Lieutenant. I mean the dame who left the Vogel apartment. We've got six witnesses who saw her board the Atlantic Highland's boat. She was a little, gray-haired old lady in a light gray wool dress and she kept mumbling to herself."

"You picked her up when the boat docked?"

Gilman shook his head. His face and his hat were still wet with spray. "Naw. That's the hell of it, Lieutenant. You see, she gets on in New York all right, but she ain't on the boat when it docks in Highlands."

There was a moment of strained silence.

"You mean she went overside?" Miller asked.

"That's what we think," Hollis told him. "One of the deck hands thought he heard a splash. He sees something gray sweep by. Then the fog settles down again. Whatever it was went out to sea on the tide."

Miller shook his head as if to clear it. "Maybe I am mad. Still, she kept talking of an appointment with the Farmer. It could be that she kept it. She'd said what she came back to say."

"That could be," Pierce admitted. He cleared his throat. "Look, Larry. You didn't stab those four guys, did you?"

"Stab them?" Miller puzzled. He shook his head. "Hell, no."

"And you didn't see a knife in the apartment? Cynthia wasn't carrying one?"

"She could have been," Miller admitted. "But I doubt it."

He demanded, "Why?"

"You didn't kill them," Pierce said quietly. "You shot all four of them, yes. *But none of those wounds were fatal.* You see, I just came from the autopsy. Vogel, Schlacter, Prager, and Harsch all died of identical wounds. Someone who knew his business stabbed all four of them through the heart with a long, thin-bladed knife."

Miller thought of the big bulk he had seen, a man even bigger than Prager, a wraith, a shadow, through whom his shot had passed. He thought of Prager sagging in his arms. He had gasped, *"Ach Gott!"* and died.

Lieutenant Pierce fingered the pages of the statement until he found the page he wanted, then read from it aloud:

"I had been foolish to be afraid. I had been foolish to think that we had failed. He had told me that he would come when the Highwayman came riding. Remember?

"Look for me by moonlight;
Watch for me by moonlight;
I'll come to thee by moonlight, though hell
should bar the way."

He inserted the page in the report and stacked it neatly.

Miller's lips were dry. He licked at them with his tongue.

"Then you think—"

"That it was Cynthia who killed them" Lieutenant Pierce said curtly. "I'm a cop. if it isn't in the book, it couldn't happen." He mopped the perspiration from his forehead, and wrote *Closed* on the report.

Miller shut his eyes. The morning traffic flooding past the window sounded almost like the rumble of presses. He could read the pages as they fell:

Three dead mice ... Hitler, Himmler, and Goering dead ... they all ran after the Farmer's wife ...

Chief Deputy Inspector Kelly cleared his throat. He had a boy in Italy. "If it's so, they can't keep it a secret long. All murder, good or bad, must out. Do you believe that they're dead, Miller?"

Miller wanted to say that he did. He wanted to print it in banners. But he had been a reporter too long.

His hands, like Pierce's, were tied. He had to have proof of his stories.

"I hope so, sincerely," he said. "What do you think?"

A CORPSE FOR CINDERELLA

CHAPTER ONE

A Visit from Dahut

BUSINESS WAS STINKING. I wasn't so good either. I'd been stinking the night before. Opening the office had seemed like a good idea at the time, but I should have been warned by Barnum. There's one born every minute. People *like* to be trimmed. They *want* to believe that Uncle Charlie's ghost can come back through the medium of Mrs. Crystal or Swami Barn Boozle to tell Aunt Minnie how she should invest his insurance. So help me—the things that I could tell you.

I was considering dropping the whole thing and going down to the City Hall to see if I could promote a renewal of my old license without greasing too many palms when Mitzie Faber walked into the office.

Even with a hangover I knew her. She looked just like her picture—only more so. A vivid, pint-sized, brunette with big black eyes, she has what it takes, and all of it in the right places.

I didn't know the old hag with her. She looked like a witch to me. And if the weight that was sagging her reticule wasn't a rod, my name wasn't Tommy Martin.

I got up and offered them chairs. If I'd had some rose petals I'd have sprinkled them on the floor. It was the closest that I had ever been to sixty million dollars.

"Imagine meeting you," I smiled. "Where's the pumpkin coach and six white mice?"

She smiled, but it was wan. "I don't feel much like Cinderella," she admitted. "You are Tommy Martin?"

I admitted that.

The old hag sniffed and dusted off her chair before she sat on it. That was all right with me, it needed dusting. I *didn't* like the way she hauled her reticule around and sat with one hand in it, the muzzle of her gun pointing at my middle.

Miss Faber introduced us. "Auntie, dear, Mr. Martin. Mr. Martin, my aunt, Miss Tabatha White."

Auntie dear said, *"Hmph."*

I said, "Hello."

You've heard of Mitzie Faber. At least you've read about her. She's the kid that was dealing them off the arm in a Sixth Avenue hash-house when they unraveled old man Faber's will and discovered that she was his dead ne'er-do-well brother's child and sole heir to only Morgenthau knows how many millions. Even after death taxes had been paid, she still had sixty million clear. So far as I could see they hadn't spoiled her any.

"You wanted to see me?" I asked. "Perhaps a skeleton in your closet?"

I mean it to be funny. It wasn't. Her black eyes flooded with tears. "I've lots of them," she said quietly. "You see, I have reasons to think I'm a killer. That's why I've come to you. You *must* help me."

I felt my pulse—normal. It must be the hangover, I thought; maybe I only imagine she's here.

Auntie dear sniffed, "Stuff!" she pointed her witch's nose at me. "It's all her imagination. And I want you to tell her, so." She added dryly, "Although I must admit that I see no reason to pay out good money to a charlatan when Doctor Morris has assured us—"

The girl stopped crying. "Damn Doctor Morris. Can he explain the dog I killed? Can he explain the skeletons?"

"There are two men," she told me, "a tall man and a short man with no nose at all. I always see them first. They are Dahut's guards." She stopped to dry her tears on the handkerchief I offered her. "I have come to the right office? You *are* Tommy Martin, the former private investigator, who debunks spiritual fakers—for a fee?"

I admitted that was the general idea of my practice, such as it was.

She took a sheaf of bills from her purse and laid them on my blotter. The top bill was a fifty.

"I'm haunted and I'm cursed," she told me flatly.

Auntie dear admitted, "I found the curse in an old book on Druids in the library." Her thin lips tightened. "I had a mind to burn it then. I wish now that I had."

Mitzie began to cry again. "That wouldn't have helped me," she sobbed. "Don't you understand, Dahut's taken possession of my body. And she's evil. *She* killed the kitten. *She* kissed the dog that died!"

"It was a cocker spaniel," she told me. "Jim gave it to me shortly after Auntie found the curse." She began to cry as if her heart would break. "And when I kissed it on its little nose, it died."

That was enough for me. I pushed the bills back across the desk and poured myself the last inch of rye in the bottle without offering them a drink. I needed it worse than they did.

Auntie dear sniffed, "A drinking man. *Hmph.* I knew it."

Mitzie pleaded, "I know that it sounds fantastic. But you must believe me. Don't you understand? I want to marry Jim. And as things stand, I don't even dare kiss him!"

Auntie dear's thin lips formed a smug line.

"That's one blessing. John would never rest easy in his grave if he knew that his granddaughter was even contemplating marrying a common Broadway gambler."

"You wouldn't mean Jim Ryan?" I asked.

Mitzie nodded.

I pulled the bills back again and put them in my top desk drawer. Ryan had been a friend of mine for years. As gamblers go, he was square. Once in a while he even gave a sucker a break.

"That's different," I told Mitzie. "Let's start over. Who's this Dahut? You don't mean Dahut The White, the wicked princess of Ys?"

She said that she didn't know. This is the story as she told it. Two hundred years before, one of the early Fabers had married a woman named Dahut. Legend had it that she was as beautiful as she was fickle. Her husband had finally killed her in a fit of righteous anger. But before the woman had died she had confessed she was really a witch and cursed the house of Faber. The curse had taken the form of a threat that once in every generation, she would inhabit the body of a Faber woman, and that all whom that woman loved—all whom she kissed would die.

It sounded cockeyed to me. I said so.

Mitzie continued. Shortly after Auntie had found the legend of the curse, a cat whom Mitzie had loved had died. Then a parade of skeletons had begun to haunt her dreams. Each night they paraded her bedroom, pointing bony, accusing fingers, muzzling her with cold noses from which the flesh had long since rotted. Next had come the dog episode.

I told her I thought I could help her. Hell, I had the whole picture right then. "You run along home," I told her. "I'll throw a few things in a bag and drive up in a few hours."

When they had gone, I considered the case. It looked fairly simple from where I sat. Someone wanted money and they wanted it damn bad. I reached for the phone to call Ryan and the office door opened again. I didn't know either man, but Mitzie had described them. One was tall with a vacant stare. The other one was a dwarf with a fold of flesh where his nose should have been.

"You're Martin?" the dwarf asked. His voice sounded like a rusty file rasping over steel.

I said that I was.

The tall lad crossed the office and sat down on one corner of my desk. There was no expression in his eyes or in his voice. "About those women who just left." I asked what about them, sharply, and he leaned over mechanically and tapped my chest. "You are not to take the case, understand? Dahut does not will it so."

I tried to get up and the dwarf pushed me back in my chair.

"You will be well paid." He laid a sheaf of bills on my desk.

I looked at the spot where his nose should have been and shuddered. There were only two slits in the flesh. "Look," I protested. "Enough is enough. What's the gimmick? Who's in back of this freak show?"

The dwarf hit me then, not hard, but hard enough. Then he pulled back his coat lapel and showed me the handle of a gun. "You see that?"

I'm not blind. I told him what he could do with it. "I don't know who the hell you are, or what this is all about," I stormed, "but—" And that was as far as I got.

The tall lad reached across the desk and slugged me with a fist like a ten pound sledge. It sent me sprawling to the floor. Before I could get to my feet, the dwarf kicked me in the belly, then slugged me with his gun barrel, while the tall lad came from behind my desk and informed me in his monotone:

"This is just a warning. See? The next time you will die!"

This wasn't real. It couldn't be. I got to my knees and said, "Boo!"

Then the dwarf's gun barrel landed again and all three of us exploded in a tangled mess of bony arms, legs, and skulls, that suddenly flew and became jabbering skeletons that ringed me in a circle.

I tried to break through and couldn't. A scantily dressed woman who looked a lot like Mitzie except that she was blond, was clinging to my arm.

"I am Dahut," she whispered. "Remember me, darling? Kiss me!"

I could feel her breath hot on my cheeks, her lips searching for mine—then everything blacked out . . .

CHAPTER TWO

Kiss of Death

IT WAS COLD on the floor of my office. It was also hard. I got up and looked at myself in the mirror. Real or fancied, the noseless dwarf and the tall lad had done a job on me. One of my eyes was completely closed; the other was narrowed to a slit. My nose would never look the same.

The sheaf of bills on my desk was gone. So was the sheaf that I had slipped into my drawer. That made me feel some better. When a lad plays with the supernatural as much as I do, he sometimes gets screwy ideas. But the lads who had slugged me were flesh; spirits haven't much use for money.

I got Ryan on the phone. "This is Martin," I told him. "How do you stand with Mitzie Faber?"

He wanted to know what I meant by how did he stand and I laid as much as I knew on the line, including a description of the two lads.

Even over the phone, his voice sounded strange. "Look. I'm headed up there tonight," he said. "Why don't I stop by for you, Tommy? Say, in about thirty minutes?"

That was fine with me. I wanted to talk to him before I saw Mitzie again. I spent most of the thirty minutes in the back room of the little drug store downstairs. When Benny got through with the arnica and plaster, I looked almost as bad as the dwarf.

Ryan pulled up with the first of the rain. A big man in his early forties, gray at the temples, with a wisp of mustache, he looked more like an old stock heavy than a big-time Broadway gambler.

He greeted me glumly. "This is one hell of a mess."

I asked if he was telling me. He pointed the car up the Hudson toward the old gray stone heap near Crum Elbow that old Israel Faber had built in 1880. I rolled up the window on my side of the car as it started to rain harder.

After we had passed Yonkers, traffic began to thin out. I described the dwarf and the tall lad and asked him if he could place them.

He told me no, then added, "I mean I don't know their names or who they're hooding for. But they dropped in on me one night about two months ago and spent almost half an hour telling me what would happen if I persisted in marrying

Mitzie."

"They mentioned this Dahut?" I asked.

He nodded. "Yeah. But that's a lot of bunk as far as I'm concerned. And so is this kiss of death stuff. But it puts me on a spot."

I asked him what he meant.

"I like the kid," he told me. "Maybe I even love her. I don't know. I liked her when she was slinging hash in a greasy spoon." He sighed. "But this marriage is all her idea. And she only thinks she loves me. I can tell. She likes to have me around because she knows that she can depend on me, because she knows that I don't give a damn if she has sixty million dollars or minus sixty cents."

That was something to chew over.

"What she really needs," Ryan concluded, "is some husky young punk like you. Hell. I'm ten years too old for her. And as soon as I can get her squared around so that she isn't afraid of her shadow, I'm going to tell her so."

I chewed on that for another five miles.

He broke the silence. "About this kiss-of-death stuff. And those skeletons that she sees. How do you explain that?"

I told him that I didn't, that I'd have to know more about the show before I could go to work. The first thing I wanted to know was who controlled her money.

"She does," he said flatly.

"And her will leaves it to whom?"

"Me," he told me tight-lipped.

I said, "I see." I did, with reservations.

That changed the whole picture again. There could be some good reason why he couldn't marry her. And few men with an in like that could bring themselves to kick sixty million dollars in the nose.

"And after you?" I asked.

"Her Aunt Tabatha," he told me. "She was her mother's sister. And from what I hear, she took it hard when all the money went to Mitzie."

I remembered a name that Auntie dear had mentioned.

"And this Doctor Morris?"

Ryan chuckled. I was to know why later.

"He's been with the family for years," he dismissed him. "He was old Faber's doctor. I wouldn't let him lance a boil, but I like him."

I said, "Now this puppy you gave her?"

"There wasn't a mark on it," he said tight lipped. "A moment before it had been raising hell like puppies do. Then Mitzie kissed it on the nose and it died."

I looked sideways at him. His forehead was wet with sweat.

"I saw it happen," he said quietly. "There was no one near the dog. She kissed it, put it back on the floor, and it died."

I jeered, "Don't give me that. You said yourself that this kiss-of-death was bunk."

"I like to think so," he said. "But I don't like anything that I can't figure out."

He had me there, so I shut up.

Rain was falling in torrents and a high wind had sprung up to twist and lash the naked branches of the trees by the time that we swung off the highway into the Faber lane. The house itself, a little gray stone shack of some forty or fifty rooms, had been built on a high bank overlooking the Hudson. Turrets, and towers and battlements loomed.

The butler who met us at the door was almost as old as the house. He looked like a walking corpse and his skin was the color of parchment. "I was with Mr. Faber for many years," he told me grimly.

I didn't doubt that in the least.

Ryan led the way into the living room and introduced me to Morris. I liked the little fat man on sight. He might have been straight out of Dickens, with his tight stand-up wing collar and stock. Only thing modern about him was a long, ebony cigarette holder and his breezy conversation.

He shook my hand as if I'd just carried a message to Eisenhower. "This is a pleasure, Martin. Positively. I've read of you, of course. And you're doing a splendid work—

splendid. Ghosts! Spirits! Bah! When a man's dead, he's dead, and that's an end to it."

"Even to Dahut?" I grinned

"Even to Dahut," he agreed. He poured cocktails from a frosted shaker. "But for heavens sake snap Mitzie out of it before the child goes mad."

Ryan said, "But the puppy—"

"Tut-tush. And also tish!" the little fat doctor snorted. "Puppies die every day. It is all in her head, I tell you. If Tabatha hadn't found that fool curse, none of this would have happened. The whole thing is imagination."

I doubted that. The dwarf without any nose and the tall zombie who had slugged me weren't the products of anyone's mind. I asked if he happened to have a copy of the alleged curse, and he got the original from a drawer.

It was written much as Mitzie had told it, in a fine Spencerian hand. The paper was properly aged and yellowed. It was either authentic or well-faked.

"If only Tabatha hadn't found it," Morris moaned.

He got to his feet and I saw that Auntie dear and Mitzie were coming down the stairs. Mitzie looked like a dream in sea-green chiffon. But evening clothes failed to improve Auntie. Her dress was black and so was her face when she saw me and Ryan. She simpered like a school girl, though, when Morris told her that she looked charming.

Mitzie came straight to me and fingered the tape on my face. "They hurt you. They came to you after we left?"

"Who came?" the old lady asked sharply.

"Dahut's guards," Mitzie told her bleakly.

"Stuff!" The old lady sniffed. "There are no such persons. Likely he fell over a bottle."

I told her I'd done that, too, but that if these were bottles, both of them had had legs, also automatics. "But they weren't spooks," I assured Mitzie. "They looked like a pair of freaks who'd escaped from some sideshow."

She said, "Oh," as if she wanted to believe me, then rested her hand on Ryan's arm, and smiled, "Hello, Jim."

I could see what Ryan meant. She liked him—trusted him.

She thought she was in love with him, but she wasn't. He was just a sturdy oak against which she had grown accustomed to leaning.

She started to turn away and Ryan caught her arm. I give the guy credit for nerve. Sweat was beading his forehead. He didn't know. His hunch was all against it. But he was spreading his cards for a showdown, not for his sake, but hers.

"Look, little honey," he told her. "Don't be like that. We're settling this kiss-of-death stuff once and for all, right now."

She fought against him. "No!"

He said, "Yes," and pulled her to him. Then he tilted her chin with one hand and kissed her soundly on the lips. Her arms slid over his shoulders and she returned his kiss hungrily.

For some reason I felt jealous. And I wasn't thinking of her money.

When Ryan released her, her face was flushed and she was half-laughing, half-crying. "I guess that proves it," he grinned.

"Yes, sir," Doctor Morris beamed.

Mitzie turned to me, still flushed, as the old butler announced from the doorway that dinner was served. "I guess that you and Jim," she smiled, "will have to take me in together. I—" She stopped short at the look on my face and swung back to Jim Ryan.

He didn't look right to me. Sweat was standing en his forehead in big drops. His jaws were working. He hunched his shoulders.

Mitzie clapped the back of her hand to her mouth. Then she screamed.

It was an effort for Ryan to talk. "I will be damned," he muttered, took one step toward the girl, and crumpled slowly to the carpet.

Doctor Morris straightened from his study of the body and stuffed a cigarette into his long ebony holder with fingers that shook slightly. "It's beyond me," he admitted. "The man *can't* be dead. But he is."

I looked across the hall to where Mitzie sat sobbing in a chair. She had kissed Ryan. None of the rest of us had been within ten feet of him. Maybe this Dahut had something!

Ragan, the old butler, read my mind. "She's evil," he told me. "Evil. She carries death like a typhoid carrier. The dead dance for her every night. I've heard them."

"There's some logical explanation," Doctor Morris insisted.

"There has to be," I told him. I asked him to call the police and went in to talk to Mitzie. The old witch in the black evening gown sat glowering beside her.

"Well—?" she demanded of me.

I told her that Ryan was dead.

"I killed him," Mitzie wailed.

I told her that I doubted that very much. But I wondered what I'd tell the law. They seldom believe in the supernatural. And if a post-mortem proved that Ryan had been poisoned, the timing had been perfect.

I thought of something that I had meant to ask before. "Who was with you when the puppy died?"

She told me Ryan, her Aunt Tabatha, Doctor Morris, and Ragan.

"And who fed the puppy?" I asked.

Auntie dear snapped, "I did. But don't think you can prove that I poisoned him."

I asked, "Do you trust Ragan?"

"Implicitly," Mitzie sobbed.

Auntie dear changed her tune. "It was Dahut who killed the puppy," she told me with conviction. "It was Dahut who killed Mr. Ryan." She sniffed. "And if you're going to earn your fee, you had better drive her out of Mitzie before one of the rest of us dies."

I could see a jury rolling over that one.

Mitzie sank deeper in her chair. "I can't stand it anymore. I wish that I were dead."

I started to pull her to her feet and shake some sense into her, then changed my mind. Her 'I wish that I were dead' had rung a bell. If my original line of reasoning was correct, someone else wished it, too. But whoever wanted her out of the way couldn't kill her. There is a law against such self-help. You can't profit by the estate of anyone whom you have murdered.

I walked back into the hall. Doctor Morris, his face florid, was still shouting 'Operator' into the phone. He turned to me, worried. "I can't get the operator. Either the storm has blown down the wire, or else it has been cut."

I said it probably had been cut and asked him if he had a gun that he could lend me. He said that he had and went up-stairs. When he came down again he had a pearl-gripped, gold-inlaid, .45 Colt in his hand. I stuck it into my belt.

"If anything should happen to Mitzie," I asked him, "who gets the Faber money?"

"Tabatha," he answered promptly.

"And if anything should happen to her—?"

That stumped him. "I really wouldn't know," he told me, "unless it would be her two half-brothers." He puckered his forehead in a frown. "And that brings up a legal point. *Can the insane inherit?*"

I said, "Insane?" and he told me that although she seldom mentioned them, he believed they were in a New Hampshire asylum. I asked him to describe them. He said that he was sorry but he hadn't the least idea what they looked like.

I thought of the noseless dwarf and the tall zombie and shuddered. If they weren't crazy, I was. "You stay with Mitzie," I told him. "Get her to bed and give her an opiate."

"You're going for the law?"

"Not in this storm," I told him. "I'm just going to see if the wire is cut. If it is, we're in for more murder. This is the showdown."

The storm was worse than I thought. It swept me off the porch into some dripping bushes. I used them to pull myself hand-over-hand back to the house wall.

I paused to get my breath. Through a crack in the shutter I could see the dynamic little doctor talking earnestly to Mitz-ie, She objected but went with him, leaning heavily on his arm. Auntie dear sat where she was.

I studied her features for some trace of a resemblance to the two hoods who had slugged me in my office, but could find none. Still, Morris had said they were half-brothers and she had openly objected to Mitzie coming to me. More, now that Ryan was dead, if anything happened to Mitzie, the Faber millions came to her.

She got up and left the room. I plowed on through the wet underbrush to the end of the phone wire. It had been cut.

I found the loose end of the wire and followed it back to the house. Even by pulling it as taut as I could, a ten-foot gap of wire was missing. What was done to stop this little murder-chain, I would have to do myself.

It was then the light flashed over my head as a shutter banged open in the wind and was promptly pulled in again. I leaned out from the house and looked up. A faint light was showing in a room on the top floor. Whether it was an attic room or not, I couldn't tell because of the false battlements and towers. But I knew—or thought that I knew—all that I needed to know.

I made my way back to the front door and fought it open. Ragan hadn't moved. "What was that," I asked him, "that you told me about the dead dancing in the attic?"

"It happens almost every night, sir," he assured me. "That's why the staff left. You see, they're afraid of the dead. I'm not."

The second floor was dark but light showed under a door. As I reached the stairhead, Doctor Morris came out of the room.

"You stay with Mitzie," I told him. "The wire was cut and I'm going on up to the attic."

I admired the man's nerve. "You'd better take a torch. Wait. I'll get you Mitzie's."

He pressed it into my hand and I climbed another flight. Eight doors led off a hall. I opened them one by one. What I wanted wasn't there. This was the deserted staff-quarters.

Then I saw the door I did want, set back in an alcove, up one stair. I picked the lock.

A rush of stale, damp air swept out. The stairs were covered with dust but the dust had been recently disturbed. Here and there I could see a drop of water.

I kicked off my shoes and walked up. Old fashioned camel-humped trunks and outworn furniture stood desolately against the eaves. At the far end of the attic, around one of the numerous bends caused by the turrets and towers, I could see a faint light.

I cocked the Colt and walked toward it. All of my cases ended the same. The spiritual manifestations all turned out to be humans with a financial axe to grind. Something rolled underneath my foot. I stooped and felt it. It was the leg bone of a skeleton. More, the skeleton was intact.

I walked on slowly and a pair of bony arms reached out of the dark and wrapped themselves around my neck. I fought back an impulse to scream. The skeleton was wired. The boys were putting on a good show.

Then I rounded the bend and saw them, both staring blankly into the dark behind me. "Hold it just as you are, boys," I called.

Neither one moved a muscle.

The noseless dwarf walked slowly towards me now. "It's Martin," he whispered to the zombie. "Dahut has sent him to us. It must be that she wants to kiss him."

The tall zombie kept pace with him. "Let's take him to her," he droned. "He can dance with the others tonight."

They kept coming and I fired. At that distance, I couldn't miss; I didn't. I saw the slug dust the left breast of the noseless dwarf but it didn't even slow him.

"You can't kill us, Martin!" he said wearily.

"We're dead," the tall zombie intoned.

I shot again and again, watching each slug as it smacked. But for all the good that they did, I might have been throwing confetti instead of .45's. Both men kept right on coming, their hands reaching for me now. A sudden stench of the grave rose rank and rotten around me.

Someone screamed. I wondered who it was.

I screamed again and knew. Cold hands reached for my

throat. I tried to fight them off, and couldn't. Then something solid smashed out of the dark and Dahut was whispering in my ear and trying to kiss me . . .

CHAPTER THREE

Out of the Grave

I WAS COLD AND WET. It was difficult to breath. I tried to raise my hand to brush away whatever was pressing against my mouth and couldn't. A weight seemed to seal my eyes. Then I smelled the wet earth.

The noseless dwarf and the tall zombie had buried me alive.

I lay fighting panic. *This was it.* Then I heard the beat of rain over my head. A trickle of water ran into my mouth, gagging me. I choked and the earth moved slightly. They hadn't buried me very deep and the rain soaked clods of earth with which I had been covered were allowing enough air to seep through to keep me from being smothered.

I tensed my muscles and heaved. The dirt gave some but not much. In blind panic I tried again and popped through the surface.

I had been left for dead. Dahut was slipping.

A hundred yards from the main house, the old carriage house loomed against the night.

There were three cars, including Ryan's, in the converted stalls. The second floor, as I had hoped, was still half-filled with musty hay. I forked some down the stairs to form a train to the gas tank of Ryan's car. Then I lit of wisp with my lighter and tossed it into a corner. On my way out I kicked the feedline lose from Ryan's tank.

Sure it was arson. So what? I was up against a killer and a smart one. Those few minutes in the grave had worked wonders with my brain. The whole thing was so clear now I could have drawn a blueprint.

Outside again, I studied Mitzie's window. There was a

small false balcony outside of one of the windows and the wall was covered with ivy. It wouldn't hold me, but a near-by down-spout would.

Through the shutters, I could see the bed. One bare arm thrown over her head, Mitzie was asleep, her lips twitching nervously. Auntie dear sat in a rocker in the shadows.

Under the bed, I could see the pumps that Mitzie had been wearing with the sea-green chiffon. The sole of one of them was wet and stained with mud. I was willing to bet that somewhere in a tool shed was a muddy shovel with her fingerprints on the handle.

I opened the shutter with my pen-knife and started to raise the window when the nose-less dwarf walked into the room. He tip-toed toward the night stand by the bed and laid down three objects I couldn't distinguish.

He beckoned toward the door. The tall lad came in with a wire that became taut when he fastened the loose end in his hand on a hook screwed into the wall. The other end was out of sight in the hall.

He flipped a long black cord along the floor as if to make certain that it was clear, then both men took up stations, one on each side of the bed. I slid up the window gently.

Auntie dear still sat in the shadows. I couldn't see her face. Noseless shook Mitzie.

She sat up, drugged, and clapped the back of her hand to her mouth, her face contorted with fear. She had seen these men before.

"No!" she pleaded. "No!"

"They come, Dahut," the tall lad said in his monotone. "They come to do you honor, the dead whom you have killed."

She screamed, "Tommy! Mr. Martin!"

"You forget, Dahut," the dwarf whispered respectfully, "that Mr. Martin is dead." He picked up her wet slipper and showed her the muddy sole. "Don't you remember—you killed him. We helped you to bury him."

She moaned, "Oh, no. *No!*"

Then the skeletons came in. To the half drugged, frightened girl it must have been impressive. From where I sat it was funny. The wired skeletons ran on a pulley, manipulated by the cords that the tall lad held in his hands. They bowed and scraped and jibbered. There were two men, two women, and a dog. Then Jim Ryan's skeleton—wearing Ryan's clothes—came into the room.

Mitzie screamed and fainted.

The tall lad gathered the skeletons in one arm, unhooked the wire and disappeared into the hall, grinning at Noseless, "That ought to do it."

The old witch in the chair didn't stir. The dwarf poured water in Mitzie's face, then chafed her wrists until she sat up and moaned.

"At your command, Dahut," he said. "I have brought you the things you asked for." He pointed to the night table. I could see what the objects were now. They were a vial marked poison, a straight-edged razor and a gun. "Come to us, Dahut," he pleaded. "Flee from the law that will pound on the door."

He strode from the room and closed the door. As I watched, the bolt slid shut, worked by the old pin hole and string trick. Either way, they couldn't lose. They had her now.

Whimpering like a frightened child, Mitzie studied the objects on the table, then reached for the vial of poison. Then I came in.

"Put that back and don't be frightened," I called softly. "This is Tommy Martin."

She turned her big eyes on me. "You're dead. They told me that you were dead."

"They've told you a lot of things." I said. I dropped the vial of poison and the razor in my pocket and thumbed the safety off the gun. "If you killed yourself, that was fine. If you didn't, you were still framed for murder. And once you trotted out Dahut and the dancing skeletons, any sane jury would send you to the chair for *pretending* you were crazy."

"What are you doing in Mitzie's room?"

It was Auntie dear's voice from the shadows. As I turned a
.32 slug burned my ear. I'd forgotten she carried a rod. The
old lady shot again before I could cross the room and slap
the gun out of her hand.

The small slug burning through my shoulder, I unbolted
the door and stepped into the hall. Noseless and the tall lad
were standing at the head of the stairs.

"You boys ready for the next rubber?" I called.

The tall lad's face wasn't blank now. "You're dead!" he
screamed. "We buried you."

"But not deep enough," I told him.

Noseless went into his act. He walked towards me slowly,
rasping, "Put down that gun. You can't kill us. We're dead!"

He slipped his own gun from his holster and I let him have
it right between the eyes. "You're damn right, you are," I
told him.

These slugs weren't confetti. They slapped him into the
wall, his brains dribbling down.

The tall lad said, "Oh, God!" and let one fly that creased
my cheek.

I gave him the remaining three slugs. He took off backwards down the stairs.

Ragan called, "Fire!" from the floor above. "Fire!" The
carriage house is on fire!"

A door down the hallway opened and Doctor Morris
popped out, rubbing his eyes. "What were those shots? And
where in the world did you go to?"

"Hell," I told him shortly. I motioned him into Mitzie's
room. "Get in there and stay with Auntie until the law gets
here."

He was wearing an old-fashioned, long white night gown
stuffed into a pair of pants. "The law?'" he repeated blankly.
"I thought that the wires were down."

I told him I'd fixed that. Just then the fire reached Ryan's
tank and the car blew up with a dull boom that blasted the
carriage house windows. I hoped that it wouldn't be long.

Morris walked briskly into the room and his face lighted in
comprehension. "Tabatha. You." He pointed an accusing

finger. "How could you, Tabatha? It's been you behind this all. You and your insane brothers!"

The old lady looked as if he had slapped her. Tears leaped to her eyes. "Oh, Doctor—Vincent—how could you?"

"You have two brothers?" I asked Auntie.

She nodded, her eyes wet with tears. "But it isn't true what Vincent says. Both boys have been dead for years."

"And still are," I assured her. "I don't know where Morris got his freaks. That can come out at his trial. I do know that he was gambling for sixty million."

The fat little man's face turned purple. "You're crazy! I have no interest in the Faber estate. I am only a salaried retainer."

I told him what I thought of that.

Ragan poked his head in the door. "There are two dead men in the hall," he whispered.

I whispered back, "I killed 'em."

I told the story as I saw it, Mitzie listening wide-eyed. "Dahut was all Doc's idea," I told her. "So were the skeletons. He filled you up with dope, under the pretense of giving you a sedative, every time he wanted to stage a séance. Then his stooges did the rest. He didn't want you to marry Ryan. That would have cost him money. That's why he invented this kiss-of-death stuff. That's why his stooges tried to buy me off. He knew that a blind man would see through his scheme, and I did. It was Doc who killed both the puppy and Ryan."

A second car exploded in the carriage house. In the distance a fire siren wailed faintly.

The little man was certain of himself. "And I suppose," he sneered, "that you can tell us how I killed them." He was fumbling with his cigarette holder as he spoke. When he had finished he put it in his lips.

I slapped it out of his mouth. "Sure I can. But not if you puff one of those darts into me." I picked up the ebony tube. It was a cleverly constructed miniature blow gun with a needle-sized dart inserted. "You were the first to reach the dog;

you were the first to reach Ryan. And you didn't want to feel their pulses. *You knew they were dead. You wanted to recover your dart.* I can't name the poison you used but there are several that would work. We'll know after the post-mortem."

Auntie dear wiped at her eyes. "I can't believe it."

"You should," I said. "Because if anything went wrong, he planned to blame the whole thing on you. He drugged you the same as Mitzie, only heavier. That's why you never saw Mopey or Dopey or the skeletons."

Mitzie had shaken off some of the effects of the drugs. "But why should Doctor Morris want me to die?" she puzzled. "If I did, the Faber millions wouldn't go to him. They would go to Aunt Tabatha."

I said, "Exactly. And Doc had Auntie dear wound right around his finger. I asked her if that wasn't right and so help me, the old witch blushed.

"We—er—had an 'understanding'," she admitted.

Heavy fists began to bang the downstairs door. I told Ragan to admit the law. They could carry it on from here.

"But how did you know?" Morris asked.

"I should have known," I told him, "when I saw you kiss Auntie dear's hand and tell her she looked charming."

The old witch looked at me blackly. "I wish I'd shot you through the head," she said. Then she began to cry.

"But I really knew," I told Morris, "when slugs from a Colt .45 wouldn't stop those hoods up in the attic. *You wanted me to get it, so you loaded the gun with blanks.*"

By now I'd lost a lot of blood. I sat down on the bed and Mitzie sobbed. "You're wounded."

I told her that I had been shot worse and lived and that if she would pay me the rest of my fee that I would write off Auntie dear's mistaken slug to profit and loss.

She said, "Oh," tight-lipped, and picked up a checkbook. "And just how much more?"

I told her one kiss like the one she'd given Ryan, and she said "Oh," again, and kissed me. But it wasn't like Ryan's.

All in all, it turned out pretty well. Getting a girl like Mitzie was a pretty big fee for what I'd done. It's even worth being related to Auntie!

CLAWS OF THE HELL-CAT

CHAPTER ONE

The Voice That Wasn't There

IT BEGAN AS A MISSING WIFE CASE. Harry had taken the call, and all that I knew about it was what he had told me over the phone. That wasn't much. Shortly after two o'clock a lad who had introduced himself as the confidential secretary of a Mr. J.E. Hare had phoned and asked if the Mercer Agency would send one of its best men to 247 Willow Road on a matter of some importance. He had refused to give any further information other than to say that any reasonable fee would be paid promptly, whether or not the agency decided to accept the assignment.

Being in the Willow Road neighborhood, I had dropped over. I didn't know J.E. Hare. But, whoever he was, he had money. Number 247 was a sizeable stone house set well back from the road on a plot of landscaped ground, enclosed by a six foot high wall well-iced with broken glass. The wrought iron gate was large and impressive, but open. I drove in up a tree-lined drive, still trying to place the name. The only Hare whom I could remember had been a hall-caste hare-lipped barman in Sydney.

The house was in keeping with the grounds. A white-haired butler let me in, one eyebrow cocked in disapproval. Even after he had heard my story he didn't seem any too certain that I had come in the right door.

"You say your name is Mercer? A private agency man?"

"I have my own agency," I corrected.

He waved the point aside as immaterial. "And according to

your story," he accused, "someone representing himself as Mr. Hare's confidential secretary phoned your office an hour or so ago and asked yon to call on a matter of some importance."

I didn't like his tone and said so. "Look," I told him. "I don't know about you or your boss. But I have things to do. Now either take me to this J.E. Hare or tell me that he has changed his mind and doesn't want to see me."

He hesitated.

"Okay. That's that," I said. I opened the door and started down the stairs.

"No. Please, Mr. Mercer," he stopped me. "I didn't mean to be rude. Just a moment, sis. I am certain that Mr. Hare will see you."

He walked down the hall past the stairs leading to the second floor and disappeared through a pair of carved doors before I could tell him to skip it. I debated taking a powder, and didn't.

I lit a cigarette and sat down in a high-backed chair facing a suit of armor. I had waited perhaps three minutes when a good looking pint-sized blonde pointed her sweater down the stairs and saw me. She stopped in front of my chair, exuding an aura of friendliness and gin.

"Hello, man."

I said, "Hello." The kid wasn't over eighteen but she was so high that she was having trouble in getting her eyes to focus. More, though I couldn't call her name, her face was vaguely familiar.

"You want a drink?" she asked me.

I told her thanks but that it was a little early for me. Then she wanted to know if I had a cigarette.

I offered her one, and lighted it for her. "I like you," she confided. "Who are you? What's your name?"

I said that my name was Matt Mercer. Then she wanted to know what I did. I told her, and she stopped being friendly.

"Oh. A private detective, eh? What sort of a jam is she in now? Gwen wants some money, I suppose."

Not knowing who Gwen was I didn't say anything.

The kid was wearing a dirndl skirt with patch pockets. She fished a silver flask out of one of them and tilted it to her lips without taking her eyes from my face. She suddenly wasn't pretty anymore. Her eyes were too old.

"And he'll send it," she continued. "My money." She nipped at the flask again, quick tears plowing through her make-up. "My money! Understand! Well, give her this for me!"

Before I could duck she slapped me with the flask and ran on back upstairs. I got to my feet spitting blood.

"What the hell!"

The butler reappeared and handed me a folded handkerchief. "Forgive her, please, Mr. Mercer. Miss Hope is not herself. She has been under considerable strain. I am certain that you understand."

I didn't. But I was too busy looking in one of the hall mirrors to make certain that my bridge work was still intact to press the point.

"Look," I asked him, "who is Gwen? Why should she want money? And on what page of whose rotogravure have I seen that young refugee from a Keeley cure who just belted me?"

He smiled thinly. "I am afraid that you are being—facetious, sir. This way, if you please."

I followed him down the hall, mentally cursing Harry.

Hare was a big, good-looking, man, almost too good looking, in a theatrical sort of way. He was sitting behind a desk in a book-lined library. But he wasn't reading a book. He was riffling a deck of cards. In his middle or late forties, all he needed was a pink coat to climb into one of the English hunting prints on the wall and begin yipping "Tally Ho."

His eyes were a cold, steel-grey. His accent was strictly old school tie. "I don't believe, Mr. Mercer," he said coldly, "that I have had the pleasure of meeting you before. To what do I owe this honor?"

He continued to riffle the cards. I started to get hot under the collar—then I began to smell a rat. "You are J.E. Hare?" I asked him. "And this is 247 Willow Road?"

"I am, and it is." The red showing above his collar began to spread into his cheeks. "Come, come. Speak up! Stop beating about the bush. Never mind repeating your story about someone sending for you." He got to his feet and leaned on his knuckles. "Speak, damn you! What kind of a mess is Gwen in this time? And how much is it going to cost me?"

I looked from him to the butler. The white haired lad was holding a gun. "Just a precaution," he informed me.

"Sit down and cool off," I told Hare. "Believe it or not, I'm leveling. Someone did phone my office representing himself to be your confidential secretary."

"You talked to him?" he demanded.

I shook my head. "No. But Harry, my partner, did." I sat down on the edge of his desk. "Now suppose you climb off your Tally Ho and tell me what this is all about."

Hare looked at the white haired lad. He studied my face and put his gun away. "If I may venture an opinion, sir," he told Hare, "I am very much inclined to believe him."

Hare spread his hands in a futile gesture. "But that fails to make sense, Dawson. Why should anyone phone Mr. Mercer and say that I wished to see him, unless—" He thought better of what he had been about to say, sat back in his chair again and resumed his shuffling of the cards.

"Unless what?" I demanded.

Dawson wet his lips. "Unless you are to be used as a contact, sir," he told me. "Frankly, I thought you were. That's why I acted as I did."

Hare glanced up and said sharply, "Tell him nothing. It's none of his affair. And I won't pay him a ruddy dime."

I said that was fine with me and got up to go.

"No. Please." Dawson begged me. He turned to Hare. "We can't go on like this much longer, sir. We don't know the customs of the country. And we either have to confide in someone, or call in the police."

Hare said he was damned if he would. But Dawson insisted, and he did. It wasn't an unusual story. I had heard it before, but never in the confiscatory brackets. Hare told it in beautiful English but broken down into every day language it

summed up Mrs. Hare as a dipsomaniac and a tramp of the
first water whom he wished to God that he had never met.

I could have kicked myself for not having recognized the
little blonde. Gwen was the much-married Cordovan heir and
the little blonde was Hope Cordovan, her daughter, who had
been dragged from one count to no account all over Europe,
Gwen having married some six or seven times. And before
Hare was well started I recalled reading some six months
before that Gwen's last marriage had been to an English
colonel of Lancers whom she had met in India.

I looked at Hare as he talked. If he had ever had any illu-
sions, he had lost them.

"And then about a fortnight ago," he continued, "after
promising on her word of honor that she would abstain from
drinking I returned to find her gone. She phoned around
midnight, intoxicated, and informed me that she was staying
in town with," it was a bitter pill for him to swallow, "with a
friend." Color crept into his face. "I told her that I'd bloody
well divorce her if she did, and that if she had no considera-
tion for me she might at least think of her daughter. She
called me a name and hung up." He continued to handle the
cards. "And that is the last that we've heard from her, directly."

I asked, "And indirectly?"

He hesitated briefly, took a scrap of paper from his wallet
and tossed it across the desk. Typed on a piece of Chalmer's
House stationery were the words:

Dear Johnny:
    Please cash a check for ten thousand and give same to a
messenger whom I will send. In one of my usual messes.
Believe me, dear, I am sorry. Your repentant—

                                                    Gwen

The name was scrawled in a shaky hand. I handed it back
to Hare. "So—?"

He said, "So I cashed a check as she requested. After all, it is Gwen's money, rather she holds it in trust for her daughter. But no messenger has appeared. And the note came three days ago."

Dawson looked at me hopefully. "Just what do you think that we ought to do, sir? Should we inform the police?"

"I'll be damned if I know," I admitted. I nodded at the note. "The signature is hers?"

Hare nodded. "Indubitably." Color crept into his cheeks again. "But I'm in a bit of a spot you know. I'm damned if I do, and damned if I don't."

I said that I understood.

Dawson suggested. "Perhaps, sir, as long as you have your own private agency, and have been called into the case so mysteriously, you might consider a commission."

I agreed that I might. But I made it plain. "No key-hole peeping. I'm not that kind of a detective."

Hare thawed completely for the first time. "Thought not. You don't look like that kind of a Johnny. See it now. Former soldier, what?"

"Yeah. But that's neither here nor there," I told him. "Just what would you want me to do?"

"Find Gwen," he told me promptly. "If she is in need of assistance, aid her. If she is merely being indiscreet—" he shrugged. "Then that would be my problem."

I said that was fair enough and named a fee. He said it was damned high, but he'd pay it.

"And you wouldn't have any idea," I asked in parting, "who might have called my office and posed as your secretary."

Hare shook his head. "I would not."

And that was that. I put his check in my pocket and Dawson led me past the armor to the door. "You will do your best, sir."

"I'll do what I can," I told him. "How about phone calls? Have there been any for Mrs. Hare since she has been gone?"

He shook his head. "None out of her social circles."

He said that he would have to consult Miss Hope and

would mail a detailed list to my office.

"Okay. I'll keep in touch," I told him.

I walked on down the steps to my car. It could be just one of those things. Or it could be a snatch. But if some mob had intended to use me as a contact, something had slipped up somewhere. Or it could be that now that I knew the facts I'd be contacted.

I was. But not in the way that I expected. The slug smashed through the rear window of the car, fanned my cheek, and starred the windshield. I slipped out from under the wheel, my own gun in my hand. The shot had been fired from the wrought iron gate. But whoever had fired it was gone. On the far side of the wall a motor roared into high and quickly faded out.

Dawson opened the house door.

"Did you see him?" I demanded.

"Only his back, sir," he told me. "But I gathered that he was short and stocky. And I *know* that he dropped his hat."

I whipped the car in a sharp U turn and drove up the drive to the gate. The hat was lying on the grass. It was an expensive Stetson with the initials J.C. stamped in gold on the sweat band. I picked it up.

Joe Connors was the only short stocky hood I knew whose initials were J.C. and kidnapping wasn't his line. He was a gambler. More, it had been fifteen years since Joe had done his own shooting. I tossed the hat into the car. It wasn't much. But it at least was a starting point.

CHAPTER TWO

Trail of the Golden Girl

TOMMY MORRIS, one of Connors' boys, was shooting the breeze with a pert young redhead under the marquee of the Parisian. He nodded cordially as I parked. I asked him if Joe was inside. He said that he was and went on talking. If my showing up worried him any, he was concealing it well. And he was Connor's driver.

Maybe you know the Parisian, maybe not. It is a big brick former warehouse that looks like a barn but isn't. It's one of Chicago's show clubs and a must on every visiting fireman's list. The prices are high but the food and the liquor are good, and the floor show is young and stripped as far as the moral code will allow. Joe's real take came, however, from the games on the second floor.

It was only later afternoon so the tables were still stacked, a porter was mopping, and a line of cuties in rompers were rehearsing a new routine. I watched them for a moment then asked the porter if he knew where I could find Connors.

He said that he thought that he was upstairs.

"Just go up?" I asked, off hand.

"No, sir," he informed me. "So far as I know, sir, Mr. Connors been upstairs all afternoon."

At night when the games are running the stairway is lousy with guards. There is even an electric eye to spot any concealed gun that the boys may overlook. But both the eye and the guards were off.

Lord and Mason, two more of Connors' boys were drinking their breakfast at the gambler's bar. A short, stocky man, in his middle forties, Connors, in his shirt sleeves, was examining a warped roulette wheel, peering down critically.

"What's the matter? Won't the gimmick work?" I asked him.

He looked up sore, then saw who I was and held out his hand, smiling, "No damn it, it won't. It gives the sucker an even break. Long time no see, Matt. I thought I told you and Sherry to drop around anytime and the check would be on me."

I shook hands saying that he had, but that the twins hadn't been very well and we had been spending our evenings at home. Then he saw the hat in my hook, looked at the initial in the sweatband, mildly puzzled, and wanted to know what I was doing with one of his hats.

If it was an act, it was good.

"I'm back-tracking the hat," I told him. "Believe it or not,

Joe, somebody wearing this Kelly just took a shot at me."

I hadn't raised my voice but Lord and Mason heard me. They sauntered up with their hands in their coat pockets. I unbuttoned my coat.

Connors shook his head. "Cut it out. What's the idea, Matt? Trying to hang something on me?"

"No. I'm just stating a fact," I told him.

"And this shooting happened where?"

I gave him the Willow Road address, adding, "At present the residence of one J.E. Hare who would seem to be Gwen Cordovan's current husband."

Connors said, "Ah," very softly and looked at Mason.

The hood took a note book from his pocket and thumbed through it. "That's the address," he told Connors. "You get in to see the dame, Mercer?"

I said that was none of his business, that I had called regarding a hat. He told me not to get so wise. I said I wasn't getting wise.

"You're always too wise," he sneered. "And too tough. You think that just because you used to be a top kick of marines that you can get away with murder." He took hold of my coat lapel. "Look. I asked you a question."

I told him to take his hands off me. He didn't. So I hit him. He caromed off a craps table, spitting curses, and making motions toward his gun. But he didn't quite dare to pull it. Mine was in my hand.

"Cut it out, both of you," Connors roared.

"The hat, remember?" I said. "Also the butler who sees the shooting tells me that the lad with the gun is inclined to be short and stocky."

Connors nodded. "That's me. I mean I describe that way. But I haven't left the joint all afternoon. And I can prove it. Besides, why should I shoot you?"

I admitted I didn't know. It didn't seem logical that he had. "Okay," I agreed. "So it wasn't you—who flipped that shot at me. Then who did? Why was he wearing your hat? And what the hell's eating on Mason?"

Connors shook his head. "I'll pass on the first two. But the answer to number three is a rubber check for five grand."

According to his story, Gwen, who through the years and at times when she wasn't in Europe had pushed a lot of money across his tables, had gone broke bucking the tiger and had asked Mason, who was running the game, to okay a check.

Mason told me, "And like a fool, I did. Now all I get is a run-a-round from a butler who tries to tell me that she isn't home. Look. I'll ask nice this time. Did you, or didn't you, see her?"

I told him that I had not. "And she cashed this check in here, when?"

"The night before last," he said.

"She was alone?"

"No," he said. "She was not. She was with a good-looking young Army sergeant."

"And she was wearing how much jewelry?"

"Quite a bit, as I recall," he said.

"And this Army sergeant was a big tall guy?"

Mason shook his head. "No. He was short and stocky. He—" He stopped short and looked at me.

"I wouldn't know," I told him. "I'm not the deducing type. All I can do is ask questions."

Connors accused, "She's missing. The butler wasn't stalling. She hasn't been home since then."

"Since long before," I told him. I used his phone to call Hare and asked him if he knew that his wife had given the Parisian a bum check for five grand.

When he stopped swearing he wanted to know when it was dated. I told him the night of the day that he had received her note.

Then he asked the same question I had.

"No," I was forced to tell him. "She was with a young Army sergeant. I'm going to check on that angle now. But before I do I wonder if you can tell me just which of her jewelry she was wearing on the day that she left home."

He said most likely her daughter could. There was a brief pause before she came to the phone. She sounded almost sober.

"Hello, man. I'm sorry I hit you. Honest!"

I said that was all right and explained what I wanted of her. She said that her mother had been wearing a pair of five carat diamond earrings, her engagement ring, and a diamond and emerald bracelet.

"Worth how much?" I asked.

She said that she hadn't the least idea but that there were forty-four diamonds and eight emeralds in the bracelet. She didn't sound very worried. "Something has happened to mother?"

I told her I didn't know. Then Hare came back on the wire and asked what I thought that he had better do about the check. I said that if I was him I would pay it and he said he would.

"And you've still no idea who phoned you?" he asked me in conclusion.

"I have not," I told him.

He hung up without even mentioning the shooting in front of the house. I figured at the time that it was one of two things. Either Dawson hadn't told him, or he didn't give a damn.

Both Connors and Mason insisted on buying me a drink for straightening out the check matter. I had a couple, meanwhile asking Mason for the young sergeant's description. He said the lad had been short and stocky, in his twenties, and handsome in a rural sort of way. "Why? You think he bumped her for her rocks?"

I shrugged and let it go at that.

"They were both high as a kite," he admitted. "And if she hadn't dropped so much dough in here, I'd never have taken the chance." He shook his head. "Those society dames. Fifteen years she's been coming in here. Almost always with a different guy, and every year she looks younger."

Lord made a crack about hormones and Connors wanted to know if I knew how many times Gwen Cordovan had been married. I said that I thought that it was six times, finished my drink and walked on out of the club.

It was still hot and still light. Tommy was still talking to the redhead. A few feet down the street a bunch of little girls, their short summer dresses swishing with their movements, were jumping rope and playing sky-blue on the sidewalk with a well-mashed tin can for a lagger. Hearing them laughing and screaming, like kids will, made me think of Gwen Cordovan's kid. Hope had probably never jumped rope or played sky-blue in her life. All that she's ever had was money.

I drove down the outer drive to Randolph, cut west into the Loop toward the office, then changed my mind and drove on down Michigan to the Chalmers House. Gwen's note had been written on its paper. And it might be that Al Gandy could give me a line on Gwen and the young sergeant.

I had a feeling that I was overlooking something. Then I suddenly realized what it was. Gwen was holding the Cordovan money in trust for Hope. It amounted to plenty of millions. Yet a five thousand dollar check of hers had bounced while Hare could write a good one for ten thousand. He could even offer to pay off the one that she had given to Connors.

More, Hope had said:

" '*And he'll send it. My money! My money! Understand! Well, give her this for me.*' "

I changed my mind again, swung back through the Loop and parked in front of the *Times-Examiner*. Harry Gold was on the city desk.

"I'm chiseling information," I told him. "Give with the loquacious. What do you know about this J.E. Hare whom Gwen Cordovan married in Cairo?"

"Not a damn thing," he admitted, "except that he was a colonel, or former colonel, of Lancers or something." He eyed me shrewdly. "Why?"

I said that I was interested in knowing if he had money of his own.

Gold shook his head. "I doubt that very much. But neither has Gwen for that matter. The way that I understand it, she only holds the Cordovan money in trust until Hope is nineteen."

I asked, "And if something should happen to Gwen, and then a little later to the kid?"

He was all ears. "What could happen? Why should anything happen?"

I said, "This is off the record," and told the whole story to date, concluding, "I'm not overly bright. I admit it. I don't think 'em out. I wear 'em down. But the whole case smells fishy to me. How come Hare can write checks on the kid's money while those that Gwen writes bounces?"

He thought a moment, picked up his phone and asked Miss Hanelley, the society page editor, if she would mind stepping out to his desk for a moment. He asked her the same question.

She smiled, "That's really very simple. As I understand it, due to her unfortunate, shall we say, craving, in the past Gwen Cordovan has always run through whatever sum of money has been allotted her by the estate long before the end of the year. So, as I understand it, as a curb and a protection, the board of trustees representing the estate asked Colonel Hare if he would mind administering the allowance. I hear he agreed, unwillingly." She smiled wryly. "But I doubt he'll be bothered much longer. I understand they are parting."

I asked her if she had heard of Gwen's latest romance with a youthful Army sergeant. She said she had not and wanted to know his name. When I said that I didn't know it, she lost interest.

I persisted. "One more question, Miss Hanelley. What if something should happen to Gwen before she and Hare separate?"

She said, "The money still goes to Hope. And that will be in the next few weeks, on the day that she is nineteen."

"But if something should happen to her before she is nineteen?"

"The money reverts to the Cordovan foundation."

"And Hare wouldn't get a dime?"

She shook her head. "Not a dime."

"Thanks. It was just a thought I had."

I called the office from the lobby. Harry said he was just locking up and wanted to know how I made out at 247 Willow Road. I briefed the case for him and asked if the party who had represented himself as Hare's confidential secretary had contacted the office again.

He said he had not but pointed out an angle that I hadn't known. The caller had said he was calling from River Forest, the suburb in which Hare lived. It was possible that he had been. If so, it was a toll call and the phone company would have a record of the station from which it had been made. I told him to find out what he could and if he turned up anything interesting in the next few minutes to call me at the Chalmers House. Otherwise I would be back at the office inside of half an hour.

The Chalmers House is old but still expensive and caters to the General-Grant-slept-here set. I found Al Gandy parked in back of a potted palm watching a group of slim young things trip in and out of the elevator. "Women ain't what they used to be, Matt," he complained. "There ain't enough meat on their bones to set a tasty table. Let alone, one a guy would hate to get up from."

I said that I hadn't noticed any of the younger male generation pushing back their chairs and asked if the Chalmers House had had the honor of housing Mrs. J.E. Hare, nee the Countess Anzelli, nee Gwen Cordovan lately.

The question seemed to amuse him. "So they've got you bird dogging, eh?"

I pointed out that I had asked him a question.

"No. Not since before the war," he told me. "Although, while I didn't see it myself, according to one of the barmen, Gwen raised quite a scene in there a few nights ago. In fact they had to ask her to leave."

He went in with me to talk to the barman. The lad was still sore about the incident and voluble.

"So she has money," he expounded. "In my book she still is a tramp. And I am very nice about it, Mr. Mercer. 'If you will excuse me, lady,' I tell her, real polite, 'I think that you have enough and I will not be able to serve you a drink.' "

"Then what happened?" I asked him.

"Then she calls me names no lady ought to know. And so does the young punk who is with her. In fact they are very nasty and I am forced to ask them to leave."

I asked him if he was certain that the woman was Gwen Cordovan.

He grinned, "I should be. She tells me fifty times she is Mrs. Hare, the former Gwen Cordovan, that she has enough money to buy the joint if she wants, and that she has been drinking for too many years not to know when she has enough."

"That dame," Al swore admiringly. "What I wouldn't give for her stomach."

I could have made a wise crack, but I didn't. I had a hunch I'd run into pay dirt. "Her escort didn't identify himself?" I asked the barman.

He shook his head. "Not to me personally. But he is a sergeant. Mrs. Hare called him Mike—" He fished in a drawer in the back-bar. "And after they are gone, the porter finds this on the floor where Mrs. Hare drops her purse and spills everything all over, she is that tight."

He handed me an envelope with the typed address—

Sergeant Michael Slavin
6331 S. Shannon St.
Chicago, Illinois

"That's back of the yards," Al said.

There wasn't any letter in the envelope. There was some small hard object. I spilled it out on my palm. It was an earring with a broken screw bob.

"Costume stuff," the barman explained. "But I spoke to the night manager and he said we had better keep it in case she should call around."

Al picked it out of my palm. "That's good paste, if it is paste."

"It isn't. It's a diamond," I told him. "It's one of a pair of five carat stones that her daughter said Gwen was wearing."

Al laid it gently on the bar as if he was afraid he might break it.

I copied the Shannon Street address and walked out to my car. The missing woman had been gone two weeks. It was certain she had been on a binge. It was equally certain, as Hare had put it, that she had been indiscreet.

When she had left home she had been wearing a fortune in diamonds. Still, she had passed a bad check at the Parisian. She had sent her husband a note, stating that she was in a mess, and had asked him to raise ten grand. To my mind that suggested collusion on her part with a party or parties unknown.

But the fact that the ten grand had never been called for made it another matter. Then, there were the phone call and the shot at me to consider. They suggested a snatch with the snatchers losing their nerve, which happens in three cases out of five.

I checked the time element. She had been in the Parisian on a Wednesday. It had been later that same night that she had made a scene in the Chalmers House. Both times she had been accompanied by a stocky young Army sergeant— whose name, it would seem, was Slavin. That had been three days before. No one had seen her or heard from her since.

I let in my clutch and rolled south. I wanted to talk to Mike Slavin. But even then I was beginning to grow a suspicion that by the time that I caught up to the convivial Mrs. Hare she would be beyond any assistance I could give her.

CHAPTER THREE

Where's the Blood?

IT WAS STILL LIGHT but growing dark when I drove under a Belt Line viaduct and parked in front of 6331 South Shannon. The kids had begun to gather under the street lights,

some just talking and some playing games. The group nearest me were playing shinny with a tin can and some taped-up
sticks. It was the closest that most of them would ever get to
golf, or to hockey for that matter. It was that kind of neighborhood.

The house was as poor as the street. An unpainted frame
story-and-a-half affair, it was set closer to the alley than the
street and leaned wearily toward its nearest neighbor.

Almost every house in the block had service stars in their
windows, some of them three and four. It was also that kind
of neighborhood, poor but fiercely proud.

As I slipped out from in back of the wheel a grimy faced
ten year old demanded, "How's about watching your car for
you mister?"

I flipped him half a buck, grinning, "Sure. Why not?"

He grinned back like the dirty-faced little pirate he was. So
it was a hold-up. So what? Even poor kids like spending
money. I knew. I'd been born on a similar street.

There was a light in the rear of the house but none in the
front room. I unbuttoned my coat and banged the door.

A broad-faced young Slav opened it. "Yeah? And what do
you want?" he asked coldly.

I said that I wanted to see Mike Slavin.

He hesitated briefly, said, "Come in."

The hallway was hot and stuffy and smelled of cabbage
and fried pork. An open door leading off the hall disclosed a
tumbled unmade bed. If Gwen Cordovan was there, it was
one hell of a love nest.

My guide told me, "Right back this way."

I followed him down the hall into a lighted kitchen. Three
men were sitting around a table drinking beer and playing
cards. None of them were in uniform. None of them answered Slavin's description.

"This guy wants to see Mike," the lad who had let me in
told them. "For my money, he's the dick Mike warned us
might show up."

I didn't get the set-up. The faces of the men at the table had
been friendly. Now all three stood up. The oldest, a big man

with a drooping white mustache, tapped my chest with a finger the size of a pistol barrel.

"You detective?" he asked me in broken English.

I said I was.

He poked at my chest again. "You come make trouble for Mike?"

I was getting fed up with the case. "Look. I'll make plenty of trouble," I warned him, "and that damn fast! Start talking. Where is Mike holding Mrs. Hare?"

That struck one of the lads as funny. He bent over slapping at his thigh. "He wants to know where Mike is holding Mrs. Hare."

His small eyes ugly over his high cheek bones, the old man started to poke at my chest again. I slapped his hand away. And that was a mistake on my part. His other hand came up like a counter-balance and belted me into the table. It broke under my weight and I landed in a foam of beer and cards, trying to get at my gun and not being very successful because all four of them had jumped me.

"Kill him! Kill the dirty shamus!" the lad who had let me in screamed.

All of them did their best. The only thing that saved me was the fact that they all were so eager to kill me that they were kicking each other's shins as often as they were me. More, killing is a science. I was an expert at it. And they were amateurs.

I rolled, knocking one of the lads off his feet, snatched a chair by a leg and beat a clear path around me long enough to get at my gun.

The old man was shouting, "Mike good boy. You no make him trouble." He began a hefty kick, saw the gun in my hand and stood on one foot poised like a dancer. The blood drained from his cheeks like someone had pulled a stopper. "No shoot, please," he begged. "Just get mad for Mike. No mean to hurt you."

The other three lads fell back against the wall, their palms raised shoulder high.

"Of course not," I told the old man. "I'll bet you tell that to all your corpses." I put a slug into the baseboard to whet their memories, then turned my gun on the lad who had let me in. "What's your name?"

"Tom," he gulped. "Tom Slavin. I'm Mike's brother."

"Where's Mike?"

"In Valdaro," he said promptly. "Valdaro, Indiana. You know, the place where you get married."

I asked why the hell he was going there.

He said, "Getting married."

That one stumped me for a moment. "He's getting married? To whom?"

The kid stared at me wide-eyed. "I—you said—we thought that her family sent you. That's why we—" he stopped, embarrassed, and not a little frightened. "Look. You ain't a city dick, are you, mister?"

There is a difference. I let him sweat while I turned over to the new joker I had drawn. Gwen knew that Hare was through with her. She had no inhibitions, and few morals. And drunks, especially women, did do the damndest things.

"Stand right where you are," I told them. "Don't move an inch." I walked on through the house, looking in every room. It was poor but it wasn't as dirty as I had thought, just the untidy house men keep. And there were no signs of any woman having been there recently.

I walked back out to the kitchen. None of them had moved. They didn't look like kidnapers to me. I pointed my gun at the old man. "What do you do, Stanislaus?"

"Please, mister. I Stepan," he told me. "I Mike's father." He made a vague gesture at the night. "Twenty years I work in Yards. No ever make trouble before." I'll be damned if he didn't start crying. "Just want Mike be happy."

I put my gun away. "All right. Let's have it," I said. "Someone tell me the story."

Their eyes elected Tom. He managed to be coherent with some prompting from the old man and the other two lads, who turned out to be neighbors. Boiled down, Mike Slavin, home on furlough, enroute to the Pacific, had met a swell queen, 'society stuff', as he called it, in one of the better Loop bars. Having only two weeks of his furlough left and being no fool, Mike had made hay while his star was shining. She was, he said, a widow with plenty of money. That afternoon he had brought her home to meet his father and his brother and had told them that he and Mrs. Hare were on their way to Valdaro, Indiana, to be married.

"This was when, what time?" I asked.

He told me about six-thirty. I looked at my watch. I'd only missed them by an hour, I found.

"She told us," Tom concluded, "that her family didn't want her to get married again. And that if a private dick should show we should rough him up a bit to discourage him from butting in on her and Mike's honeymoon." He spread his hands in a futile gesture. "So—we tried to."

I reached for a cigarette I didn't have. One of my eyes was swollen shut. Sherry had told me that morning that the Elberts were coming for dinner. I knew what she'd say when I called her. What Hare might want to say, he couldn't say over the phone.

"Okay. So it's a mistake all around," I admitted. "But just to make sure, one of you describe the blushing bride."

The old man said she was blonde and pretty and very jolly. She had insisted they all have a drink.

I said, "I'll bet."

Tom whistled. "And did she have diamonds. A green and diamond bracelet and rings, and a big diamond in one ear."

The old man followed me to the door. "My Mike. He don't do anything wrong?"

"I don't think so, Dad."

I didn't. The whole onus, as I saw it, was on Gwen. She had wanted Slavin. She'd got him. But the case was sour in my mouth. Two and two still made three. Nothing I had heard yet explained the phone call, the star in my windshield, or Joe Connors' hat.

There was a phone booth in the saloon on the corner. Hare answered the phone himself. I gave him what I had, concluding, "So I guess it's up to you."

He rose considerably in my estimation. Instead of cursing, all that he said was, "Well, she's rather jumped the barrier this time."

I said that it would seem so.

"No, please, Mercer," he stopped me from hanging up. "Name your own fee, but carry on. Locate Gwen. Hold her by force if necessary. Then call me back again. I'll be waiting at the phone."

I reminded him of our bargain.

He said, with quiet dignity, "I'm not asking you to peep in key-holes. I'm not even thinking of that aspect of the case. I'm thinking of her daughter. The poor child has gone through Hades. She mustn't be hurt anymore. All that I am asking you to do is to locate Gwen and phone me. I'll start for wherever you are immediately. With me on the scene, whether this bigamous marriage has taken place, or not, I may be able to run a bluff, pass it off as a joke or something, and thus keep it out of the papers. In her right mind and sober, Gwen wouldn't do this to Hope."

I thought of the kid's wistful, "Hello, man," and her equally wistful, "I like you." Then, there was the phone call, the slug, the hat. Walking out on the case now would be like leaving in the middle of a picture.

"Okay. I'll play chump," I agreed. "But it's going to cost you plenty. And you stay close to your phone all night."

He promised that he would. I bought a drink and a handful of slugs. But something was screwy somewhere. I didn't have much better luck with the slugs. Harry wasn't at the office or in any of the bars that he supported.

I used the next to the last slug to call Sherry, told her I was on a case, that she and the Elberts had better sit down if the roast was still fit to eat, and to expect me when she saw me.

Having quite an extensive vocabulary, and having squandered quite a few points on the roast, she taught the operator a few new words and banged up the receiver.

I called her back with my last slug. "But you still love me?"

She smacked a kiss into the mouthpiece, said, "Yes, God help me!" and banged up her receiver again.

I walked out chuckling and built up the dirty-faced little pirate's movie and ice cream fund by another half a dollar, asking as an after-thought, "You wouldn't happen to remember the kind of a car that Mike Slavin was driving?"

He wanted to know if Mike was in trouble. When I said that he wasn't, he grinned.

"Then he was driving a maroon Buick club coupe with white side-wall tires."

The trail wasn't hard to follow. I drove the most direct route to Valdaro, stopping from time to time at likely looking roadhouses that I thought might have attracted Gwen's eager eye.

The other side of Deep River a barman said, "Yeah. They was in here. They have three drinks apiece." He winked. "Then they remember where they're headed and blow out in a cloud of dust."

I wasn't hooting. Even the farms were few and far between.

It was after nine when I reached Valdaro. The town hall and the license bureau were closed but one of the group of men gassing in front of the building admitted to being the town clerk and wanted to know what he could for me.

I told him that I was supposed to be the best man for a young friend of mine but it was beginning to look like I'd missed him. He wanted to know his name.

"Sergeant Mike Slavin," I told him.

He let go a stream of tobacco. "He and Miss Hare got a license not over ten minutes ago." He peered across the street at a pair of lighted windows over a hardware store. "I think they went over to Charlie's. He's one of our J.P. s," he explained.

I started to cross the street, stopped as one of the men asked him, "That the couple in the red Buick, the sergeant and the blonde with all the diamonds?"

The clerk said that was the couple he meant.

The other lad told me, "Then you've missed 'em all right,

Mister. I was just locking up when they came down. Both of them were pretty high. Him especially. But she slid in back of the wheel and seemed to be doing okay." He pointed up the street. "The last I seen of them, they was headed out 45 toward Michigan City."

I debated calling Hare and asking him if he knew if Gwen had a cottage in the dune country and decided to let it wait, figuring that if I hadn't caught up with them by then that I could check the angle from Michigan City.

But I didn't get that far. Five minutes out of town a state patrol car whipped by me with its siren wailing. I found out why a half mile down the road.

There was a sharp right curve over a culvert, but the red Buick hadn't made it. It had plowed off the road instead, torn up dirt for fifty yards and smacked into a big oak so hard that the whole front end had telescoped.

As I parked, the white-faced farmer who had called the law was telling the young trooper, "They must have been going about ninety."

"You see it, chum?" I asked.

He said he had not. His story was that he had heard the squeal of brakes and the crash, while he was at the far end of the curve and had stepped on his own gas only to have another car roar around the curve almost forcing him off the road. "They was racing, I think," he said.

Gwen had been thrown from the car. There was a nasty gash on her forehead that exposed white bone. She was dead. The sergeant was still in the telescoped mess.

The trooper gagged and turned away. "And sudden death."

Other cars were stopping now. A fat little Doc Yak who had been one of the group in front of the Valdaro Town Hall and who turned out to be the local coroner, waddled up to the wreck, glanced at the dead woman perfunctorily and waggled the dead lad's head. *"Hmm.* It's the couple that Charlie just married. Fractured skull and a broken neck. Both died instantly. Damn this drunken driving." He picked his jury before the gathering crowd. "You, Sam, Bill, Jake—"

When he asked if anyone knew them I told the same lie that I had told in Valdaro, adding that if he would impound the jewels and what money they might have on them, as a favor to their families, I would see that their bodies were taken back to Chicago.

So they were dead. I was still working for Hare. I had some influence in Chicago, but none in Indiana. And I wanted the bodies out of sight before some smart Joe of a reporter put booze, the name Hare, and the diamonds, together—and came up with the correct score.

He said that was impossible, that their bodies would have to be claimed by their next of kin and that I'd better try to get them on the phone.

So I'd made my try and failed. Both Hare and her kid would have to face it. I got the robe from my car, started to cover Gwen's body, looked at the wound in her head again and suddenly realized why it looked so strange.

There wasn't any blood.

The wound was deep enough to have killed her. But it hadn't. I lifted one of her arms unobtrusively, then laid it back on the ground, the short hairs on my neck tingling.

She had reputedly been driving the car. She and Slavin had reputedly been married only a few minutes before. A dozen witnesses, including the coroner, could testify to that fact. But something was screwy somewhere. Rigor mortis was setting in.

She had been dead when the car had crashed. She had been dead for at least an hour.

CHAPTER FOUR

The Knife-Cure for Harry

THE HOTEL WAS JUST NORTH of the Loop, not far from the Parisian. Gold sat on the edge of his bed nipping at the pint I'd brought with me, but not enjoying it very much. "You're crazy, Matt. Either crazy or drunk."

"Yeah? I just came from Valdaro," I told him. "Call your sheet and check. One of the press services should have the flash on the wire by now."

He did as I requested, hung up, sobered. "They're dead all right," he admitted. "But that doesn't prove it was murder. The local coroner has signed a certificate reading accidental death."

I pounded, "For God's sake use your head, man. I don't care how many people swear she was driving the car. I don't care how many saw them getting married. Gwen Cordovan was dead when the car smacked into that tree. She had been dead long enough for rigor mortis to set in."

He wanted to know what I wanted him to do about it.

I said, "Get in touch with your Cairo correspondent. Get him on the overseas phone. Find out all you can about this J.E. Hare and I'll pay all the charges."

"You've talked to Hare?" he asked.

I said I had. "I phoned him from Valdaro to come down and get the body. That's why I'm here."

Gold looked at me sharply.

"I haven't a thing," I admitted. "He's treated me fine so far. He is taking it like a man. But . . . " I tried to explain, and couldn't. It was one of those things you feel but can't put into words. It's a tilt of an eyebrow, a gesture, a tone of voice, the way that a man shuffles cards.

I got up to go. "And find out especially, if you can, if he had a wife or a girl friend who somewhat resembled Gwen."

He swore, "By God—!"

"There could have been a switch," I pointed out. "She could have been in that other car that almost ran down the farmer."

"And young Slavin—?"

"Duped, drunk, or doped," I told him.

He reached for the phone on his night table, hesitated. "But Hare can't possibly inherit. Miss Hanelley told us this afternoon that according to the estate—"

I admitted, "That's an angle I've still got to hurdle. And I can be all wet. Maybe the gremlins did it. But I *know* Gwen

Cordovan was murdered."

He picked up his phone again and asked for the overseas operator. "Okay. The story is worth a gamble. Where can I reach you?"

I told him I didn't know but that I would call him back in half an hour.

"Better make it an hour." He cupped his hand over the mouthpiece. "Where are you going now? Over to see Harry?"

I turned, one hand on the door knob. "And why should I go to see Harry?"

He said, "I thought you knew. A squad car picked him up in front of the Parisian a little after eight tonight. It seems he was crossing the street and a hit and run car—" he stopped, his eyes gone wide. "He was working on the case?"

I nodded. "He was straightening out an angle." The sour taste was back in my mouth. The case refused to run straight. I'd had the same feeling before, sitting in on a rigged poker game and not being able to spot just who was dealing the seconds but with too much in the pot to quit. "Where have they got him? How bad was he hurt?"

Gold told me, "Mercy Hospital. And the last I heard he was still unconscious but they said that he'd pull through."

I said, "He'd better." Corny, sure. But I meant it. We'd been through too much together for me to feel any other way.

The night was as black as hell and almost as hot. I stopped under the hotel marquee to light a cigarette and try to untangle my thoughts. The lad I was looking for could be Hare. I had a hunch it was. He was too smooth, a sharper. After his seeming reluctance to bring me into the case he had kept my nose on the trail until I'd wound up with a pair of corpses and a perfect alibi for him.

"But I couldn't have slain her, your honor. I was home, and Mr. Mercer can so testify."

The only thing that threw that off was that only the lad who had killed her, myself, and Gold knew that she had been murdered. Her death was listed as accidental and would remain so unless I could dig up enough evidence to demand an autopsy.

On the other hand, Harry getting it where he had, brought Joe Connors back into the picture. And according to what Miss Hanelley had told me, Hare *couldn't* inherit the money. But God knew Connors couldn't. It was a mess.

"Cab, sir?" the doorman asked me.

I told him no, I had my car. Both Sherry and Beth were in the Mercy waiting room, dry-eyed but they had been crying. Harry was stronger, they said, but still unconscious. Beth, for a bride, was taking it well. I asked if I could see Harry and Sherry said that she'd take me up and for Beth to stay where she was.

In the cage, Sherry touched my face, her eyes wet with tears. "They've hurt you, Matt. This is a murder case?"

I said it was and she pressed closer to me. That was all. It was enough.

"It was a car that hurt Harry?"

I said that I doubted that very much. They had him on the fifth floor. The long corridor was hushed, and dark, except for an exit light here and there and the light over the night nurses' desk. All hospitals make me gag. They also set my left wing to aching. That is, it feels like it's aching. It isn't. Cork and steel don't ache and they'd sawed off my real wing in Shanghai.

"This is Mr. Mercer, my husband, the partner of the patient in 512," Sherry told the night nurse. "Is it all right if we just peek in?"

The nurse said it was, as long as we just peeked.

I started down the bed-pan alley, turned back and asked the nurse if she had been in surgery when they had dressed Harry's wound. She said she had not but that it was down on his medical chart as a multiple concussion with the X-rays showing no pieces of skull pressing against the brain.

"And he was hit by a car?"

She said so she understood.

"But in your opinion," I persisted, "could his injuries have been caused by a beating? In other words could he have been slugged with a sap and pushed out into the street?"

She said she was certain she didn't know but that it seemed very unlikely as the police officers who had brought him in had listed it as a hit and run case. I made a mental note to stop at the office on my way out and get the prowl cops' names from the record.

Sherry brightened. "Oh. I see you did get a male special."

The nurse looked at her blankly.

Sherry explained, "The male nurse in the white coat that just went into Harry's room."

I didn't hear what the nurse said. I was racing down the hall tugging at my gun, Sherry's heels clacking behind her. By the time I reached the doorway of 512 the lad was bending over the bed. I couldn't see his face. I could see the knife in his hand.

"You! Drop it! Quick!" I barked.

He turned instead, dropping the knife but whipping a gun from a shoulder holster. I didn't know who he was. I didn't care. I let him have four—in the face.

The shots rocked the hall like a cannon. Patients began to scream. All the lights over the doors went on.

I walked in, switched on the bed lamp, and looked at Harry. The knife, a razor-sharp stiletto, was lying on the sheet. But I'd been in time. It hadn't bothered him any. Neither had the shots for that matter. His eyes were still closed but he was breathing normally.

I kicked the lad on the floor over. There wasn't much left of his face. But what there was left was strange to me. Just as I'd thought I was getting my darned hand straightened out, I'd drawn another joker.

"You've killed him!" the nurse screamed in my ear.

"Yeah. I meant to," I told her. I walked back out in the Ball, making a snap decision. In another three or four minutes the joint would be lousy with cops.

Sherry's fingers were hot on my wrist. "This means more trouble, Matt? Trouble with Inspector Haig?"

I shook my head. "No. Not tonight." So far I'd been working for a fee, because I'd been sorry for a poor little rich kid whom I had felt was getting a bad break, and because I was naturally curious. But the attack on Harry had made it personal. And if they wanted to play that way, that was all right with me.

"No," I repeated to Sherry. "This thing is breaking too fast." I thumbed a fresh clip in my gun. "Put this in your bag and shoot any son who tries to get in that door before the cops get here. Harry knows something. Something damn important."

She took the gun without question. "And you—?"

I kissed her fast. "I'm scramming. Tell Haig that I'll see him sometime tomorrow."

I had wanted to stop at the office, find out the names of the cops who had picked up Harry, and ask to look through the stuff that had been in his pockets in the hope that he might have written down something. But by the time that I hit the lobby Doyle and Corrigan, riding No. 23 out of East Chicago Avenue, were effervescing through the door.

"What's up?" Doyle demanded.

"It's terrible," I told them. "Up on the fifth floor. Someone just cut a nurse's throat."

They boiled on into the elevator. I walked on out the door. I had nothing to fear from the law. But I hadn't any time to waste on a lot of official red tape.

A few blocks up the street I parked in front of one of the all night bars that dot the near-north side and called a couple of lads who sometimes worked for me when there was too much for Harry and me to handle. I told them both to get down to Mercy as fast as they could make it, one to stay close to Sherry and 512, the other to wait in the lobby of the hospital for a phone call from me in case the cops were able to identify the dead hood.

Then I bought a couple of drinks, a ham sandwich, and a beer, and headed for the office to pick up my spare gun, damning Gwen Cordovan, Hare, and Connors. The nightmare was getting me down.

Starting at two o'clock that afternoon I had been lied to,

shot at, punched, and kicked. It was almost four in the morning. And after fourteen hours of bars, diamonds, and red herrings, I was beginning to reach a point where very little more would push me off my chump.

If nothing had detained him, Hare should have returned from Valdaro with the body, and once I had re-heeled myself I meant to have it out with both him and Connors.

I rode up to the office thinking that I had better start with Joe to give Gold time to complete his phone call. If Hare was a phony I'd have a lever to work with. But first of all I'd contact the phone company. Whatever they had told Harry had been enough to get him slugged—if he had been slugged.

The hall was hot and stuffy. My heels made hollow clicking sounds. Even my key sounded unnaturally loud in the lock. I slammed the door behind me, reached for the switch—and froze. Moonlight was streaming in the windows. All of them but one. Two black hulks blotted that out.

Someone was waiting for me. And there was no use reaching for my gun. I hadn't any.

CHAPTER FIVE

Mr. Hare—And the Hounds

MASON'S VOICE cut through the dark. "Hold it, Mercer. Just like you are. So far, you're doing fine."

I asked if it was all right if I switched on the lights. He said it was. There were two of them, Mason and Lord. Both of them had guns in their hands.

"You got the key out of Harry's pocket when you slugged him," I accused.

"It dropped out," Lord admitted. His anger was genuine. "What the hell are you trying to pull? What are you trying to pin on Joe? And while I'm at it, where have you got him?"

I closed my eyes at that and sat down at my desk without being told I could. "One of you wouldn't have a cigarette?"

Lord hesitated, pulled a pack from his pocket and tossed it

on my desk, the gun in his other hand never once leaving my belly.

I lit the cigarette, remarking that I thought there was some mistake; the last time that I had seen Joe being in their presence at the Parisian.

"Don't give us that," Lord sneered. "Harry tipped your hand when he barged into the joint wanting to know why one of us had called you up representing ourselves to be this guy Hare's confidential secretary. Start talking. What the hell are you trying to pull?"

"Then you did slug Harry?"

"We roughed him some," Mason admitted.

"But you didn't make the phone call."

"You know damn well we didn't."

He wasn't lying. There was no reason for him to lie. He had the gun. "No, I didn't know," I said. "I never even thought of you lads in that connection." I spread my good and bum palms on my desk. "And I don't know what's happened to Joe. That's my story. If you don't believe it, you'll have to shoot. How long has he been missing, and from where?"

Both of them chewed that over.

I continued, "We've had our disagreements. But have I ever lied to you boys? Have you ever heard of me lying to anyone on anything of importance?"

Mason was forced to admit he had not.

"More," I told them, "I just came from Mercy Hospital where somebody tried to finish the job that you boys began, tried to finish it with a knife."

"What the hell?" Lord demanded.

I said, "I've been wondering that for hours." I opened my bottom desk drawer and took out a bottle. "Now either shoot, give me the whole story, or get the hell out of here."

I had a drink while they talked it over between them and decided to tell me as much as they knew.

Shortly after Harry had barged into the Parisian accusing Joe of making the phone call, and wanting to know why, Connors had taken Gwen's bad check and had gone out to see Hare himself to try and find out what was cooking.

When he hadn't returned in two hours Mason and Lord had followed him only to be told by Hare that after collecting for the bad check Connors had left for my office with the avowed intention of beating my face in.

I wanted to know why.

"You and Harry," Mason said thin-lipped.

Lord told me that Hare had told them that he had told Joe Connors, that I had phoned him and had positively identified Connors as the short stocky man who had flipped a slug at me. More, I had said that I was undecided between beating in his brains and swearing out a warrant accusing him of attempted murder.

Mason said, "So we checked with headquarters, found out that no warrant had been issued, and when Joe fails to show up we reason that you snagged him. But he didn't shoot at you, believe me."

I told him I did believe him, that the way that I saw the picture someone was running a whizzer on both Joe and myself. "But tell me this. Could anyone have made that phone call from the Parisian?"

"Anyone," Mason shrugged. "There's a phone booth in the downstairs bar."

"And they could have picked up one of Joe's hats at the same time?"

He said that could be, Joe being very careless with his hats.

"Then it was Hare for my money," I told them. "But I wouldn't begin to know why he should want to snag Joe." I looked from their guns to my phone. "But Harry Gold is phoning Cairo in an attempt to smell out Hare's background, and it could be that his call's gone through."

Lord said for me to call him.

Gold was biting his nails waiting for me to call. "You named it, Matt," he crowed. "Boy, what a story. Hare is a former English colonel, all right, but he was cashiered some years ago. Since then, and up until the time he married Gwen, he made his living as a con man and trans-Atlantic gambler. He always worked with an older man who would seem to answer the description of the lad posing as his butler. More he did have a blonde girl friend by the name of Stella. But she is supposed to have died some months before Gwen and Hare were married."

I said I guessed that sewed it up except for a few details.

"But damn it, man," Gold protested. "You've still got a hole in your case big enough to drive a tank through. I just got one of the Cordovan lawyers out of bed and he swears that there is no way that Hare can get his hands on any of the estate other than what is left from this years' allowance."

"I'm headed out to work on that angle now," I told him.

When I hung up Lord and Mason had holstered their guns. "We'll tag along," Mason said.

I said that was fine with me, and slipped my spare gun in my holster.

A siren was wailing down State Street by the time we reached the street and I told them that we had better use their car, as Haig was probably burned up because I hadn't stuck around Mercy.

Mason wanted to know why that should burn Haig up. I told him and his lips grew thinner. He knew that he and Lord had a beating coming.

Dawn wasn't far away. There was a milk truck but no cars on Willow Road. The big gates of 247 were closed and locked. The wall was too high to climb, even disregarding the glass.

"So—?" Mason asked.

I told him to drive the car up on the sidewalk, as close to the wall as he could get it and we could use the top of the car as a ladder. It wasn't a perfect arrangement but it worked. And the jump on the other side wasn't too bad, the ground being soft and springy.

The house was built in an H. The middle and left wings were dark. So were the upper floors. But light streamed out onto the lawn from the open right wing French window. Somewhere a girl was crying as though her heart would break.

I had told them what had happened in Valdaro on our way

out to the house and Lord wanted to know if it was the dead woman's daughter who was crying. I said I imagined it was. I also said that I wanted to talk to her, if possible, before we went to work on Hare, it being just possible that she could furnish the missing pieces of the puzzle.

Then Mason coughed and the sobbing stopped abruptly. A window was opened or closed on one of the upper floors. We froze as close to the house as we could but when nothing more happened I figured that it was just one of the maids trying to get more air.

I tiptoed across a flower bed to one of the lighted windows. The little blonde who had popped me with the silver flask was stretched out on a chaise lounge, alternately sniffling and sipping at the flask. There was no one else in the room. I tapped lightly on the glass then stepped out where she could see me.

She opened her mouth to scream, saw who I was and said wanly, "Hello, man."

I asked her if Hare was home. She said that he was not.

"Then I want to talk to you," I told her.

I walked on into the room. She stood up weaving slightly. "My mother's dead," she told me. "That—that's where he's gone. Down to bring her back."

She buried her face on my shoulder. I patted her bare back, feeling like a damned old fool, and glad that Sherry couldn't see me.

"I like you," she repeated her crack of that afternoon.

"I like you, too," I told her. "Now pull yourself together."

She wanted to know who Lord and Mason were. I introduced them as friends of mine. Then Mason, trying to be pleasant, told her that she looked a lot like her mother and started her off crying again.

When she had quieted down I asked her who was home. She said that she was alone, Hare having taken Dawson with him when they had left for Valdaro. Then Lord described Connors to her and asked her if she had seen him.

She bobbed her head and told him between sniffles, "He was here tonight, about eight o'clock, I think. He and Mr.

Hare quarreled dreadfully. But I couldn't hear what it was about because Mr. Hare came out in the hall and told me to go to my room."

I looked at the boys.

"He played us for suckers," Mason said. "But we'll be here when he gets home."

Lord wondered if one of us hadn't better open the gate from the inside and move the car, it being a dead tip-off that there was someone inside the grounds.

I said I thought it was wise and started for the window but the kid caught at my arm.

"Don't leave me. Please. He won't be home for hours. There was some delay in Valdaro, I know. Because he just called up from there about five minutes ago and wanted to know if you had been here looking for him."

"He's wise that you're wise," Mason said. "But why drag Joe into the picture?"

I said I was damned if I knew, and picked up the stitches of my own knitting by asking the kid if her relations with her step-father had been friendly.

She said she didn't know him very well, her mother having left her in Spain while she had gone on to Cairo. In fact she had never even seen him until she had returned to Chicago the month before after having been abroad since before the beginning of the war.

I said, "In other words, you were twelve when you were home last."

"Twelve going on thirteen," she corrected. "And while I guess Mr. Hare married mother for my money like all the others did, he is an improvement over the count."

I asked her if he had ever tried to get her to sign any legal-looking papers.

"A few," she admitted.

"It only takes one," I told her. I hesitated, debating whether or not to tell her that I believed that Hare and his girl friend had cleverly murdered her mother in the first steps of a bid to gain control of the Cordovan fortune. I decided to spare her that, but Lord upset the apple cart with the best intentions.

"You watch what you sign. And you watch your step, kid," he warned her. "The way that Mercer has it figured out, this guy Hare and his girl friend Stella, did away with your mother. And you may be next on his list."

She busted out weeping again and buried her face on my shoulder. "You won't let him hurt me. You won't, will you, Mr. Mercer?"

I assured her that I would not but she leaned on her flask for a double take only to find it was empty.

"In that cabinet," she sniffled to Mason. "Hand me a bottle, please."

There was only one left, rye. Mason glanced at the bond date and whistled. It had been old enough to register when war had been declared. I tore off the seal, uncorked it, and handed it to the girl. She poured herself a stiff slug, started to raise it to her lips, then tardily remembered her manners.

"Excuse me. Won't you gentlemen join me?"

None of us refused. It was good but I'd tasted better. I downed mine looking at the little blonde and thinking, "If you were my kid I'd spank some sense into your pretty pink panties and put you on a buttermilk diet." She was a scant nineteen and travelling the same pace that her mother had traveled before her.

Mason and Lord had a second drink. I said that I'd had plenty and that we'd better run in the car.

"Check," Mason said. He tried to get to his feet, and couldn't. He looked at his glass, then me, a swift scowl twisting his lips. His hand inched up toward his gun only to drop to his lap as his head lolled back against the cushion.

Lord raised himself to his feet, stood wavering a moment, then crumpled to the floor.

I shook my head to clear it but it wouldn't clear. Five hundred B-29's were roaring in my ears. The floor of the room was tilting like the deck of a battle-wagon.

I looked down at the girl beside me. She was watching me, amused, her lips drawn back from her teeth, her eyes cold and calculating. She wasn't pretty any more.

I knew how Hare meant to inherit. I knew whom I had heard sobbing. I knew a lot of things. The hell of it was, it looked like I'd learned them too late.

CHAPTER SIX

Until Death Us Do Part

I WAS COLD. I was stiff. I was tired. My chest hurt so badly I could hardly breathe. I thought I could see old man Stepan persisting in shaking his fist in my face, shouting that Mike was a good boy. I pushed him away and panted on—smack into the fat little coroner.

"It was an accident, hear me?" he screamed. "They were drunk. And she drove into the tree. Don't you make a fool out of me in the papers."

I tried to push him away and couldn't. Somehow he'd fallen flat on my chest. Then I realized it was all in my mind. Full consciousness returned slowly.

The place I was in was dark. The air was foul. I was lying on my back, my cork arm twisted under me. And there was something or someone on my chest. I wriggled out from under, found a match and struck it.

Lord had been piled on me like a length of cord wood. His face was bloody but he was breathing soddenly. Mason was lying a few feet away. I couldn't tell if he was dead or alive. Joe Connors lay beside him, a puckered brown hole in his forehead. There were rows of racked bottles along the wall. Pending future and permanent disposal, we'd been tossed into the wine cellar.

In the last flame of the match I tried the door. I had expected to find it locked. It was. There wasn't any window.

Now that it was too late the whole thing was crystal clear. I had been played for a sucker from the start. The only thing that I couldn't figure was why I was still alive. Then I touched the side of my head and knew. It was sticky with clotted blood and swollen like a balloon.

My being alive was strictly accidental.

We would be missed, of course, but there was little but my conversation with Gold to point the finger at Hare. And by the time that the finger was pointed, three hoods and one private detective would be planted deep in the earth somewhere.

I broke a neck off one of the bottles, drank some, and palmed the rest to the side of my head. It burned but the pain cleared out the rest of the cobwebs. Whatever I did, if anything was possible, I would have to do fast. The air in the vault, or lack of it, was burning holes in my chest.

I frisked my pockets without much hope. But in even cleverer murders there is usually one mistake. And they had made one with me. They had taken my knife and my gun, but whoever had frisked me had somehow overlooked the small piece of stiff celluloid in one of my upper vest pockets. It was as good as a key to the vault. In seven states out of ten it's considered a burglar tool and possession can get you one to ten. I had taken it away from the 'loid' man of a ducat mob and forgotten I even had it.

As it was, it was close. By the time I had gimmicked the lock I was too weak to even crawl. I wormed out of the vault on my belly sucking in lungs full of air.

The basement was large and dark. It was night. I had no way of knowing how long I had been out. When I was able I dragged out Lord. There was no use fooling with Mason. He and Joe had gone to keep Mike Slavin and Gwen Cordovan Company. From a single well-planned murder, as often happens, the breaks had caused them to pile one corpse on top of another.

I was out of the vault and on my feet. But I still wasn't in the clear. The lads upstairs were well-heeled. I wasn't. I picked up the furnace shaker, laid it back and broke the neck off another bottle. It makes a nasty weapon.

The stairs opened into the kitchen. These was no one in the kitchen but in the butler's pantry just beyond I could see Dawson uncorking a bottle of Scotch. I slipped out of my shoes and stalked him. It was a pleasure.

Unaware that I was behind him, he wiped the neck of the bottle with a napkin, put it on a tray with five glasses, picked it up then turned and saw me.

His face went a fish-belly white. "You're dead!"

"Don't bet on it," I told him.

He set the tray down and went for a gun. I gave him the glass in the face, at the same time stoppering his gurgled scream with my steel left fist. He made some small noise in falling, but not much, I pried his gun out of his hand.

The dining room opened on the hall and was across from the library with the big carved doors. At the far end of the hall I could see the little blonde offering her cheek to a hatchet-faced old dowager whom curiosity had pried away from her evening of contract bridge.

The only make-up the blonde was wearing was a smear of lip stick. Her hair hung in a girlish bob. She was wearing a plain black dress with a touch of white at the throat. She looked slim, and young, and pathetic.

"So sorry, my dear," the old bat lied. "But when our time comes we must all pass on."

The little blonde agreed that we must and they both disappeared into the living room. I couldn't see it but I knew what was in there.

I started across the hall, stopped as I heard, or thought that I heard, Sherry's voice.

"Then Matt did not come here this morning, or at any time during the day?"

Back of the doors, Hare lied, "He did not."

It was Sherry. "I think he's a damned liar," she said. "Harry Gold told me—"

"Inspector," Hare cut her short, "I must protest and terminate this scene. Mrs. Mercer's charges are fantastic and so are those of this newspaperman Gold. I loved Gwen very dearly. And I have not seen nor heard from Mercer since he phoned me from Valdaro. If he has disappeared, I'm sorry. But why in the name of time would I spirit him away?"

"Because you murdered your wife," Sherry told him. "Matt told Harry you did."

"This is fantastic," Hare scoffed.

Haig rumbled, "It would seem so to me. But you do admit Gold's charge that you are a former confidence man and gambler?

Hare made a good point. "I do. I have never tried to conceal my identity. But it certainly isn't a crime for a gambler to fall in love."

A voice that I didn't know broke in, "Gentlemen and Mrs. Mercer, please, I think I can settle this matter. Because of Mr. Mercer's rather mysterious disappearance, Mrs. Mercer has made a serious charge. She, because of an alleged conversation between Mr. Mercer and this newspaperman, has accused Mr. Hare of killing Mrs. Hare, his motive being the Cordovan money. But the charge is palpably absurd for two reasons. In the first place, Mrs. Hare's death has been established as accidental, and fifty miles away. In the second place, I can give you my word as one of the Cordovan Foundation lawyers that Mr. Hare will not inherit one penny of the money."

Haig asked, "Who gets it?"

"Her daughter," the other lad told him. "According to the terms of the trust, it is to be turned over to her in just a few more days."

Hare said, "Thank you, Mr. Phillips."

"Well, I guess that's that," Haig said. "But I'll be damned if I know where Matt's gone to. Or Joe Connors and Lord and Mason for that matter."

I still wasn't quite certain of Connor's place in the picture. But having botched the actual killing, Hare was doing a good cover job. He might be suspected of a lot of things but no one could ever prove it with me dead. I was the fly in his ointment, and very pleased about it.

The voices except for Sherry's sunk to polite murmurs and I knew that Hare was suggesting a drink before Haig left. Sherry kept insisting that I couldn't "just disappear."

Then the buzzer rang in the butler's pantry. I crossed the hall, walked into the library and closed the door behind me, asking Hare, "There was something that you wanted, louse?"

He said, "Oh, God!"

"Yeah. There goes the ball game," I agreed. I crossed the room in three steps, belted him off his feet. "Now get that blonde in here," I said, "And don't give me an argument."

Curry and Johnson were with him. He sent Curry for the girl. Sherry didn't say anything but her eyes were wet and shining.

The blonde's eyes grew wide when she saw me and she nibbled hard at a knuckle to keep from screaming. I sat on the edge of the desk where I could kick Hare again if he showed any interest in rising.

"Now I'll tell the story," I began. "This louse on the floor here married Gwen with all of this in mind. It's Gwen out there in the coffin. But it wasn't Gwen who toured the bars, or passed out bad checks, or made love to young Slavin. That was Hare's girl friend Stella wearing Gwen's clothes and diamonds and making damn certain that she left a wide, broad trail. Gwen had been out of the country for years. And Stella got away with it fine merely by staying away from the cafe society group one of whom might have been sober enough to spot the deception.

"It was Stella who talked young Slavin into marriage. It was Stella who drove to Valdaro and married him. Hare stayed behind to make good the alibi that he had suckered me into providing. But Dawson—his partner and not his butler—followed in a second car with the real Mrs. Hare who had been kept out of sight and on a whiskey diet for two weeks. What happened in the car, or possibly before they started, I wouldn't know. But Gwen grew unmanageable and Dawson was forced to slug or choke her. Her heart rotten with booze, she died. And that is what cost them the ball game.

"I know how a head wound bleeds. And Gwen had been dead for an hour when Dawson rendezvoused with Stella the other side of Valdaro transferred her to the death car along with the passed-out young sergeant pointed the car off the road, jammed the accelerator, then jumped off the running board."

Hare whimpered "Don't believe him. He's crazy."

"You were crazy when you brought me in on the case," I corrected. "I'm not brainy, but I'm persistent. And you made a second bad mistake by dragging Joe Connors into the case by having one of your stooges sneak one of his hats and drop it to point to his joint as the starting place of Gwen's trail."

It was coming too fast for Haig. He wanted to know where Joe figured. I told him I wasn't certain, that at first I had figured Joe in on the deal but that after talking to Lord and Mason I had changed my mind.

"After Harry accused him of being in on the deal," I told him, "I think Joe came out here to see what was cooking, recognized Hare as a former trans-Atlantic shark and demanded to be cut in. He was, for a piece of lead."

"Joe's dead?"

"He's down in the basement," I told Haig, "along with Lord and Mason."

Haig told Johnson to go see. He went out in a hurry.

I called after him, "And there's another stiff out in the butler's pantry. At least I think he's stiff. I hit him with that in mind."

Haig said, "Damn you, Mercer. No matter what has happened you have no right to take the law in your own hands."

Sherry hooted. "What should he have done? Wait for you to identify his body?"

I told the rest of the story fast, admitting that three things still struck me, one the phone call having been made from the Parisian, the second who made it and the last the attempt on Harry's life. I said that I believed, however, that after Hare had been forced to shoot Connors, the attack on Harry had been an after-thought, hoping that the police would trail Harry back to the Parisian and thus forge a plausible reason for Connors to disappear, giving the impression that he was laying out a murder rap until the heat had cooled.

Hare repeated, "The man is crazy. What would I stand to gain?"

I asked the lawyer how much there was in the Cordovan

estate.

"But this is insane," he protested. "I told you before. I tell you again." He pointed at the little blonde. "Everything goes to her."

"Yeah. That's what I mean," I said quietly.

Sherry got it then. "Oh, oh."

"It was you, wasn't it, baby," I asked the blonde, "who took that shot at me and dropped Joe Connors' hat. All that you had to do was to go out the back and drive around in front."

She told me to go to hell.

Phillips was shocked. "You mustn't let this get you, Miss Cordovan," he said primly. "No matter—" He broke off abruptly, staring at the blonde. "You mean to say," he asked me, "that—"

"That's what I mean," I said. "They gave this year's Oscar to the wrong actress. That's why they had to get rid of Gwen. Hope having been abroad for years, it was easy enough for Stella to play daughter-following-in-mama's-foot-steps to the general public and old buddle-duddies like Phillips. *But they couldn't get Gwen drunk enough to pass a tart off on her as her daughter!*"

Sherry said, "With her hair up and wearing high heels, she was Gwen. With her hair hanging she was Hope. But she wouldn't have fooled me a minute." I refrained from pointing out that she had. "Look at those crow's feet around her eyes."

Stella called her a name. Sherry slapped her. And the battle was on. Not being able to slug her myself, I was glad to let Sherry do it. But Haig stepped in and stopped it.

"Cut it." He leveled a finger at me. "All right. You know so much, Mercer. Where is the real Hope Cordovan? Dead?"

I shook my head. "No. You'll find her locked in one of the upstairs rooms. I wouldn't know, never having been an heir to millions, but I imagine that they had to keep her around for her signature and such."

Phillips held out a hand on behalf, he said, of the Cordovan Estate. I told him where he could put it. Then I yanked Hare to his feet.

"We had an agreement, remember? I was to locate your wife and tell you. Then I could name my own fee." I slipped his wallet out of his pocket and counted out ten one-hundred dollar bills.

"This will just cover it nicely. Your wife's in a coffin in the front room. You married her for better or for worse, until death should you two part. But I wouldn't grieve about the separation, rat. It shouldn't be too long."

"You're a hard man, Matt," Haig said.

I touched the clotted blood on the side of my head. "Yeah? And where would I be if I wasn't?"

I knew what he was thinking. So did Sherry.

"Don't you dare tell him," she said.

RAMBLE HOUSE's

HARRY STEPHEN KEELER WEBWORK MYSTERIES

(RH) indicates the title is available ONLY in the RAMBLE HOUSE edition

The Ace of Spades Murder
The Affair of the Bottled Deuce (RH)
The Amazing Web
The Barking Clock
Behind That Mask
The Book with the Orange Leaves
The Bottle with the Green Wax Seal
The Box from Japan
The Case of the Canny Killer
The Case of the Crazy Corpse (RH)
The Case of the Flying Hands (RH)
The Case of the Ivory Arrow
The Case of the Jeweled Ragpicker
The Case of the Lavender Gripsack
The Case of the Mysterious Moll
The Case of the 16 Beans
The Case of the Transparent Nude (RH)
The Case of the Transposed Legs
The Case of the Two-Headed Idiot (RH)
The Case of the Two Strange Ladies
The Circus Stealers (RH)
Cleopatra's Tears
A Copy of Beowulf (RH)
The Crimson Cube (RH)
The Face of the Man From Saturn
Find the Clock
The Five Silver Buddhas
The 4th King
The Gallows Waits, My Lord! (RH)
The Green Jade Hand
Finger! Finger!
Hangman's Nights (RH)
I, Chameleon (RH)
I Killed Lincoln at 10:13! (RH)
The Iron Ring
The Man Who Changed His Skin (RH)
The Man with the Crimson Box
The Man with the Magic Eardrums
The Man with the Wooden Spectacles
The Marceau Case
The Matilda Hunter Murder

The Monocled Monster
The Murder of London Lew
The Murdered Mathematician
The Mysterious Card (RH)
The Mysterious Ivory Ball of Wong Shing Li (RH)
The Mystery of the Fiddling Cracksman
The Peacock Fan
The Photo of Lady X (RH)
The Portrait of Jirjohn Cobb
Report on Vanessa Hewstone (RH)
Riddle of the Travelling Skull
Riddle of the Wooden Parrakeet (RH)
The Scarlet Mummy (RH)
The Search for X-Y-Z
The Sharkskin Book
Sing Sing Nights
The Six From Nowhere (RH)
The Skull of the Waltzing Clown
The Spectacles of Mr. Cagliostro
Stand By—London Calling!
The Steeltown Strangler
The Stolen Gravestone (RH)
Strange Journey (RH)
The Strange Will
The Straw Hat Murders (RH)
The Street of 1000 Eyes (RH)
Thieves' Nights
Three Novellos (RH)
The Tiger Snake
The Trap (RH)
Vagabond Nights (Defrauded Yeggman)
Vagabond Nights 2 (10 Hours)
The Vanishing Gold Truck
The Voice of the Seven Sparrows
The Washington Square Enigma
When Thief Meets Thief
The White Circle (RH)
The Wonderful Scheme of Mr. Christopher Thorne
X. Jones—of Scotland Yard
Y. Cheung, Business Detective

Keeler Related Works

A To Izzard: A Harry Stephen Keeler Companion by Fender Tucker — Articles and stories about Harry, by Harry, and in his style. Included is a compleat bibliography.

Wild About Harry: Reviews of Keeler Novels — Edited by Richard Polt & Fender Tucker — 22 reviews of works by Harry Stephen Keeler from *Keeler News*. A perfect introduction to the author.

The Keeler Keyhole Collection: Annotated newsletter rants from Harry Stephen Keeler, edited by Francis M. Nevins. Over 400 pages of incredibly personal Keeleriana.

Fakealoo — Pastiches of the style of Harry Stephen Keeler by selected demented members of the HSK Society. Updated every year with the new winner.

Strands of the Web: Short Stories of Harry Stephen Keeler — 29 stories, just about all that Keeler wrote, are edited and introduced by Fred Cleaver.

RAMBLE HOUSE's Loon Sanctuary

A Clear Path to Cross — Sharon Knowles short mystery stories by Ed Lynskey.

A Corpse Walks in Brooklyn and Other Stories — Volume 5 in the Day Keene in the Detective Pulps series.

A Jimmy Starr Omnibus — Three 40s novels by Jimmy Starr.

A Niche in Time and Other Stories — Classic SF by William F. Temple

A Roland Daniel Double: The Signal and The Return of Wu Fang — Classic thrillers from the 30s.

A Shot Rang Out — Three decades of reviews and articles by today's Anthony Boucher, Jon Breen. An essential book for any mystery lover's library.

A Smell of Smoke — A 1951 English countryside thriller by Miles Burton.

A Snark Selection — Lewis Carroll's *The Hunting of the Snark* with two Snarkian chapters by Harry Stephen Keeler — Illustrated by Gavin L. O'Keefe.

A Young Man's Heart — A forgotten early classic by Cornell Woolrich.

Alexander Laing Novels — *The Motives of Nicholas Holtz* and *Dr. Scarlett*, stories of medical mayhem and intrigue from the 30s.

An Angel in the Street — Modern hardboiled noir by Peter Genovese.

Automaton — Brilliant treatise on robotics: 1928-style! By H. Stafford Hatfield.

Away From the Here and Now — Clare Winger Harris stories, collected by Richard A. Lupoff

Beast or Man? — A 1930 novel of racism and horror by Sean M'Guire. Introduced by John Pelan.

Black Beadle — A 1939 thriller by E.C.R. Lorac.

Black Hogan Strikes Again — Australia's Peter Renwick pens a tale of the 30s outback.

Black River Falls — Suspense from the master, Ed Gorman.

Blondy's Boy Friend — A snappy 1930 story by Philip Wylie, writing as Leatrice Homesley.

Blood in a Snap — The *Finnegan's Wake* of the 21st century, by Jim Weiler.

Blood Moon — The first of the Robert Payne series by Ed Gorman.

Bogart '48 — Hollywood action with Bogie by John Stanley and Kenn Davis

Calling Lou Largo! — Two Lou Largo novels by William Ard.

Cornucopia of Crime — Francis M. Nevins assembled this huge collection of his writings about crime literature and the people who write it. Essential for any serious mystery library.

Corpse Without Flesh — Strange novel of forensics by George Bruce

Crimson Clown Novels — By Johnston McCulley, author of the Zorro novels, *The Crimson Clown* and *The Crimson Clown Again*.

Dago Red — 22 tales of dark suspense by Bill Pronzini.

Dark Sanctuary — Weird Menace story by H. B. Gregory

David Hume Novels — *Corpses Never Argue, Cemetery First Stop, Make Way for the Mourners, Eternity Here I Come*. 1930s British hardboiled fiction with an attitude.

Dead Man Talks Too Much — Hollywood boozer by Weed Dickenson.

Death Leaves No Card — One of the most unusual murdered-in-the-tub mysteries you'll ever read. By Miles Burton.

Death March of the Dancing Dolls and Other Stories — Volume Three in the Day Keene in the Detective Pulps series. Introduced by Bill Crider.

Deep Space and other Stories — A collection of SF gems by Richard A. Lupoff.

Detective Duff Unravels It — Episodic mysteries by Harvey O'Higgins.

Diabolic Candelabra — Classic 30s mystery by E.R. Punshon

Dictator's Way — Another D.S. Bobby Owen mystery from E.R. Punshon

Dime Novels: Ramble House's 10-Cent Books — *Knife in the Dark* by Robert Leslie Bellem, *Hot Lead* and *Song of Death* by Ed Earl Repp, *A Hashish House in New York* by H.H. Kane, and five more.

Doctor Arnoldi — Tiffany Thayer's story of the death of death.

Don Diablo: Book of a Lost Film — Two-volume treatment of a western by Paul Landres, with diagrams. Intro by Francis M. Nevins.

Dope and Swastikas — Two strange novels from 1922 by Edmund Snell

Dope Tales #1 — Two dope-riddled classics; *Dope Runners* by Gerald Grantham and *Death Takes the Joystick* by Phillip Condé.

Dope Tales #2 — Two more narco-classics; *The Invisible Hand* by Rex Dark and *The Smokers of Hashish* by Norman Berrow.

Dope Tales #3 — Two enchanting novels of opium by the master, Sax Rohmer. *Dope* and *The Yellow Claw*.

Double Hot — Two 60s softcore sex novels by Morris Hershman.

Double Sex — Yet two more panting thrillers from Morris Hershman.

Dr. Odin — Douglas Newton's 1933 racial potboiler comes back to life.

Evangelical Cockroach — Jack Woodford writes about writing.

Evidence in Blue — 1938 mystery by E. Charles Vivian.

Fatal Accident — Murder by automobile, a 1936 mystery by Cecil M. Wills.

Fighting Mad — Todd Robbins' 1922 novel about boxing and life

Finger-prints Never Lie — A 1939 classic detective novel by John G. Brandon.

Freaks and Fantasies — Eerie tales by Tod Robbins, collaborator of Tod Browning on the film FREAKS.

Gadsby — A lipogram (a novel without the letter E). Ernest Vincent Wright's last work, published in 1939 right before his death.

Gelett Burgess Novels — *The Master of Mysteries, The White Cat, Two O'Clock Courage, Ladies in Boxes, Find the Woman, The Heart Line, The Picaroons* and *Lady Mechante.* Recently added is A Gelett Burgess Sampler, edited by Alfred Jan. All are introduced by Richard A. Lupoff.

Geronimo — S. M. Barrett's 1905 autobiography of a noble American.

Hake Talbot Novels — *Rim of the Pit, The Hangman's Handyman.* Classic locked room mysteries, with mapback covers by Gavin O'Keefe.

Hands Out of Hell and Other Stories — John H. Knox's eerie hallucinations

Hell is a City — William Ard's masterpiece.

Hollywood Dreams — A novel of Tinsel Town and the Depression by Richard O'Brien.

Hostesses in Hell and Other Stories — Russell Gray's most graphic stories

House of the Restless Dead — Strange and ominous tales by Hugh B. Cave.

I Stole $16,000,000 — A true story by cracksman Herbert E. Wilson.

Inclination to Murder — 1966 thriller by New Zealand's Harriet Hunter.

Invaders from the Dark — Classic werewolf tale from Greye La Spina.

J. Poindexter, Colored — Classic satirical black novel by Irvin S. Cobb.

Jack Mann Novels — Strange murder in the English countryside. *Gees' First Case, Nightmare Farm, Grey Shapes, The Ninth Life, The Glass Too Many, Her Ways Are Death, The Kleinert Case* and *Maker of Shadows.*

Jake Hardy — A lusty western tale from Wesley Tallant.

Jim Harmon Double Novels — *Vixen Hollow/Celluloid Scandal, The Man Who Made Maniacs/Silent Siren, Ape Rape/Wanton Witch, Sex Burns Like Fire/Twist Session, Sudden Lust/Passion Strip, Sin Unlimited/Harlot Master, Twilight Girls/Sex Institution.* Written in the early 60s and never reprinted until now.

Joel Townsley Rogers Novels and Short Stories — By the author of *The Red Right Hand: Once In a Red Moon, Lady With the Dice, The Stopped Clock, Never Leave My Bed.* Also two short story collections: *Night of Horror* and *Killing Time.*

John Carstairs, Space Detective — Arboreal Sci-fi by Frank Belknap Long

Joseph Shallit Novels — *The Case of the Billion Dollar Body, Lady Don't Die on My Doorstep, Kiss the Killer, Yell Bloody Murder, Take Your Last Look.* One of America's best 50's authors and a favorite of author Bill Pronzini.

Keller Memento — 45 short stories of the amazing and weird by Dr. David Keller.

Killer's Caress — Cary Moran's 1936 hardboiled thriller.

Lady of the Yellow Death and Other Stories — More stories by Wyatt Blassingame.

League of the Grateful Dead and Other Stories — Volume One in the Day Keene in the Detective Pulps series.

Library of Death — Ghastly tale by Ronald S. L. Harding, introduced by John Pelan

Malcolm Jameson Novels and Short Stories — *Astonishing! Astounding!, Tarnished Bomb, The Alien Envoy and Other Stories* and *The Chariots of San Fernando and Other Stories.* All introduced and edited by John Pelan or Richard A. Lupoff.

Man Out of Hell and Other Stories — Volume II of the John H. Knox weird pulps collection.

Marblehead: A Novel of H.P. Lovecraft — A long-lost masterpiece from Richard A. Lupoff. This is the "director's cut", the long version that has never been published before.

Mark of the Laughing Death and Other Stories — Shockers from the pulps by Francis James, introduced by John Pelan.

Master of Souls — Mark Hansom's 1937 shocker is introduced by weirdologist John Pelan.

Max Afford Novels — *Owl of Darkness, Death's Mannikins, Blood on His Hands, The Dead Are Blind, The Sheep and the Wolves, Sinners in Paradise* and *Two Locked Room Mysteries and a Ripping Yarn* by one of Australia's finest mystery novelists.

Money Brawl — Two books about the writing business by Jack Woodford and H. Bedford-Jones. Introduced by Richard A. Lupoff.

More Secret Adventures of Sherlock Holmes — Gary Lovisi's second collection of tales about the unknown sides of the great detective.

Muddled Mind: Complete Works of Ed Wood, Jr. — David Hayes and Hayden Davis deconstruct the life and works of the mad, but canny, genius.

Murder among the Nudists — A mystery from 1934 by Peter Hunt, featuring a naked Detective-Inspector going undercover in a nudist colony.

Murder in Black and White — 1931 classic tennis whodunit by Evelyn Elder.

Murder in Shawnee — Two novels of the Alleghenies by John Douglas: *Shawnee Alley Fire* and *Haunts*.

Murder in Silk — A 1937 Yellow Peril novel of the silk trade by Ralph Trevor.

My Deadly Angel — 1955 Cold War drama by John Chelton.

My First Time: The One Experience You Never Forget — Michael Birchwood — 64 true first-person narratives of how they lost it.

Mysterious Martin, the Master of Murder — Two versions of a strange 1912 novel by Tod Robbins about a man who writes books that can kill.

Norman Berrow Novels — *The Bishop's Sword, Ghost House, Don't Go Out After Dark, Claws of the Cougar, The Smokers of Hashish, The Secret Dancer, Don't Jump Mr. Boland!, The Footprints of Satan, Fingers for Ransom, The Three Tiers of Fantasy, The Spaniard's Thumb, The Eleventh Plague, Words Have Wings, One Thrilling Night, The Lady's in Danger, It Howls at Night, The Terror in the Fog, Oil Under the Window, Murder in the Melody, The Singing Room*. This is the complete Norman Berrow library of locked-room mysteries, several of which are masterpieces.

Old Faithful and Other Stories — SF classic tales by Raymond Z. Gallun

Old Times' Sake — Short stories by James Reasoner from Mike Shayne Magazine.

One Dreadful Night — A classic mystery by Ronald S. L. Harding

Pair O' Jacks — A mystery novel and a diatribe about publishing by Jack Woodford

Perfect .38 — Two early Timothy Dane novels by William Ard. More to come.

Prince Pax — Devilish intrigue by George Sylvester Viereck and Philip Eldridge

Prose Bowl — Futuristic satire of a world where hack writing has replaced football as our national obsession, by Bill Pronzini and Barry N. Malzberg.

Red Light — The history of legal prostitution in Shreveport Louisiana by Eric Brock. Includes wonderful photos of the houses and the ladies.

Researching American-Made Toy Soldiers — A 276-page collection of a lifetime of articles by toy soldier expert Richard O'Brien.

Reunion in Hell — Volume One of the John H. Knox series of weird stories from the pulps. Introduced by horror expert John Pelan.

Ripped from the Headlines! — The Jack the Ripper story as told in the newspaper articles in the *New York* and *London Times*.

Robert Randisi Novels — *No Exit to Brooklyn* and *The Dead of Brooklyn*. The first two Nick Delvecchio novels.

Rough Cut & New, Improved Murder — Ed Gorman's first two novels.

R.R. Ryan Novels — Freak Museum and The Subjugated Beast, two horror classics.

Ruby of a Thousand Dreams — The villain Wu Fang returns in this Roland Daniel novel.

Ruled By Radio — 1925 futuristic novel by Robert L. Hadfield & Frank E. Farncombe.

Rupert Penny Novels — *Policeman's Holiday, Policeman's Evidence, Lucky Policeman, Policeman in Armour, Sealed Room Murder, Sweet Poison, The Talkative Policeman, She had to Have Gas* and *Cut and Run* (by Martin Tanner.) Rupert Penny is the pseudonym of Australian Charles Thornett, a master of the locked room, impossible crime plot.

Sacred Locomotive Flies — Richard A. Lupoff's psychedelic SF story.

Sam — Early gay novel by Lonnie Coleman.

Sand's Game — Spectacular hard-boiled noir from Ennis Willie, edited by Lynn Myers and Stephen Mertz, with contributions from Max Allan Collins, Bill Crider, Wayne Dundee, Bill Pronzini, Gary Lovisi and James Reasoner.

Sand's War — More violent fiction from the typewriter of Ennis Willie

Satan's Den Exposed — True crime in Truth or Consequences New Mexico — Award-winning journalism by the *Desert Journal*.

Satans of Saturn — Novellas from the pulps by Otis Adelbert Kline and E. H. Price

Satan's Sin House and Other Stories — Horrific gore by Wayne Rogers

Secrets of a Teenage Superhero — Graphic lit by Jonathan Sweet

Sex Slave — Potboiler of lust in the days of Cleopatra by Dion Leclerq, 1966.

Sideslip — 1968 SF masterpiece by Ted White and Dave Van Arnam.

Slammer Days — Two full-length prison memoirs: *Men into Beasts* (1952) by George Sylvester Viereck and *Home Away From Home* (1962) by Jack Woodford.

Slippery Staircase — 1930s whodunit from E.C.R. Lorac

Sorcerer's Chessmen — John Pelan introduces this 1939 classic by Mark Hansom.

Star Griffin — Michael Kurland's 1987 masterpiece of SF drollery is back.

Stakeout on Millennium Drive — Award-winning Indianapolis Noir by Ian Woollen.

Strands of the Web: Short Stories of Harry Stephen Keeler — Edited and Introduced by Fred Cleaver.

Summer Camp for Corpses and Other Stories — Weird Menace tales from Arthur Leo Zagat; introduced by John Pelan.

Suzy — A collection of comic strips by Richard O'Brien and Bob Vojtko from 1970.

Tales of the Macabre and Ordinary — Modern twisted horror by Chris Mikul, author of the *Bizarrism* series.

Tales of Terror and Torment #1 — John Pelan selects and introduces this sampler of weird menace tales from the pulps.

Tenebrae — Ernest G. Henham's 1898 horror tale brought back.

The Amorous Intrigues & Adventures of Aaron Burr — by Anonymous. Hot historical action about the man who almost became Emperor of Mexico.

The Anthony Boucher Chronicles — edited by Francis M. Nevins. Book reviews by Anthony Boucher written for the *San Francisco Chronicle, 1942 – 1947.* Essential and fascinating reading by the best book reviewer there ever was.

The Barclay Catalogs — Two essential books about toy soldier collecting by Richard O'Brien

The Basil Wells Omnibus — A collection of Wells' stories by Richard A. Lupoff

The Beautiful Dead and Other Stories — Dreadful tales from Donald Dale

The Best of 10-Story Book — edited by Chris Mikul, over 35 stories from the literary magazine Harry Stephen Keeler edited.

The Black Dark Murders — Vintage 50s college murder yarn by Milt Ozaki, writing as Robert O. Saber.

The Book of Time — The classic novel by H.G. Wells is joined by sequels by Wells himself and three stories by Richard A. Lupoff. Illustrated by Gavin L. O'Keefe.

The Case in the Clinic — One of E.C.R. Lorac's finest.

The Strange Case of the Antlered Man — A mystery of superstition by Edwy Searles Brooks.

The Case of the Bearded Bride — #4 in the Day Keene in the Detective Pulps series

The Case of the Little Green Men — Mack Reynolds wrote this love song to sci-fi fans back in 1951 and it's now back in print.

The Case of the Withered Hand — 1936 potboiler by John G. Brandon.

The Charlie Chaplin Murder Mystery — A 2004 tribute by noted film scholar, Wes D. Gehring.

The Chinese Jar Mystery — Murder in the manor by John Stephen Strange, 1934.

The Cloudbuilders and Other Stories — SF tales from Colin Kapp.

The Compleat Calhoon — All of Fender Tucker's works: Includes *Totah Six-Pack, Weed, Women and Song* and *Tales from the Tower*, plus a CD of all of his songs.

The Compleat Ova Hamlet — Parodies of SF authors by Richard A. Lupoff. This is a brand new edition with more stories and more illustrations by Trina Robbins.

The Contested Earth and Other SF Stories — A never-before published space opera and seven short stories by Jim Harmon.

The Crimson Query — A 1929 thriller from Arlton Eadie. A perfect way to get introduced.

The Curse of Cantire — Classic 1939 novel of a family curse by Walter S. Masterman.

The Devil and the C.I.D. — Odd diabolic mystery by E.C.R. Lorac

The Devil Drives — An odd prison and lost treasure novel from 1932 by Virgil Markham.

The Devil of Pei-Ling — Herbert Asbury's 1929 tale of the occult.

The Devil's Mistress — A 1915 Scottish gothic tale by J. W. Brodie-Innes, a member of Aleister Crowley's Golden Dawn.

The Devil's Nightclub and Other Stories — John Pelan introduces some gruesome tales by Nat Schachner.

The Disentanglers — Episodic intrigue at the turn of last century by Andrew Lang

The Dog Poker Code — A spoof of *The Da Vinci Code* by D.B. Smithee.

The Dumpling — Political murder from 1907 by Coulson Kernahan.

The End of It All and Other Stories — Ed Gorman selected his favorite short stories for this huge collection.

The Fangs of Suet Pudding — A 1944 novel of the German invasion by Adams Farr

The Finger of Destiny and Other Stories — Edmund Snell's superb collection of weird stories of Borneo.

The Ghost of Gaston Revere — From 1935, a novel of life and beyond by Mark Hansom, introduced by John Pelan.

The Girl in the Dark — A thriller from Roland Daniel

The Gold Star Line — Seaboard adventure from L.T. Reade and Robert Eustace.

The Golden Dagger — 1951 Scotland Yard yarn by E. R. Punshon.

The Great Orme Terror — Horror stories by Garnett Radcliffe from the pulps

The Hairbreadth Escapes of Major Mendax — Francis Blake Crofton's 1889 boys' book.

The House That Time Forgot and Other Stories — Insane pulpitude by Robert F. Young

The House of the Vampire — 1907 poetic thriller by George S. Viereck.

The Illustrous Corpse — Murder hijinx from Tiffany Thayer.

The Incredible Adventures of Rowland Hern — Intriguing 1928 impossible crimes by Nicholas Olde.

The Julius Caesar Murder Case — A classic 1935 re-telling of the assassination by Wallace Irwin that's much more fun than the Shakespeare version.

The Koky Comics — A collection of all of the 1978-1981 Sunday and daily comic strips by Richard O'Brien and Mort Gerberg, in two volumes.

The Lady of the Terraces — 1925 missing race adventure by E. Charles Vivian.

The Lord of Terror — 1925 mystery with master-criminal, Fantômas.

The Melamare Mystery — A classic 1929 Arsene Lupin mystery by Maurice Leblanc

The Man Who Was Secrett — Epic SF stories from John Brunner

The Man Without a Planet — Science fiction tales by Richard Wilson

The N. R. De Mexico Novels — Robert Bragg, the real N.R. de Mexico, presents *Marijuana Girl, Madman on a Drum, Private Chauffeur* in one volume.

The Night Remembers — A 1991 Jack Walsh mystery from Ed Gorman.

The One After Snelling — Kickass modern noir from Richard O'Brien.

The Organ Reader — A huge compilation of just about everything published in the 1971-1972 radical bay-area newspaper, *THE ORGAN*. A coffee table book that points out the shallowness of the coffee table mindset.

The Poker Club — Three in one! Ed Gorman's ground-breaking novel, the short story it was based upon, and the screenplay of the film made from it.

The Private Journal & Diary of John H. Surratt — The memoirs of the man who conspired to assassinate President Lincoln.

The Ramble House Mapbacks — Recently revised book by Gavin L. O'Keefe with color pictures of all the Ramble House books with mapbacks.

The Secret Adventures of Sherlock Holmes — Three Sherlockian pastiches by the Brooklyn author/publisher, Gary Lovisi.

The Shadow on the House — Mark Hansom's 1934 masterpiece of horror is introduced by John Pelan.

The Sign of the Scorpion — A 1935 Edmund Snell tale of oriental evil.

The Singular Problem of the Stygian House-Boat — Two classic tales by John Kendrick Bangs about the denizens of Hades.

The Smiling Corpse — Philip Wylie and Bernard Bergman's odd 1935 novel.

The Spider: Satan's Murder Machines — A thesis about Iron Man

The Stench of Death: An Odoriferous Omnibus by Jack Moskovitz — Two complete novels and two novellas from 60's sleaze author, Jack Moskovitz.

The Story Writer and Other Stories — Classic SF from Richard Wilson

The Strange Case of the Antlered Man — 1935 dementia from Edwy Searles Brooks

The Strange Thirteen — Richard B. Gamon's odd stories about Raj India.

The Technique of the Mystery Story — Carolyn Wells' tips about writing.

The Threat of Nostalgia — A collection of his most obscure stories by Jon Breen

The Time Armada — Fox B. Holden's 1953 SF gem.

The Tongueless Horror and Other Stories — Volume One of the series of short stories from the weird pulps by Wyatt Blassingame.

The Town from Planet Five — From Richard Wilson, two SF classics, *And Then the Town Took Off* and *The Girls from Planet 5*

The Tracer of Lost Persons — From 1906, an episodic novel that became a hit radio series in the 30s. Introduced by Richard A. Lupoff.

The Trail of the Cloven Hoof — Diabolical horror from 1935 by Arlton Eadie. Introduced by John Pelan.

The Triune Man — Mindscrambling science fiction from Richard A. Lupoff.

The Unholy Goddess and Other Stories — Wyatt Blassingame's first DTP compilation

The Universal Holmes — Richard A. Lupoff's 2007 collection of five Holmesian pastiches and a recipe for giant rat stew.

The Werewolf vs the Vampire Woman — Hard to believe ultraviolence by either Arthur M. Scarm or Arthur M. Scram.

The Whistling Ancestors — A 1936 classic of weirdness by Richard E. Goddard and introduced by John Pelan.

The White Owl — A vintage thriller from Edmund Snell

The White Peril in the Far East — Sidney Lewis Gulick's 1905 indictment of the West and assurance that Japan would never attack the U.S.

The Wizard of Berner's Abbey — A 1935 horror gem written by Mark Hansom and introduced by John Pelan.

The Wonderful Wizard of Oz — by L. Frank Baum and illustrated by Gavin L. O'Keefe

Through the Looking Glass — Lewis Carroll wrote it; Gavin L. O'Keefe illustrated it.

Time Line — Ramble House artist Gavin O'Keefe selects his most evocative art inspired by the twisted literature he reads and designs.

Tiresias — Psychotic modern horror novel by Jonathan M. Sweet.

Tortures and Towers — Two novellas of terror by Dexter Dayle.

Totah Six-Pack — Fender Tucker's six tales about Farmington in one sleek volume.

Tree of Life, Book of Death — Grania Davis' book of her life.

Triple Quest — An arty mystery from the 30s by E.R. Punshon.

Trail of the Spirit Warrior — Roger Haley's saga of life in the Indian Territories.

Two Kinds of Bad — Two 50s novels by William Ard about Danny Fontaine

Two Suns of Morcali and Other Stories — Evelyn E. Smith's SF tour-de-force

Ultra-Boiled — 23 gut-wrenching tales by our Man in Brooklyn, Gary Lovisi.

Up Front From Behind — A 2011 satire of Wall Street by James B. Kobak.

Victims & Villains — Intriguing Sherlockiana from Derham Groves.

Wade Wright Novels — *Echo of Fear, Death At Nostalgia Street, It Leads to Murder* and *Shadows' Edge*, a double book featuring *Shadows Don't Bleed* and *The Sharp Edge*.

Walter S. Masterman Novels — *The Green Toad, The Flying Beast, The Yellow Mistletoe, The Wrong Verdict, The Perjured Alibi, The Border Line, The Bloodhounds Bay, The Curse of Cantire* and *The Baddington Horror*. Masterman wrote horror and mystery, some introduced by John Pelan.

We Are the Dead and Other Stories — Volume Two in the Day Keene in the Detective Pulps series, introduced by Ed Gorman. When done, there may be as many as 11 in the series.

Welsh Rarebit Tales — Charming stories from 1902 by Harle Oren Cummins

West Texas War and Other Western Stories — by Gary Lovisi.

What If? Volume 1, 2 and 3 — Richard A. Lupoff introduces three decades worth of SF short stories that should have won a Hugo, but didn't.

When the Batman Thirsts and Other Stories — Weird tales from Frederick C. Davis.

Whip Dodge: Man Hunter — Wesley Tallant's saga of a bounty hunter of the old West.

Win, Place and Die! — The first new mystery by Milt Ozaki in decades. The ultimate novel of 70s Reno.

Writer 1 and 2 — A magnus opus from Richard A. Lupoff summing up his life as writer.

You'll Die Laughing — Bruce Elliott's 1945 novel of murder at a practical joker's English countryside manor.

RAMBLE HOUSE

Fender Tucker, Prop. Gavin L. O'Keefe, Graphics
www.ramblehouse.com   fender@ramblehouse.com
228-826-1783 10329 Sheephead Drive, Vancleave MS 39565